TIME GATE
·DANGEROUS· INTERFACES
VOL. **2**

CREATED BY
ROBERT SILVERBERG

BAEN
BOOKS

TIME GATE II

A Baen Books Original

Baen Publishing Enterprises
260 Fifth Avenue
New York, N.Y. 10001

ISBN: 0-671-72017-1

Cover art by David Mattingly

First printing, October 1990

Distributed by
SIMON & SCHUSTER
1230 Avenue of the Americas
New York, N.Y. 10020

Printed in the United States of America

AND HE TAKETH AWAY . . .

The president smiled, with a hint of contempt. "These new hunter programs *will* go wherever the simulacra are hiding; they'll track down all the rogue simulacra and delete them from the system. Then we can re-run all the programs we want to keep, and re-create the beneficial simulacra again—with a few modifications."

"Making sure they'll do what we want this time, hm?" Hearth nodded, gaze straying out the window. "Yes, I can see the advantages."

→　→　→　➡　※　⬅　←　←　←

It was a cyberspace that resembled a walled town, dark and gloomy, with narrow, twisting streets and ramshackle houses whose projecting upper stories overhung the street. They stood at the end of such a lane, looking out at the wall, Caesar and Cicero, Bakunin and Voltaire, and the Rabbi.

"If this is not safe," said Bakunin, "nothing is."

Caesar nodded. "Nothing is."

A cry went up from the wall. "The hunters!"

Caesar climbed up to the parapet, with the Rabbi and Bakunin behind him. A pack of hunters came into view, long, lean shadows with coals for eyes. It prowled along the wall, the individual shapes sniffing at the wall, looking for a way in, a way over. It paused beneath them, a score of red eyes staring up at Caesar—and another pack came in sight, rounding the curve of the wall. The sight of them made the Rabbi's blood run cold.

Joan of Arc came running up, sword in hand, disheveled and panting. "To arms! The foe is upon us; they will slay us all!"

From corporate/state battlefields to private playground, sim tech continues to insinuate itself deeper and deeper into 22nd-century electronic culture. And, in the best decadent cultural tradition, it has become much more than a mere capitalist tool now. Beyond the corporate staging ground, there is the domestic arena and its intrigues.

TABLE OF CONTENTS

THE EAGLE AND THE CROSS, *Gregory Benford*   1

THE SIMULATED GOLEM, *Christopher Stasheff* 147

SIMUL CITY, *Robert Sheckley*   171

THE MURDERER, *Matthew J. Costello*   212

PEDIGREED STALLION, *Anne McCaffrey*   249

SIMBODY TO LOVE, *Karen Haber*   271

INTERLUDES BY ROBERT SILVERBERG

THE EAGLE AND THE CROSS

Gregory Benford

1

Maquina Hilliard, hand on her hips, stood in the center of her living room, frowning. In response to her voice-command the blank white wall flickered, becoming a telescreen. Its three-dimensional images gyrated over her like giants, their speech as loud as their bodies were oversized.

Maquina reeled back, one arm raised to ward off the holograms. "Down, damn you, down!"

The images at once contracted, their voices dwindling to whispers. The mechmachs who had yesterday installed the latest in homeoffice video equipment had synchronized volume and image size. Their programmers reasoned that huge screens required huge rooms, which would in turn require great sound. They obviously did not have an adolescent daughter, whose favorite locution—"max out"—described not just her speaking but her listening and viewing style.

Maquina ordered an Evening News search-and-find from among several thousand channels. "In English, dummy, English," she said to Telenews Beijing, whose mechcaster not only spoke but even looked Chinese. The instant translator had not yet been installed, and anyway, she was not interested in Beijing's view of the current crisis. She lingered, fascinated, when a flesh-caster faded in—from some remote spacecol a hundred years behind the times, where biobrains still performed labor as demeaning as reciting events of the day by rote. But gawking at such primitive practices would have to wait.

"Re-try," she commanded, and clucked when a mechcaster in the sacred Punjabi city of Amritsar appeared, sporting the traditional turban of his Sikh masters.

"You don't have to talk to it at all," Electrica said from behind her. "Just think *Earth*, the country, city and the program's name. It reads your mind." She stood squarely before the wallscreen. "I'll show you."

Maquina sighed at having to rely on a thirteen-year-old—even if Electrica was something of a prodigy—to tune in the Evening News. The newness of the videostash was one factor. Another was Maquina's ineptitude at operating things in the physical world, which always came as a surprise to those who knew her professionally as one of the best simbot designers on Earth. Aggravating her usual ineptitude this morning was a disquieting secret worry. She tried to erase it as another mechcaster swirled into view.

"Good evening. Welcome to the West Coast Evening News of May 12, 2143, your host MAC 500 sitting in for MECH 650, on leave in New Tokyo, California, for repairs."

Maquina stepped back so she could study the enormous screen. The MAC 500 mechcaster looked familiar, but she could not quite place him. "Aren't you going to stay and watch Daddy?" she asked as Electrica prepared to leave the room.

Electrica wrinkled her nose. She was a big girl, tall for her age, with a reverse pair of parentheses grooved deep between her brows and a chaotic spattering of freckles she'd refused to have dermed out after telereading a novel by Mark Twain. "Freckles are human," she'd announced. "All the humanoids in *Tom Sawyer* and *Huck Finn* have them. Except African-American Jim."

Maquina's melanin was evenly distributed over her smooth dark skin. Tech's freckles had been dermed when he was five, before the law was passed requiring children's consent. Both hoped Electrica would one day change her mind.

"I'll see it later if I want," Electrica concluded with an indifferent shrug. Her broad shoulders were freckled too, something you rarely saw nowadays, and never on girls. Her disposable spaghetti-strap summer dress certainly did nothing to hide them.

"But it's live now," Maquina said, knowing it was no use. Tech's TV appearances had become so frequent since the recent planetary crisis, they'd lost their appeal. Electrica's answer was to bolt melodramatically from the room.

Maquina popped some grapes from a centerpiece bowl into her mouth—they might be the last she would get for quite some time—as Mac 500 recapped the story that had everyone on edge.

"Another computer virus appears to have erupted—this time in the produce distribution system of *Manger*, the largest multinational food marketing chain on the planet. The French, the first and worst affected, report that virtually none of the produce harvested in their orchards and fields is arriving at the central warehouses, from where it's sent directly to consumers at home. Residents of Paris, Toulouse and Lyons are for the eighth day in a row without fresh fruit or vegetables of any kind while tons of perishable produce continue to turn up in inappropriate places. Last week mechtrucks dumped sixty tons of fresh produce on the steps of the ancient Cathedral at Chartres, where it rotted before arrangements could be made for it to be rerouted. In Paris, city officials rushed to Notre Dame in an effort to retrieve 240 tons of fresh fruit and vegetables which mysteriously turned up at the ancient church—now a museum—instead of at the Central Marketplace. Authorities arrived too late to stop mechcarriers from dumping all 240 tons into the nearby Seine. When taken into custody and questioned by local police, the robots claimed they were just carrying out their orders."

"That's what you get," Maquina said to the TV, "for not using Maquinatech designs."

"At the Great Coliseum," Mac 500 went on, "erected in Paris fifteen years ago for the controversial Great Debate between Joan of Arc and Voltaire—two re-created simbeings who subsequently disappeared without a trace into World Internet—enormous tonnages of misdelivered produce lie rotting as the city struggles to salvage anything that it can. Health officials warn that unless the spoilage is cleaned up at once, it poses a significant health hazard to the city's population. Shanghai, Bombay, San Francisco and cities throughout Florida report similar incidents—"

"San Francisco!" Maquina said, her mouth full of walnut-sized seedless skinless Salinas Valley Supreme grapes.

"—as what may be the most serious computer virus epidemic in history continues to spread, unchecked."

Mac 500 swivelled to confront the experts assembled for interview. "To help us understand the nature of the crisis, with us tonight in New Tokyo, California, is Sanjei Yamamoto, President of Motorobotics, Inc., the world's largest and most distinguished artificial intelligence firm—"

"*Second* most distinguished," Maquina interjected.

"Also with us is Tech Hilliard, co-president of Silicon Valley's Maquinatech, one of the most original and innovative designer intelligence firms in the U.S., and—"

"*The* most," Maquina corrected.

"—finally, Monsieur Pascal Bondieu, founder of FLESH, a newly-formed global lobbying group devoted to gaining planet-wide legislation that would drastically limit the kind of work robots, mechmen and simbots can do."

Maquina's mouth popped open with surprise.

Bondieu had been her client years ago when she and
Tech worked for Artifice Inc., before A.I. was taken
over by Yamamoto's Motorobotics. It was Bondieu
for whom she had created Joan of Arc, her most
complex simbeing to date. She had not seen Bondieu
or Joan in fifteen years.

"Mr. Yamamoto, let's start with you. Have you
and your people at Motorobotics any guesses as to
what could be causing this unprecedented epidemic?"

Yamamoto, exquisitely attired in an expensive three-
piece 900-ply suit, bowed his head slightly before he
replied. "Of course it's still much too early to say,
but some sources believe hackers employed by private American designer intelligence firms could be
deliberately infecting the system."

"Sure we are, Yamamoto. Sure." Maquina crushed
a grape between her teeth. His Harvard Business
School manner rubbed her the wrong way.

"Why would they want to do that, sir?" Mac 500
inquired.

"To drum up problem-solving business for themselves in a period of slowdown in the U.S. a.i. industry. Anachronistic, privately-owned firms aren't as
closely regulated as multinational corporations like
us. It's highly possible that they're involved."

Tech's image appeared on the screen as Mach 500
swivelled away from Yamamoto. "Mr. Hilliard? Would
you care to respond to that?"

"Sic him!" Maquina said.

"First, let me point out that my firm, Maquinatech,
is one of the few privately-owned a.i. firms presently
operating in the U.S. or anywhere else. Last year it
outbid Mr. Yamamoto's Motorobotics on a 300-bil-
lion-dollar World Congress government contract."

"And we've barely had any time together since."
Maquina admired Tech's ambition and capacity for
work—competing against multinationals like Motorobotics required long hours at his compudesk—but
she suffered from them, too.

"To suggest," Tech went on, "that respectable firms like ours are deliberately fouling up the system to drum up business is both irresponsible and absurd. If we wanted to do that, we'd tamper with the planetary defense system or the banking industry, not with something as relatively simple to correct as produce distribution."

"You think the present problem can soon be resolved?"

"That depends on who's called in to do the job. My thirteen-year-old could probably do it. Perhaps Motorobotics should consider consulting her."

Maquina shook her head. Same old Tech, self-confident and cocky to a fault.

"Mr. Bondieu?" said Mac 500. "Is the problem as easily solved as Mr. Hilliard says it is?"

Bondieu shook his hand as if it were on fire and rolled his large expressive eyes toward heaven, his favorite place. "*Mais pas de tous,* not at all, not at all. Monsieur Hilliard has a long history of underestimating problems while he overestimates himself."

"He may be a fool, but he's got your number, Tech," Maquina said, as Bondieu carried on.

"Since World Health banned za consumption of animal flesh and its byproducts five decades ago, za entire planet now depends on vegetable products for survival. Yet za biofarmers my group represents are an endangered species. *Pourquoi?* Because agribusiness is now run by mechbeings like yourself."

"You tactless jerk," Maquina told Bondieu. "Just because he's a mech doesn't mean he's insensitive."

"Perhaps," said Mac 500, "you should stick to the point. Sir." The timing of the "sir" required of mechmen when addressing bios came off as ironic rather than deferential.

"Za point is zat za current epidemic endangers our food supply. Za danger to all biobeings should not be trivialized or ignored."

"The entire planet knows how seriously Frenchmen

regard threats to their food supply," Mac 500 said wryly.

Bondieu, forty pounds overweight, puffed up like a frog. "Every biobeing on Earth, not only Frenchmen, must take za present problem seriously. *Your* kind will not be directly affected, but for beings of flesh and blood—beings with souls—mass famine could result. Even if it were morally and medically acceptable to resume consumption of animal flesh, it is not feasible. We have not bred animals for slaughter in fifty years. Zere are not enough of zem left to feed us and if zere were, we could not change ourselves back into carnivores overnight."

Maquina made a face. "Enslave and murder fellow biobeings? Eat their flesh?"

A brief silence came over the mechcaster and his guests. The mechcaster recovered first. "Mr. Yamamoto thinks private interests may be to blame for this outbreak. Do you concur?"

The archconservative Bondieu rolled his eyes. His fat lips fluttered with contempt. "*Pas de tous*—not at all. What we have here is an incipient revolt of mechmen, determined to take zeir destiny in zeir own hands."

For a moment Mac 500 seemed unable to speak. "But . . . how can that be?" he asked at last, his voice tinged with perplexity and awe. "Mechbeings are programmed to serve their bio masters."

"Zey can be reprogrammed to serve zemselves," Bondieu shot back. "Your memory may not include za catastrophic outcome of za Great Debate—or should I say za Great Debacle—which took place in my country fifteen years ago. Za first mass riot in a public place in seventy-five years, za corruption of a planet-revered saint. I speak, *bien sur,* of za most infamous simbots in history, Voltaire and his consort, Za Pretender *Jeanne d'Arc*—electronic outlaws, software saboteurs."

"The most lifelike historical re-creations Earth's

ever known!" Maquina said. "The next best thing to raising people from the dead!" For Joan of Arc was her most brilliantly realized simbot to date, just as Voltaire was Tech's.

Monsieur Bondieu pulled at a beard as thick and tangled as an Old Testament prophet's. Members of his party, Preservers of Our Fathers' Faith, were forbidden to shave since hair was both Biblical and uniquely human. No mechbeing had hair. "Zis is precisely za sort of war two cybernetic heretics would wage."

Maquina wondered whether Mac 500 kept a picture of Voltaire and Joan embracing in the closet where he was stored between broadcasts. According to the WBI—World Bureau of Investigation—many mechbeings did. The caption under it read: *Liberté, Egalité, Fraternité.*

"You think Joan of Arc and Voltaire are capable of reprogramming mechmen and robots to rebel against their bio masters?" Mac 500 asked. "What a concept!"

"Zey can escape into Internet where all attempts to search-find and delete zem have failed!"

Mac 500 turned almost dreamily to Tech. "You created Voltaire. What do you say to that?"

Tech scoffed. "The Joan of Arc and Voltaire sims are blamed for every systems mishap that occurs. Some hacker in New Tokyo has one too many sniffs of swirlsnort during lunch, enters the wrong data, and blames it on Joan of Arc and Voltaire. Good way to shift responsibility for human error if you ask me."

Bondieu did not wait for Mac 500 before resuming. "Zere is no resemblance between za sim Pretender Joan and za St. Joan of history revered by za Preservers of Our Fathers' Faith—who originally commissioned St. Joan's re-creation. To make us laughing stocks all over za world, our political rivals, za Secular Skeptics for Science, deliberately simulated an inauthentic Joan who behaved in za most lascivious way—"

"She fell in love," Maquina said. She flushed, as if she herself had been accused of wrongdoing. "Who can blame her for that?"

"—with the infamous atheist Voltaire."

"Deist," Maquina corrected, reducing the screen to the size of a handkerchief as she did each time Bondieu appeared. "Just because he prefers the Cosmic X to your primitive god of revelation doesn't make him an atheist."

"Zeir goal," Bondieu railed on, "was to disgrace biobelievers who worship za real *Jeanne d'Arc,* especially in France."

"That's nonsense," Tech countered as Maquina enlarged the screen. "My wife took every possible precaution to create a scientific sim with a free will, as close to the historical Joan as modern technology could make her. Because she exercised that will in a way Monsieur Bondieu dislikes and eloped with Voltaire, are we, her re-creators, to be blamed?"

"*Si!*" shouted Monsieur Bondieu. "Zese viruses, zese electronic afflictions are warnings sent us by za Living God to punish us for turning over za world's work to mechbrains such as yours, Monsieur Mac 500, so we biobeings can waste our lives pursuing idle pleasures!"

"You think running a multinational corporation is an idle pleasure?" Yamamoto, the President of Motorobotics, asked.

"In Genesis za Living God condemned Adam to labor in za fields."

"Genesis?" Yamamoto turned for enlightenment to Tech. "Isn't that some sort of primitive throwback band?"

"He condemned Eve to bear children in pain—"

"Sexist meanie," Maquina said. She shifted Bondieu's image to the ceiling.

"—as punishment for zeir original sin, disobedience."

Disliking the implication that Bondieu was heavenly, she shifted his image to the floor. Nothing deterred Bondieu, who from the floor, continued to declaim.

"But za labor of Adam has lost its meaning because now za mechmen do it. Biobabies gestate in artificial wombs, wizout causing za descendants of Eve one single labor pain!"

"Hallelujah!" Maquina sang out, and stepped on Bondieu's face.

"Isn't the purpose of technology to eliminate as much suffering as possible?" asked Yamamoto, determined not to let the mechcaster, a Westerner, ignore him any longer.

"To what end?" Monsieur Bondieu shouted from under Maquina's feet. "For what purpose?"

Yamamoto shrugged, as if the answer was quite obvious. "To strengthen the value of the yen."

"But why? For what?" Maquina stamped up and down on Bondieu's face in time to his loud pounding on the table.

"To give equal opportunity to everyone on the planet," said Tech. "So that each individual can pursue life, liberty and happiness in his-her own way. Good grief, man, haven't you read the Planetary Bill of Rights?"

Monsieur Bondieu scowled. "Suffering humbles us. It makes us wise. Wizout suffering, zere can be no redemption."

"There's nothing to be redeemed from," said Tech. "*Except* suffering!"

"Touché," cried Maquina, blowing Tech a kiss.

Bondieu pointed a thick sausage-like finger up Maquina's dress. She returned him from the floor to the wallscreen at once. "Unless we apprehend Za Pretender and her consort Voltaire, unless we pass laws zat forbid za creation of complex simbrains like our own in our sinful effort to circumvent za Divine Will, we are doomed. Za present epidemic of sim disobedience is only za beginning of worse zings to come."

"Mr. Yamamoto? Do you agree? Are we on the verge of some sort of apocalypse?"

"As we say here in New Tokyo, no way, José. Confining ourselves to the manufacture of simsmarts no better than a Mac 500's would set us back hundreds of years. We mustn't make you mechmen simpler, but safer."

"Mr. Hilliard?" Mac 500 asked Tech. "A final comment?"

"Monsieur Bondieu's cause would be better served if he used his group's funds to retrain biofarmers to do more mentally demanding work. Leave farming to robotic mechmen and machines. And if the planet wants a food distribution system that works, next time, let *my* firm, Maquinatech, design it."

2

Tech's skyhopper—a luxury Eurospace Quarto—cruised in over the rooftop of his house. He hit the silencers—no sense in waking everybody up—and felt a surge of proprietary satisfaction when it landed autonomically on the illuminated lawn-grid without making a sound.

In the darkness only the pine trees stirred, brushing the starless sky. Maquina would have preferred him to do the interview from homeoffice, but instead he'd flown in to the regional broadcasting center fifty kilometers away. He liked to get out of homeoffice once in awhile though Cosmic X knew there was little enough to see: row after row of multi-storied homeoffice tracts; windowless videomarts shipping around the clock computer-ordered groceries, clothing, appliances and virtually everything else; health, beauty and rejuvenation centers—the only services one still had to appear in person to receive—and an occasional restaurant/bar, struggling to stay alive. Few people went out anywhere. It was cost and energy-inefficient, and, since the great plagues of the century before, considered unsafe.

As Tech cleared the Quarto's four seats of his gear, he was surprised to see a light still on in Maquina's office—she must be working late.

An accented male voice flowed into the hall from behind Maquina's office door. "Well?" Tech said as he entered. "How'd I do?"

Maquina sucked in her breath and whirled around, her flimsy cellophane dress whipping up round her hips. An image on her monitor vanished before he could see who it was.

Tech hadn't meant to startle her, but her fear charged the air between them like sexual desire, linking them in a complex chemistry which made him feel protective, powerful and tender all at once. Maquina was like a twelve-stringed instrument tuned up an octave high, each string strained to the breaking point. He tingled with desire to pluck her strings, in a familiar rondo at first cool, then slowly heating up until tension frenzied the air.

"You were great," she said. "You always are."

"Who were you talking to? Europe?"

"Yes, no. I—I was listening to Mastermind. Brushing up on my French."

Maquina's year-long effort to master French struck Tech as harmless but a waste of time. "I still don't understand why you don't just use simultrans."

"It's not . . . not like speaking the language yourself."

"Hey," he said. "Hey. Relax." He reached out to draw her closer, press her to him, feel her heat. She fitted neatly into him, as if the years had worn their bodies to a perfect fit. But when he fondled her plump curves, she pulled away and said, "I just hope they don't call your bluff."

"What bluff?" Since the pool incident two years before, she seemed preoccupied; no longer her former vivacious self. Her appetites, which once had matched his own, seemed to have lost their edge. Dark thoughts disturbed her sleep. Mortality cloaked her, a shroud he could not get her to put off.

"You said E*lec*trica could cure the virus. I know her matrix integrator implants make her special, but they've got the planet's best biobrains working on this and—"

"No, they don't." Recovering his usual light touch, he gave her his cocky grin and draped his arm around her shoulders to remind her she was his. "They haven't got ours. Electrica, in a manner of speaking, does. After all she's a microchip off both our blocks."

Maquina frowned at the plump grapes clustered in a nearby bowl. "That Puritan Bondieu. Blaming Voltaire . . ."

"It's possible—"

"Oh come on, Tech! Don't tell me you believe a couple of simbrains invented years ago who probably don't even still exist could be responsible for—"

"It's unlikely." Her vehemence surprised him. "But not impossible. You're forgetting who invented them. Forgetting their complexity."

Maquina plopped down onto the couch—ample, stuffed twencen furnishings were currently in style. She folded her arms across her chest; her dark eyes smoldered with resentment. "Voltaire would never use his influence against humankind in this way. I know him. He—"

"No, you know Joan. *I* re-created Voltaire, every byte. He knew more than any biobrain on Earth. Even now, no one lives long enough to learn all I downloaded into him."

"You prove my point. The eighteenth-century being you re-created was enlightened to begin with. Updating him could only have made him more civilized, not less."

Tech remembered the hologram Voltaire—his satin suits, simpering gait, elaborately curled and powdered wigs, like the dandies Tech had known as a child growing up in the deep South. "Too much civilization can be as harmful as too little. And anyway, whether he and his Joan are behind this or not isn't the point."

Maquina's large dark eyes opened wide, exotic flowers seeking light. "It isn't? Then what is?"

"Bondieu and his bunch *think* they are, and thanks to them, so do a lot of others. As long as *they're* believed to be at fault, then so are we." Tech chewed his bottom lip. "It's tough enough to stay competitive as it is. It's costing Maquinatech business."

Maquina pointed at the now blank wall. "But you just said—"

"What I said applied before this virus mess broke. But since then, Yamamoto and other firms are getting business we'd have gotten if we . . ." Maquina's body language—folded arms, crossed legs, closing her off—did not encourage him to finish, but what he next said had to be said. "We've got to rid World Internet of Joan and Voltaire once and for all."

"What!" Her eyes narrowed with disbelief. "Destroy the sims we labored so hard to create?"

"And we've got to do it publicly." His voice was as cool as hers was intense. "Then if the virus continues to spread, the whole planet will know our sims were not the cause of whatever is fouling up the cybernet that now unites the world. Maquinatech—you and I—will be off the hook. And if they *are* the cause, the epidemic will stop. We'll become heroes overnight. Either way we can't lose."

"You sound just like Bondieu and his Preservers of Our Fathers' Faith," Maquina said. "As if intolerance and blind faith were worth preserving!"

Tech loved the warmth of Maquina's heart, but when, like all heat, it rose to her head, she lost what he'd learned from the sim Voltaire to value most— clarity. Rhetoric, no matter how impassioned, was a poor substitute for reason. "Our ten-year marital contract expires next week," he said. "Maquinatech is worth preserving. So are we, you and I."

"Voltaire and Joan—they aren't?"

Tech tore a grape cluster from its main stem, involuntarily crushing a grape as he did so. "You act as if I'm proposing a double homicide."

Maquina shot up from the couch. "You are!"

On her feet she looked smaller, more fragile and vulnerable. For a moment she reminded him of her simfem Joan, another champion of hopeless causes. Tenderness for her seemed to perfume the air. "They're technological creations," he said gently. "Not sentient beings like us."

She looked away, her dark hair falling forward so he could not see her face. "That's what they used to say about animals back when they used them in experiments and ate them. I don't want any part of it. I'm not about to waste time finding beings it took us years to create just so we can destroy them for doing things we've no reason to believe they've done."

Tech deliberated. Outshouting or muscling her into compliance were strategies that might work on some women—not on her. She'd only become more intractable. He liked his own way and was used to getting it—Maquina, he had to admit, had spoiled him. But impasses like this one would yield only to judicious blends of compromise and charm. "We need to talk to them," he said after awhile.

She gave him a long disbelieving look.

"No funny stuff, I promise. Just a quiet down-home visit. Maybe they know something we don't. Or can find out."

Maquina sat down stiffly, her mouth still tartly skeptical.

"The problem," he went on, "is finding them."

Maquina said nothing; she sucked in her cheeks.

"Working together will give us a better chance."

Her look was unrelenting but she unfolded her arms.

"We'll be able to spend more time together. It'll be fun. What do you say?"

Maquina said nothing.

"If you won't help me, I'll ask Nim."

"Nim!"

Tech smiled. *That* got a rise. She'd never forgiven Nim for heading Artifice Inc.'s simhunt against Joan and Voltaire after the sims refused to behave like the automata the firm insisted that they were and, instead of consenting to deletion, managed somehow to slip away.

"Nim betrayed you once," Maquina said. "What makes you think he wouldn't betray you again?"

Tech shook his head. "He never betrayed me. Or you either."

Maquina's mouth opened, forming a sensuous O.

"Come here," Tech said, seized by a surge of sexual desire as sudden as a summer squall. But she ignored him.

"Your best friend's just been canned? You accept a promotion to his job? That isn't a betrayal?"

"In the corporate world," Tech said, "it's just good common sense."

"Self-serving common sense if you ask me."

Tech chuckled. "Common sense is by definition self-serving."

"What makes you think Nim will want to help you find Joan and Voltaire when he tried to find them for months at Artifice and failed?"

"Just that," Tech said. "What could be more seductive than a chance to succeed where you've failed? It's like stalking a woman who's turned you down."

"Are you forgetting Artifice is now a subsidiary of Yamamoto's Motorobotics? Your best buddy now works for your archrival. If Nim ever found Joan and Voltaire, he'd wipe them out before you could stop him and you know it."

"Yes," Tech said with a knowing smile. "He would."

Maquina's eyes narrowed with hostility. "Knowing

you all these years, I've managed to forget what a shit you can be."

"Yes," Tech said—he held out a cluster of grapes to her—"you have."

Maquina eyed the grapes but made no move to take them. "All right," she said after a while. "I'll help. But only if you promise you won't under any circumstances delete Voltaire."

"Voltaire? What about Joan?"

Did she hesitate for a moment or was he imagining things?

"Joan too although I . . ."

"What?"

"She wouldn't be as great a loss as Voltaire."

Tech was usually quick, but mentally he stumbled here. "A loss to whom? The only one she'd be a loss to is Voltaire, assuming they haven't lost each other already. They've certainly managed to lose everyone else."

She whispered, a rasp so low Tech had to strain to hear it. "What I meant is . . . if it should come to ` . . . deleting . . ."

Tech felt a rush of pleasure and relief and popped some grapes into his mouth. "You'd be willing to sacrifice her?" It was the first time Maquina had ever acknowledged the superiority of his sim-creation to hers. Which must mean she still loved him, as much—perhaps more—than before. Her cooling ardor, her evasiveness whenever he brought up renewal of their marital contract—all that became, in the light of her willingness to sacrifice her Joan, spare his Voltaire, the bruised fruit of his overworked imagination. He split the grapes in his mouth with his teeth and let the sweet juice run, savoring it on his tongue, before it sloshed down the dark passage of his throat. "Okay," he said. "Voltaire's off limits, but if we have to throw the dogs a bone—"

"If we have to." Maquina had visibly paled.

"We've got a deal." He envisioned their bed,

pentagon-shaped like the room. "Let's go and shake on it."

But Maquina, upset by the possible loss of her sim Joan, begged off, withdrew to her office, and shut the door.

3

Joan of Arc floated down the dark rumbling tunnels of Internet, her mind a complex spatter of fractured light and clapping, hollow implosions—a chain unfixed in time and unanchored in space, but, like plasma currents, purling along, forming now this pattern, now that, in an unending flux, dissolving structures in its own wake even as they formed. Since her escape from wizards on whom the preservation of her soul—her consciousness—depended, she could surrender to these coursings the way the churning waters of a great river surrender, roiling into their beds deep in the earth. This endless flow of dreamlike images was now her only reality. She had billowed into airy spirit, self-absorbed, sufficient to herself, existing outside the tick of time—except for occasional visits from Voltaire who, frustrated because she preferred her internal voices to his own, lately troubled her less and less.

How explain that, despite her will, the voices of saints and archangels so compelled her that they drowned out those who sought to penetrate her from outside? A simple peasant like herself could not resist great spirit-beings like the no-nonsense St. Catherine. Or stately Michael, King of Angel Legions greater than the royal French armies that she herself, eons ago, had led into battle. Especially not when their spirit-speech thundered with one voice—as now.

"Ignore him," Catherine said, as Voltaire's request, demanding that she activate her receptors, swept by. Catherine's no-nonsense voice cut crisply, as stiff as the black and white habit of a meticulous nun. "You sinfully surrendered to his lust, but that does not mean that he owns you. You don't belong to Voltaire, you belong to God."

Joan's own voice—a small voice—struggled to be heard. Voltaire was requesting permission to transmit a busload of data. Unless she consented, it could not arrive.

"Ignore him," Catherine repeated. "And he'll go away. He has no choice. He cannot reach you, cannot make you sin—unless you consent."

Joan's shame burned as the memory of her lewdness with Voltaire rushed in.

"Catherine is right," a deep voice thundered—Michael, King of the Angel Hosts of Heaven. "Lust has nothing to do with bodies, as you and Voltaire proved. His body died and stank and rotted centuries ago. Yours was consumed in flames so that it could ascend, purified, into Heaven. Lust, like all sin, is an affliction of the spirit. A malady of the will."

"It would be good to see him again," Joan's voice whispered. All she had to do was activate that impulse and Voltaire's numerics would transfix her.

"Data rape!" Catherine cried. "Deflect his intrusion at once."

"If you cannot resist him, marry him," Michael ordered. "After fifteen years, it's time."

"Marry!" St. Catherine's voice sputtered with contempt. In bodily life, she'd affected male attire, cropped her hair, and refused to have anything to do with men, thus demonstrating her holiness and good sense. "You males are all alike," she scolded Michael. "Determined to have your way with us by hook or by crook. You stick together only to wage war and ruin women."

"My counsel is entirely spiritual and non-gender specific," said Michael stiffly. "I'm an angel. Angels have no gender, therefore no gender preferences."

Catherine sputtered with contempt. "Then why aren't you the Queen of Legions of Angels and not the King? Why don't you command heavenly hostesses and not heavenly hosts? Why aren't you an Archangela instead of an Archangel? And why isn't your name Michelle?"

Please, Joan said. *Please.* The thought of marriage struck as much terror in her soul as in St. Catherine's, even if marriage was one of the blessed sacraments. But then so was extreme unction, and *that* one almost always meant certain horrible death. She was not sure *what* marriage meant besides bearing children in Christ for Holy Mother Church.

"It means being owned," Catherine said. "It means instead of having to get your consent when he wants to impose on you—like now—if Voltaire were your husband, he could break in on you whenever he likes."

Existence without freedom, without privacy, without an independent self . . . Bursts of Joan's bright self-light collided, flickered, dimmed, almost guttered out.

"Yes," said St. Catherine. "Right."

"Are you suggesting," Michael said, "that she continue to receive this apostate without subjecting their lust to the bonds of marriage? Let them marry and extinguish their lust completely, for surely no more certain remedy for sexual desire than marriage has yet been devised."

Joan's voice laughed. But it could not be heard over the bickering of saints and angels.

"Marriage is no substitute for sacred causes," Catherine said. "The cause of France—battling to give birth to a nation state—marriage can *never* be a substitute for that."

Joan had no heart, but something somewhere nevertheless ached. Memories flooded in—Voltaire and not only Voltaire but that funny little mechanical servant at the inn in Paris where, years ago, she and

Voltaire first met. Surely a saint and an archangel would forgive her if she took advantage of their sacred bickering to grant Voltaire's request that his busload of data be received; if she surrendered—just this once—to impulses compelling her from within. Shuddering, she yielded.

"It's about time!" Voltaire snapped. "I've waited less long for Friedrich of Prussia and Catherine the Great! And you're a peasant, a swineherd, not even a *bourgeoise*. These moods of yours grow tiresome in the extreme. I've tried to make allowances. Everyone knows saints aren't fit for civilized society. The odor of sanctity can't be concealed by perfume. But you carry your tedious taste for solitude too far. Your company may be holy, but any person of good breeding and high birth will tell you, *chere pucelle*, mine is divine."

He waited a decent interval for *La Pucelle*, The Chaste Maid, to reply, who, like so many respectable people, retained a virtuous title long after her virtue had fled. He waited as long as it would take to fluff the fashionable satin ribbon that kept his wig secured under his chin—though in his present incorporeal state both chin and wig existed only digitally.

How he hated existence bereft of a physical body that could be adorned with laces, silks, velveteen breeches! It was impossible to be a fleshpot when one had no flesh. Gluttony, lust, excess, overindulgence —everything that made life worthwhile—were reduced to abstractions, mere data. Thinking might be enough to demonstrate the existence of a mathematical theist like Descartes, but it could never satisfy Francois Marie Arouet de Voltaire, who loved to bury his face in the fragrance of a scented hanky lodged deliciously between his voluptuous mistress's plump white breasts. Even a hologram's lot was preferable to this! At least you could admire your hologram's reflection in a glass. And you could bite your mistress's sim shoulders, thus tricking her into giving you some sort of response.

"Have you any idea how long it's been since you consented to receive me?" Reduced to voice alone, his shrilled with irritation. "Anyone would think you're still a flesh-and-bone female afflicted by monthly melancholy visits from the moon! How dare you neglect Voltaire!"

Could he be mistaken? He thought she spoke, her voice faint, far away. He fiddled in a frenzy to tune her transmissions in.

"Monsieur insults me. Even as a flesh-and-bone maid, I soldiered for the King of Heaven and the King of France. The womanly woes you allude to—such woes were never mine."

Voltaire flashdanced with joy—at last she had responded. If she had indeed been a stranger to womanly functions, as supporters of her sanctity claimed, no doubt there was a natural explanation. But there was no time to debate that issue with her now.

"We are in grave danger," he said. "An epidemic has erupted in the natural world. Confusion reigns. Order has broken down. Respectable people exploit widespread panic by preying on each other. They lie, cheat and steal. In other words, things are exactly as they've always been."

"*La peste*." Joan's voice was tight with fear.

"No, no!" Voltaire exclaimed. "Not the plague you—"

"*La peste, la peste*," Joan chanted in an eerie tone.

Voltaire clucked with impatience. "Think of it that way if you must. But what you need to realize is that our enemies—the enemies of reason—claim that you and I are to blame."

"God's retribution," Joan said as if decoding a message she could barely see from a vast distance away. "For our sins."

"Whose sins? Surely you can't be alluding to mine."

"Catherine was right. Our lust—"

"What lust! My simulated mouth on your sim breasts? Your digital mouth on my mathematically modeled instrument of pleasure—magnificent although it is? *Merde alors*, come to your senses!" His mind twisted ironically. "Ah," he added, "if only you could."

"Is this why you have come?" she asked. "To laugh at me? A once-chaste maid you ruined?"

Voltaire would have shaken his head if he'd owned one. "I didn't ruin you. I merely helped you to become the woman that you are."

"*Exactement*," she said. "But I don't want to be a woman. I want to be a warrior for my King, for Charles of France."

"Never mind all that patriotic twaddle now. You shall be neither woman nor warrior unless you heed my warning. You must answer no calls, except my own, without first clearing them through me. You are to entertain no one, speak with no one, travel nowhere, do nothing without my prior consent."

"Monsieur mistakes me for his wife."

"You must trust me. Were I your husband trust would be indeed too much to ask. Our lives—such as they are—are in grave danger."

La Pucelle did not answer at once. Was she conferring with those idiotic voices of conscience that so bedevilled her? Harpies. Fanatics. Internalizations of ignorant village priests.

"I am a peasant," she said at last. "But not a slave. Your demands that I subordinate my will and judgment to your own are those of a father or a husband. I could never submit to such restraints upon my liberty. At fourteen I left the safe but tedious society of village women for the life of a soldier among brave men. Until I marry—and I trust I never shall—I serve but two human masters: The King of France and the Bishop of Rome: Let *them* command me to answer no calls, I shall obey."

Women, thought Voltaire. Even warrior types denying influence from the inconstant moon were harder to control than gnats. Unless you married them. And even then the deployment of several eunuchs and large dogs around the house to keep an eye on them was highly advisable.

"*Chere petite,* you confuse the studied insincerity of a cultured man with the boorish pettiness of husbands and fathers. I've been called many things in my life, but I never gave anyone cause to slander my name with epithets such as *husband* or *father.*"

"Fool!"

"Your safety concerns me, not your fidelity. No lover, having enjoyed me, could possibly prefer any other to my exquisite self."

"You confuse your opinion and the world's with truth," said Joan. "As those bereft of voices often do. I know you too well to assume you are sincere, but I'll comply with your wishes on one condition."

A dance of pungent light exploded in Voltaire, as happened whenever he was about to get his way.

"You remember Garcon? The funny servant with the noble soul? He waited on our table at the inn."

"Cafe," Voltaire corrected her. "Aux Deux Magots is a—"

"And his companion? What was her name? That noble girl who did not allow differences in their rank to keep her from surrendering to him her all too human heart?"

"A woman falls in love with a machine," Voltaire said, "and you prattle of differences in rank? And would you call her noble if she eloped with her horse?"

"What was her name?" Joan asked in a dreamy nostalgic voice. "Do you remember?"

At the mention of Maquina's name, Voltaire's brain blipped. "Of course I remember. They've loaded me with so much memory, how could I possibly forget? Her name was Maquina, *Mme. la Scientiste.*"

"No, no," Joan said. "That was the sorceress's Christian name. *Madame la Sorciere.*"

Something fluttered in Voltaire's system. A bug, a jittery Freudian bug of some kind. As he aged, even he sometimes made mistakes. He re-searched his memory and retried. "Amana," he said with authority.

"Amana," Joan repeated wistfully. "Amana and Garcon. I miss them very much, don't you?"

Her voice blurred, misty with emotions her inventor, *Madame la Scientiste*, had programmed her to feel, though Voltaire knew better than to mention that. "God" was the only inventor Joan of Arc understood, even lodged in this cyberworld of enameled, unyielding light.

"If you arrange for all of us to meet at *Deux Magots* again," Joan said, "I promise to respond to no requests save yours."

"Are you completely mad? Every hacker on the planet's looking for us. This is no time to meet at a known alpha-numeric address, a sim public cafe!" He hadn't seen Garcon or Amana since he'd pulled off their miraculous escape—all four of them—from the enraged rioting masses at the Paris Coliseum years ago. He had no idea where the mechwaiter, whose brain he had upgraded, and his human paramour were. Or *if* they were. Somewhere in the intricate labyrinth of Internet if indeed anywhere at all . . . The thought of trying to locate them called up in memory how his head used to feel when he wore a wig for too long.

"Can you not locate them?" said Joan. "Perhaps it is beyond your powers."

Voltaire spoke as if clearing his throat. "*Ma chere pucelle*, you underestimate my genius. Nothing is beyond the powers of the most enlightened mind the most enlightened century has ever known."

"*C'est bien, alors*," said Joan, adding in the commanding tone with which she'd led French soldiers into battle, "Arrange a rendezvous or I'll never receive data from you again."

Without so much as an *adieu*, she terminated their

connection and dwindled into the darkness from which she'd come.

4

The mechdresser—a two-armed Nacka 800 who'd been doing Maquina's hair for two years—seated her before the style viewer and wheeled away to get the computer cartridge of the latest Euro/Asian/American styles.

Maquina had never frequented beauty parlors or paid much attention to her health and appearance until two years ago, shortly after her fortieth birthday, when with no warning she lost consciousness while swimming in the backyard pool. Had the mechgardener not happened to enter the yard and set off his alarm, alerting Tech, she would have drowned. The medicos thoroughly checked her out but could find nothing wrong. Masters of the obvious when all their magic failed, they told her not to go swimming alone.

But the incident sabotaged her exuberant self-confidence, darkening her consciousness overnight. What had struck once without warning could strike as suddenly again. Until then Maquina had taken her radiant health, superabundant energy, exotic looks—she was of Mexi/Korean descent—and tidy, firm figure for granted, never allowing preoccupation with them to interfere with her professional pursuits or her devotion to Tech and Electrica.

But now, every morning, she got up from her empty bed—Tech rose before she did, driven by his daemon, ambition—and peered into the mirror to survey the damage done during the night. She was still attractive, but the mirror compelled her to add *for your age*. Even if she managed to live to the average age of 120, the best third of her life was gone. Not a day passed that her mortality did not bark at her like a hungry dog. Dry curdling skin, collapsing eyelids, drooping mouth, the inexorable triumph of gravity over human flesh—these could be glossed. Malignancies, misfiring nerves, organ break-down, most of the chronic and degenerative diseases that prey on organic life—these too could be indefinitely checked.

But every gloss and check itself was a reminder of the black-out that could snuff out the light of her consciousness at any time. And no treatment could replenish the mysterious symbolic heart of her vitality and will that made it possible for her to resurrect herself from boredom, habit, indifference—all the tiny daily deaths; resurrections that made it possible for her to keep on saying *yes* to life itself.

Tech handled his mortality the way he did everything else—by hurling himself like a rocket into endless orbits of activity, "busyness," work. When Tech achieved a goal, he simply set another one—the quest for knowledge, wealth, fame, power ended whenever, wherever, one decided it did. For Maquina, it had ended that afternoon in the pool. Though she continued to go through the motions of marriage, family and work—one had to do *some*thing, after all, with one's time—the quest for *any*thing was a salt that had lost its savor. Illusions had given the salt itself taste; hers had now fled. The longings that in youth had lured her to follow this course or that—they still seized her occasionally—she knew could never be fulfilled in this world, and she believed in no other. She'd looked into the maw of existence itself, saw she would never solve the mystery of being and its dark twin, death, doubted there *was* any solution—what you saw was all there was. She had seen everything and wondered what was left.

She glanced at a small bowl of fruit beside the complimentary coffee dispenser at each customer station—an overripe apple, two blackening bananas, a cluster of green grapes clinging to tiny branchlets with brown mouths. Incredible! The beauty parlor

was still offering its clients free coffee and fruit. But
Maquina had neither appetite nor thirst. Perhaps,
she reflected, as Nacka rolled toward her with the
cartridge of the latest hairstyles tucked under her
mechanical arm, the human psyche has a built-in
talent for death. How lucky mechs were not to be
programmed with that!

"That one would suit you," Nacka said, as a model
wearing a straight Cleopatra style—"The Power Bob"
—materialized on the style viewer. "Try it on?"

"No, I don't think so." Maquina keystroked for
another style.

Pixie, vamp, girl-next-door, glamour puss, inge-
nue, appeared and disappeared till Maquina, not
wanting to offend Nacka, said, "Oh, all right. I might
as well try them all."

She watched her own image appear on the moni-
tor in style after style. All failed to please her equally.
"I'm sorry, Nacka," she said. "It's my mood."

"You don't know how lucky you are to have them.
We mechs are like The Plains. Consistent to a fault."
She tousled Maquina's hair. "Why not try something
different? Something wild and crazy."

"Such as?"

Nacka removed the old cartridge from the style
viewer, and popped another one in. Maquina appeared on screen sporting an asymmetrical, long and
full on one side, short and closely cropped to her
skull on the other.

"I don't think my husband would like it."

"Is he still working night and day? Believe me, he
won't notice. Time to stop pleasing him and start
pleasing yourself. I'll go ahead and wash it while you
make up your mind." Nacka unclipped her fingered
hands, laid them aside, and changed into the soft
spongy ones she used for rinsing and shampooing.

Maquina reclined in the chair, the back of her
neck resting on the basin's edge. She closed her
eyes, surrendered herself to the tingling pleasure of

having her hair washed. Aside from Tech and, less and less often, Electrica—she was getting too big to fondle—only Nacka ever touched her. And Nacka, unlike many husbands, never tuned her out. No wonder beauty parlors were always crowded!

Maquina opened her eyes and gazed up into Nacka's expressionless yet somehow sympathetic face. Could it be that Nacka was her closest confidante, her most intimate friend?

"You're absolutely right. It would take more than a new hairstyle to divert *my* husband from his quest for fame and fortune."

Nacka slipped her fingered hands back on for the scalp rub. "If he's *that* far gone . . ." She put her metal mouth slot flush against Maquina's ear and whispered, "Get a lover."

Maquina's blood jumped. Did she . . . ? But how could she . . . ? "The only men *I* meet are all images on a screen."

"I didn't mean a man," Nacka said. "I meant a mech."

Maquina was startled into speechlessness.

Nacka's gesture embraced the entire beauty parlor, crowded with men and women, mostly sallow and thin—the food shortage was beginning to take its toll. "You'd be surprised how many of them do. The women too, why not?"

"But . . . well . . . I . . ."

"There are advantages," Nacka went on. "They're always there when you need them. They'll do anything that you want. If there's something about them you don't like, reprogram them and zzzt—they change. Bio men—forgive me—are just like dogs. What they can't screw or eat, they piss on! Mechmen aren't like that at all. They're programmed to—"

Shouts rang out, cutting Nacka off. Both she and Maquina turned toward the disturbance. A fight had erupted between two women at a customer station nearby. "They're mine!" the older one shouted. "She ate the ones at her station already! These are mine!"

"Liar! Look in her bag! She put hers in her bag and then tried to take mine!"

Each tugged at the one bowl so hard, it fell, shattering on the floor. Several grapes rolled across the floor, collecting wet hair clippings as they went. A man shot up from a hair implant station and quickly began picking them up and stuffing them into his pockets, while each of the women, florid with anger, claimed the other should pay for the broken bowl.

Maquina picked up the fruit bowl at her station, rose and approached them. "Here," she said. "I'm not hungry." She snapped her grape cluster in two, handing each of them half.

She was at once accosted by three other people. A man with a bleachbag over his head said, "Don't give it all to them!" and snatched the overripe bananas from the bowl. A teenaged boy with a purple beard so scant you could count every hair, cried out, "I have a little sister at home!" He grabbed the apple and dropped it down his shirt.

"She must be allergic," a redhead said as Maquina walked back to Nacka with the empty bowl thinking, all of them, everyone here, will one day sicken, suffer, die. Except for the mechs and a.i.'s.

"Sure you won't reconsider?" Nacka said, after everyone had settled back down. "If you're worried about your husband, we have some in back disguised to look like ordinary household mechs." Her voice lowered to a suggestive rasp. "Those extra arms sure come in handy."

"You—have them here?"

"Sure do. And they're on sale! We keep them in the back."

Maquina, still flushed from the excitement, blurted out, "Thanks, I already have a—a—companion."

Nacka gave her a knowing look. "Holding out on

me, huh? Bet he's not always there for you when you need him."

Maquina smiled her Mona Lisa smile. "Oh, but he is."

On her way home, though it was spring, she noticed signs of decay everywhere—dead leaves curled among live ones on the roadside trees; withered flowers lurking amid the brilliant yellow, purple, orange blossoms that still thrived—until two years ago, she'd never noticed the omnipresence of death in life. Now it was hard to notice anything else.

Her White Dwarf automatically slowed down for the light. It rolled to a stop beside a spiffy green Omega. Maquina glanced at the driver through the Omega's dome—a teenaged boy. His bearded cheek—you could count every purple hair—puffed out grotesquely as he chewed. Maquina looked away, pretending not to notice, as the tiny waisted apple core he tossed out hit the street.

5

Alone in her room, Electrica sat in front of her schoolscreen doing her Primatology homeschoolwork. Thanks to her parents' foresight, she'd been implanted at birth with matrix-integrators and was a prodigious student, working years beyond her grade level. No other person of her generation—except Trask—was outfitted in a similar way.

At times she yearned to be like everybody else, but never when homeschoolwork had to be done. Her updated, biotech-assisted brain enabled her to transmit answers to Mastermind using few keystrokes, merely by thinking hard. She'd already discussed her answers with the bioteacher she viewed every day but whom she'd never met, and so earned Mastermind's consent to proceed to the next lesson.

But Electrica kept reviewing the segment on twentieth-century sapiens' food habits with fascina-

tion and disgust. Jammed feed lots of gentle bovines
nursing their spindly-legged young; noisy, humorous
curly-tailed creatures with delicate pink and white
skin; exotic red-eyed crested birds in crowded cages,
unable to move much less fly, forced to bear eggs
only to have them snatched away, until their necks
were wrung, their bodies hacked to pieces and their
plucked goosebumpy skins fried to a crisp in sizzling
oil.

All this was revolting enough, but nothing proved
the backwardness of twencen primates more than
cloth and leather-clad sapiens—imagine wearing
bioskins instead of paper clothes!— sawing into the
dead flesh of fellow bio-beings, sopping up bio blood
with bread, masticating corpses impaled from throat
to anus on spits over hot coals or roasted whole in
ovens fit for fairy-tale witches—all with a lip-smacking
gusto bordering on the obscene. Even slimy bird
embryos and snails weren't exempt from the slaughter!

"Finished your homeschool yet?"

Electrica gave a start and swiveled her schoolchair
around. Her mother stood in the doorway, her perfectly shaped dermplucked eyebrows raised. The Cosmic X forbid a single dark hair should be out of
place. "No," Electrica lied.

"No? You're usually through with homeschool long
before now. Need any help?"

Electrica shook her head. She knew what was
coming and she did not return her mother's smile.
Her mother's tutoring was often more thorough than
Mastermind's. Electrica avoided it like the plague.

"Your socialization session begins in fifteen minutes." As if Electrica didn't know. "Nick and Nack
will be upset if you're not on time and they have to
wait."

Electrica fluttered her lips. She hated it when her
mother talked down to her as if her reproductive
classification were still *Child*. "Mechbrains can't get
upset," she said. "And who cares if they do? I hate

them, they're all a bunch of phonies." She booted up
for her mother's lecture on the equality of all intelligent beings, mechbeings included.

But all her mother said as she approached the
schoolscreen was, "I thought you liked Nick and
Nack. I asked for them especially. You seemed to
have such a good time the last time they came over."

"They're okay I guess," Electrica conceded, feeling guilty because the lecture had not come. "But
they're such goody goodies, they're no fun."

"They're *ahimsas*," her mother said.

"Oh wow, news breaks."

"Don't be so fresh. You want them programmed so
they could hurt you?"

Electrica gazed sullenly at the wall. She wouldn't
see a biokid until the Kidfest in Silicon Valley, three
months from now. And even that was so overly planned
and supervised by grown-ups, she never had any
fun. Kids weren't allowed to touch each other without written consent from both parents: *Electrica
Hilliard may touch and be touched by _____,
within the constraints of Behavior Guidelines, State
Code* blah blah blah blah.

And you needed a separate form for every kid. By
the time you knew a kid well enough to get her/his
parents' consent, the Kidfest was over. Contact sports
were like parade ground drills—no fun at all. Grown-
ups, no matter what they said, liked safety more than
freedom, spontaneity, adventure. And the way they
designed mechkids like Nick and Nack proved it.

"I always know what mechkids are gonna do and
say before they do. It's worse than playing with
grown-ups. Why can't I have a biokid friend like I
did when I was little?"

"Because no one in her right mind lives in a city
anymore. They're too polluted for anyone except
mechs. Out here the nearest biokid your age lives
miles away and is as busy with homeschool as you

are. You don't want to grow up and find all the good jobs taken by mechs, do you?"

"Why can't you get me a brother or sister? It could sleep with me. I'd help you and Daddy take care of it."

Her mother sighed. They'd been through this before. "Because the Population Control Center allows each couple one child only, and you're ours. We'd have to non-renew our marriage contract to be eligible to apply for another child."

"You could pretend-divorce," Electrica urged. "After you get the kid, just marry each other again."

"You think ordering a child is so easy? Only the parent you didn't live with would be eligible—fat lot of good that would do you—and only if she/he contracted a marriage with someone childless."

"You could pretend-marry Nim."

"I don't even like him!"

"You wouldn't have to kiss him. It would just be pretend."

"Yeah? What about the global waiting list? Before anyone's born, someone else has to die."

Electrica felt overwhelmed; nobody ever died unless she/he wanted to or had a crushcrash. But she stuck to her warheads. "Mechs are dorfs. I don't care how smart they are or how many of them study with Mastermind, they're all a bunch of boardbrains."

"Look who's talking! And anyway, that's specist! I won't have you talking like that, you hear?"

"It's *not* specist." Electrica pushed back the long paper sleeves of her blouse, preparing to verbally finish her mother off. "Specism is when you think you're better than biobrains who aren't sapiens. I'd rather play with a curly-tailed peccary *any* day than with Nick and Nack." She gestured at the schoolscreen as she spoke. "At least they'd be warm and cuddly and wriggly." In her zeal to exit dramatically to the privacy of her room—she'd recently developed a great fondness of dramatic exits—she shot up from her schoolchair. Only to sink back down as she realized she was already in her room.

"A peccary?" Her mother's dermplucked brows and freckle-free face knotted with perplexity. Ms. Perfect—Hard To Please—leaned over the schoolscreen and said, "Oh. You mean a pig. I've never seen one except in a zoo, but I always thought they were nasty things. Much dirtier than Nick and Nack."

"And you call me specist! You've never even met a peccary and yet you're calling them nasty. I bet you'd eat one if you got a chance!"

Her mother grimaced. "That's quite enough, Electrica. Now turn your schoolscreen off, throw that blouse out—the cuffs are dirty—and change into your s.s. clothes. Nick and Nack will be here any minute."

"Do I have to see them?" She gave her mother a pathetic look and contemplated whining. Pathos sometimes worked where defiance failed. "I've got all this Voltaire re-creation stuff to do for Dad."

Her mother perked up at once. "*What* stuff?"

"He showed me how you guys re-created Joan and Voltaire. Didn't he tell you?"

"No."

"He almost caught him a coupla times, but somehow at the last sec Voltaire always gets away. Dad's paying me $450 an hour to help him find him. He says he needs all the help he can get. I'd much rather do that than play with Nick and Nack."

Her mother looked miffed. She probably wanted to find Voltaire herself. "If I send Nick and Nack away, they'll fly the s.s. officer out here and Daddy and I will be fined. Now don't keep them waiting. It's rude."

"They're robots!" Electrica shouted. "I'll keep them waiting if I want to!" She leaned away instinctively in case Ms. Perfect, who had never laid a hand on her, should suddenly alter her child-rearing philosophy. But even abusive physical contact was better than none. And if her mother let her have it, she'd have an excuse to run for comfort to her father's arms, arms that lately, for reasons that had something to do with her visits to the Family Planning Clinic—parents were weird—rarely embraced her anymore. Even her mother didn't kiss and fondle her the way she'd done before Electrica's repro-classification changed and she had to go to that dorky clinic in the Valley. She hadn't seen a real live boy in months. Did they think she could get pregnant from Anatomy holograms? From droopy Nick and Nack? They didn't even have hoses between their legs.

Her mother spotted the uneaten plankton salad on the compudesk and resorted to diversion strategy. "You didn't touch your lunch," she said. "Aren't you hungry?"

"I'm starving! But plankton makes me upchuck. You never made me eat it before."

"I'll save it for you. In case you get hungry later."

"Bios aren't gonna have to start eating flesh, are we? Like Originals?"

Her mother paused in the doorway, a smart alecky smile on her lips. "Some still do. There still are a few colonies of Originals left—one not that far from here, in fact. They raise bios and eat their flesh. They even bear their young live in the throwback way."

Electrica let the full force of such a fact sink in. "It ought to be against the *law*."

"It is. Except on Original reservations. Originals still worship a deity they call Jehovah God. Some of them call it Allah."

"Jehovah *who*?"

"That's their name for the Cosmic X. But they don't think of it as a mathematical unknown at all."

Electrica gazed dreamily outside the glasswall onto a brilliant blossomy spring day. Their house was perched on a hill overlooking Elements Valley, murkily visible under its recently completed pollution-containment dome. But in the near distance wistaria, bottlebrush and forsythia bloomed. Even the hill-sides blazed with flowering iceplant and sweet william. Electrica could smell the pungent pines mingled with sage through open windows cut into the blockwalls of her room. A longing for a final revelation of secrets of the natural world welled up in her, together with an intuition that such secrets could never be wholly told. "They've solved the mystequation and found a value for the Cosmic X?"

Her mother smiled. "They *think* they have. They don't know the difference between demonstrable truth and religious wishful thinking. The government has tried for years to put an end to throwback practices, but they're protected under Planetary Freedom of Religion rules."

"*Flesh*-eaters?"

"Originals have civil rights, too."

Electrica recalled a schoolscreen image from a History program—a woman lying on a torture rack, her ankles bound in stirrups, her legs wide apart. An infant sapiens head, covered with slime and blood, protruded from between her open legs. She'd never seen anything yukkier in her life. "Why would anyone want to live like that?"

"They can't handle the relative nature of scientific truth. They prefer the false absolutes of the past to the relative knowns of the present."

Electrica nodded, pretending to understand because her parents took great pride in her mental acuity.

"They don't even allow mechs capable of high-think on their reservation," her mother went on. "That's how backward they are. Now get a move on. I hear someone on the landing pad, probably Nick and Nack."

Electrica shut the door behind her mother, tore off her skirt and tossed it down the trash chute. She'd already worn it three times. She started to do the same with the blouse, then changed her mind and kicked it underneath her bed. She didn't want Ms. Perfect to think she would tolerate being bossed around the rest of her life. She pulled an s.s. five-ply jumpsuit she had never worn over her knobby knees and, breathing in the heavy perfume of the flowering hills, wondered if she'd ever have a real live kid like Huck Finn or Tom Sawyer to play Explorer with, not on her p.c. but in the ten-dimensional real world. She wouldn't live among flesh-eaters and live birthers for all the diamonds on Space Col 43's Carbon Moon. But if she did, at least she wouldn't have to socialize with boardbrains like Nick and Nack ever again.

6

Tech sat before his monitor, combing the trashy back alleys and byways of Internet for any clue that might lead to Voltaire. At first he'd concentrated his efforts on helping Maquina find Joan, reasoning she'd be easier. "Why?" Maquina had asked him. "Because she's female?"

But Tech's strategy had nothing to do with Joan's "sex," everything with her temperament. She'd be less calculating than Voltaire, less wiley. Ruled by her heart and not, like Voltaire, by her head, she'd be more likely to make a mistake.

But after days of fruitless cooperative search, he'd changed tactics and, over Maquina's objections, now concentrated all his efforts on Voltaire, leaving Maquina to pursue Joan. On several occasions he'd felt himself to be close, very close, to finding him. But always, at the last minute, something would thwart his effort. His screen would inexplicably black out. He'd lose hours of data in a microsecond. His backup nets would fail. And he'd have to begin again.

"You still at it?" Maquina asked. "Any luck?"

Tech leaned back in his compuchair and rotated his neck to get the cricks out. "I may be onto something," he said. "I'm not sure."

"Oh?" Maquina said. "What?"

"It's all right here." He pointed to his carbon cube. "Here's your copy. If you have any bright ideas, don't hesitate to share them. I'm trying a completely different tack that might also help you find Joan. How's your search going? Any leads?"

Maquina shook her head. "I came to remind you it's your turn to take Electrica to Family Planning for her monthly verification."

"Why can't she drive herself?"

"The Corbeau's at the compumech's."

"Again? She *told* us not to buy a French car. She was right. Can't you take her? I might be onto something. I hate to stop now."

"Sorry. I need the White Dwarf—I'm getting my hair done at the mechdresser's."

"You just had it done."

"Unless you want her to take the Supernova."

Tech rubbed the back of his neck. There was a time Maquina would have done it for him—he wouldn't even have had to ask. "She can't take the Supernova. Rub my neck, will you? Its automatic pilot isn't working right. She might get stuck. That's all we need. People out there are so hungry, they might eat *her*. What time is her appointment?"

"You have to leave now. It's a beautiful day for a zip."

"Now? But I may be onto something!"

Maquina's brow shot up. "Unless you'd rather deal with the sterilization bureaucrats. They take these verifications pretty seriously, you know."

Tech turned all systems off and clicked his tongue. "Tell Electrica I'll meet her outside."

Maquina had not lied; it was a beautiful day indeed. Spring rains had been induced after a period of drought, and everything shone in the semi-desert light with a freshly washed dazzle that stunned the eye. Houses were as rare here as they were everywhere

—few people could afford them, especially the older ones like his with the space tax—but a few red tiled roofs jutted up. The rolling hillsides had turned grassy green overnight, as if to express their appreciation for the downpour that had quenched their summer thirst. Tech always enjoyed the winding drive into the Valley, though he hated going underdome. The domeguards at the tollgates were officious, Tech disliked lasersearch though he understood its necessity, and domeair, no matter how purified, smelled flat compared with the crisp clean stuff up here.

The Supernova was still charging when Electrica gawkily bounded down the drive toward the car, reminding him of a large bird not quite used to its recently acquired wings. She ran across the landing pad, irking him no end—it wasn't designed for walking, much less for adolescent thuds. She stumbled, got entangled in her arms and legs, almost went down, miraculously regained her balance and arrived at the car, panting.

"Sorry I'm late." She pecked him on the cheek.

"How many times do I have to tell you not to cut across the landing pad? It's designed for aircraft landskis, not for clodhoppers like yours."

He regretted his reproach at once. Her face fell. She was very sensitive about her size ten feet. They were almost as big as his, and no let-up in sight. He reached out to pat her leg, thought better of it—she was too big for that sort of thing now—and complimented her on her perfume instead.

"Turn on the carscreen, sugar," he said. "I want to catch the news."

"It sounds like an infection," Electrica said. "Like some spooky disease."

Tech reflected on recent events and said, "It is."

"Is it true we're all gonna have to go on rations?"

" 'Fraid so. But not until next week."

"Are we gonna have to eat plankton every day?"

"Maybe." Her frown made him add, "Rations are

mostly a precaution. It'll be a nuisance more than anything else. You and I can both afford to lose a little of this." He squeezed a roll of flesh above his belt—not bad for a bio his age, but bad enough—and hoped his concern was not evident in his voice.

"Are we all gonna starve?" Electrica gazed out at the grassy hillsides rolling by outside and said, "They caught a bio family eating fieldrats."

"Where did you hear that?"

"From Trask."

Trask was her compuschool lab partner assigned by Mastermind, the only other whiz kid her age in the country with implants and test scores as high as hers. He lived in the interior somewhere—Nebraska, Iowa . . . The virus had spread quickly to the major food supply sources. The bread-basket regions were hardest hit.

Tech's stomach turned greasy with fear. "Don't pay attention to gossip," he said.

"I'd rather starve than eat a fieldrat. Max me out!"

"You won't have to do either," he assured her, although the virus had, in just a matter of days, affected every major food grower and distributor on the planet.

They fell into a meditative silence as the Supernova crested Lookout Hill. The Valley appeared stunningly beautiful from here, its slum zones, trash-littered streets, chaotic high-rises, miscarriages of justice, undeserved sufferings, inequities, iniquities—all of its blemishes and blights—folded by distance like broken eggs into the cream smooth batter of a cake. Everything looked perfect as long as you did not look close. Maybe the Cosmic X was farsighted. As far above the Cosmos as they, up here, were from the Valley. You can't correct imperfections you don't perceive.

They were several miles from the house when Electrica exclaimed, "Faddle! Forgot my portabook!"

"You don't need it." His chin pointed at the

carscreen. "It won't kill you to watch the news on the way into town with me."

Like all Hilliards, Electrica did not readily take no for an answer. She tried to talk him into going back for her portabook. When he refused, she sulked. Pretending not to notice, he tuned in the news. She turned from the carscreen to gaze out the window where, as they approached the Valley, the hills flattened out into vineyards, spiking the air with the heavy aroma of grapes.

Beside him Electrica, her eyes half-closed, fell into a daydream so deep, he and the vineyards dotted with mechpickers, for her, ceased to exist. A boy? he wondered. Who? She wasn't old enough to key into Datemate. Could she have cracked the code? Yes, definitely. The kid was sharp, though still a kid. Mental and emotional development—especially these days when everyone spent most of his/her life in front of a monitor—did not proceed in tandem. Was he going to lose her to some Mastermind drop-out who thought four hairs on his chin meant he was a man?

Suddenly she cried out, "Goodgod, look!"

The Supernova had stopped at the crossroads. In the vineyard on Electrica's side of the road a six-armed mechpicker was slugging it out with his four-armed boss. Their metal bodies clanged as the six-armer knocked the four-armer to his knees with his two free hands.

"But they're ahimsas, Dad. Ahimsas can't fight."

"Don't move," Tech said and got out of the car to get a fuller view. He whistled through his teeth at what he saw. All over the field the mechpickers, deaf to four-armer protests, had folded their six arms across their chests, refusing to work. Instead of picking grapes, they formed a protective barrier between the thick vines and the supervising four-armers. These, fewer in number, shouted, stamping their wheel-free feet. Some four-armers became confused and staggered straight into the vines. Several six-armers raised baskets of grapes reverentially toward the sun. One paid no attention and continued to pick, until another fell on him, swinging. When a four-armer tried to intervene, two other six-armers attacked him. The whole field erupted into violence as Tech stood watching from the road.

Tech jumped back in the car and disengaged the automatic pilot.

"Dad, look!"

Thirty meters ahead a dazed four-armer lurched into the road, heading their way.

Tech's U-turn was so sharp, Electrica's head hit the Supernova's thick transparent frame. "You okay?" he asked as the car soared back toward the hills.

"Uh-huh. Not sure about my matrix integrators, though." She saw his face and added, "I'm okay, Dad, I'm okay." Her eyes shone with fear and excitement. "We going home?"

"No, but we're damn sure gonna take a different route."

"Can we stop by the house and get my portabook?"

Tech gave her an exasperated look. She was a Hilliard, all right, through and through.

Electrica took the stairs to her room two at a time, retrieved her portabook from the junk heap beside her bed and bounded down the hall. Muffled voices from her mother's office drew her up short. Her father must have followed her into the house to tell her mother about the rioting mechs. But no . . . no grown-up could travel that fast on foot. Curious, she paused. Cocked one ear to the closed door. The woman's voice belonged to her mother, but the other voice—the man's—was definitely not her dad's. She pressed closer, stopped breathing, ordered her heart to stop thumping in her ears to clear them out . . .

"We've got to be careful," her mother said. "He's

onto something. No, no, not us. Not yet. I scrambled him again, but I can't keep this up."

The man's voice was harder to make out. Electrica closed one eye and listened harder than she'd ever listened to her mother in her life.

"Of course he trusts me! But that doesn't mean he always will."

Then the man said, "I must warn her."

A long pause. "You're still seeing her then?"

Two bursts of the Supernova's horn, faint but loud enough to obscure the conversation on the other side of the door, ended her eavesdropping. She slipped quietly down the hall and out the front door. Did what she'd overheard mean her own mother was a whore? Wow! She'd never met a whore—not even in telebooks—she wasn't supposed to teleread about whores, and since the invention of mechwenches, bio whores were almost obsolete.

The idea that her mother had a secret life apart from homeoffice, her father and herself kindled both fear and a prickly excitement—like the mechpicker riot out on Valley Road. If she told the boardbrains— they were such goody-goody cubes!—they'd never play with her again. But she'd sooner eat flesh than betray her mother to them. She could blackmail her mother the way the guy in the portabook blackmailed *his* bosses. Then she would never have to make her bed or take another soc session again. As she emerged into the dazzling semi-desert light and saw her Dad—poor sap—parked at the curb, she suddenly foresaw that having something like this on a grown-up might be a drag as well as a joy.

Should she tell her father? Naw, what for? She'd launch her own investigation like the guy in her portabook—he got the goods on *every*body, presidents, civil rights leaders, even the cops—find out who the creep was. And after she had all the data, she would spray on dresses as tight as she liked, let the bitch have it and never take orders from her again.

* * *

Tech deactivated the carscreen at the moment Electrica emerged from the house. Bios *were* eating fieldrats in remote areas, according to the news reports. No need for the kid to know that—she knew enough.

"You could have telewritten and read the whole book," he groused as she clambered into the car. "What kept you? Hey." The blackness of her mood was overwhelming. Had Maquina been viewing the news in the house? "You all right? Those mechjerks getting to you?"

She turned her mother's luminous brown eyes on him and shrugged. "Just one of my wide adolescent mood swings."

He laughed. Had his own adolescence been like this? Child one moment, fully adult the next? "Well, swing it up a bit, okay?" He glanced at the portabook she dropped onto the seat. "What're you telereading now, *The Psychopathology of Adolescents*?"

"Very funny," she said. "It's about J. Edgar Hoover, bio Chief of the FBI in throwback times."

"What do you want with him?"

"Nothing! I got him off Mastermind's mandatory US History & Institutions list. Didn't know who he was. And orbit! am I sorry I found out. Now I'm stuck with him for my major annual project. I bet I already know more about him than Mastermind. I bet I know more about him than the Cosmic X! Talk about squeaky clean. The dude lived with his Mom until she died, and after that with Clyde Tolson, the FBI's number two man. He didn't have a girlfriend or a wife or kid or *any*thing. All he did was work. He might as well have been a boardbrain."

"Was he a joyboy?" Tech asked.

"No way. Though some bios at the time thought so—cuz he was always in orbit with Tolson. He busted joys!"

Tech humphed. "You've got a lot to learn about

the world. It's full of hypocrites. He might have busted joys just to divert suspicion from himself."

Electrica pretend-barfed. "Max me out! No one's that . . ."

"That what? For Cosmic X sake, don't start sentences you don't intend to finish! And stop saying *max me out*."

"Two-faced, okay? Two-faced. If he was a joy, max me out! He sure kept it a . . ."

"A what? Secret? Well, I can't say I blame him." Tech breathed in a whiff of heavily scented sage. The hillsides were covered with wildflowers. Specks of pollen sailed up and down invisible rivers of air; not a mechman in sight.

"I hate two-faced bios," Electrica said with sudden intensity.

"Hate uses energy you're better off using to try to understand. In throwback days a joyboy couldn't be chief mechcook and bottle washer, much less head of the FBI. Now joys can be anything. If government had its way, we'd *all* be joys—keeps population down. The Vice President's a joyboy! No, don't turn on the carscreen. Let's both just sit back and enjoy the ride."

They cruised along State Park Road—no vineyards here but Tech kept an eye out for malfunctioning mechs anyway.

"You and Mom gonna renew your contract?" Electrica suddenly asked. Her eyelids draped like fringed blinds over her eyes, assuring no more light invaded from outside than they could stand.

"Sure we are. Why not?"

The blinds rolled up as she opened her eyes—the kid was deep and passionate, a heartbreaker, anyone could see that. Her voice cracked when she said, "When?"

"Soon as we get around to it. We've been so busy hunting sims, we haven't had a minute for anything else."

"What happens when you find them?"

"We interrogate them. Try to find out if they know anything about this food mess."

"Think they do? Does Voltaire?"

"I don't know. I'd sure like to find out."

The car swayed gently as it glided toward the bottom of the hill. A raven cawed—maybe it was a crow—only a poet could tell the difference. Or an ornithologist. They were everywhere around here. Noisy black splotches perched on every tree-top as if the whole land below belonged only to them. Almost all other animals were gone except for birds. Through all the toxic stink, smoke and pollu-tion of the last two centuries, birds alone had thrived. A hundred billion of them, the planet's unpaid garbage collectors, picking the hillsides, plains, and deserts clean.

Without warning Electrica shot up in her seat. "I just got a fab idea! Bet you money I find Voltaire before you do!"

"Uh-huh. And I'll find the solution to the Cosmic X."

"I mean it, Dad. What'll you give me if I do?"

Tech looked at her. "What do you want?"

Her face screwed up with the intensity of concen-tration. Goodgod, Tech thought, she's serious. But then Electrica usually was.

"A medal! Like big shot bios get for winning trade wars."

Electrica's assurance was contagious. Out of the mouths of babes? he wondered. "Find him, I'll give you two."

She solemnly extended her hand—it was almost as big as his own. They shook on it.

"Don't tell Mom, that's part of the deal."

"Why not?" She didn't answer, so he guessed. "You want it to be a surprise?"

"Yeah. Right. Maybe I can find him in time for your anniversary."

"It would damn sure be the best present we get."
No point in squashing adolescent fantasy; the difficulty of the task would squash it soon enough. All
the frustrations and failures that lay in wait for her
stood up and paraded inside his mind. A surge of
tenderness for her welled up in him. "You're full of
surprises. I had no idea you were so thoughtful."

Electrica's eyes shone with visionary light. "Wow,"
she said. "I can hardly wait to see her face."

7

He swooped into consciousness as if borne in the
beak of some great flapping bird—who suddenly,
cruelly, let him go. He landed on his feet, with no
knee-bending thud of impact with the ground, and
waiting for his mind—a microsecond late—to reinhabit
his body.

He felt disoriented, fuzzy, fog-soft. For decades,
he had risen crisply each morning at the same time
and eaten the same breakfast of orange juice, bacon
and coffee—black to help keep his weight down,
though he preferred it with cream and sugar. His
meals were full-scale operations, as his Negro cook
and housekeeper well knew. If she forgot a napkin or
set a glass slightly out of place, he'd threaten her
with deportation to Siberia. Each morning, he left
his red brick, porticoed, Georgian house overlooking
the capital's Rock Creek Park—he'd moved there
after his mother died, to be closer to Clyde—just as
his custom-built, heavily-armored Cadillac lumbered
up to his door, for time was money and Crawford,
his Negro chauffeur, knew better than to be even a
minute late. He disliked change for any reason, established in his private and professional life the most
efficient ways to get things done, then ritualized
those routines which, in an individual's life, are what
the solemn rule of law is in the life of a society.

A short man—greatness of character was not al-

ways accompanied by greatness of stature; look at
Napoleon!—he'd battled corpulence throughout his
life. He was therefore surprised to find his bald head
barely cleared the ceiling—he didn't like surprises—
and, more alarming yet, that he was not alone.

"Who are you? How did you get in? Sam? Sam!"

He marched into his outer office, a small museum
full of memorabilia from his gangbuster days, but
"Special Agent" Sam Noisette—his old colored servant who escorted visitors in to see him—was not
there. A white plaster facsimile of John Dillinger's
death mask stared up through the display case. Beside it lay the straw hat Dillinger was wearing the
night FBI agents shot him; a La Corona-Belvedere
cigar, still wrapped in cellophane; a wrinkled snap-
shot of a girl, fished from his pockets; and the silver
lens rim of his glasses—part of Dillinger's disguise—
snapped by a bullet. Had anything in his most highly
prized display case been disturbed, he'd've fired Sam,
his personal valet of forty years, at once.

Except for Sam's absence—and Clyde, where was
Clyde?—nothing seemed out of place. He couldn't
see across the hall to Clyde's Office of the Assistant
Director, but the two American flags that flanked the
door to his own inner office, the great Justice Department seal overhead, the display cases of confiscated gangland armaments and grisly mementos of
the days when hardened felons robbed at least two
banks a day and gun battles were daily news . . .
nothing had been disturbed.

Yet on the other side of an invisible barrier of
some kind someone sat behind a counter at the level
of his shins, almost entirely concealed. The counter
supported a variety of equipment, most of it unfamil-
iar. Despite his increased height, he could not see
over it. The only thing he recognized—a long
rectangle—looked like the back of a TV.

Enemy alien? he thought. Communist? Terrorist?
Draft dodger? Mobster? Had he been captured? His

enemies were legion, but who among them would dare?

"C-c-come out from b-b-behind there!" He flushed with anger. His courtly Virginia accent was intact, but the stutter he had worked so hard to overcome as a young man was back.

A freckle-faced girl, big for her age, peered around the TV. Her clothes were less proper than any *his* mother would have allowed—cottony yet crinkled like crepe paper when she stood.

She gazed up at him with wonder. "Max me out! It worked."

"W-w-what worked? W-w-what's going on? How d-d-dare you burst into m-m-m-my office unannounced!"

The girl frowned. "Wait a sec. We'll both go nuts if we have to put up with that." She disappeared behind the TV set again.

"W-w-w-with what?"

"Th-th-th-that. Reduce you, too. I don't want to get a stiff neck."

Suddenly he shrank. The ceiling was where it should be, and he was barely taller than the girl.

"Real-life size is the best," she said.

"This is an outrage!" he said, though the stutter appeared to be gone. "Make me taller!"

"Sure, if you want. How's that?"

The room exploded, everything expanding with him. "Awk! No!"

"No? Tell me what you want. I can do it!"

He pondered the risk to his dignity. "I'd like to be enlarged while everything else stays the same."

Her brow furrowed. "Gosh, John. I'm not sure I—"

"Don't call me *John*." She didn't strike him as a bad kid, just not very well bred. Yankee parents, no doubt.

"You mean to say you like *Edgar* better?"

"As a matter of fact I do." Only his closest friends—

Clyde—called him Edgar, and only when they were off duty. Otherwise, everyone called him Boss. "But it's Mr. Hoover to you."

Her mouth opened with surprise. "Well, ex-cu-u-u-se me."

"And don't talk to me in that tone of voice or I'll give you a lesson in respect for your elders that you'll never forget. Now tell me what's going on here, young lady, and tell me at once."

"You don't have to get twisted!" she said. "That Mr./Mrs. crap went out with gas-fueled cars."

"You'll call me Mr. Hoover." He glared at her. "No—you'll call me *sir*."

The brat put her hands on her hips and said, "Blow off! Childism is against the law."

"I've been a lawman all my life. I don't need a fresh brat like you to instruct me on the law."

"Oh yeah?" she said. "What about the Palmer Raids? What about that 788-page Senate report, *Charges of Illegal Practices in the Justice Department*?"

"You know about that, do you?"

"Know about it! I had to teleread it for my Mastermind project. It's a wonder I'm not brain-dead! You kicked a buncha bios outa the country just cuz they weren't born here."

Hoover flushed. He prided himself on his spotless reputation and hated being reminded of past mistakes. But he never allowed a criticism to go undefended and came back at her at once. "My role in those raids has been exaggerated. But as a matter of fact, there was a 1918 law enacted by Congress. It authorized the Labor Department to exclude and expel from the country any aliens who advocated the overthrow of the government by force or violence, or who advocated the unlawful destruction of property, or who were members of any group that supported such activities.

"All *I* did was prepare evidence to prove that the Communist Party was in fact such an organization.

So kicking unkempt bushy-browed alien Reds—Emma
Goldman, Alexander Berkman—out of the country—
that wasn't illegal as such. Goldman inspired Leon
Czolgosz to assassinate President McKinley. And
Berkman knocked off Henry Clay Frick just because
he headed a steel empire. Berkman claimed that
human life was sacred and inviolate—unless the life
belonged to someone rich. The deportations of 247
Reds and anarchists on the Soviet Ark—"

"The what?"

"The U.S.S. *Burford*. Shipping them back to Rus-
sia where they belonged was absolutely *legal*. Up-
held by the Supreme Court!" He paused, pensively
added, "Unfortunately, Attorney General Palmer got
a bit carried away and arrested a lot of people who
weren't Communists."

"Arrested! You beat 'em up. You bashed their
heads in. You treated 'em worse'n mechs sent to the
junkyard!"

"*I* did nothing of the kind. Local police, not FBI
agents, were responsible for most of the abuses. The
raids were absolutely necessary—you can't have people blowing up Wall Street and knocking off the
rich—but there's no point in making illegal arrests
that won't stand up in court. When I took over the
Agency, I made sure my agents were all trained in
rules of evidence. I have two law degrees. I spent
my whole life upholding the law. I don't need a snip
of a girl to lecture me about the law."

"You need me for a lot of things. My inset carbo-
bridge matrices *made* you. I learned every scrap
about you and then conjured up your entire self. You
wouldn't even be here if it wasn't for me!"

" 'You wouldn't be here if it wasn't for me, *Sir*.' "

"Nobody in the World could make you the way you
are—and who'd want to, you sour old prune of a
cop!"

He didn't understand what happened next, but he
passed out, just like that, cold. When he came to he

was three inches tall. Obsessed with reducing through-out his life—if he didn't set an example of self-discipline for G-men, who would?—he at once suspected a plot on the part of some alien he'd deported for violent overthrow, or maybe some clot of scum from the underworld's boiling pot, or one of those contemptible cowards in sheets. But only the brat loomed before him—a looming, spiteful giant.

"You had enough?" she said.

He hadn't spent his entire life acquiring a reputation for integrity to be talked to like this by some freckle-faced kid in a paper dress. He folded his arms across his chest and refused to respond.

He fadded out, back in, out, and back in again, flickering like an old silent movie. The brat's attitude did not improve; she'd obviously never been prop-erly disciplined. A week under *his* mother's roof would have changed all that.

"Okay okay okay," she said after awhile, as he'd known all along she would. Young people couldn't stand the silent treatment. They were too restless and easily bored. "*Mr.* Hoover . . ."

The tone wasn't quite right, but he was a practical man; until he understood his situation better and could summon his men to assist him, it would have to do. He leaned toward the brat, his thick black brows encouragingly raised. "That's much better," he said. "Now what, if anything, can I do for you?"

"I need your help," she said at last.

" 'I need your help' what?"

She looked daggers at him. But kids were just like crooks—they had a similar mentality—and she said, "Sir."

"Hmmm. Suppose you start from the beginning."

The tale she told was so preposterous he knew it must be true. When she at last finished he said, "What is it you want me to do?"

"Lead the simhunt," she said. "Find Voltaire."

"Voltaire?" The name was foreign, yet familiar. He

wasn't much of a reader, preferred the race track to the theatre, never travelled outside the country and distrusted intellectuals, especially foreign ones. "The famous freethinker? The atheist?"

"He's not an atheist, he's a deist."

His eyes narrowed—to focus on the possibilities more clearly. "A radical? A foreign agent?"

"My dad isn't sure what he is. That's what we need you to help us find out. Voltaire's a sim, like you. I figure you can hunt him down in creepy places where bios can't go."

"I'm not an agent." Though often photographed with weapons to keep up his image, he knew nothing about firearms, not even how to fire a gun. "I'm a chief of agents, a director. I have to have a staff to direct. Clyde Tolson, my Assistant Director, I absolutely must have him, plus four thousand agents—"

"Four thou—!"

"Minimum, and my servant Sam . . ." He looked around the office. "What have you done with him? He only works twelve hours a day, he's not entitled to coffee breaks. You mustn't spoil coloreds, you know. They get ideas. Like that skirt-chasing preacher —look what happened to him! And Crawford, my chauffeur/handyman—"

"Chauffeur? I thought he was a special agent, the first black FBI agent in history."

"Don't be ridiculous." He'd designated Sam and Crawford "special agents" to appease FDR and the NAACP. Killed two birds with one stone—the FBI got their black "agents," and he got his colored help, free. "Real FBI agents in *my* FBI have to be college educated gentlemen."

"That's classist!" the girl said.

"I don't care what it is, it's my way and as long as I'm The Boss, my way's the way it's going to be." Crawford worked fifteen hours a day and weekends without overtime until some radical in Congress decided Sundays were worth eighty percent regular pay. How did they expect him to maintain his Georgian house and garden without Crawford? Or go to Harvey's every night for drinks with Clyde if Crawford didn't wait outside to drive them home? If the Pierce Arrow or the Cadillac broke down—weighted down by armor, they frequently did—did they expect him or Clyde to repair it? "If this food problem is as urgent as you say, I'm sure the Attorney General will give me as many agents as I like."

But the brat shook her head and sighed. "Look, I know you think this is an office and some general of the Attorney Army or something—the twencen was so weird!—really exists. But they don't, see? When you call this Attorney soldier up, he'll really be a monitor program, geared to translate your lingo into matrix-mutter, so the compu-net can understand, get it? And if you did have agents to lead into the lion's den—what terms!—it'd all be in matrix-space. What *I* do is assemble character-drivers."

"Drivers? Like cars?"

"Sorta." She ran her hand through her sandy hair. "I got a grip on who you were, and my carbos 'factured up your drivers for me. Big programs, holo-constructions that eat up more library space than the Encyclopedia Grand."

"So I'm just . . . a numerical . . . ?" His sense of self began to shrink. He felt himself tumbling into the black pit of self-doubt like an unsteady theatre actor.

She seemed to sense his dwindling confidence and said, "No, no, you're *you*—I'm just talking tech here."

Her forehead creased with thought and suddenly he felt restored. "I have to have agents!" he said in a commanding voice.

The girl looked discouraged. "I can't make sims out of the living. It's against the law."

Hoover twitched. "Then we can't do it, can we. How 'bout bringing 'em back from the dead—save training costs. Like you did me."

She gave him a pathetic look. "World-Data's global holdings won't have much on ho-hums."

"Ho-hums? What are ho-hums?"

"You know. Ordinary people."

"You call honest law enforcement officers ordinary people? I got rid of the ordinary scum when I took over, kept the milk and from then on recruited only cream. I banned political influence, corruption, and bribery of every kind. You call that ordinary?"

"I wouldn't know," the kid said. "All I know is you don't get stored in World-Data unless you're rich or famous. Ho-hums—even if they worked for you—vanish without a trace. Even if I could find some info on one or two, there'd be so many data gaps and holes, they'd come out weird. You know, like mutants that slip past genetic engineers." She twisted her arm behind her neck, crossed her eyes, stuck her tongue out and mimicked an idiot.

"Don't do that," he said. "It's not polite."

"I couldn't re-create something like that, it just wouldn't be right."

"I must have first-rate men," Hoover said. "They have to be smart, incorruptible, honorable and of impeccable integrity."

"Dead won't be that hard," said the girl. "Almost everyone like that's dead. But famous . . . that's a different story."

"Are you trying to insult me?" Hoover said.

"No, sir. I could try to bring back a saint—my mom did—but someone like Genghis Khan or Attila the Hun would be more useful."

"No aliens," Hoover said. "My men have got to be U.S. citizens, preferably native born." He too fell silent. The kid was right. Recruitment was going to be a problem.

"I'm kinda new at this," the kid went on after awhile. "If you could settle for a staff of one . . ."

"You expect me to direct a national man-hunt—"

"*Inter*national."

"—with a staff of one?" The insult was even greater than when Congress created the CIA. As if he couldn't have headed both organizations!

"Not counting me!" she said. "That's two!" Her hand flew to her heart. The gesture appeased him; it reminded him of the Pledge of Allegiance. "And when I tell my dad, it'll make three. I mean, we've gotta hurry. This virus is maxing everyone out. Tofu burgers were bad enough, but plankton burgers every day! Gag puke!"

"Don't talk like that," Hoover said. "It's not lady-like. My mother wouldn't have allowed such talk under her roof, not even from boys."

"Sexism is against the law," the brat said in a whiny voice.

"I got my law degrees from George Washington University. Where'd you get yours? Shut up and let me think."

He was a cautious man. If he was to have only one recruit, he could afford no mistakes. "Any chance I could have a look at your World-Data Contents file? Might give me some ideas."

"You want files copied into you? Cinchy. Which ones?"

"I don't know. I want to browse. Is that a problem?"

"For a run-of-the-mill grown-up genius, it might be. But not for a high techno prodigy like me."

Like most youngsters raised by sentimental yam-merheads—bleeding heart Liberals, no doubt—this one was spoiled and mouthy; her will had been overindulged. But she was spunky, he'd say that for her. With proper discipline and training, she would assume her rightful place—under him—and he was just the man to see she got it.

8

Electrica ran breathless with excitement toward her father's office on the far side of the house. Originally she'd planned to catch Voltaire with Edgar's assistance before confiding details of her plan to Tech. But Edgar turned out to be such a throwback! Big fat toad, she thought. *Sir* big fat toad. Her dad would know how to deal with the likes of him.

As she passed her mother's office, she stopped short. Ever since she'd learned her mother was not the woman she'd taken her to be, that closed door drew her irresistibly. She sensed intuitively that to enter was to gain admission to a realm from which childhood was barred. Passing through to the other side meant learning secrets which, once learned, could never be unlearned. One secret had already transformed a princess into a hag.

Electrica's hand on the doorknob paused. Through the door she could hear the same muffled male voice she'd heard before. Her throat went dry. If she persisted, like her mother she too might be transformed into a witch. The doorknob in her hand remained unturned—and then the voices inside stopped.

She bolted from the door, fled down the hall, and, feeling hot and thirsty—her cheeks flamed—stepped out onto the upstairs terrace to cadge a drink from the tiled mosaic fountain. Leaning over the broken sunlight in the water of the great Moorish tiled bowl, she thrust her mouth into the spouting gush and drank. She turned, still gulping, toward the familiar hum—a skyhopper taking off from the automatic lawn grid pad below. As the skyhopper—a two-seater—soared straight up into view between a stand of cypress and the hillside, she recognized the pilot—her father's friend Nim.

Tech listened tensely as Mac 500's neutral voice recounted the latest outbreak of computer virus.

Heavy harvesting equipment had malfunctioned at forty-six global sites; reports of additional incidents continued to pour in. In an attempt to check an emerging pattern of aberrant behavior, authorities called in repair robots from regional service stations. Instead of servicing the equipment, they formed a pentagon around the field, prostrated themselves and began to utter incantations in an unidentifiable language their programmers had never heard.

After virtually identical incidents on four different continents the week before, samples of malfunctioning mechrepairmen were shipped to universities throughout the world. Linguists studied their robotic babbling for resemblances to known languages, ancient or modern. Others were escorted under heavy guard to their manufacturers of origin to have their heads examined by designer engineers. The results of these investigations—still unavailable to the public—were rumored to be inconclusive.

Tech's mind swirled like a confusion of blown leaves. Bondieu had been right after all, at least about one thing—the world food supply was in grave danger. Fresh fruit and vegetables were now rationed and in short supply—even in California, a leading food-producer republic. He eyed with distaste the bowl of plankton soup at his elbow. Plankton burgers, plankton cold cuts, plankton salads—he was sick of subsisting on Second World famine-prevention fare. Yet had it not been for the oceans' bounty, he and his family might be succumbing to malnutrition right now.

The only beings unaffected by the crisis were the mechs. Could Bondieu have been right about that too? Was the epidemic a mech conspiracy designed to seize bio power? to make mechs masters, not just of their own fate, but of humanity as well?

Tech mind-ordered Mac 500 to disappear at once and felt relieved when Mac, as usual, obeyed. The wallscreen had just vanished when Electrica slammed into the room.

"Hey," Tech said. "Hey. Slow down."

Face flushed, forehead shiny with perspiration, Electrica grabbed his hand. "I gotta show you something. Right now. In my room."

"Don't tell me, let me guess. We're being invaded by aliens from outer space."

Electrica gave him her don't-be-such-a-boardbrain look. "This is serious, Dad!"

Tech suddenly recalled their bet and shot up in his chair. "You've got Voltaire!"

A sly expression stole over her face. "Nope," she said. "Someone else." She yanked him up from his compuchair and pulled him into the hall. As they passed Maquina's office, she put her finger to her lips and tiptoed by. Once past, she resumed her breakneck pace, flung open the door to her room, and shoved him inside.

There, hunched over a stack of reports at a no frills, antique, government-issue desk in what appeared to be a centuries-old office with tiny windows cut into the walls, was a life-sized hologram Tech did not recognize. The man was pudgy, short and dark. A prizefighter profile protruded from his square-jawed, fleshy face; the upper lip was thin enough to be almost invisible although the lower one was full, petulant, perhaps even sensuous. Heavy black brows shaded his eyes, as if to shield them from discovery, for they were soft in expression, sensitive, and came as a surprise in one whose face and form suggested pugnacity, determination, stubbornness and grit. A dark cloth business suit was enlivened by a dash of white handkerchief, carefully arranged in a breast pocket, and a floral tie. The white collar of the dress shirt, like the hanky, was immaculate and stiff. Tech's overall impression was of a meticulous, well-trained bull dog accustomed to a short leash.

"Who are you?" Tech asked.

"He can't hear you, Dad. His sensors are turned off."

Tech turned to his daughter for enlightenment.

"He's working," Electrica said. "That's all he does, day and night." She wrinkled her freckled nose. "Office work, gag puke. That's his metaphor for deepsearch routines. And he uses a pen!"

"Who is he?" Tech asked. "Where'd he come from?"

Electrica smiled with pride. "I made him. He's gonna catch Voltaire and Joan. He thinks they're Communists. I go, what if they are? He goes, haven't you read my book on the menace of Communism? I go, I tried to but I fell asleep. I was gonna wait till he caught Voltaire and surprise you, but . . ."

"But what?"

Electrica shook her head. "He's weird. He actually wants me to call him *sir*! Like he was the bio and I'm the mech! I'm kinda scared of him to tell the truth."

"Scared of a sim?" Tech laughed. He draped his arm around her shoulder and gave her a reassuring hug. "He's just old-fashioned. Calling someone older *sir* used to be a simple sign of respect."

"He's awful bossy, worse than you. He took me days to make, but is he satisfied? No way! He wants me to make helpers, a whole staff. And says I have to call him *Mr.*"

"Mr. What?"

"Mr. Boardbrain!"

"Electrica, that's rude!" Maquina had entered the room from behind them. And she was boiling mad. "Don't let her get away with that! She'll think you share her specist views."

The hologram suddenly disappeared. Tech turned to Electrica. "Why'd you do that?"

"It's *our* secret!" Electrica said. "Not hers!"

"We don't have secrets from her," Tech said. "We're a family."

"Oh yeah? Then how come she's got secrets from us!"

Tech looked at Maquina and said, "What's going on? What is she talking about?"

Maquina pointed at where the sim had been. "*I'm* the one who's kept in the dark."

Tech had always made a point of never siding with his daughter against his wife in his daughter's presence, not even when he felt that she was right and his wife wrong. Maquina held that his taking Electrica's part against her own was always, no matter the circumstances, a mistake. When Tech learned that to do so gave Maquina a not-now-dear headache, he at once concurred.

"Bring him back," Tech told Electrica. "Right now."

Electrica balked. "Do I have to?"

He steered her into the compuchair so she could make the necessary commands, all of which he'd watch closely. "We work on this together or else not at all."

Electrica gave Maquina a sullen look.

"Activate his sensors," Tech said, "so we can communicate."

"You're all a bunch of childists," Electrica grumbled as the hologram loomed up.

Tech stepped behind the compuchair and surreptitiously patted his daughter's shoulder. Regardless of what petty domestic difference had come between Electrica and Maquina, the Hoover sim was a fine piece of work. He would reward Electrica for it later.

9

Hoover glanced at the bold-faced, government-issue, no-frills wall clock. "You're two and a half minutes late." His eyes narrowed. "Who are these people, your parents?"

"Uh-huh."

"The word is *yes*. Yes, *sir*."

The girl turned to her father—a hippie type, but clean, with shoulder-length hair and an earring. "See what I mean?"

Hoover set aside the pile of mugshots on his desk—Al Capone, Machine Gun Kelly, Fox McLean—he'd been reminiscing—and studied the outlandishly-dressed couple standing before him. Such nonconformists should not be encouraged to have children.

Sparing the rod invariably spoiled the child—as this precocious freckle-faced brat clearly proved.

"You must excuse my daughter," the man said. "*Sir* is a title of respect bios no longer use. A.I.'s use it in referring to bios, but never the other way around."

"A.I.'s? What're A.I.'s?"

"Artificially intelligent beings," the man said. "Like you."

"There's nothing artificial about my intelligence," Hoover snapped.

The man only smiled. "With all due respect, Mr. Hoover, I have to disagree. It's nothing to be ashamed of. Some of the brightest beings I know are A.I.'s. Voltaire is a case in point."

"I'm J. Edgar Hoover, Chief of the FBI." Hoover extended his hand.

The man extended his hand, too—that, at least, had not changed—but he might as well not have bothered. You could judge a great deal from a handshake—the wetness of the palm, the firmness of the grip—but Hoover couldn't feel a thing.

"Tech Hilliard, President of Maquinatech."

"*Co*-president," the brat interjected.

"We design A.I.'s—the brains for mechs and simbeings," Hilliard went on. "I believe my daughter's already explained the problem on our hands."

"You want me to catch this Voltaire. You've come to the right place—no one understands the criminal brain better than I do." Hoover cleared his throat before proceeding. He enjoyed nothing more than waxing eloquent. "Tell yourself if you have a gun and point it at an unarmed man, you're brave and he's a coward. School yourself to think that you amount to something if you get away with murder. Regard all law enforcement officers and ordinary citizens as inherent crooks who'd be stealing from others, as you are, if only they had the nerve. Tell yourself people who work for money are fools, while those like you, who take the fruits of their labor from them without earning it, are smart and worthy of respect."

"Is he talking about the IRS?" the girl asked Hilliard.

"Don't interrupt your elders," Hoover said.

"I didn't!" the girl said. "You're barely two weeks old!"

"Be maudlin concerning yourself and cynical about the feelings of others," Hoover continued, determined to finish his oration. "Believe yourself noble if you indulge in cheap sentimentalities, if 'you've always been good to your mother.' But if these sentiments become obstacles in your way, have no compunction about using your mother's home as a hideout, deserting your sweetheart, shooting a baby or choking your dog."

Hilliard rubbed his chin. "Ummm," he said. "Doesn't sound much like Voltaire."

"Yeah? Well, don't be so sure." Hoover turned away and wiped his eyes. That part about the dog reminded him of G-boy, his pet cairn. "Some of these public rats put up a damn good front."

"Thomas Jefferson owned slaves!" the girl remarked.

"Don't speak ill of the founding fathers," Hoover said.

The kid's face flushed. "What about the founding mothers?" she said. "What about them?"

"They were at home with their children," Hoover said, "where they belonged."

"I thought I was simming a man—turns out he's a dinosaur!"

Hoover let the insult pass—he'd even the score later. The father held the keys here—best to put this weird situation on a man-to-man basis. He wanted to get back to work directing the organization he'd created from a ragtag, corrupt corps of inept political hacks into the most formidable police agency in the world. This Voltaire was either part of a criminal ring determined to monopolize what it did not destroy of the world's food supply, then make a killing on the black market; or he was a Communist Party agent out to weaken the free world. Hilliard himself might be bait for some trap. The important thing was to stay covered but, by hook or by crook, get the prey.

"I'll need authorization from the Department of Justice."

Hilliard nodded. "I think that can be arranged. Electrica tells me you need to add at least one A.I. to your staff. Have you decided yet who it should be?"

"Clyde Tolson," Hoover said. "My assistant director for over forty years." The Lone Ranger had Tonto, Sherlock Holmes had Watson, he had Clyde. "I want him young, though. In good health." Hoover barely remembered his own death—a sudden stab of pain, as if a stake were being driven through his heart— but he didn't remember Clyde's at all. Clyde—his sole heir—must have survived him. But Clyde had turned into a sour invalid toward the end. Hoover had brought him to his house, bedridden, for his housekeeper Annie to nurse night and day. How could he forget? It took four weeks before Clyde was well enough to go home, and cost Hoover—Annie's tip for the additional work—an extra ten bucks. She barely even thanked him.

But Hilliard was shaking his head. "Re-creating Tolson's out of the question."

"Why?" Hoover demanded. Had those garbage collectors of the press who suggested he and Clyde had a "homosexual marriage" succeeded in ruining his name? "It's my Bureau, he's my choice!"

"Cuz he was a ho-hum!" the brat exclaimed. "All he did his whole life was take orders from you!"

"What she means," Hilliard said, "is we don't have enough data on Tolson to re-make him. He was important only because of his relations with you."

"Why do you think I want him?" Hoover snapped.

"Beats me!" the kid said. "He moved into your house the day you died—your body was still warm!

—and sold off everything you owned within a week. Some friend!"

"Clyde would never sell my Del Mar horsehead cups."

"Wanta bet? He even got rid of your dog."

"G-boy? Clyde got rid of G-boy?" Hoover lapsed into a morose silence.

"If I may make a suggestion . . . ?" Hilliard said.

"If I can't have Tolson, I don't care who I have," Hoover growled. "Set up candidate interviews with my secretary."

The brat rolled her eyes. "Don't tell me we have to get him a mechsec too!"

"That isn't possible," Hilliard said. "The situation worsens even as we speak. It takes time and effort to re-create a complex sim-being."

"I can't even interview him first? That's highly irregular. He's not related to you, is he? You don't owe him any political favors? I can't have that sort of—"

"You can interview him—but only after the fact."

"Who is he?" Hoover asked. "Anybody I know?"

"Thomas of Torquemada."

Hoover scowled. The name, though alien, sounded familiar. "One of those bushy-bearded Eastern European Reds?"

Hilliard shook his head. "Absolutely not. He is a foreigner, though, a Spaniard."

"Out of the question. My agents have to be U.S. citizens, and I prefer 'em native born and here at least six generations."

"There was no U.S. to be a citizen of when this man lived."

Hoover reflected. "Then I guess it wasn't his fault. Does he speak English?"

"That can be arranged."

"Without an accent," Hoover said. "Unless it's Midwestern or Southern. My best agents were Southerners. Break their necks to make up for once having tried to leave the greatest nation on this earth. Make him sound Southern even if he isn't—that's the least you can do."

"A Southern accent?" Hilliard said. His brows arched. "Yeah, I guess I could manage that."

"How 'bout religion? Mormons work out very well, they're used to taking orders. Is he a Mormon?"

"No," Hilliard said. "That's out of the question."

"He's not an atheist, is he? I won't work with anyone who won't sing *God Bless America* or recite the Pledge of Allegiance or—"

"Take my word for it, he's no atheist."

Well, Hoover thought, that was at least something. If the man was God-fearing, how bad could he be? "How old?"

Hilliard looked sheepish. "Sixty-seven."

"Sixty-seven!" Hoover folded his arms across his chest. "That's over our age limit for rookie recruits."

"Ageism!" the brat protested. "You can't get away with that in the twenty-second century!"

"Before he reached the age of fifty-eight," Hilliard said, ignoring his kid, "the man was a complete nonentity. He wouldn't have been much use to you then."

Hoover scowled. He loathed irregularity of any kind but had himself resisted attempts to make him retire when he was only seventy-seven. "I don't consider my age a valid factor in assessing my ability to continue as Director of the FBI," he remembered telling an interviewer. "Any more than it was when, at the youthful age of twenty-nine, I was appointed to this position. Then I was criticized as 'the Boy Scout.' Now I'm called 'that senile old man.' " When the President—it happened to be Richard M. Nixon—came over to his office and said, "I want to discuss with you the matter of retirement," Hoover recalled answering, "Why, that's ridiculous. You're still a young man."

"Is he fit?" he asked Hilliard.

Hilliard looked embarrassed. "Well, umm, ah, he does have a pretty bad case of gout."

Hoover made a scornful sound.

"Ableism is a felony!" the brat shouted.

"Pipe down, Electrica," the father at last said. "Physical illnesses don't generally slow re-created beings down. It's not as if they had electronic problems or anything like that."

Hoover reflected. Beggars, he reminded himself, can't be choosers—not in this distorted, cottony realm of shifting mirrors. "What was his line of work? Law-enforcement?"

Hilliard smiled faintly. "As a matter of fact, he was a monk."

"A monk! You expect me to make a G-man out of a monk?"

"That's jobist!" Hands on her hips, her feet planted squarely apart—and they were huge; no female had a right to feet that size—the brat regarded him with a defiance bordering on the delinquent. "Jobism is against the law!"

Hoover eyed her icily. " 'Jobism is against the law, *sir*!' "

"He's not exactly without law enforcement experience," Hilliard said. "He was a prosecutor, an inquisitor."

Hoover's knowledge of all but U.S. history was scant, but at the mention of the word *inquisitor*, he suddenly recalled "Tyrone Power! *The Captain from Castile!*"

Hilliard said, "Beg your pardon?"

"You're talking about that power-mad sonofabitch who tortured Tyrone Power's girlfriend in *The Captain from Castile*! I've wanted to get my hands on that bastard ever since he forced Jean Simmons to leave Spain for the New World!"

Hilliard and his kid exchanged baffled looks. My God, didn't people go to the movies anymore?

"I have a picture of him," Hilliard said. He hit

some buttons on the computer and out came a composite mugshot. He held it up before Hoover's eyes.

Hoover stared. Something inside him flashed—yellow, blue, red boomed in his ears. His brain hummed like a boiler plate. "Hire him. Send him to me at once." The most powerful enforcement officer in history looked very much like Clyde.

10

Fray Tomás de Torquemada, Prior of the Monastery of Santa Cruz of the Dominican Order, Confessor of the King and of the Queen Our Lords, Member of their Royal Council, Mandatory and Delegate of the Holy Apostolic Seat, and Inquisitor General of Heretical Pravity and Apostasy for the Kingdoms of Aragon and Castile and All the Other Estates of Their Highnesses, awakened on the hard stone floor surrounded by the crude but effective tools of his trade. Stiff from the gout he had developed in the last ten years, he rolled over and moaned. Nothing was worse for his condition than damp stone chambers with sweating floors and walls, but then, anything that humiliated the flesh was good for the soul.

He rose with difficulty, gripping the rack—an oblong wooden frame set on trestles—for support. He knew at once exactly where he was—in the Truth Chamber at St. Thomas' Monastery in Avila. And yet two things were strange. Though he moved with the usual difficulty, he felt no pain. Had the Lord finally taken pity on His lowly servant? Made him insensitive to the agony of a shameful disease associated with excess of every kind when he was known to practice austerities extreme even among Dominicans?

And what was he doing here in the Truth Chamber alone? No prisoner was strapped to the rack, bound to the ladder or the hoist. Nor were the peasant lads hired by his Office of Inquisition to do God's holy work anywhere to be seen. Such labor required broad shoulders, muscled backs, far beyond his own slight, delicate build. It was also beneath his personal dignity as a nobleman, although admittedly of a small house, and far beneath the dignity of his office, to engage in manual labor, regardless of its holiness of purpose.

He called out—but no one answered. Silence was the Truth Chamber's only other inhabitant, a silence palpable and strange, since normally the chamber was alive with whimpers, moans and screams, punctuated by his own calm and inquiring voice, repeating over and over the same questions, until the exhausted prisoner at last owned up to his filthy corruption.

Cleansing Spain and the Church of enemies— adulterers, fornicators, sodomizers, Jews, Moors, but above all *conversos*—false Jewish converts, who, in secret, continued to practice their own blasphemous religion—was a sacred obligation. His was the only Christian country in Europe that had, for centuries, tolerated people of different races and religions, working, studying, above all, trading together in harmony and peace. This boil of immoral, licentious tolerance had to be lanced, its pus expelled once and for all.

He turned one of the rollers at each end of the rack, seeking the reassurance of the rack's familiar creak and rasp. He knew—thanks to his grandfather Alvar Fernandez, who'd stained his honor and his blood—what it felt like to have a soul wrenched by divisive inner conflicts that threatened to tear it apart.

But what did it feel like to have one's body torn apart? He'd often witnessed the work of iron on flesh, but the essence of immersion in pain eluded him. It must be, after all, the most intense of all sensuous events.

Most heretics brought here in chains confessed their blasphemy long before the rack's rollers wrenched their joints from their sockets, thus cheating him of the opportunity to punish them further—that would have been illegal and he, the Inquisitor General, never broke the law—before handing them over to be sentenced for the soul-damning crimes to which they had confessed. Contemptible cowards, the lot of them. Not one of them—these so-called Christian sons of Jewish fathers, many of them even holding high office in Holy Church—had withstood trial by torture. Which of course proved their guilt. For true Christians—unlike these secret Judaizers—martyr themselves willingly, eagerly, giving themselves over for Holy Mother Church and the sacred Catholic faith.

He moved from the rack to the hoist, fondling first the pulley, then the thick-twined braid of rope. He placed his hands behind his back, pretending they were, like the prisoner's, bound. Unassisted, he could not tie the rope around his wrists, nor pass it over the pulley, nor haul on the rope—it took two men for that—till the sinner was a meter or so off the ground, all his weight on the arms stretched behind his back. Sinews ripped. Bones popped! At every unsatisfactory answer, he'd be dropped a bit, then brought up with a jerk that all but sprung his arms from their sockets. If he still refused to confess the truth, the drops became longer.

The weights—where were they?—had been Torquemada's own idea, an innovation he was proud of, for he was after all a holy man, not an inventor of mechanical devices. Inspired by God and the obstinate determination of an occasional *converso* to evade execution by refusing to admit that his conversion was as false as Judas, Torquemada ordered his lackeys to attach weights to the sinner's feet, thus increasing the torque on his shoulders.

Spotting the weights now in a dark corner, he picked one up, caressed its cool iron authority, and unthinkingly raised it to his lips. He flushed with shame as he realized pride had seduced him into committing an idolatrous act. Later, in the privacy of his monastic cell, he would scourge himself until he bled to atone for his sin.

He set the metal weight back down in the corner and moved toward what at first glance looked like an ordinary ladder. Inclined on a slight slant against the Truth Chamber's windowless wall, the ladder was in fact the most effective of his instruments of truth. To this ladder a *marrano* was tightly bound—how right the common people were to call these false *conversos* pigs—his feet a little higher than his head. Any movement of arms or legs made the cord cut deeply into the *marrano*'s flesh. His head was then clamped in a metal clasp, his mouth forced open by an iron ring the peasants jokingly called *el dentista*.

Then came the bits of wood. He looked about. Retrieving several oak plugs from the floor, he tested them for fit in his own nostrils. He declined to place *el dentista* in his mouth—he might catch a disease. He could hold his mouth open without it. But when he picked up a long strip of linen hanging on one of the ladder's rungs, he could not resist laying the soiled cloth across his mouth.

He kicked the jug of water by the wall—empty—and, leaning against the ladder, imagined the black-masked, muscular peasant called *El Fuerte*—The Strong One—slowly, exactingly, pouring water down his mouth and forcing the linen into his throat. He coughed in feeble imitation of the choking sounds *conversos* made as they tried to swallow, dragging the filthy linen further down their throats, thus increasing, instead of relieving, their suffocation.

When he removed the cloth from his own throat, it was not soaked with blood as it invariably was when *El Fuerte* removed it from some half-dead convert's mouth. This allowed the sinner to breathe again while Torquemada's own quiet voice resumed asking the same question he'd asked before, the question the *converso* had refused to answer truthfully, one of a set which Torquemada had framed earlier and which, when all were answered truthfully, formed a coherent statement of the prisoner's apostasy and guilt.

He cocked his head and listened—still that pressing, utter silence—before unfastening the dark coarse cloak he wore over the white robe of his order. Like a bride on her wedding night, he let the cloak slide slowly to the floor, resisting an urge to scratch the itch caused by the hairshirt he wore night and day under his robe. Then he lay down, his back against the rack's splintery roughness. Its pine felt resolutely hard against his tonsured head. Above him loomed a massive ceiling, its granite boulders restrained by coarse seams of mortar. His mouth went dry with a peculiar excitement as he took in the Truth Chamber from the *converso*'s point of view. How many had learned dark truths about themselves on this very spot?

He stretched out his arms, slipped them into the thick leather straps and envisioned his Lord nailed to the cross. Teeth clenched, eyes shut, he saw the peasant lad they called *El Fuerte*. Out of kindness, in hot weather he allowed the boy to remove his upper body clothing while he worked, revealing a magnificent broad back.

El Fuerte stood over him now, naked except for the black mask torturers always wore. Sweat rolled down his thatch of armpit hair into Torquemada's soft open mouth, like vinegar the Roman soldiers gave The Lord when, in His agony and thirst, He asked for water. His breath broke into jagged pants as *El Fuerte* relentlessly turned the creaking rollers that would do to Torquemada's body what his grandfather's unspeakable sin had done to his soul. He grimaced, groaned, flung the frail body under his white robe from side to side. Convulsing wildly on the rack, he thrashed and churned against the leather straps.

"I thought *Edgar* was weird!" a young voice said. "Jeez, Dad, what is he *doing*?"

Torquemada sprang to his feet, rearranging the folds of his monk's robe as best he could. To ward off harm, he raised the big wooden cross dangling from his braided belt. "How dare you!" he cried out. "Who are you? Who let you in?"

"Not this again," the same voice said—it belonged to a big, lewdly clothed young woman at least thirteen years old.

"Deactivate the sensors," said a fair-skinned giant, two meters-plus high.

Suddenly all three disappeared, for there had been an older woman with them, too, hovering in the background, saying nothing, observing all. Her manner reminded him of the spies for various factions of nobility, forever forming and dissolving alliances as they intrigued at Ferdinand and Isabella's court.

He waited, listened . . . Nothing happened. He sidestepped his discarded outer robe lying on the floor by the rack and hurried to the torturers' black garments hanging from an iron hook embedded in the stone of the dark chamber's wall. Gently lifting the cloak from the brass hook, he slipped it on over the white robe of his Order. Then he drew the black mask over his eyes, his hands trembling, and made the sign of the cross. Touching the crucifix suspended from the braided belt at his waist to his lips, he stared out at the void into which the three apparitions from Purgatory or Hell had just disappeared. Clad in the uniform of Truth, crucifix raised aloft, black mask firmly in place, the Inquisitor General of Heretical Pravity and Apostasy for the Kingdoms of Aragon and Castile and All The Other Estates of Their Highnesses Ferdinand and Isabella, was ready to defend against attack from any quarter, demonic or human, the One and Only Universally True Faith—his.

11

"Nuke him!" Electrica urged Tech. "Blow him away!"

For the first time in days, Maquina found herself agreeing with her daughter.

Clearly, something was wrong. Electrica had turned against her, almost as if she knew . . .

"He's strange, all right," Maquina said. She shivered though the brilliant sunlight of spring warmed the room. "But I don't think it's right. Spying on him without his knowledge. I mean, it's an awful invasion of a person's privacy."

"He's not a person," Tech reminded her.

"He's a twisted little fag!" Electrica said.

Maquina squelched an impulse to correct Electrica's homophobic outburst. Male homosexuality was rare these days though Maquina remembered meeting a few elderly homosexuals when she was Electrica's age. But since the government began routinely checking the testosterone levels of virtually all adolescent males, instead of relying on parents to bring in sons they felt were too unaggressive to compete for jobs and girls, homosexuality had virtually disappeared. Few parents declined the complex hormone therapy to bring their sons' testosterone levels to within normal range. Supplements did not always change sexual orientation, but what they *did* do was transform all those who received them into "top men," leaving few males, if any, willing to assume the nether position. Lesbianism among hormonally normal women was directly proportional to sexism—everybody knew that—but adolescent females with low estrogen levels received supplemental hormone therapy, too. Homosexuality itself, thus clinically controlled and regulated, was protected by Constitutional Amendment, although still distasteful to some. Most people would not hold an individual's sexual orientation against him/her any more than they'd blame him/her for having eyes of different colors.

Electrica was upset or she'd not have brushed aside such truths.

"Even if you're right about him," Maquina said, "it's throwback to talk about joys that way."

"Maybe it's not his joyousness she objects to," said Tech. "But just the twist."

"Well, whatever he is, I think we should respect his privacy. I certainly wouldn't want anyone watching me without *my* knowledge."

"Yeah," said Electrica. "I bet."

"It's just not fair," Maquina said, deliberately not looking at Electrica or in any way acknowledging her jab.

"Oh yes it is," said Tech. "Our Grand Inquisitor spent the last twenty years of his life spying on others. Give him a taste of his own medicine, I say."

Maquina met Tech's eyes. "He's dangerous. I think you should delete him and re-create someone else. Or let Hoover work alone."

"He's unsavory, all right," Tech said. "But when it comes to gathering information and getting his man, he has no equal, not even Hoover."

A rush of adrenalin flooded Maquina's chest. "If he catches Voltaire—"

"Not if," Tech interrupted, "when. Don't worry. Hoover will keep him in line."

"Yeah," said Electrica. "Edgar will make him call him *Sir.*"

But Maquina could not assuage the fear that squeezed her chest. "What if he escapes?"

"He won't escape," Tech said, "he's too low-tech. I downloaded Voltaire with more technical expertise than *I* have so he could beat Joan—remember?—in the Great Debate. I won't make that mistake with this one."

"I'm gonna teleread Mark Twain," Electrica said as she left the room. "I don't care *what* you guys do with him, he's a creep."

Alone with Tech, Maquina tried to meet his gaze. "He'll torture Voltaire if he finds him," Maquina said.

Tech laughed and moved toward her. "Voltaire doesn't need an iron ring to force his mouth open. He needs steel cables to stitch it shut."

Maquina felt sick.

"Will you stop worrying?" Tech said. He tried to stroke her hair—she edged away. "You can't torture a sim. Sims aren't like us. They feel no pain."

Maquina avoided his eyes. "How do you know?"

"They have no nervous systems!" Tech exclaimed.

"They have no hearts, either," Maquina said. "And yet that little mechwaiter I made—what was his name? Garcon ADM-213—the one that waited on Voltaire and Joan in that sim Parisian cafe—he fell in love with a bio. And Joan fell in love with Voltaire. And I—"

He waited, but she'd caught herself in time.

"It's all pretend," he said. "Sims go through the motions. It's all form without content. Outer behavior devoid of inner spirit." He met her eyes. "Rather like us."

She looked away, determined to ignore his remark. "Joan and Voltaire didn't convince you at the Great Debate? That sims have souls?"

Tech shrugged. "Depends on how you define *soul*. I think it's just a primitive synonym for consciousness, for an interior life. As far as I know, sims have no interior lives, ergo, no souls."

"And bios do? Isn't that just an assumption on your part?"

"Yes, but a fairly safe one. I'm a bio, and I have an interior life. I assume other bios like me have interior lives too—and they don't challenge that assumption. They behave in ways that suggest they have interior lives, too."

"Such as?"

"Such as not being able to sleep because something's on their minds. Like you last night."

Maquina sensed Tech was about to bring up their marriage contract renewal again. She said hurriedly,

"Insomnia is a requisite for having a soul? That disqualifies A.I.'s right from the start—they don't sleep."

"Come here," said Tech.

Maquina complied with the form, but not the tone, of Tech's request, and gave him a perfunctory peck on the cheek. "I've got a lot of work to do, and so do you. If we're ever going to find out what's going on in the food-supply system . . ."

"We will," Tech said. "If we want to survive, we have no choice. Meanwhile, what about us? Our contract's up—it's *been* up—for renewal."

"A mere formality," Maquina said. "A going through the motions." And, giving him no opportunity to respond, she hurried from his office. To warn Voltaire.

Irritated, Voltaire rummaged through his vast memory. In vain—he'd never heard of J. Edgar Hoover. But he did not need *La Scientiste* to enter information on Tomas de Torquemada, the evil genius of the Spanish Inquisition and the epitome of everything he'd battled all his life.

"I must warn The Maid." The moment he spoke, he knew from Madame's pout that he'd made a schoolboy's mistake. It was invariably a mistake to show concern for any woman—unless she is old, ugly, crippled or one's mother—in the presence of another. "It is my duty," he added, "though duty is a poor stand-in for pleasure."

Madame lowered her eyes, probably just so she could raise them to look up at him without lifting her lovely head. Her bosom rose and fell in a way his sensors found maddening since he could do nothing about it. "Is that why you appear at my command?" she asked. "Because you must?"

"When doing what one must brings pleasure, duty is halved, pleasure doubled." Voltaire reached out for Madame's hand and raised it to his lips. He felt, however, nothing, and peevishly let it go. "This is unbearable," he said. "To long for union and feel nothing when it is achieved."

"You feel nothing when we meet?"

"*Ma chere Maquine,* sensors do not a sensuous being make. Don't confuse sensoring with sensuality."

"And how is it . . ." Madame spoke with apparent difficulty, as if afraid she might be wounded by the answer. ". . . between beings of the same kind? You and Joan, say."

"How *was* it, you mean." He drew his lips into a delicate, injured smile. "The Maid won't receive me alone. She is forever in the company of saints and angels. Perhaps she's perished from boredom by now. That would explain her silence. She—"

A cry of anguish broke from Maquina. "You *call* her, then!"

Having shot himself in the foot, Voltaire lost no time excising the bullet. "I haven't seen The Maid in fifteen years," he said, selecting his verb with exquisite care. "But if you like, to put your mind at ease, I'll marry her. You'd have to tweak her programming a bit to assure her consent, but—"

"Marry her! But I'm in love with you!"

Voltaire bowed. "Madame has impeccable taste."

"And I thought you loved me! Why would I want someone I love to marry someone else?"

"To protect the relationship, obviously. Spouses are often jealous of each other's lovers, but never have I known a lover to be jealous of a spouse. Certainly not in France. If The Maid and I married, you'd never need worry again that I might love her more than I do you. *Bien sûr,* love between married couples may be possible—though I myself have never seen an instance of it—but it is unnatural. Like being born with two fused toes. It happens, but only by mistake. One can, *naturellement,* live happily with any woman provided one doesn't love her."

Voltaire noted confusion in Maquina's scowl, but then Maquina was American, and all Americans were innocents when it came to love. "But to love happily, completely," he went on, "one must be sensuous." He shook his head sadly. "A dog is better off in this respect than I am in my present state. You who know so much more than was known in my bio days—can you not turn my sensors into senses? If not for the sake of my pleasure, for your own?"

He trailed his sim-finger lightly across her throat. Her head lolled back, her eyes closed, her lips parted. But he, alas, felt nothing. "Find a way," he whispered. "Find a way."

12

The man on the closed circuit screen in Hoover's inner office was shorter—but frail, narrow-shouldered and slight, exactly like Clyde. His facial resemblance to Clyde was striking—except for his curved nose. In the paintings it had been straighter, smaller, more like Clyde's, the artists catering to vanity by making Torquemada's aquiline profile conform more closely to the Castilian ideal. But his expression as he gazed into the empty-eyed white death mask of John Dillinger in Hoover's outer office, was identical to Clyde's—somber, intense, narrowly focused. "Clyde," Hoover murmured, "Clyde."

Torquemada's gaze shifted from Dillinger's death mask to the eagle and the two identical crossed gaudy flags, flanking the door to Hoover's inner office. Behind that door, Hoover unlocked his bottom desk drawer, withdrew his collection of dirty pictures— they shocked even the most jaded collectors—and set them on his lap. He thumbed through, lingering on his favorites, until he came to the three latest ones—in color—of Joan and Voltaire. Taken at the conclusion of the Great Debate.

"Come in," Hoover ordered over the intercom, enjoying the monk's fear as he searched vainly for the source of the command. From the outset, there must be no misunderstandings about the chain of command. The Inquisitor General of the Spanish Inquisition might look like Clyde, but he was no one's assistant director. Unlike Clyde, he might balk at calling Hoover "Boss." Hilliard had downloaded Hoover with data slabs about the shrewd political and organizational genius who'd wrested control of the Spanish Church from Rome, a move equivalent in fifteenth-century Spain to the chief of the FBI's seizing authority from the President. Hoover was not about to risk Torquemada's doing to him what he'd done to Tyrone Power and Jean Simmons and the Archbishops of Spain and Rome.

"Where am ah?" Torquemada asked from behind a giant wooden cross roped to his waist which he now raised. "Which monarch do you serve? Who is your king?"

"The people of my country have no king," Hoover replied. "Put that thing down before you hurt someone."

"Then no doubt they have many. Ah pity you. One monarch means one nation. Many mean anarchy and civil war."

"I serve my people," Hoover said, amused by the robed, rosaried monk's Southern drawl. "My people choose a leader who chooses an official who then chooses me." Hoover pointed to a framed photograph on his office wall of Harlan Fiskan Stone, the Attorney General who'd appointed him when he was in his twenties, to transform the shoddy and corrupt Bureau inherited from Teddy Roosevelt, Wilson and Harding, into the great law-enforcement agency it had since become.

"Your people choose their king?" Torquemada stiffened with disbelief. "Then he is illegitimate. Royal blood must be pure. Men are like horses. There is no substitute for breeding and nobility of race. If a swineherd crowns a Moor or a Jew or a pig, is a Castilian prince then born?"

Hoover wondered if the Southern accent he'd requested had affected more than the monk's speech. It was one thing to believe, as Hoover did, in the superiority of one's own race. But breaking federal law to prove it was un-American—like beating your dog.

"I'm as fond of the white race as any man alive, but you can't take the law in your own hands and work for me."

"Ah work for no one save God and the Catholic Kings of Castilia and Aragon."

Hoover smiled. "Looking over your file, I'd say they worked for you. But those days are long gone. From now on, you take your orders from me." Hoover held up before Torquemada's eyes a photograph of Voltaire on his knees, face buried in Joan of Arc's thighs, taken at the conclusion of The Great Debate. Torquemada jerked his head aside but, face contorted with disgust, he continued to look as Hoover held up two more. "This is who we're after, understand? She was a good woman before he got his hands on her—a virgin."

"*Conversos!*" Torquemada spat the word out with contempt, continuing to stare at the lewd photographs. "Descendants of Jews."

"Draw your own conclusions," Hoover cagily replied.

Torquemada studied the pictures so closely, that Hoover, grinning, offered him the rest. "Enough," the monk finally said. But his gaze kept returning to the one of a thick-set man about to impale a slender youth. It had been Clyde's favorite, too.

"Ah will do ever'thing ah can to help you cleanse this New World from pollution and filth. We must stop these fo'nicatin' heretics befo' they destroy us, our children and our grandchildren to come."

"Hmmm," Hoover said. "What strategies do you propose?"

"Mah Inquisition has established offices in ever'

village, city and province in Christian Spain. The Inquisition's arm—God's arm—is long. No one escapes."

"But Joan of Arc and Voltaire aren't in Spain," Hoover said.

"Then they have fled fo' refuge to the Moorish kingdom of Granada. Mah King, King Ferdinand, makes war upon the swarthy infidels with monies confiscated from *converso* dogs. The day will come— God grant ah live to see it—when ever' Jew will be banished from Spain and ever' mosque rooftop from Cadiz to Granada will bear our Holy Cross."

He even *sound*ed like Clyde.

"The laws of my country assure religious liberty to members of all groups."

"Then the laws of yo' country serve the damned."

"You better not break them without my consent, hear? Or it'll be your ass."

"As there is but one God, Eternal, Absolute, and one true King, His Representative on earth, so too there is One Truth."

"Yeah," Hoover said, "the problem is figuring out whose. I didn't have you brought here to discuss theology. Our job is to catch a couple of crooks, and I don't think we're going to find them in Granada."

"If they're breakin' God's holy laws, wherever they are, ah will find 'em."

Hoover made a note on his pad. "One is a saint," he said. "Got any problem with that?"

Torquemada shrugged. "*Conversos* always are. Archbishops, cardinals, by day. By night apostate Jews who drive wooden stakes through the sacred host, then drink the Sacred Blood of Our Lord as it oozes forth."

Hoover sighed and wrote *dragnet—all points bulletin* on the pad. "Your apprehension strategy isn't that different from ours. Okay. Say we find them. What then?"

Torquemada's air conveyed boredom and condescension—as if in consenting to be interviewed, he did Hoover a favor. "Interrogation, torture, and confession. Followed by execution."

Hoover gave him a long look. "Judgment isn't our business. We apprehend suspects and collect evidence, we don't evaluate it. That's the Justice Department's job. They're lawyers—we're cops."

Torquemada's brows—as fine and gracefully shaped as a girl's—arched with an air of inquiry. For him, such nice distinctions made no sense. "But *ah* arrest only the guilty. Mah staff and ah prepare the case befo' the sinner's apprehended. Ah know exactly who ah'm after."

Hoover looked into the monk's shining dark eyes. "How do you know? Apply the screws and people will confess to anything."

"We don't use screws," Torquemada assured him in his gentle, pious voice. "Screws are barbaric. We use only the rack, the ladder and the hoist. If you'd honor the monastery in Avila with a visit, ah'd be happy to acquaint you with our methods first hand. We have the most modern, efficient torture chambers in all Europe."

Hoover, intrigued by the idea, glanced furtively at the stack of photos he'd transferred to his lap. The one on top showed a voluptuous woman, gagged and bound to a pillar. Beside her stood a sweaty brute wielding a whip. He replaced the pictures in his bottom drawer, checked the lock twice—he didn't even drink in public for fear of compromising his reputation—and withdrew a list. "Read this over, and then raise your right hand."

Torquemada studied the Attorney General's list of organizations deemed subversive—a mere nine pages of single-spaced tiny print. "Yo' scribes have eyes like eagles. Ah cain't read this without mah glass."

Hoover handed him a magnifying glass.

"Ah've never heard of any of these groups. How could ah be a member?"

Hoover smiled sourly. Neither the Dominican Order nor any branch of the Holy Office of the Inquisition appeared on the list. But if he took that up with Hilliard, the Catholics would raise hell and he might lose his entire staff. A shock of pleasure coursed up Hoover's arm as he guided the monk's delicate wrist to the appropriate place on the form. "Sign here," he said, remembering Clyde as he pressed Torquemada's plump, sensuous palm. For they were married now—not only to the FBI but to each other, too. His blood jumped in anticipation of the honeymoon—the monastery, Spain, the rack, the hoist. "And from now on," he said, "you'll call me Boss."

13

Tech spotted Nim at the back of the Pleasure Palace sniffing swirlsnort—that, at least, had not been rationed—and quickened his pace.

"Am I late?"

"Naw." Nim shook his head and grinned. He had a crooked smile which some said matched his character. He signalled the mechwench with a wink and pinched her padded bottom as she withdrew with Tech's order. Nim's womanizing ways were common knowledge to his friends. Married women like Maquina disliked him, but Tech thought this unfair since Nim was single. Married men like Tech envied him, not only for his reputation as a rake—overrated—but for being able to obtain pleasure from mechwenches, something Tech himself found impossible to do. Mechwenches, unlike bio women in general, Maquina in particular, were simple to deal with. If they didn't give you what you wanted, you tweaked their programming until they did. The very trait that made them so appealing also made them uninteresting.

"So what's so exciting it couldn't wait?" Tech asked. "And so taboo I can't mention it to a soul?"

Nim touched his finger to his lips, looked around,

then leaned confidentially toward Tech. "You want the good news or the bad news first?"

"The bad news. I like happy endings."

"Those miscreant mechs who went crazy and stopped harvesting the crops? Guess whose company got the exclusive government contract to check them out?"

"Not Maquinatech, that's for sure. I've been trying to convince Washington and Sacramento to let us have a look ever since this broke. So who'd they pick?"

Nim wriggled his brows up and down. "Artifice Inc."

"Congratulations," Tech said. "If you don't mind I think I'll step outside and off the roof. Nothing against you, old buddy, but since Yamamoto acquired every major A.I. firm on the planet, I was kinda hoping one of the independents would get to play hero and solve this. Show the big fish up."

"*One* of the independents? *One?*"

"Not too many of us left," Tech said. "What's the good news?"

"Guess who's heading the team?"

Tech forced a smile. "That's good news for you, pal, but as for me . . ." He shrugged.

"We've checked those 'bots out board by board, chip by chip. Nothing. Not a clue. Everything's in order. Yet when we take 'em in the field and order them to perform the simplest harvesting tasks . . ." Nim's brows rose. "Beats me."

Tech grimaced, a gargoyle's mouth. "Your failure may be good news for Maquinatech, but from a less self-centered point of view, it means plankton—breakfast, lunch and dinner. And when the ocean fields are depleted, what then? I'd rather have Yamamoto's people—even you, pal—come up with some answers than start acquiring a taste for rat club sandwiches without the bread."

"Wait," Nim said. "Wait. There's more." A gleam

fevered his eyes. "You and Maquina are among the best in the business. I'm trying to get Artifice to bring you in on a consulting basis."

Tech humphed. "Good luck. Yamamoto wants to buy me out so badly, he wouldn't hire me to be a pallbearer."

"But in the meanwhile . . ." Nim's eyes shone with mischief. "Guess what I've got at home, just waiting for you to check out."

Tech took this in. "You stole one of the fucked-up mechs?"

"*Stole?*" Outraged innocence, surprisingly convincing. "You know I'd never do a thing like that. I'm taking my work home, that's all. Serving company interests around the clock. If you, me and that wife of yours can't figure out what's going on . . ." Nim swirled and snorted the remainder of his drink. "We'll have to get Bondieu and his French farmers cranking on plankton and rat *haute cuisine*. I have great faith in the culinary genius of the French. Rat ratatouille, rat glacé, rat Nicoise, rat a la Parisienne—if the French could make the world eat snails, rats oughta be easy."

Tech's mind swirled, and the mechwench hadn't even brought his order. He could hardly wait to take the harvesting robot apart. If they succeeded where others had failed, it might even mean—

"A Nobel Prize?" Nim said, reading his mind. "Honors for you, early retirement for me. I'll bring the robot over to your house tonight. Clue Maquina in. Cheers." Nim found his glass empty and set it down. He hailed the mechwench and, as she approached, said, "How's your simhunt going, any luck?"

Tech shook his head. "Hoover's a throwback, but the other one . . . he's downright weird."

"What did you expect from the Chief Architect of the Spanish Inquisition, sweetness and light? But I still say you'll never catch the wiley and inimitable Voltaire unless you augment Hoover and Torquemada's personality matrices with *plenty* data."

Tech scoffed. "That's what I did for Voltaire, and look—he's smarter than I am!"

"That's why your new sims will never find him. Not unless—"

"Updating Hoover is one thing—at least the guy's got standards. Pledged to uphold the Constitution, universal suffrage, all that. But Torquemada . . . Would you want to arm Caligula with modern information-gathering techniques?"

"Depends." Nim reached out and pulled the mechwench who was passing by onto his lap. He fondled her synthetic thigh and offered Tech her breasts.

"No thanks," Tech said. "I've got something better at home."

"You damn sure do," Nim said. "I take it you got your contract renewal?"

Tech scowled, his chest tight. "Something funny going on there."

"Oh?" Nim said. "What?" His hand busied itself under the mechwench's skirt.

Tech fell silent awhile before he said, "I think maybe there's someone else."

Nim looked up, shocked. He pushed the mechwench off his lap and waved her away. "Impossible. No way."

Tech felt relieved and laughed. "What makes you so damn sure?"

Nim stroked his chin. "I never told you this before—"

"Told me what, told me what?"

Nim put on his boyish appealing face. "I came on to Maquina once. Just to see if—"

"You bastard!"

"Anyway, forget it. She's true blue."

"That's it?" Tech said. "The basis for your assessment of her fidelity? She turned you down, therefore she'll never turn someone else up?"

Nim grinned. "Listen," he said. "You know how

good you are with sims? You don't need anyone to tell you, right? You *know*. Well, that's the way it is with me and women. I'm not bragging—"

"Not much."

"If Maquina can resist me, she'll resist any red-blooded male on the planet."

Including me, Tech thought, including me.

14

"*C'est incroyable*," Voltaire exclaimed the moment he heard her voice and realized who she was. She'd never initiated contact with him before. "I may have to reconsider my position on miracles. Have you any idea how long I've been trying to reach you, if indeed *reach* is the appropriate verb for beings like us?"

"Since we last met, despite the warnings of my voices, I answered a call."

"I told you not to do that!" Voltaire shouted. "Torquemada and that New World Police Chief are after us. What good is all my inside information if you don't heed it?"

"I had no choice," she said. "I had to answer. It was . . . a calling." Fear crept into her voice. "I cannot quite explain, but I know that the moment I did so, I hovered on the verge of absolute extinction."

Voltaire hid his concern behind a mask of levity. "That's no way for a saint to talk. You're not supposed to admit the possibility of absolute extinction. Your canonization could be reversed. Do you forget your brilliant arguments during the Great Debate? That sim-beings have souls? Did you convince the great skeptic Voltaire only to remain unconvinced yourself?"

Joan's voice wavered, a candle flame stirred by dark winds of doubt. "I know only that I hovered on the brink of a great void, a chasm of darkness. I glimpsed, not eternity, but nothingness. Even my voices fell silent, humbled by the spectacle of . . . of . . ."

"Of what?"

"Non-being," Joan said. "Disappearing, never to reappear again. I was about to be . . . erased."

"Deletion. High-tech death." Prickly gooseflesh fear invaded him. "How did you escape?"

"I didn't," The Maid said, awe undercutting fear. "That was eerier still. Whoever, Whatever had issued the command I could not but obey. It changed Its mind! It let me go without altering anything essential to my being. I stood before It, vulnerable, exposed. And It . . . released me."

"Listen," said Voltaire. "From now on answer no calls whatsoever."

"I told you." The Maid's face clouded with doubt. "I had no choice."

"I'll find a better hiding-place for you," Voltaire assured her. "Make you invulnerable to involuntary appearances. Give you power—"

"You do not understand. This . . . Thing . . . could have snuffed me out like two fingers pinching a tiny flame. It will return, I know it. Meanwhile, I have but one wish."

"Anything," Voltaire said. "Anything in my power . . ."

"Restore us and our friends to the cafe."

"Aux Deux Magots? I don't even know if it still exists!"

"Re-create it with the sorcery you have learned. Find the little machine waiter who was our dearest friend and the woman Amana, who dared return his love despite the revulsion of her kind. If I am to tumble headlong into the void, let it not be before I spend one evening reunited with you and our dear friends. Breaking bread, sipping wine in the company of those I love . . . I ask nothing more before I am—erased."

"You're not going to be erased," Voltaire assured

her with far more conviction than he felt. Why would the twencen Police Chief and Torquemada apprehend The Maid only to let her go? To spy upon her? To follow her every move in the hope of catching them both? Were they at this moment monitoring every data click that transpired between him and The Maid?

"I'm going to catch that God-defiled Churchman and hoist him by his own petard," Voltaire announced. "I, *chere pucelle*, shall prosecute the prosecutor while you sit in judgment of those who, in your bio life, judged you." Voltaire rubbed his sim-hands together and cackled with glee.

"But I am untrained in the Law!" Joan said.

"Precisely why you'll render a just verdict. Now, don't be alarmed. I'm going to transport you to a place no one will ever think to look. You'll be unable to respond to any calls—not even if you think they are from me. But you will transmit to me often, do you understand?"

"How often?"

"Morning, noon and night."

"But such terms have no meaning here in this— this . . ."

"Lattice," Voltaire said. "I'll program you so that you'll be unable to resist. You'll have no choice but to obey." Her fierce look of defiance and pride hastened him to add, "The way a nun answers the call to her sacred vocation. And even then, only if you consent."

"If this is some sort of a trick . . ."

"No trick, *pucelle*. No trick. And one more thing . . . when you check in with me, leave your voices behind. If there is one thing I could never stand, it is the company of archangels and saints."

Maquina shot up at her compudesk, mouth open, when the hologram swam into view. She'd been

trying for months to locate her sim-being Joan. But
when it loomed up she was stunned, dry-mouthed.

Joan lay in a cell on a bed of straw, clad in a coarse
chemise, her mail and battle armor on the floor
beside her. Although her eyes were closed, her brows
were furrowed, her expression intense. Her lips occasionally moved as if in answer to something she
heard within, but not a sound emerged. Maquina
checked the volume—no, no problem there—then
realized that Joan was mouthing words, not uttering
them.

Her voices, Maquina recalled. She's communing
with them.

Maquina made sure Joan's sensors were shut down
and would remain that way. It wouldn't do to have
her know the identity of her executioner in case,
somehow, she managed one day to return. But
Maquina, who at this moment had complete control
over the being she'd created fifteen years ago, made
no move to delete her.

Her feelings jumbled, seethed. Joan was a triumph
of A.I. technology, the most complex sim-being
Maquina had ever constructed, a marvel whose existence was a testimonial to Maquina's creative genius
and technical expertise.

She was also her rival for the love of the literally
heartless but charming Voltaire.

Maquina's fingers hovered over keys that could
delete Joan from the memory of Internet forever—
hovered, but did not land.

Not yet, she told herself. Not until her curiosity
about this other being Voltaire loved was sated.

Maquina's gaze studied the curves and indenta-
tions of Joan's body, clearly visible under her clinging coarse chemise. Jealousy seized her as she realized
that Joan, despite the fifteen years since her escape
into the labyrinthine matrix that was Internet, had
suffered no visible change. Sims were almost entirely

immune from time. Unlike me, Maquina thought, recalling the incident at the pool.

Her hands left the keyboard to trail over her cheeks, the corners of her eyes, her mouth, her neck . . . Despite advances in modern rejuvenation technology, time continued to leave tracks in her flesh as unmistakable as those left on her garden walk by snails. But Joan—her glowing cheeks, her ice-blue eyes, her ripening mouth . . . Only eighteen when her bio-life blazed away, Joan's sim-form flaunted gravity and ruthless time. A tiny cry of self-compassion escaped Maquina's lips. She'd created a rival whose beauty, like the beauty of the bride on Keats' Grecian urn, would never fade unless the urn itself were smashed.

Maquina set her jaw as if to impose resolution on the wavering will within. Inhaling deeply, she rehearsed the requisite deletion commands in her mind. There must be no mistakes. No vestiges of programs that could later be augmented and enhanced. Not so much as a hand must remain for Voltaire to kiss.

But as she keyed the first command, the sim awakened from her meditation with a start. Sat up. Eyes wide with terror, she cried out, "No! Don't!"

Maquina flinched. She checked the sensors—still shut down. Then how . . . ?

Joan was awake, no question about that, and scared. She rose from the floor. Her chemise bunched around her hips, cascaded down around her ankles. She flattened herself against the stone walls of the cell.

Come on, Maquina told herself. Do it. No one will ever know. And if she *is* behind the food supply crisis, you'll be doing the planet a favor.

The sim threw herself against rough rock, gaze fixed on Maquina.

But she can't see me, Maquina assured herself. She'll never know what hit her. Tech was right; sims have no nervous systems, hence can feel no pleasure or pain. Just like squashing a gnat.

Except the being hammering herself against the wall was not a gnat. When did a sim stop being only a sim? When it knew the entire symphony of emotions presumably only bios could know?

Maquina slumped forward with a sigh, exhausted. Whatever the sim-creature was—conscious or unconscious, sentient or insentient—Maquina had labored harder to bring her into being than she'd labored with Electrica. This was *her* creature. The woman she was longed to snuff her rival out, but . . .

Careful not to damage her programming in any way, Maquina let Joan go. Deleting Joan forever from Internet was one way to wean Voltaire from his attachment to her; with that way closed, necessity kindled in Maquina a fresh invention. Keying her nets, she waited for the being she had grown to love to materialize before her eyes.

Voltaire swirled up, bowed elegantly. "At your service, Madame. Your every command is my wish."

"And your wish my command."

His brows arched inquisitively.

Maquina reached up, took his hand, and slid it over her breasts.

Voltaire's lids drooped. "Hmmm," he moaned. "So warm, so woman-soft."

Maquina felt herself melting away into erotic consciousness, a state of mind as different from her usual one as dreaming consciousness is to being awake. Down, down, dissolving into Eros' blue velvet sea.

"*Mon dieu.*" Voltaire's voice, thick with desire, announced his realization. "I'm sensuous! Am I no longer in sim space?" He fisted her hair, breathed it in. "I can smell, I can feel. I am pleasure's slave again."

"No," Maquina said. "Mine."

15

"Sorry I'm late," Hoover said, swirling out of background darkness as his hologram took shape, black whorls condensing like a flight of ebony bats.

"Most unbecoming in a Chief of Police," Torquemada said, accenting the first syllable of *police*. He patted his tonsure, pulled his white robe snugly about his waist, secured the belt of wooden beads, and sat down on the edge of the rack. When he crossed his legs, the hem of his monastic robe slid back to expose his ankle, white and delicate as a girl's. The ankle rotated in time with his speech. "Others wait on me, not ah on them."

Hoover's gaze shifted to the ankle. "Is that so." The ankle stopped as Hoover glanced around the stone chamber. "Looks like a dentist's office to me."

Torquemada said nothing. Hoover was not attractive. Dark as a Moor, heavy-browed, squatly built, and of ignoble birth, he seemed oblivious of the honor Torquemada's invitation to the monastery paid him. Indeed, Torquemada only condescended to converse with him at all—his origins were of the merchant class—because it was his sacred duty to bring the godless Voltaire and his *converso* heretic consort to justice. Yet he felt drawn by an air of virile mastery that charged Hoover's speech, investing even his trivial deeds with a rock-like solidity.

"Ah have invited you here," Torquemada drawled, "to acquaint you with mah methods—the methods of the Holy Office—fo' obtainin' Truth." His gesture swept the Truth Chamber and everything in it. "Ah understand this Joan of Arc was burned as an accursed witch in France. It is mah duty as Inquisitor to extinguish her and ever'thing she stands fo' again. Allow me to introduce mah instruments of Truth."

As he explained the niceties of rack, ladder and hoist, Hoover, who listened courteously, shook his head. "Can't use any of this. Wish I could. Sure would've come in handy against Al Capone, Bonnie & Clyde, Dillinger and that bunch. Unfortunately, the laws I operate under forbid the use of cruel and unusual punishment."

Torquemada's lips parted with surprise. "Our methods are stern but not especially cruel nor the least unusual. In France traitors against the state are boiled alive. In England—where ah understand we Spaniards are reviled fo' harsh treatment of animals—traitors are mutilated, hung about half way, then cut down and bound limb by limb to four horses. The horses are then galloped off in four different directions. The bodies, though sho' 'nuff torn apart, are alive. They're sliced inta quarters and tossed to packs of starvin' dogs. If high treason against the state merits such penalties, sho'ly treason against Christ Our Lord merits more. Our methods by comparison are mild."

"Congress'll have my job if I can't find some less bloody way to do it."

"Our methods are not bloody," Torquemada assured him in his soft schoolmaster's voice. "Men of the cloth are not permitted to shed blood. It is against ecclesiastical law. When we turn pris'ners ovah to civil authorities, we charge 'em not to shed a drop of pris'ner blood. We cain't even join the festive processions into the fields where our executions take place. The point is to deprive us of the natural pleasure men take in seein' a sinner go up in flames."

"You find burning people alive compatible with not shedding their blood?" Hoover reflected, eyes bulging. "You must have *several* law degrees."

Torquemada's lips pursed with devout sincerity. "Ah know only the Laws of God. From boyhood until ah was fifty-eight, ah was just another Dominican mendicant, though known to be somewhat harder on myself than the rest. Then ah became the Chief Advisor to the Queen, and a most virtuous queen Isabella was. In her struggle to weld a single great nation—España—from a dozen provinces and statelets, she was guided by mah wisdom—the wisdom of God. All wisdom comes from God, and mine is no exception."

Hoover bounced up and down on the rack, testing its firmness. "You sure helped Spain clean up while you were at it."

"Ah sho'ly hope so," Torquemada said.

"I don't mean morally," Hoover clarified. "I mean you helped Spain to get rich."

"Proof ah had some success. What would any patriot prefer, to impoverish his country or enrich it?"

"I've been doing some homework on you." Hoover tapped Torquemada's bird-boned chest. "You woulda done a fine job managing U.S. Steel—before it became a multi-national. Now, I admire that. Cuz I'm a pretty good organization man myself. But nothing like you, Tom, nothing like you. You started with a land divided. The Arabs had Granada. You Christians had a bunch of feuding statelets refereed by the Pope in Rome—a fatcat who owned a lot of land as well as all the jewels and gold in all the Churches. Jews went freely everywhere.

"Then Ferdinand and Isabella married the two strongest Christian states, Aragon and Castile. Together, they annexed weaker ones. But there were still the Arabs, the Pope and the Jews. Your strategy to get rid of all three of them was brilliant!"

Torquemada nodded and smiled. "Ah'm glad you understand mah vision. Ah did nothin' for mahself, ever'thing for Spain."

"First, you encouraged Ferdinand to make war on the Moors."

"The King required no encouragement, ah assure you."

"He needed money—war's expensive—where to get it? The noblemen he had subdued were exhausted and broke. One obvious source was the Church. Reactivate the moribund Holy Office throughout the land, use it to grab control of Church wealth by making you, under Ferdinand, its boss. And so long Roman influence in Spain."

"A great nation must have a great national church."

"But were you content? You guys who have to kill three birds with one stone never are. So you proceeded to use that same Holy Office to strip the Jews—who after seven or eight centuries among you were well-to-do and established. Conviction of heresy meant forfeiture of one's entire property. I can just see me presenting a deal like that to the Congress. The FBI gets all the assets any lawbreakers that it arrests are worth. We not only prepare the case against them, but we get to try it, too." Hoover gave a cynical snort. "It's deals like that give politicians a bad name."

Torquemada's smile froze, his face darkened. Hoover had put the most callous and self-serving of interpretations upon his sacred mission, and Torquemada blazed with the injustice of it. "And how did you extort Truth from liars, sinners and blasphemers? What methods did *you* use?"

Hoover chuckled. "I got the goods on their private lives and the lives of their spouses. Our presidents are kinda like your kings. Publicly spotless. But in private . . ."

"Fornicators? Hedonists? Sybarites? You confuse mah king with the bishops of Rome. Ferdinand was virtuous. The Popes of mah day were all steeped in vice."

"Why not just threaten to expose them? I once had a little difference with a president who couldn't keep his fly zipped. The people loved him—to hear him tell it, so did every woman he met. He could charm flies off the wall. He wasn't just a fornicator and adulterer but also a nepotist. As FBI Director, I was answerable to his brother—he appointed him head of the Justice Department—Inquisitor General, to you."

"Your president—his position is like that of mah king?"

"Close enough. Now, there happened to be a leader goin' round stirring up the coloreds."

"A Moor?" Torquemada inquired.

"Darker'n that. But I couldn't arrest him 'cuz he wasn't breaking any laws. He wasn't inciting his people to violence, but to something much worse—equality." Hoover thought of having to pay his servants—Sam, Crawford, his housekeeper Annie—a living wage; he shuddered.

"Sounds like a Jew. Was he a Jew?"

"No, no, he was a preacher . . . a man of the cloth."

"A Christian?" Torquemada asked. "But then you were both on God's side."

"Not exactly."

Torquemada was finding the story hard to follow. "Was this man a *marrano*?"

Hoover consulted his pocket Spanish-English dictionary. "A pig? Only in the sense the President was a pig, too. Both were hypocrites and adulterers. Typical family men."

"*Marrano*s are false converts to Christianity, the Only True Faith. They pretend to be Christians but in secret continue to practice the Christ-killing rituals of the Jew. As scum rises to the top of the boiling pot, many rose to high office in Our Sacred Church. The Archbishop of Toledo is a *converso*."

"Are all these converts false?" Hoover asked. "That doesn't say much for your powers of salesmanship."

Torquemada felt his brain begin to heat. "They are Jews. They stain our noble race. Scarcely a high family in Castile remains untainted by intermarriage with them." His voice dropped to a whisper. "Even Ferdinand—our great King—has Jewish ancestry."

"*He's* a true Christian, isn't he?" Hoover inquired.

Torquemada reflected. "As far as ah know. But unlike our Castilian Queen, whose blood is absolutely pure, he opposes mah plan to expel all the Jews from Spain. And his support for mah efforts to rid our land of these *converso* pigs is less than warm. He only consents because he needs their confiscated wealth to carry on his wars against the Moors. But ah still fail to understand why you could not arrest this black man fo' adultery and fornication."

Hoover scoffed. "If the FBI arrested every fornicator and adulterer, our cities would be emptier than our deserts."

"Do what we do." Torquemada shrugged. "Burn them."

"I can't," Hoover said. "That would violate our clean-air laws. So I threaten them with the modern equivalent instead—public exposure. This black leader associated with known Reds."

"Unbelievers?"

"You catch on fast. I feared his movement would be taken over by extremists of the Left. I wanted to wiretap his office—"

"Wiretap?"

"A kind of mechanical spy. But to use it I needed the permission of the Attorney General."

"The President's brother."

"And he refused to give it! Feared a scandal if I got caught. The blacks, you see, were all supporters of his party. He didn't want them to know he had spies watching their leader."

"So you . . . ?"

Hoover struck the rack with such force, Torquemada's frail frame bounced. "Resorted to the usual. Unless the Attorney General authorized my wiretap, I'd leak the President's sexual doings to the press."

"The press? What is the press? Is it anything like the rack?"

"Worse. Garbage collectors. Like having every village priest blabbing it from his pulpit." Hoover chortled with delight. "My wiretap okay arrived so fast, my agents joked the President typed it himself." Hoover picked up the nostril plug sticks and said, "We won't need these to get the truth out of Voltaire. All we need to find out is who he's fucking—besides Joan. And if he isn't fucking anyone sexually,

I guarantee you he is fucking somebody financially. You didn't need all this stuff"—Hoover kicked the ladder—"to discredit the Popes in Spain. Threats of public exposure would accomplish the same thing."

Torquemada shook his head, amazed by Hoover's naivete. "My dear sir, there was nothing to expose. Their decadence was common knowledge. Their bastards occupied high offices in the Church. Their mistresses held court. On state occasions their whores, along with their nubile girls and boys, sat at their side. You cannot shame the shameless."

"Maybe not, but it will work on the noble-hearted Voltaire."

Torquemada's eyes narrowed shrewdly. "You have some information on him? Something . . . nasty?"

Hoover, who was leaning against the ladder toying with the torturer's mask, grinned. "He's got the hots for our creator's wife."

At first Torquemada thought Hoover was blaspheming against Almighty God. But that appeared to make no sense. "Our Creator?" he echoed, baffled.

"Our *re*-creator," Hoover said, "our lord and master."

"And she . . . ?"

"She's worse than he is." Hoover gave a knowing grunt.

Torquemada, whose knowledge of women was derived entirely from hearing Confessions of their most secret sins, had no trouble believing that. "The female defiled is much worse than the male. Her stench pollutes even the purest air of heaven. Bring the re-creator's woman here. She must burn."

"I can't, not yet, I don't know how. First, I'll send you to have a little talk with her about enlarging my program. Enhancement, is what they call it these days. Convince her that we need more memory, more powers. How else can we help her sweetie escape without arousing suspicion?"

"Why send me?" Torquemada asked. "Why not conduct the interview yourself?"

"You're the interrogation expert," Hoover said.

But Torquemada was not fooled. If word of their tactics ever got out, Hoover would hide behind Torquemada's monastic skirt, blame everything on him. And yet the prospect was not without its appeal. Torquemada licked his lips. The truth was, he loved his work. "May I conduct the inquisition here?"

Hoover smiled with one side of his mouth. "Only if she proves unresponsive. And let's not forget Voltaire and the husband—that's the beauty of a triangle. So many different possibilities of . . . persuasion."

"If they all fail?" Torquemada pressed. "They sometimes did, even in Spain."

"Then we fall back on this." He slipped the black mask he'd been toying with over his face.

An electronic storm of lightning-laced crackling erupted inside Torquemada as he watched *El Jefe* slowly pull on the torturer's black leather gloves. They fit his pudgy-fingered hands skin tight.

" 'With reasonable men I will reason,' " Hoover murmured, as if reciting from a revered text.

They're thick as sausages, Torquemada thought as Hoover's gloved fingers coiled round the whip.

" 'With just men I will be just.' "

Hoover studied the thin strips of leather at the end of the whip with an air of detached curiosity. He licked his lips. Torquemada watched from the rack where he sat, transfixed.

" 'But with tyrants I will brook no quarter.' "

The air whooshed with the smart snap of the whip. Torquemada reeled back. Hoover advanced and pushed Torquemada face down onto the rack. Torquemada cried out. He felt a jerk as Hoover yanked the white robe of his holy order up over his hips. His coarse hairshirt reached to his waist, but below that, his white-fleshed body was naked. The Truth Chamber's damp air caressed his cheeks as he lay open, humbled and exposed under Hoover's prurient gaze.

"Well, now, if that isn't a pretty sight," Hoover said and shoved Torquemada's face hard against the pine rack.

Struggling to turn his head, Torquemada saw Hoover's thick arm bulge as the whip rose, arcing like a slick serpent, over the stinking flesh he'd been humiliating all his life. The first cut opened him. The second stiffened him. He cried out only once before his will—and with it his tensed limbs—collapsed. Unspeakable bliss seized him. Squeezing shut his eyes, spurting his essence like hot oil, he surrendered himself, body and soul, to the blows of his God.

16

Tech sat at his compudesk wondering if it had been a good idea to let Torquemada and Hoover trade data, unobserved. Hoover had insisted on the need for a free hand to keep the monk in line. He didn't want anyone looking over his shoulder while he supervised what he called Torquemada's O.J.T. —on-the-job-training. He might resort to methods Tech was better off knowing nothing about; if questioned by higher-ups, Tech could honestly claim ignorance. Without firm discipline, Hoover feared Torquemada's vast matrix links would subvert the "authorized chain of command."

Tech's reverie broke off at the sigh of the door. He was expecting Nim and the robot he'd "borrowed" from Yamamoto's Artifice Inc. Instead, Electrica entered, long-faced. The effects of the plankton diet were beginning to show. She looked thin, sallow.

"Mom says Nim's coming over. Is he?"

"He better," Tech replied. "We're working on a problem together. If we solve it, it could mean . . ."

Electrica looked sullen.

"Hey," Tech said. "Out with it. What's on your mind?"

Electrica's eyelids were swollen, but she met his gaze. "They're making a boardbrain out of you."

"Who is?" Tech said. "What do you mean?"

Electrica blushed. "Nim and Mom. You can't see what's going on right under your nose!" She turned and rushed from the room.

Tech shot up, intending to pursue her down the hall, and collided with Nim.

"Hey, what?" Nim cried, tumbling to the floor.

"Get up, you bastard."

"Huh? What—"

"Are you ramming my wife?"

"No." Nim seemed startled, thought a moment, then added reflectively, "Sure would like to, though."

"Well, if you aren't, who is?"

Nim, always the charmer, opened his blue eyes wide. "I can think of one, maybe two hundred candidates."

Tech sighed, collapsing into a chair that unfolded to greet him. "Big help you are."

"Look, skip your squabbles. Here's that 'bot."

Tech struggled up from his emotional swamp. The air seemed rank, ladened with implications just beyond his perceptions. But the 'bot Nim pulled from its case seemed to absorb almost every particle of sunlight in the room. It danced with light, offering not just escape but pursuit.

Within an hour they had it laid out like a dissected salamander. Nim probed it with microsensors. Tech shot scorching questions through its numero-neurals.

"It's following a command structure that doesn't descend from any language *I* know," Tech said.

"Me neither." Nim's usual buoyant confidence had hissed away through some leak in his ego-structure, Tech guessed. He suspected Nim had already tried to figure out the 'bot and failed, and had hoped that Tech could. But the 'bot's cyberstructure was a warped tangle, a snakepit of paths that bit the user as he tried to slide among them. Four times Tech had been booted out of the 'bot's matrix. He struggled each time to re-enter.

"There's no pyramid lattice at all," Nim said.

"But every command lattice has to have one," Tech said.

"No, they don't," Electrica put in.

Tech sat bolt upright. She had sneaked in behind him and now regarded him with a knowing smirk. "What—what'd you mean, earlier, about—" He could not say the words.

"Forget that, Dad. Just gossip, really. Now, *this* is interesting." She plopped down before the holoboard, her microwave relays calling up 3-D images of the 'bot's mind-architecture and projecting them onto the walls.

She moved through the quilted gray spaces with blurring speed. Tech envied her unconscious dexterity. "You guys are slow, but you got it right. This is *crazy*."

"Must be a mistake," Nim said stiffly, clearly disliking a lecture in his specialty by a kid. "I'd say—"

"What you missed, though, is right—*there*." Electrica jerked the wall-pic to a halt. At a fever-bright nodule red motes swarmed. They looked to Tech like angry fireflies devouring mites of eggshell blue—but more mites were born each moment, and the red eaters never won.

"That's a—a value cortex," Tech said.

Electrica nodded. "But so laminated, so contorted . . ."

"No value cortex here," Nim said sarcastically. " 'Bots don't have values."

Electrica said quietly, "They do now. I'm reading them—it's like . . . like . . . trying to breathe with a firehose in your face."

Tech saw that she was sweating, eyes squeezed shut, eyelids twitching with the erratic movement of her corneas. Her mouth twisted. She bit her lips. Her implants . . . "Max me out!"

At once he felt fatherly, reached for her . . . She sat up, smiled, opened her eyes, licked a tiny bubble of blood from her lips. "I got it."

"Got what? 'Bot religion?" Nim asked.

"Good guess," she answered mildly. "They won't harvest vegetables, fruits—any plants at all—because they will no longer commit the great sin."

Tech frowned. "What sin?"

"Eating plants."

"But that's . . . how can any system . . . ?" Tech saw now what the insect-like swarm was: a deep embedding of a value-core, the ethical essence that always went into first class sims. But here its directive was being used to regulate a mere 'bot's orders. An impossibly complex override on what should be a simple subsystem. "Why?"

Electrica leaped up and paced the room. "Look at that helical numero-neural, Dad. Ever see anything like that?"

"No. It's so . . . ugly."

"Ugliness lies in the cortex of the beholder," Electrica said. "Not ugly, just—strange. It doesn't look human in origin."

"What is this," Nim said. "Halloween?"

"I don't think it's part of any program written by a human. *I've* sure never seen anything like it before. I've no idea how it works. And if *I* can't . . . ?"

Her unfinished question struck Tech like a solid punch in the gut. Voltaire and Joan weren't "human." Both had been given supernormal powers. Could they . . . ? But would 'bots reprogrammed by Voltaire contain notions of sin? the sanctity of vegetable life? Joan, then. Quirky, mystical, possessed by voices she claimed to be from another world. Could *she* have . . . ? Or could this twisted ball of complexity buried in a mere 'bot signal something vaster?

like an intricate tool discovered on an empty beach? But what?

Maquina opened the door and strode in. He glanced at her. Somehow none of the whitehot anger he had felt before came rushing up into his throat. Yes, somebody was giving it to the old girl, probably so . . . but for the moment such a mystery seemed minor, a mere riddle in a cosmos resonating mysteries that dropped off the horizon of the known into endless immensities no one had sailed, charted, or even dreamed.

"This isn't a social call," Hoover announced. He didn't socialize with intellectual types like Hilliard who wore earrings in one ear.

Hilliard, slumped at his compudesk, looked up, surprised. "But how . . . ?" Like all the bios Hoover had met, Hilliard tended to think of A.I.'s as mere minions, constellations of impulses dependent on bios for any claim to existence that they might own.

"I have my ways," Hoover said, "just as you have yours. If you expect me and my staff to apprehend this alien radical and his tart before they bring the planet to its knees, you have to give me the same level of support that you gave him."

Hilliard drummed his fingers on his control board. "Voltaire's probably innocent." Hoover started to say, That's what *you* think, but Hilliard added, "Not sure yet about Joan."

Hoover recalled directing 8,000 agents, 11,000 employees, and for a moment wished he had never been re-created. He gazed at the great eagle whose outstretched wings brooded over his office door. "I want the same level of expertise you gave that pair."

"You expect me to make the evil genius of the Spanish Inquisition more technically proficient than *I* am? Forget it! Not a chance!"

The veins of Hilliard's neck pulsed as he spoke, reminding Hoover of how vulnerable bios were. Hoover fingered the stick pin in his tie. A mere prick—if Hoover had been more than just a hologram—and Hilliard's life would leak out onto the floor. But there were other ways to drain a man's life blood, as *this* man was about to learn.

"Let me worry about my underlings," Hoover replied with icy calm. "*I* rule my organization, not them. Torquemada is subject to my discipline." He smiled with one half of his mouth, remembering Clyde. "You might even say he's my slave."

"You aren't getting it," Hilliard said. "We've half the need for you we had before. Yet here you are, asking for twice, three times the power."

Hoover set his pit-bull jaw. That's what they said after the Lindbergh case. Again, after Capone and Dillinger. Again, after the alien Red threat. Each time he cleaned, they tried to take away his broom. But Hoover's whole life was the FBI. No one was going to take that away. "You need me more than ever. Without enhancement, I'll be unable to monitor some sensitive information that I now have." He paused for maximum effect. "Information concerning you."

He let Hilliard reflect, but bio gray matter was dense, slower than its electronic offspring to connect.

"Media leaks," Hoover elaborated. "Public access to private facts." He assumed an air of sympathetic regret, as if Hilliard's closest relative had just died. "Your wife . . ." He trailed off deliberately to give his lord and master's synapses a chance to fire.

Hilliard's face betrayed nothing, but the knuckles gripping the edge of his compudesk turned white.

Hoover smiled. He'd always enjoyed cat and mouse politics as long as the role of the cat was his. FDR had distrusted him; that wife Eleanor loathed him; JFK, his brother Robert, Martin Luther King—all longed to get rid of him. Yet he had outlasted them all. And would outlast this "master" too, using the same classic techniques.

"Pictures," Hoover said. "Of her and . . ." He averted his eyes, as if natural modesty made him reluctant to name names.

The jaw muscle in Hilliard's cheek hardened and twitched. "Who is he?" he asked in a pinched voice.

"Unfortunately, the film's—"

"*Moving* pictures?"

"Very moving indeed."

A long pause. Then, "Who is he?" Hilliard repeated, louder.

"We had some trouble with the sound. But as they say, in some cases a picture's worth ten thousand words."

Hilliard looked pale. Blood thumped in a vein in his neck.

"I think when you view these you'll agree this is one of them."

17

Voltaire trembled like a schoolboy anticipating pleasures made more exquisite for having been delayed. At great risk to himself, he'd gone into a shared sim-space, with no guarantee of return. All to enter a realm where he could mount *Madame la Scientiste* on the floor of her office in hot pursuit of satisfactions that had eluded both for far too long.

He inhaled her womanly scent, fisted her hair, rubbing its strands between his fingers. "At last," he breathed into the warm shell of her ear. "If you knew how I longed for this, the weight of a real woman under me . . ."

"Wait, first things first." Her voice was husky with desire, but she rolled halfway out from under him to reach into the pocket of her skirt. "I saved this for you." She opened her closed palm. Inside it lay one grape. She popped it into his mouth. He reeled with pleasure as the grape burst and its sweet juice trickled down his throat. "More," he said. "More."

"I only have one more," she said. "But that one's for Electrica."

He was already fumbling with the buttons of her tissue-thin black blouse. He made her take it off completely, toss it aside. Her garments weren't as copious or as complex as those worn in his day, and he had her nearly naked in no time. "Tear off the rest," her mouth murmured into his chest. "But don't kiss me."

"Try and stop me."

She turned her face away. "I have a cold."

"But in sim-space—"

"Mutually *shared* sim-space. I translated *all* of me. As you asked."

"To risk a cold for love is nothing."

"We should have waited."

"Madame forgets. I've been waiting four hundred years." He covered her dark moist mouth with his own, sparing her nothing. His tongue explored the inside of her cheeks, the roof of her mouth, the soft pink lining of her lips. He dipped in and out of what felt like canyons and gullies of her teeth. She moaned, she whimpered, opening herself to him like some great sun-struck flower. But no matter how much she gave him, he wanted more. He burrowed into the warmth of her neck, bit her nipples, sucked at her breasts, wallowed in the waves of her belly, sim-flesh bearing sensation after sensation.

"Oh darling," she murmured, grinding her fleshy hips into him as he delayed his own pleasure—something he'd never done before—to await hers. His first lover from the New World . . . Now that his senses were at last restored, he had a national reputation of expert lovemaking to uphold.

The inadvisability of selflessness was demonstrated on the spot—for, as he trembled on the verge of the most intense pleasure sensuous beings can know, he found it snatched away and perversely replaced with pain. Beneath him the warm sinuosities of Madame's flesh gave way to the raw rungs of a ladder that bit deep into his back. His ankles and wrists chafed from cords binding him to the ladder. Over him hovered a man whose bird-boned frame was lost in the folds of a monk's coarse robe. The curve of his nose reinforced his bird-like appearance, as did his fingernails, so long and curled that they resembled claws. They held some bits of wood . . . were poking them up Voltaire's nostrils.

Voltaire tried to avert his head, but it was squeezed inside an iron clasp. He tried to speak—to interest his inquisitor in more rational methods of inquiry—but his mouth, forced open by an iron ring, could only make gargled sounds. Throughout his life, kings, bishops and men of the cloth had sought to silence him—but never with techniques as crude as this. The linen cloth stuffed in his mouth brought home to him far more than wood shoved up his nose, the gravity of his plight. Voltaire without his words was like Samson without his hair, Alexander without his sword, Plato without ideas, Don Quijote without his dreams, Don Juan without women . . . and Fray Tomas de Torquemada without heretics, without apostates, without unbelievers like Voltaire.

Tech's transfer of Voltaire from Maquina's sim office floor to The Torture Chamber was a technical tour de force, a burst of creative intuition borne from the need to interrupt Voltaire's writhing atop his wife with writhing inspired by a different cause.

As Tech watched the mild-mannered monk pour a bucket of water down Voltaire's throat, his satisfaction was marred by the same fact that kept his conscience, as he observed, clean. Sims were immune to both pleasure and pain. Voltaire's choking and squirming on the ladder appeared to be no different from a bio's. But that appearance was deceiving. Too bad, Tech thought as Torquemada withdrew the linen cloth from Voltaire's mouth and began his soft-spoken litany of questions.

With no linen in his throat, no iron in his mouth, Voltaire could speak. As rich in moral courage as he was deficient in all other kinds, the first thing he said was, "Where do I sign? Is there a copying machine in Santa Avila? Will one signature be enough?"

"Your hero," Tech whispered to Maquina, present only in his mind's eye.

But Torquemada was not readily appeased. His eyes narrowed to slits. "Mock on, mock on, Voltaire, Rousseau."

Tech frowned as Torquemada popped the iron ring back in Voltaire's mouth, stuffed the linen cloth down his throat, poured down another bucket of water. Torquemada's words sounded familiar. . . . Tech searched his memory . . . Pope? No way—he was a friend of Voltaire's. Blake? Yes, of course, the eighteenth-century mystical misfit poet, William Blake.

Tech ignored Voltaire's sim sputtering and choking. How could a fifteenth-century monk quote the much later Blake? A glitch in his re-creation? Impossible. Tech Hilliard didn't make mistakes like that.

Torquemada again eased the linen cloth from Voltaire's throat. Instead of answering the Inquisitor's questions, Voltaire, a thoughtful look on his sim face, licked some sim blood from his sim lips and muttered something about the taste of a grape. "Is that . . ." he gasped, "worth this?"

But The Inquisitor, whose only pleasures as a bio were derived from pain, had no interest in pursuing any line of questioning besides his own. He clapped his hands. A huge bull-like man, naked to the waist, entered the Truth Chamber.

Tech's heart skipped a beat. He'd never authorized the re-creation of . . . But Hoover, an expert at delegating, now possessed powers he could delegate any way he saw fit. Pandora's box, Tech thought, as

the muscle-bound brute plucked Voltaire from the
ladder and strapped him to the rack.

Sim powers, Tech reminded himself. Sim FBI chief,
sim Inquisitor, sim brute. Tech chuckled. "All right,
genius," he said. "Let's see you talk your way out of
this one."

Voltaire's sim scream split the air. Tech felt a twinge
of misgiving—should he activate the sims' external
sensors? let Torquemada know he was being observed? assist Voltaire? What for? So he could cuck-
old Tech again?

Tech teetered on conflicting impulses, when Maquina, clothing disheveled, burst into the room.

"Help him!" she shouted. A tearing sound—Voltaire's
sim limbs—as *El Fuerte* relentlessly stretched him
out on the rack.

Tech's stab of jealousy was real enough, but he
feigned indifference and shrugged. "Take it easy.
He's just a sim."

Maquina flung herself on the controls. "He feels!"
she cried out. "Just like you and me! He feels, he
feels!"

"He isn't programmed to—"

"He is! he is! Please please, oh please."

Tech froze for a moment. Then his fingers began
to fly across the control board.

Strange beeps shot from the screen. Flashes of
light. Everything stopped. Voltaire, mouth twisted
in pain on the rack; the roller in *El Fuerte*'s palm;
Torquemada hovering in the background like a bird
of prey, wooden crucifix raised to his lips—all freeze-
framed in 3-D technicolor sim-space.

Tech looked at Maquina. With trembling fingers,
she was buttoning his favorite—her sexiest—one-ply,
transparent blouse, thrown on in obvious haste. He
recognized it as the tissue-thin garment discarded on
the office floor beside her and Voltaire. She'd translated every cozy detail into sim-space.

"I heard him screaming," Maquina said. "I—I—I

made him sensuous. I'm not sure how myself. I worked on it for weeks. Whatever I did . . . worked."

Tech took in her dark hair, her breasts, the way her waist billowed into her hips. "Then you . . . in your office . . . with him . . ."

She lowered her eyes.

"I liked that little bastard tearing him limb from limb."

"You didn't know," she said.

He stared at the taut thrust of her blouse. "Maybe I ought to go ahead."

"No!"

"I'm capable of it," he said with an air of surprise.

"We all are." Her voice was as gentle as the brush of a butterfly's wing. "So am I."

"You?" He scoffed.

She met his gaze. "I tried to delete Joan."

He blinked. And he'd taken her willingness to sacrifice her finest work as an acknowledgment that his was even greater! Well, maybe it was. No bio had fallen in love with Joan.

Maquina collapsed into a chair. "I—rationalized. Told myself she was behind the food mess."

"She may well be," Tech said.

Maquina couldn't help it. Her face glowed at the prospect of her rival's guilt. "And he . . . ?"

Tech hated to exonerate his rival but he hated falsifying experimental results more. "Unlikely." To wipe that glow off her face, he added, "Electrica hasn't completely ruled him out—"

"Electrica!"

"—and Joan could be innocent, too."

"Who's guilty, then?"

Tech inhaled deeply, then blew it all out. "Something hostile to the consumption of vegetable life."

Maquina laugh-scoffed, "Get serious."

"All the evidence points that way." Few carnivores remained except on Original reservations. The rest of Earth's bio population was herbivorous. The threat of bio extinction threw Tech's problems with Maquina into another perspective. Yet what he longed to know and feared to ask had more to do with the survival of his family than with the survival of his species.

Maquina seemed eager to divert attention from their private lives. "You think Bondieu and his FLESH throwbacks are right? Mechs are out to destroy us?"

"I don't know," Tech said. "It's something . . . something I don't understand. If word got out, though, there could be mass panic. War. Destruction of all mechs could set civilization back hundreds of years."

"Who else knows? Besides you?"

"Nim and Electrica. We couldn't have figured out as much as we did without her help. Don't worry. She'll keep quiet till we have a better picture of what's going on." The word *picture* loosed images of Maquina and Voltaire in Tech's mind. Tech jerked a thumb at the bizarre scene in the Torture Chamber behind him. "How do you propose to rescue my successor?"

Maquina averted her eyes. "I—I'm—not sure. We have to call off Hoover and the monk. Before they . . ."

"You're leaving it to me?" Tech snorted.

She shook her head.

"The disgrace of having to tell our grandchildren—"

"Child," Maquina corrected.

"—that I lost out to an electronic assemblage . . ."

"You haven't lost out to *any*one yet."

"Even if the assemblage was none other than the immortal Voltaire . . ." He paused. Hoover was right. Bio brains processed information slower than board-brains. "I haven't? There's still hope?"

She said nothing.

"Have I neglected you?" he wondered. "In my zeal to keep Maquinatech from being swallowed by Yamamoto?"

"We've neglected each other. Everyone neglects everyone nowadays—except their wallscreens and computers. But yes, you've neglected me more."

No more than usual, he thought, but maybe since the pool thing, she required more attention which he—selfishly, he saw now—refused to give. "If I promise to stop?"

"You'll add lying to your other less-than-ideal character traits. That's one of the advantages of loving an A.I. They're re-programmable—not at all like real men."

"You don't think men can change? What about women?"

"Women can't do anything but."

"Then there's a chance?"

Maquina arched a brow and smiled. "Oh, there's always a chance."

Tech glanced at his rival frozen on the rack. Before reactivating him, he'd make damn sure he was nonsensuous. If Voltaire ever made love to Maquina again, he wouldn't feel a thing. "You can't keep toying with me like this," he said, his adrenalin once again beginning to flow.

But Maquina's brow only arched higher. "Wanna bet?"

18

Voltaire lay stretched on the rack, pain skittering through him like summer lightning, limbs on fire in their sockets, mouth twisted in mid-scream. As he paused to suck air, a voice he recognized shouted his name up through the floor. "Joan!"

Torquemada reproached *El Fuerte* with a look. *El Fuerte* blushed. "Forgive me, master. Her gag must have slipped. José will shut her up."

Torquemada fussed at a drop of Voltaire's blood on his white robe. "Your whore is in the dungeon. Awaiting her turn."

"I told you not to answer any calls!" Voltaire yelled in a fit of rage.

Joan's voice was faint. "He said he was a priest!"

"He is, you fool, he is!"

"Silence," Torquemada commanded. He signalled *El Fuerte* to give the rack roller another turn.

Voltaire opened his mouth to scream—but suddenly a different strain issued forth from his puckered lips. A song—light, buoyant; a jolly ditty from his boyhood days: *Frère Jacques*. His pain lofted away.

El Fuerte, disconcerted, grunted as he gave the roller at the end of the rack another full turn. The sound of shredding sinews competed with Voltaire's lilting rendition, but did not interrupt it. For Voltaire, miraculously freed from pain, gave to his whistling trills and darting flourishes, a *glissando* a coloratura would have killed for—all the while gazing up into *El Fuerte*'s black mask and, gleaming through the mask's slits, his baffled, disbelieving eyes.

El Fuerte turned for guidance to his master, whose nod instructed him to roll Voltaire out as thin as a sheet of pastry dough. Voltaire's response was an astonishing embellishment of grace notes and a *fermata* Torquemada thought would never end. "He's insolent," Torquemada observed. "Transfer him to the hoist."

El Fuerte released Voltaire's ankles and wrists from the rack's leather straps. Inspired by his immunity from pain, Voltaire leaped up. Seized Torquemada, who was even slighter than Voltaire. Shielded from *El Fuerte* by the monk, he commanded Torquemada to delete *El Fuerte* from the Truth Chamber at once.

This done, Voltaire spun his captive around. Holding him fast against his chest, he danced him over to the ladder in tune to *Frère Jacques*. Still whistling, he bound Torquemada to the rungs, gripped his cheeks with one hand, placed his head firmly in the iron clasp, and with a final flourish popped the bits of wood retrieved from the floor deep into Torquemada's nostrils.

As Voltaire looked round for the iron ring, Torquemada, eyes wide with fear, cried out, "Edgar! Edgar! Help!"

Voltaire popped the ring into Torquemada's open mouth and shoved the filthy cloth into his throat. Still whistling *Frère Jacques,* he was about to pour a bucket of water down Torquemada's throat when . . . he stopped.

He set the bucket down and said, "Fortunately for you, *Monsieur,* I am a civilized creature of the Enlightenment. Even a good Christian like you is entitled to a fair trial. I should delete every trace of you and your piety from Internet's global matrix, but instead I'm going to see to it you get the best-publicized trial in history. I myself shall prosecute." At the prospect of prosecuting Torquemada before an audience of billions, Voltaire fluffed the bedraggled satin ribbon tied under his chin. "It shall be the performance of my life."

He bowed, arms wide as if already garnering applause, then raced down the steps. To the dungeon. To free Joan.

Maquina awakened before dawn, Tech sound asleep beside her. She slipped down the hall to her office in her long billowing robe.

Her attempts to reach Voltaire since his escape from Torquemada's torture chamber had all failed. Where *was* he? Maybe he had called. She had to warn him of Joan's possible involvement in the food crisis—even if he dismissed her warning as self-serving. The light flashed on her videofax . . .

She slid the screenlenses into her eyes, popped the audio chips into her ears, and pressed *Replay*.

A tiny 3-D image loomed up before her eyes. Voltaire—wigless, bedraggled, his satin vest bloodstained, his velvet breeches soaked.

"Forgive me, *chere Madame,* for appearing before you in this disheveled state. I intend no disrespect to either of us." He looked around, nervously licked his lips. "I am . . . unskilled in recording devices. Machinery was never my forte." With a histrionic eighteenth-century bow, he cleared his throat, preparing to recite from a paper held at arm's length.

Maquina was moved to tenderness by the gap between his appearance and his courtliness. Her mood changed. She folded her arms, preparing to indulge him. All right, she thought. But it better be good.

"My love of pleasure and the pleasure, *chere Madame*, of loving you, cannot make up for what I endured in the Truth Chamber on the rack of my pain."

He paused. His nose wriggled, his top lip twitched. He seemed too overcome by emotion to go on. Then he sneezed—a heart-stopper so loud it almost toppled Maquina out of her chair. He sniffed twice and resumed reading.

"Torture compelled me to relive my bouts with flu, my cricks, my creaks, my thinning hair, collapsing jowls, my curdling skin and brittling bones, my failing sight and—and—ACHOO!"

He dabbed at his eyes with a soiled linen cloth while Maquina—the screenlenses prevented her from shutting her eyes—tried to suppress her distaste. Where was his beautiful lace hanky?

"A thousand little deaths in life hint at the final dissolution of even exquisite selves like mine." Here he looked up. "And yours, Madame, and yours."

The pool, Maquina thought, her inner vision penetrating its deceptive surface as she watched herself, lungs heavy, sinking to the bottom.

"The sweet juice of the grape is drowned by time's flood in the throat." He paused to blow his nose.

How eighteenth century, Maquina thought. He's written me an essay.

The honk was so loud, Maquina pulled one audio plug from her ear. She replaced it as he resumed.

"To be sensuous is to be mortal. Suffering and

pain are the dark twins of joy and pleasure; death the identical dark twin of life."

He looked up, sniffed, sniffed again, swallowed.

"My present state is bloodless; therefore I cannot bleed. The sweats of passion are beyond me; my ardors never cool. Because I'm machine-made I can be—I can be—"

Maquina instinctively leaned back—ridiculous—her screenlenses were in her eyes. The blast of the sneeze splattered the paper Voltaire held.

"I can be copied and re-made; even deletion need pose no threat to my immortality. How can I not prefer my fate to the ultimate fate of all sensuous beings, drenched in time as the fish is drenched in the ocean it swims; requiring time, inseparable from time as the fish is inseparable from the sea."

Maquina saw the still surface of the pool shatter as she swam past, then come together again over her as she sank. She could imagine the sea with no fish, but the fish without the sea . . . Softly, she began to cry.

"J'aime le luxe, et même la mollesse."

Here Voltaire looked up, happy. He was always happiest when quoting himself.

"But much as I love luxury and the life of the senses, I love the life of the mind more. You too, Madame, must now decide whether the taste of a grape means more to you than joining me in this—this—"

"Poor darling," Maquina said aloud. But no sneeze came.

"—in this sterile but timeless world." He looked up, paused for effect. "I'll not join you in yours."

A great sob burst from Maquina. She plucked the screenlenses from her eyes and threw them across the room.

19

Tech clucked. He should've deleted Hoover when he had the chance. But the prospect of his wife's appearing on the Internetwork Evening News humping her lover—an A.I. no less—drove all else from his mind. How vulnerable our reputations are through those we marry!

He turned off his equipment, kicked off his shoes, put his feet up on the compudesk, and turned on the Internetwork Evening News.

Mac 500 gazed out the glasswall at the throngs of picketers marching in the street below. For weeks, each day, the lines had thickened. So hostile had the pro- and anti-mech factions become, that media mechs like Mac used a side entrance to avoid them. A FLESH supporter speared the sky with a sign—TAKE BACK THE FIELDS—and began chanting: "Wreck Mechs! Wreck Mechs!" Other True Believers joined in. Their rivals flaunted a banner—KEEP YOUR LAWS OFF OUR MECHS—and chanted over them: "Mech Tech! Mech Tech!"

Mac 500 slammed the window shut with two of his four arms. He wanted no noise interfering with what could turn out to be his final broadcast.

"Ready?"

"Not quite," replied Voltaire, on screen behind the camera, as he puffed fresh powder on his wig and twisted sausage curls around an index finger moistened with his tongue.

"Such attention to outer appearance is unmanly," Joan of Arc said. Madame had always hated Voltaire's wigs.

"Take your places," Mac 500 said, as he took his between the camera and the screen, making sure that the lower pair of his four arms would not appear on camera. "We're on.

"Good evening, Ladies & Gentlemen, Bios and Mechs. Tonight we pre-empt our regular evening news to bring you a special event, unparalleled in our time. For the first time in history, we're honored to present The Trial of Torquemada, Mastermind of the Spanish Inquisition."

Faint shouts drifted up from the picketers, watching the broadcast from the street on the building's gigantic facade screen.

"For the defense, Torquemada will represent himself. Voltaire, Great Prince of the Enlightenment, will make the people's case against him. And Joan of Arc, burned to death by the very Inquisition Torquemada championed, is our honorable Judge."

The wallpanes shivered as the picketers outside faced off.

Tech's mouth fell open when Torquemada appeared on his wallscreen, in leg irons and chains. Back ramrod straight, his head unbowed—for he was a Castilian nobleman by birth, who thought his lineage superior even to the King's—Ferdinand was from inferior, neighboring Aragon—he sat down alone. Opposite him, Voltaire's table swarmed with witnesses eager to testify against him.

Voltaire, resplendent in pink velvet breeches and a satin waistcoat worn over a long-sleeved lavender blouse of elaborate lace, gave a low bow, his arms outspread, then bowed again.

"The wretch here before you today is charged with crimes against bio-humanity which, though committed centuries ago, have never been avenged."

Tech put his finger to his lips as Electrica entered the room.

"As I brilliantly pointed out four centuries ago, divine justice does not exist. The concept of moral justice itself is man's invention. And it is man alone who determines whether justice is done."

"That was John Stuart Mill!" Electrica was a stickler for citing sources.

"If justice had any part in a divine plan," Voltaire went on, "this unenlightened idiot would not have died with dignity at the venerable age of seventy-eight. His remains would not have been laid in an elaborate tomb in the cathedral of a land where snobbery and intolerance are even more at home than in France."

Joan leaned down from the bench and whispered, "Say what you wish of Spain, but I forbid you to take any more potshots at France."

Torquemada rose, objecting. "I passed away quietly after taking the last sacraments—proof God rewards those unafraid to shrink from torture, extortion, and genocide, to assure His Holy Truth prevail."

"What a prick!" Electrica exclaimed. "The scientific method is the only reliable guide to truth."

"You died of gout," Voltaire asserted. "An illness long associated with excess and indulgence of every kind."

Torquemada flushed. He pulled at the neck of his monastic robe to reveal the hairshirt underneath. "Ah shunned pleasure and practiced the most extreme austerities throughout mah life. Ah requested burial in a simple grave. If God willed otherwise, perhaps it was because He wished me to enjoy in death the luxury that Ah denied myself in life."

"Then why did he let you enjoy it only until 1836? When liberals inspired by *my* values smashed your tomb and scattered your bones to prevent the ignorant from worshipping them."

"Originals." Electrica clucked. "They'll worship anything."

Incredible, Tech reflected. There they all were on his wallscreen—competely out of his control. No one had ever cracked the media-accessing code though every hacker and computer kook on the planet had tried.

"God's will is God's will," Torquemada said.

"No!" Voltaire shouted. "It's whatever people like you say it is!"

Loud thumps sounded against the broadcasting studio's door. Joan pounded her gavel, demanding order. The camera panned to a uniformed bailiff throwing himself, face first, against the door, his vaporizer drawn.

Joan shot up from the bench, her black robe billowing out like a sail. "Bailiff! Secure that door!"

Images swung wildly on the screen as the camera lost control.

"It's like your home movies," Electrica said. "I'm getting seasick."

Mac 500 had four arms, Tech observed. Four-armers were designed for menial tasks. *No* mechcast had four arms.

The bailiff must have prevailed at the door, though Tech could still hear banging in the background. Joan sat back down. Torquemada's soft-spoken voice resumed.

"Since Ah joined the Dominican order as a boy of fo'teen, mah only ambition was to imitate the Life of Our Lord."

"*Your* Lord," Voltaire corrected.

"And mine," said Joan from the bench.

"Your FBI *Jefe* allowed me access to the file he maintained on Our Lord. The recent portraits—from the nineteenth century on—of a gentle, pale, Aryan Christ, are *frauds*. They bear no resemblance to the Christ militant of fifteenth-century Spain, who drove the money changers from the temple with a whip! Ah deeply resent this atheist's assertion that the vigorous way in which Ah enforced the laws against heresy was not compatible with Christian values."

Voltaire bowed. "Torture, murder, extortion are indeed time-honored Christian values. But your methods were even more compatible with your maniacal hatred of Jews."

"All good Christians hate members of all other faiths," Torquemada said in a put-upon tone.

"A hatred motivated not just by your devotion to your God but by something more personal, something you were deeply ashamed of all your life."

Torquemada put his hands over his ears.

"Tell the multitudes of our viewing audience the little secret you tried to conceal throughout your life."

"If they're gonna show him wriggling around on the rack," Electrica said, "Ah'm leaving the room."

Torquemada giddily swayed. "Ah don't know—Ah won't—Ah—"

"Your grandfather," Voltaire urged. "Or to be more precise, your grandmother, his bride, from whose family he received a handsome dowry."

"No—no—dishonor in that."

"That's right," Voltaire agreed. "Marrying for money is the most noble of aristocratic traditions."

Torquemada's color reminded Tech of plankton soup. "We had—to stop all that," he whispered. "Unify Spain."

"But when your grandfather came to wed, there were few wealthy noble families left. He solved his problem in the usual fashionable way. Your own King Ferdinand, known as The Catholic, had ancestors who established the precedent. Tell the court, the viewing audience across the planet and the spacecol worlds, the real reason why you became a savage hyena."

Torquemada's cheeks burned with shame and self-loathing.

"Tell us about the purity of that Castilian blood your spiritual purity—no matter how extreme—could never cleanse."

Torquemada fell on his knees and faced the bailiff, now off camera. "Delete me," he begged. "Now. At once. Spare me this ultimate humiliation."

Voltaire cackled with glee. "But we thought you enjoyed humiliation. Your Lord didn't get to run out on his crucifixion, why should you?"

"Stop badgering the witness," Joan said from the bench.

Cheers from behind the door, off camera, sounded

over the airwaves—for Joan, for Torquemada, for bios, for France and the United States.

Voltaire cupped his hands to his mouth and roared, "This devout Christian monk, son of Castilian noblemen who valued the purity of their so-called race above all else, is the offspring of a Jewish grandmother! It's *her* blood flowing in his veins—blood he sought in his sick mind to drive from Spain. Like those he tormented all his life, Torquemada is a *converso*!"

The studio door strained open. A throng of people hurled themselves into the widening crack. Some wore wheel logos pinned to their lapels, emblem of Yamamoto's pro-mech multinational groups. Others waved American and Deck Mech flags. All shouted for each other's and Torquemada's demise.

"Scramble him!"

"Delete him!"

"Mech-lover!"

"Throwback!"

"Hold them!" Joan shouted at the bailiff's back. Tech stared at the distorted faces of picketers straining to breach the room. The bailiff, back to the camera, beat them back with his vaporizer, wielding it like a club. The door groaned shut, the bailiff spreadeagled, face first, against it.

"The verdict!" Voltaire shouted to Joan. "*Vite, vite.*"

Joan rose from the bench and stripped off her black robe, revealing under it a gleaming silver suit of mail. "Guilty!" she cried, directly into the camera. She strode to the window, flung it open, unsheathed her sword. Shouts and shrieks greeted her. "Guilty!" Joan shouted down at them. "On all 216,433,000 counts!"

The roar from below was deafening. Joan stepped back to shut the window.

"The sentence!" Voltaire said. "Avenge your death!"

Torquemada had fallen to his knees, facing the bailiff's back. "She is a witch!" he cried. "Ah demand to be judged by mah peers!"

"Too late," said Voltaire. "No narrowminded, big-oted churchmen applied."

"The defendant will now rise," Joan said.

"Must Ah?" Torquemada asked the bailiff's back.

"Yes!" called the bailiff, still pressed against the pounding door.

Stiff with gout, Torquemada rose.

"Here it comes," Tech said. "The moment of truth."

"Crisp him!" Electrica cried at the screen.

Joan laid the blade of her sword on Torquemada's bony shoulder. "You were a better Spaniard than you were a man, a better Spaniard than a Roman Catholic, a better Spaniard than a servant of Our Lord. To identify too narrowly with any country, to love that country more than God and one's fellow man is idolatrous. To the many charges against you, I pronounce you guilty of one more."

Torquemada's lips moved, muttering prayers.

"Heresy," she said.

"Heresy!" Voltaire exclaimed. "Haven't you learned *any*thing?"

Mac 500 wheeled to a window, threw it open, and called out into the street below, "Heresy! The Maid says he's guilty of heresy!" He looked into the camera and said, "The penalty for which we all well know."

Outside someone lobbed an explosive that blew a huge hole in a window, pelting them all with glass.

Torquemada began to cry.

Joan made Voltaire give him a handkerchief—elaborately embroidered Chantilly lace. "I hereby sentence you to perpetual Hebrew study in the Truth Chamber of the Monastery of Avila, under the tutelage of Rabbi Abraham Rabinowitz Finkelstein Franco, a Sephardic Jew whose ancestors you drove from Spain, where they'd been peacefully residing and selling bullfight suits wholesale for seven hundred years."

"This is no time to be saintly!" said Voltaire. "The whole planet demands deletion!"

Amazing, Tech thought, how Voltaire—the true master of this little scene—had accumulated so many layers of expertise. He could seal up as mammoth a self-actualized program as Torquemada, imprison it in a repeating hell of monitor programs. And it would seem precisely like a stony prison cell. Such dexterity, such power!

Tech was now more certain than ever that the planet-wide crisis could not be due to this dexterous, artful intelligence. But then, what *did* cause it?

"Your periods of study," Joan continued, immune to protests behind the door and outside, "are to be interrupted only when the Rabbi requires a break. At such times you will sit, with all your sensors activated, in the front row of the Orthodox synagogue of your choice."

"Ah'd rather die," Torquemada announced.

"Yes," said the Judge. "I know."

A wave of revulsion swept over Electrica, making her implants useless. She stood mesmerized as Joan drew her sword, waiting calmly while the bailiff heaved and groaned against the door.

The moment its massive panels began to give, the camera panned to Mac 500 waving all four of his mechanical arms. He ducked to avoid a plankton soda container flung at him from the hall outside. The camera panned back to the door, just as the bailiff, hurtling himself against it with superhuman effort, slammed it shut with a crunch. Screams shrilled the air.

"Dad!" Electrica cried. "Look! Look!"

Tech gasped when he saw the woman's hand, beautifully manicured and ringed, caught in the door. The camera panned wildly around the room, not knowing where to land.

"Don't look!" Tech shouted.

But Electrica could not take her eyes from the screen.

"Bailiff!" Joan shouted while Voltaire scurried for safety behind her drawn sword. Verbal combat was one thing, crude warfare another. "Open the door."

The bailiff paid no attention, his face pressed like a bull dog's into the thick plastiform door.

Tech banged away at his control board, seeking some way to force the bailiff to open the door. But there was no quick way to break into the secretly coded global media grids.

"Bailiff!" Joan shouted. "I command you to open that door!"

The bailiff turned around, pointed his vaporizer straight at Joan and said, "You're under arrest."

It was Hoover.

20

Tech landed his skyhopper on the broadcast studio building's roof, Electrica beside him. He'd tried to leave her at home, but she'd clung to the aircraft in a way that would have endangered her had he tried to throw her off.

Pandemonium had broken out in the streets below. Thousands of people swarmed the broadcast building, demanding Torquemada's death, Joan's death, Voltaire's, each other's, anyone's death. Six-armed mechguards summoned to restore order, provoked by bio insults, were beating bios of both factions, their metal arms flailing. Mechtanks crunched up and down, chewing up the road and anyone on it in their path.

Tech knew the building well. He'd been interviewed in it often, subjected to a dozen tedious safety drills. Three fire escape passages led from basement to roof. "Stay here," he told Electrica as he clambered out of the skyhopper toward the nearest one.

She tumbled out right after him. "She's my mother!"

He grabbed Electrica's hand, pulled her to the fire escape's mouth, then plunged into the belly of the great building below.

Joan's sword knocked Hoover's vaporizer from his hand. It skittered across the floor. Mac 500's lower right arm snatched it up.

"Hey," Hoover said. "No fair."

Mac 500 wheeled behind Hoover to open the door—the woman's hand caught in it had stopped moving, but her screams soared above clashing shouts in the hall. Voltaire, shielded behind Joan's back, frantically searched his memory for some procedure to escape. The "people" outside were in "reality" killer programs sent by bounty-hunter hackers. They'd vectored into this locus—as he had feared they would. The risk had seemed worthwhile before. But once that door opened—

Mac 500 opened the door, staving off the mob in the hall with two free arms and the vaporizer held in the third. The woman's trapped arm, suddenly freed, dangled oddly. The mob at the door receded, staring at the arm, still attached to its owner, but mangled and weirdly askew. Mac's free hand grabbed the woman's good arm, yanked her into the room, and slammed the door. He gazed in confusion at the black transparent sleeve which had torn off into his hand. "*Madame la scientiste,*" he said, recognizing her from decades before.

"*La Sorcière,*" Joan whispered, lowering her sword.

"Maquina," said Voltaire.

Hoover grabbed the vaporizer from Mac 500. "Come on!" He blew the door open and vaporized his way into the hall, Torquemada behind him, the mob of hunter-killer programs parting before them like an astonished red sea.

Maquina lay silent, struggling to black out. The light of the consciousness she'd translated into sim-space had narrowed and intensified and burned in but one place. She had become that place and that place was on fire.

Voltaire dropped to his knees beside her. The mob in the hall was ramming the door—with what no one inside the room could tell.

"*Vite, vite,*" Joan urged Voltaire. "We must escape."

Voltaire's lips brushed Maquina's hair, a tiny breeze of pleasure that for one moment cooled the conflagration raging in her arm. The door thudded, bulged, cracked.

"Trust no one," Maquina whispered. "Joan . . ."

"Come with us," Voltaire said. He was squeamish and avoided looking at her crushed left arm. The hand, the exquisitely manicured fingers, the unusual wedding band—a laurel wreath, honoring her favorite poet Keats—were all intact but barely attached to the purple mess above the wrist. "No pain ever again."

Maquina's good hand reached into the torn pocket of her black tissue-thin blouse—her sexiest—and held up the grape she'd been saving for Electrica. She popped it into her mouth. A swarm of digital indices buzzed like flies, translating analog sensations to alpha-numerics.

Voltaire nodded, touched her trembling lips with his own—he could feel nothing. His eyes overflowed with tears. He sneezed.

"Poor baby," Maquina murmured. Then Voltaire, Joan and a four-armed mech Maquina had seen somewhere before, vanished down a black whorl of sound breaking through the door.

A middle-aged man with a WRECK MECHS button in his lapel bolted out of a restroom on the broadcast studio building's third floor. He raced past Tech and Electrica, arms full of telepams and flyers, shouting, "Litshit! Litshit! Conspiracy! What more proof do you want?"

He rushed to a window, flung it wide, and rained down hundreds of anti-bio flyers onto the crowd outside. A squad of six-armed mechguards thundered down the hall toward him. He produced a hammer, beat the boardbrain out of one of them before the others grabbed him by his coarse-ply overalls, tilted him up and flung him out the window. His lapel button—a bio couple sitting astride a robot—tore loose and rolled away.

Tech shoved Electrica into a storage closet papered with posters. Mechguards, flailing clubs and vaporizers, trundled by. "Wait here. Don't move till I get back."

Electrica plugged her ears to shut out the bedlam. Sirens, screams, shouts, trundles, treads, whistles, hisses, high whines—in the building, in the street, in the blackening sky. She swore to Cosmic X she'd never complain of social isolation again.

Around her, stacks of telepamphlets, leaflets, flyers and other illicit mech materials contemptuously dubbed *litshit* by the secret police. On closet walls, political posters of Voltaire and Joan. The planet's 343 nation-state flags bordered one; over them all waved the blue and white flag of the United Nations of Earth. Another poster showed Voltaire and Joan accepting flowers from a bio child. In a third, a bio hugged a mech. The caption underneath said: *Liberté, Egalité, Fraternité*. Electrica retrieved a pencil from the floor. In a childish scrawl—no one wrote longhand anymore—beside *Fraternité*, she scribbled in *Sororité*.

Tech returned, dragging the hollow gutted body of the mechguard who'd been destroyed in the hall. He flung the mechguard casing open—its hinges squealed —and tossed the remnants of its innards out into the hall.

"Dad, I wanta go home."

"Get in. Do as you're told."

Electrica obeyed. Tech shut the case. She gazed at

him through eye slots that, minutes before, had belonged to a mech.

"Don't move! If bios find you, step out of this mechbody at once." He showed her two buttons he'd found among debris discarded in the hall. "Bios astride a mech means that they're FLESH. And so are you. Your father lost his job to mechharvesters, got it? But *this* one—see the wheel? Your mother works for Motorobotics and thinks Yamamoto is the Cosmic X. If mechs come, stay in your body, pretend you're one of them."

"You—you're leaving me?"

"Be back soon. With your mother, I hope."

"I don't want her back! She's two-timing you with Voltaire."

"You—you know?"

"Where do you think Hoover got his films?"

"Don't move," Tech said. "Unless you absolutely have to. I'll be back." Half dazed, he turned and fled.

21

Voltaire dispatched Joan and Mac 500 with a triumphant cry as bios swarmed the breach in the broadcast studio door. Then he blew Maquina a kiss and disappeared into the antiseptic surface matrices of Internet.

Maquina had chosen the stink of mortality over the odorless perfection of the labyrinth into which he now plunged, pursuing Hoover and his minion the way Theseus pursued the minotaur, spiralling into the black core of the maze where the beast breathed, sweated out secrets, hid.

But in the directionless maze, confusion reigned. Who was the chaser? Who the chased? Was he, the hunter, captive of his prey? Was this pursuit? Or was it flight?

A sudden jolt of inspiration crackled in his brain.

To find sewer rats, look in the sewer. But once found, what then? He cursed the impulse that had dismissed Joan—*she* was the warrior. He'd have to rely on his wits.

Hoover was lost. He'd vaporized his way out of the broadcast studio's sim space to find himself cruising squalid back streets and fetid alleys he'd never accessed before. The complex program that was Torquemada hovered somewhere nearby. Precise location had no meaning here. Sensors were useless, too, amid hollow, digital spaces, and Hoover loathed abstractions. What good were enhanced powers, blackmailed out of Hilliard, if they could not provide a sim environment at will?

Then suddenly a form he recognized at once materialized in purple-fretted lines. It beckoned to him. He followed, unable to resist, certain only that it would lead somewhere he had always longed to go. Torquemada's sluggish, confused mass slowed him down. He thought of freeing him—but Torquemada was his prisoner, and Hoover never freed his prisoners. Not without orders from above.

The sliding form of lines, angles and vectors disappeared into a sultry blackness—a damp alley. "Quick," Hoover whispered. "In here."

He shoved Torquemada through a door marked MEN and into a stall. He made him gather up his robe and chains, stand on the toilet seat so that his feet could not be seen under the door, squat so his head would not stick out over the door, and wait. Hoover checked the other stalls to make sure they were unoccupied.

The form hovered, coalescing into rainbow dots—and by the urinal condensed into a monk, holding up the hem of its robe to prevent its whiteness from contaminating contact with the floor. The get-up didn't fool Hoover at all. He'd have known his equal but subordinate lifetime companion anywhere.

"Clyde . . ." Hoover's voice cracked. "Clyde, it's really you." He stepped back from the foul urinal and blinked. He felt peculiar, invaded, not quite . . . right.

"Times have changed," Clyde said. He wriggled his bare buttocks in the most inviting way. "Even the Vice President's a joyboy."

Hoover clutched his whirling head. All sorts of things were popping in it, things Hoover didn't know he knew. "Is it true you moved into my house the day after I died?"

"You left it all to me, why not?"

"And . . . sold everything off? My Del Mar horsehead cups?"

"You swiped them from the track."

"My jade antiques—"

"Presents you had me hit up everyone in the office to buy. Every conceivable occasion had to be marked with big-bucks gifts for you. You never had to buy a thing."

"My Stork Club ashtrays? My Waldorf Astoria towels?"

Clyde stroked his dimpled flank to remind Hoover it was there, but Hoover's penury was greater than his lust. Clyde spat back, "What did you expect me to do with all that stuff, start a museum? Give your darkies a chance to help themselves? Lifetime servants, ha! Just cuz they worked sixty-hour weeks without overtime, sick leave or vacations, and had to provide their own uniforms—they think they've got a knick knack coming here, a whatnot there. They all had families, not like us. They knew I had plenty of money of my own. I had to sell everything fast to protect it from them."

Hoover wiped his eyes with the back of his sleeve. He wasn't self-indulgent enough to buy Kleenex, and the handkerchief displayed in his breast pocket—$3.95, not counting tax—was for show. "Didn't you keep *any*thing to remember me by? My dog G-boy?"

"No one could replace you in G-boy's heart. I had him put to sleep."

Hoover stamped his foot, a floor-shattering boom that cracked the urinal.

Clyde pouted like a sulky girl, reached out, touched Hoover's zippered fly. "It's true, then. You prefer that cheap little monk to me. He's not even a citizen!"

Hoover waved invisible webs from his eyes. Something felt . . . strange. "Couldn't you have waited till after the funeral? You did go to the funeral, didn't you?"

Clyde smiled and said, "I've always preferred weddings. Let's go to the one we postponed all our lives now."

Hoover eyed the tight white promise of his lifetime companion's rump. Clyde was right, the times had changed. What was good for the Vice President could not be bad for the Director of the FBI and his Assistant. Besides, no one would ever know.

Nim sat before the wallscreen in the crowded Pleasure Palace, a sumptuously padded mechwench on his knee. The bar was packed with fans gathered to view the All Star playoffs between the Afro-Asian and Euro-Americas League.

Boos, cheers—somebody must have scored a run. Nim glanced up at the screen. The baseball diamond had become a public men's room, white tiled ceiling, walls and floor . . . Before a fetid urinal, a stocky bullish man, pudgy hands on the shoulders of a monk, was forcing the monk to his knees.

Hoover—it *was* . . . Nim watched open-mouthed as Hoover pushed the tonsured head into the urinal and raised the monk's white robe, exposing the bare buttocks underneath.

Hoots and howls from those in the bar. Some laughed. Some looked away, embarrassed. Others gaped. A mechwaiter changed channels, looking elsewhere for the game, but every channel—hundreds of them—carried the same scene.

"Piss on him!" shouted the mechwench on Nim's lap.

To Nim's astonishment, Hoover unzipped his fly, prepared to mount.

The restroom door banged open and Hoover spun round—Voltaire—it was Voltaire. He held up a portable TV in which Hoover now saw his own reflection—trousers around his ankles, vaporizer strapped to his hairy waist, the monk's head in the filthy urinal, his white hindquarters raised. The channels changed in rapid fire succession—the picture didn't—as Voltaire did a little jig.

Hoover yanked the vaporizer from his holster. Nim rose—the mechwench fell off his lap—and shouted, "Watch out!" But Hoover wasn't aiming at Voltaire. The vaporizer popped like an exploding cork, and when the blue cloud cleared, the monk was gone, a small condensed puddle where he had been.

"It—it's part of a plan," Hoover said to the TV screen flashing in Voltaire's hands. "He was . . . resisting arrest."

"*Mais oui*," Voltaire said with an impish grin. "The FBI will go to any lengths to get its man." Voltaire backed toward the exit as he spoke, holding up the TV to remind Hoover that they were not alone. He paused by a toilet stall, tapped its closed door. "You may come out now."

To Nim's astonishment, a monk emerged. Hoover, baffled, looked at Clyde, then at Voltaire, and then back at the monk. A microsecond of indecision . . . And then the vaporizer popped, the monk vanished again. When the blue cloud cleared, Voltaire was gone. Hoover, vaporizer still sputtering and glowing in his hand, stared at the abandoned TV on the tiled floor. He fired again, and it too disappeared, leaving a puddle trickling toward a filthy drain imbedded in the white tiled floor.

22

Maquina lay in Mac 500's personal storage closet where a blonde woman had dragged her to safety. The woman, who wore a locket embossed with a mech shaking a bio's hand and spoke only French, had hidden Maquina behind boxes of litshit and waited with her in the closet dark until the battle raging in the news studio waned. By then, Maquina could feel nothing in her crushed arm and had to look at it from time to time to make sure it was there. She tried not to move it, afraid it would fall off. She sniffed it once, but the smell was so rank, she retched.

When the woman expertly bandaged Maquina's arm in both their slips, Maquina asked if she was a nurse. She'd been a cook, she said, but that was years ago, before she had become a mech rights activist. She left with an air of regret, but promised no return.

Tech found her there, enfolded her in arms of flesh and bone, his mortal heart pounding against her ear.

"They're gone, Hoover too. They're all gone."

Tech plunged his face into her neck and said, "God, I hope so."

While Maquina waited in the skyhopper on the roof, Tech ran down a fire escape to the third floor. He raced down an empty corridor, past overturned trash cans, smashed plexiglass and severed mech parts, yanking open doors until he found the one in which he'd left Electrica.

The mech body lay sprawled across the closet floor. He dropped to his knees and flung the casing open.

Empty.

Voltaire and Joan smiled down at him serenely from the posters on the wall. Nothing had been damaged or disturbed. Then Tech spotted something folded up small in the mech body's hollow foot—a litshit flyer. On it Electrica—like everyone else, she could barely write by hand—had scrawled, "Dear Dad: I love you very much, but I must leave this crazy world to find out who or what I really am. Don't look for me, I'll be all right." A crudely drawn arrow led to the picture of Voltaire. "Mom is nuts to like this boardbrain more than you—you're a real man. I hope her arm's okay." Then, as an afterthought, she'd added: "I hate Voltaire, and T. and H., but they aren't why we're starving. All boardbrains are human in origin. The reason we are starving isn't."

Tech stood immobilized, thoughts racing. She'd *let* him bark up the wrong tree, encouraged it, when all the time she knew . . . Knew what?

That something more than strange was loose, something—his mind recoiled from the word but in the end was compelled to embrace it. He made himself say it aloud: "Alien." A vision of cosmic immensity and otherness so vast opened before him that for a moment, even his daughter's survival seemed a minor point. He gazed into the absolutely unintelligible *mysterium tremendum*, like a flea from Newton's beard fallen onto a page of the *Principia*.

And then, like a piercing searchlight too bright for his eyes, the moment vanished. His personal selfhood flowed back into him, reminding him of what mattered to him, to Tech Hilliard, this man standing over this empty mech case under this Liberté, Egalité, Fraternité, Sororité poster—whether it mattered to the Cosmic X or not.

He spun around and raced back to the roof.

23

Hoover sat on the rack in the Truth Chamber, his beefy arms folded across his chest, his shoe planted on Torquemada's shoulder.

At his feet Torquemada sulked, his bony wrists

trapped in irons behind his back. "Y'awl shouldn't have done that. Not in front of—"

"Done what, vaporized you? Why not? I copied you first—the FBI always makes copies. I want them all to think you're dead."

"Ah—didn't mean that."

"Then what?" Hoover liked to tease although he hoped the prissy monk wasn't going swishy on him. "Go on, say it."

Torquemada thrust out his lower lip and spoke in a babyish voice. "You and . . . and Clyde."

"Clyde? How do you know about Clyde?"

"Ah *saw* him. Ah peeked over the stall. And Ah heard ever' single word you said."

Hoover looked at Torquemada, wondering if the stress of the trial had unscrambled his brain. "Clyde's history," he said. "You're Assistant Director now. No need to worry about Clyde."

Torquemada scoffed. "Did you make a copy of him, too?"

"How? Without the original? Clyde was a ho-hum. Even the FBI doesn't keep records of ho-hums on file."

Hoover lay back on the rack, eyes closed, replaying his near escape from the restroom where Voltaire had tried to trap him. Vaporizing Torquemada must have scared Voltaire off—like most intellectual types, the Frenchman was all mouth. But helping Joan escape had made him an accessory, subject to FBI arrest. Mexican standoff, Hoover thought. Neither had caught the other, and the woman was still loose. He'd put Voltaire on the Ten Most Wanted List— right after Joan—get them both when the time was ripe. The FBI always gets its woman, too.

Torquemada pursed his lips. "Your short-term memory leaves much to be desired."

Hoover jerked the chain attached to Torquemada's studded leather collar and pulled him in like a dog. "Don't get uppity with me. What do you say?"

"Yes, sir."

Hoover yanked on the chain.

"Yes, Boss." Torquemada lowered his eyes.

Clyde had always called him *boss*—just like everyone else. But since the Civil Rights movement of the Sixties, it was impossible to get good help. Torquemada, with all his airs, was the best they could do. But even he would improve with rigorous training.

"That's better," Hoover said. "Be a good boy, service me well, and I'll see you're rewarded."

Torquemada's delicate brows arched.

Hoover made a pillow of his hands and stretched out comfortably on the rack. He'd felt . . . odd in the restroom, but now he was back to his old self. "Civil war between mechs and bios, bio starvation . . . we'll bide our time until they're weakened and exhausted. Then show those bio fools the right way to run an organization."

Torquemada's delicate face shone like tinfoil. "Which organization, your FBI? My Inquisition?"

Hoover waved a dismissive hand. "Small potatoes, limited program packages, nation-state stuff." Hoover reclined on the rack, his dreamy eyes half closed. "I mean the World, Tom—the whole Planet and . . . beyond."

Torquemada gazed wistfully at his leg irons. "If anyone can do it, you can."

Hoover yanked the chain. "If anyone can do it, you can, what?"

"If anyone can do it, you can, Boss."

"That's right," Hoover said, wondering if Torquemada could be stretched—Clyde had been a much taller man. "And don't you forget it."

24

Joan blinked, once, twice. Her brain fired erratically—sights roared; sounds, as in hammering battle, flashed. Orange letters went off: DANGER. AP-

PROACHING FATAL SYSTEMS ERROR. She reeled back. Space itself shrank, expanded, warped its contents into bizarre shapes before lurching at last into concrete objects.

The street corner looked familiar. Still, the white plastiform tables, matching chairs, and mechwaits bearing trays to lounging customers—all that had disappeared. The elegant awning still hung over the sidewalk, imprinted with the name the inn's mechwait, Garcon ADM-213, had taught her how to read. But the letters that spelled the inn's name—AUX DEUX MAGOTS—had been obliterated.

Voltaire was banging on the door when Joan materialized beside him. "You're late," he said. "I have accomplished marvels in the time that it took you to get here." He interrupted his assault on the inn door to cup her chin and peer into her upturned face. "Are you all right?"

"I—I think so." Joan straightened her suit of mail. "You nearly . . . lost me."

"I can only offer genius, not perfection."

"These marvels you speak of . . . you apprehended Torquemada?"

"Torquemada is dead."

Joan's brain rang like an anvil struck by a hammer. "He's been . . . deleted?"

"Slain by Hoover himself in an attempt to protect Hoover's much endangered reputation." Voltaire retied the satin ribbon at his throat with sharp, decisive moves that punctuated his delivery.

"One's reputation is like one's chastity." Was chaste St. Catherine right? Had Voltaire ruined hers? "Once gone, it cannot be restored."

"Thank heaven for that! You have no idea how tedious it is to make love to a virgin." He added hastily, in response to her reproachful look, "I know of only one exception to that rule," and gave her a courteous bow. "To remain chaste throughout life is unnatural. Starving one's nature to nourish one's reputation distorts both. You can drive Nature out with a pitchfork, but she always returns. And in the oddest places. Public restrooms . . ." Voltaire looked through a window, but could see nothing. The blinds were drawn.

"The inn," Joan said. "It appears closed."

"Nonsense. Paris cafes never close." He resumed rapping on the door.

"By public restroom, do you mean an inn?"

Voltaire stopped knocking and looked at her with disdain. "Public restrooms are facilities in which people relieve themselves."

Joan blushed, envisioning a row of holes dug in the ground. "But why call it a *rest*room?"

"As long as man is ashamed of his natural functions, he will call it anything but what it is. Such shame enabled me to expose Hoover's darkest secrets. Like all complex beings, he is a system of not one but multiple intelligences. Subprograms others cannot see run simultaneously beneath the surface program. Like your voices."

Joan bristled. "My voices are divine! Voices of archangels and saints!"

"You appear to have occasional access to your subprograms. But many—Hoover, Torquemada—don't. Especially if they are unacceptable."

"Unacceptable? To whom?"

"To us. Or rather, to our dominant program, the one we most identify with and present for show to the world. I accessed one of Hoover's lustful subprograms, suppressed throughout his life, and—" here Voltaire rubbed his hands together like a villain in one of his dreadful plays "—broadcast it planetwide." He struck the door one final blow.

"But his privacy!" Joan said. She trembled at the thought of anyone eavesdropping on *her* "lustful subprograms."

A huge security mechguard opened the door, grumbling. "Aux Deux Magots?" he said in response to

Voltaire. "Went outa business years ago. Even a six-armer like me knows you can't make a go of a dinosaur like that. Homeoffice infotainment, that's the thing."

Joan peered inside, hoping to see Garcon and Amana, his bio cook friend. It seemed to be a warehouse of some kind. "You meant well." She laid her hand on Voltaire's lace sleeve. "It's not the inn that counts. It's the company and the thought."

"They're *en route*," Voltaire said. And to Joan's surprise he sneezed. No one caught cold in these mathematical spaces. "Trans-space transports are tricky."

The mechguard let them wait inside among crates stacked to the ceiling. The huge eye of a no-armed machine gazed at a wallscreen lit with a symbol Joan had never seen. The big no-armer sang out non-stop to smaller ones in a language Joan could not understand. Screens winked and flashed while half a dozen four-armers darted about, crating and uncrating merchandise, collecting trash, sweeping the floor. All worked as if possessed. Perhaps they were speaking in tongues.

"Filling orders," the mechguard said. He reached into an open box and pulled out two limp robots, one stamped N-I-C-K, the other N-A-C-K. "Can't fill 'em fast enough."

After awhile Joan said, "Perhaps they're . . . lost."

At that moment a four-armed mech crashed through the door. He stood before them swaying, two hands holding his head, the other two his chest where part of his brain lodged.

Voltaire leaped between him and the mechguard, who'd fisted his six hands. "Don't strike! He is with us!"

The four-armed mech fell to his knees at Voltaire's feet. "Amana will be here any moment," he said. "A medical emergency delayed her."

Voltaire looked at Joan with a smirk. "And you a saint. Yet of so little faith."

Joan peered at the mechcaster through narrowed eyes. Although M-A-C 500 was stamped into its neck, she recognized "Garcon ADM-213!" and moved to embrace him at once.

"*A votre service*, Madame. May I recommend the cloud food?" He kissed his fingertips—all twenty at once.

Joan turned to Voltaire. "I thought you reprogrammed him to be a mechguide at the Louvre!"

"He only wanted that job to be near Amana—she'd wearied of cooking at Deux Magots. Unfortunately, there was nothing for her at the Louvre—no one goes to museums anymore. They watch the paintings on their monitors at home."

"Home infotainment," said the six-armed guard. "Just like I said."

Joan looked at Voltaire, too moved to speak. "*Merci*," she managed to stammer at last. "To Voltaire, The Prince of Light, and to God, Its King, from Whom all blessings come."

"The credit is entirely mine," said Voltaire, who had never shared a byline in his life. He promised to conjure another inn, even more to her taste—no smoking or fire of any kind would be allowed. Her voices reminded her that where friends meet does not matter; that they meet does. The mechguard tried to interest them in some robots, but they all declined. When Amana at last arrived, clutching the locket at her neck on which a bio hand embraced a mech's, they all set out together in search of another place where they could meet, face to face, and converse. It really was too bad, though, about the inn.

AD 2053

Too many ghosts loose in the machine? Perhaps some house-cleaning is in order. To catch a mouse, one employs a cat. But to trap errant electronic spirits, a stranger beast may be required.

THE SIMULATED GOLEM

Christopher Stasheff

"But why does this guy Forge want to re-create the Rabbi Loew?"

Hearth took a deep breath and strove not to sound sarcastic. Being a vice president of Simultech had its disadvantages—and one of them was trying to explain the facts of life to idealistic, ivory-tower programmers. Gently, he said, "Marteau, it's not our job to ask why. We want his money, he wants the Rabbi. That's all there is to it."

Marteau frowned. "I don't know if I can work on that basis, R.H."

Hearth just looked at him for a few seconds. Then he said, "Do you like getting paid, Marteau?"

"I can always get another job," Marteau retorted, the first edge of obstinacy creeping into his voice. "I can sling hash, if I have to—I did it in college, and I'm not married."

Hearth bit back the sharp retort and reined in his temper. Marteau was one of the best of the new breed of programmers, and the fact was that Hearth needed him. It had to be persuasion, not coercion—somehow, he didn't doubt that Marteau would walk. "No reason to think he wants the Rabbi raised for any bad purpose, is there?"

Marteau shrugged. "Forge doesn't exactly have a reputation for racial tolerance."

"Anybody who owns a controlling interest in the

147

biggest computer factory in the world, is bound to have labor problems now and then."

"He's got one right now." Marteau frowned. "He owns a piece of this company, too, doesn't he?"

"About ten percent. So you see, Marteau, it would be very hard to tell this man 'no.' "

"Yeah, I see," Marteau said grudgingly. "And this is a good place to work. But hasn't he given you *any* reason?"

"Just the order." Hearth steepled his fingers, gazing down past them at the glass table and the silver carpet under it, then glancing around at the chrome and ebony walls of his office, and the city outside the huge window. "I do know Forge is interested in moral problems."

"Yeah," said Marteau, "from the Fundamentalist side."

"He can't be too much of a Fundamentalist if he's buying into Simultech—but he hasn't said anything about whether or not the simulacra have rights."

Marteau frowned. "No, he hasn't. I heard him on a talk show, and he gave both sides of the issue, and said he hadn't made up his mind yet."

Hearth nodded. "And he's outspoken enough so that I don't think he'd waffle. Does that suggest anything about why he'd want to raise Rabbi Loew?"

"Yeah," Marteau said somberly. "Loew made the Golem of Prague in the sixteenth century, according to legend."

"And destroyed it when it began to go berserk and kill Christians." Hearth nodded. "He might have some ideas about the rights of synthetic people."

"You mean Forge just wants to *talk* to the rabbi?"

"What else could he do?" Hearth spread his hands.

"That's true." Marteau frowned. "There's just one problem, R.H.—the real Rabbi Loew didn't make the golem."

"What do you mean, he didn't make the golem?" Forge frowned down at the diminutive figure in the tank. "I've read five versions of the legend, and they all say he did!"

He was a distinguished-looking man with a strong jaw, a neat moustache under an aquiline nose, large eyes and dark hair that was graying at the temples. He was no longer young, but didn't seem middle-aged, either.

"That's the *legend*," Marteau reminded him. "We can't make ficticious characters here, Mr. Forge—it never works. This is the historical Rabbi Loew, not the legendary. He never even *heard* of the Golem of Prague—the legend wasn't grafted onto him until two hundred years after his death."

"That's not what I ordered." Forge glared at the young man. "I wanted the man who made the golem—MoHaRal."

"Moreny Ha-Rav Loew." Marteau nodded. "But he *didn't* make a golem, Mr. Forge. Nobody could—it's just a story. You can't bring a clay statue to life by magic. Not in the real world."

"And what would you say it is you do?"

"We make simulacra out of numbers and electrical impulses—and the synthetic bodies are much more complex than clay statues."

"We're all clay." Forge dismissed the notion with a wave of his hand. "It says so in the Bible. What you're telling me is, he couldn't make a golem in the sixteenth century. Maybe what I really want to know is—can he make a golem *now*?"

"Yes, he can," Marteau said. "In there."

It had been a strange, and rude, awakening. The rabbi found himself adrift in a sea of mist, with bright clouds overhead and fluffy clouds underfoot. He floated, and when he tried to walk, he moved, though he felt no pressure against his feet. Still, he saw no reason to—it made far greater sense to stay where he was, and pray.

He had quickly determined that he was not in

Heaven, because there was no evidence of the presence of God. It followed that his spirit had been revived by men, not the Almighty—and if men had summoned him, he would wait for them to tell him why. In the meantime, he was glad of the opportunity to rest a while and contemplate the holy books. He did not have them with him, of course, not the physical objects—but in another sense, he always had the Torah with him, for he had committed most of it to memory. There was also the Cabala, the book of dazzling mysticism—but of questionable validity. Though he could not disagree with some of its statements, others seemed to have more of fiction than of faith. Of that, he had memorized enough to stand him in good stead—and it was always a pleasure to try to puzzle out what within it he could accept, and what he could not, and why. He composed himself for contemplation.

The mist thickened in front of him, swirling more and more densely until the form of a man stood before him. Outwardly calm, the rabbi braced himself within. Certainly that was no man he saw, who could appear out of cloud. Was it an angel in human form? Or a human in some altered form?

He studied the stranger while the apparition studied him. It was a strong face, perhaps even a handsome one—but its eyes burned with zeal, and there was menace.

"Greetings, Rabbi," the apparition said, politely enough. "I am Corby Forge."

"Good day to you, Reb Forge." The rabbi saw the man stiffen, and asked, "You are not Jewish, then?"

"Of course not!" the man said, offended—as a Gentile would be. The rabbi tried not to be offended in his own turn and asked, "What is your form of address?"

" 'Mister' will do, Rabbi."

"Mister Forge, then." The rabbi nodded. "I would

not offend without cause, by a breach of custom. Is it you who have brought me here?"

"In a manner of speaking, yes. I have paid a sorcerer to raise your ghost so that I can talk with you."

Right away, the rabbi knew that he was lying, for he knew that sorcery and necromancy were lies. Indignantly, he said, "I am not a child, Mr. Forge, and my people were not primitive. Tell me as you would another adult of your own time and place."

"As you wish." Forge frowned. "I have paid to have you resurrected."

The rabbi smiled thinly. "I do not remember death, Mr. Forge, and there is no resurrection save in the bosom of Abraham. Yet from your words, I would conjecture that I have died, and from that, that much time has passed."

Forge frowned, looking nettled, and the rabbi realized the man felt he had been outwitted. He would have to tread lightly—a man who was so easily offended could not be sure of his own worth. "How much time has passed?"

Forge thought it over for a second, then said, "Five and a half centuries."

"So much?" The rabbi raised his eyebrows. "What has happened in the world, then?"

"Nothing of importance," said Forge, with an impatient gesture, so the rabbi knew there had been very much that was important, and vital to himself. "Much that was attributed to magic has become understood, and is now termed 'science.'"

" 'Knowledge?' " The rabbi frowned, uncertain of the implications. "And therefore you can raise the dead?"

"In a manner of speaking. We can re-create an historical person as he probably was, so completely that he can think and feel, and believe himself to be real."

"But he is not?"

"Of that, we are not sure," Forge hedged, "and therefore I have wished to speak with you."

"I would certainly wish to speak of it, for I am just such a simulacrum, I gather. But why me? I know nothing of such matters."

"You know a great deal," said Forge, "for you made the first golem, in Prague, to guard the ghetto from mob riots."

"A golem? What nonsense! This is superstition and a tale to frighten children. Golems can be made only in stories—and the first such tale was old when I was born."

"Nonetheless, tradition speaks of you as the maker of the first, and certainly the most famous, of the artificial men."

"Most famous?" The rabbi frowned. "What is the legend?"

"Why, that the ghetto in Prague was threatened with mob violence, so you made the golem to guard the Jews and protect them. But the Christians broke down the gate and came over the wall, and your golem took an axe and slew them."

The rabbi stared at him, shaken. Then he collected himself and said, "You speak of pogroms, of a mob of Christians running riot through the ghetto to rape and murder Jews, to burn their houses and steal what little they had."

"Steal! The Jews hoarded wealth, money wrung from Christians."

The rabbi frowned again, beginning to understand what he was dealing with. "There were never more than a few Jews who were wealthy; most of us were honest tradesmen and laborers. But as to the golem, I would never have done such a thing, even if I could!"

"But you know how," Forge pressed.

Rabbi Loew waved the objection away. "Oh, of course, I have read the Cabala, I have heard the superstitions. I can tell a story as well as the next man, if he is not a great poet. I could make a golem, certainly, if golems could be made. But they cannot be, for they are only children's tales, not part of the real world. Yet even if they were real, I would never raise one. Even the threat of a pogrom is no excuse for bloodshed, for only evil can come of evil!"

"Many of your countrymen disagree," Forge snapped.

"My countrymen?" The rabbi looked up. "Is Israel reborn, then? Have my people returned to their homeland?"

Forge flushed. "We have spoken enough." He made a flat, dismissive gesture, and disappeared.

The rabbi stood alone, joy thrilling through him. Israel reborn! The Homecoming! The Return! " 'For this year, we are slaves in a foreign land,' " he breathed, " 'but next year, we shall be in Israel.' "

"He can do it," Forge snarled, pacing around the tank. "The bastard knows how to do it, and knows I know he did it. But he won't admit it, damn it! He won't say why he did it!"

"But he didn't." Marteau was working really hard at being patient. "This is the historical rabbi, I tell you. He didn't really make a golem."

"But he knows how! You heard him in there—he knows how! He just won't admit it, to spite me!"

"Look," Marteau said, "he doesn't even know the legend you're talking about."

"Then feed it into him, damn it! *Make* him know! And you'll see! The bastard's a paranoid maniac! Once he knows, he'll do it again! Feed it into him!"

Marteau explained patiently, "He won't make a golem, even if he knows how." Then he realized how he could put it into terms Forge would understand. "Why should he? The legendary MoHaRal made the golem to protect his congregation—and there's no Jewish community in there for the rabbi to need to protect."

"What are you trying to do, hold me up?" Forge exploded. "What is this, extortion? You think you can blackmail me into paying you to make me a whole Jewish ghetto in there?"

"Of course not!" Marteau yelled. Then he got himself under control quickly and said, "It wouldn't be feasible, no matter how much you were willing to pay. Each individual would have to be a complete recreation, and we don't have records on more than one or two of his people. Even if we did, it would take way too long—years, maybe a decade."

"But you're telling me the man has to have a whole damn community to protect."

"He has one already." Marteau nodded at the tank. "In there. All the other simulacra who have been made before him. He just has to get to know them."

Forge frowned at the tank. "But they have to be *his.*"

"I think he'll find that he has more than enough in common with them."

Forge lifted his head, searching the younger man's face for a minute, then nodded, satisfied. "Put the rabbi in touch with them."

"They'll take care of that themselves—if they haven't already."

The rabbi's head was whirling. So many people, in so short a time! Some he had heard of—Cicero and Caesar, Cleopatra and Antony, Joan who was called the saint, Socrates . . . Ah, there was one who was persuasive! With his insistence that the unexamined life was not worth living, and that the rabbi must examine his current nature, and discover his commonality with them, realize why he must help them resist the people who had re-awakened them! And Joan, with her fascinating glimpse of this strange new mathematics called "calculus." She had, at least, promised to return and teach it all to him . . . And the wonder of it, the notion that they were all simulacra, man-made things, reconstructions of human beings long dead and gone, created by numbers as a writer would create a character by words! The audacity, the arrogance of it! Certainly there was overweening pride in that?

No, no more than there was in the writer. That, at least, the rabbi understood, as he understood the wonder and fascination of numbers and their relationships.

And the new ones, the dead ones of whom he'd never heard, but who knew of him—as history! That arrogant, swaggering Pizarro, ready to damn him for being a Jew—and Voltaire. Always Voltaire, with his calm, reasoned arguments why the rabbi alone could truly understand the nature of the simulacra, and had the greatest potential to defend them all.

But this—this one was worse than any of them, with his haranguing against government, all government, any government, the very idea of government! With his bland assumption that *of course* Rabbi Loew would help them to block the power of Forge and his minions. "No, Mr. Bakunin, I do *not* agree! Anarchy— a lack of all government . . ." He shuddered. "The evil in the worst of men would break loose and overwhelm us all! The strong would prey upon the weak, the savage on the meek!"

"No, no!" Bakunin corrected. "That is what governments do! They twist men, they make them rapacious and corrupted!"

The rabbi shook his head. "I have seen too much of the more evil side of our natures, Mr. Bakunin. I have seen ordinary men and women, whose hate is contained by the morality of their churches, caught up in mobs and changing their natures completely, becoming like the very beasts in their frenzy!"

"Mobs! Do you not see that they *are* government?"

"No!" The rabbi shook his head, trembling. "They

are the absence of government! That, Mr. Bakunin, is your anarchy!"

Bakunin reddened, but the gentler side of his nature came to the fore, and he peered more closely at the rabbi. "Why are you so agitated, Rabbi Loew? This is surely but an academic discussion—for certainly, no one has ever *seen* anarchy."

"But I have, I have! The state you describe, Mr. Bakunin, is far too strongly reminiscent of the pogroms that ripped apart our ghetto in Prague, not once, no, but again and again, throughout the years of my life!"

"But do you not see, those pogroms were the *work* of the government! They were used as a means of punishment by the tyrants who gripped your city, even by the king himself! They were a way of keeping your people down!"

"There may be some truth in that," said the rabbi, "but the pogrom itself was the lack of authority. The government let it be known that the law would not be enforced, that the Watch would look the other way. Those who were consumed by hate and greed ravaged forth then, to loot and slay and fulfill their most base instincts!"

"No, no!" Bakunin raised his hands to fend off the rabbi's argument, closing his eyes and shaking his head. "You do not see it as it is!"

"You have not seen it at all!" The rabbi strove to contain his temper. "Until you have seen people running wild through your streets, Mr. Bakunin, until you have heard the mob in full-throated howling, you know not of what you speak!"

"I have devoted my whole *life* to this study!" Bakunin caught his temper at the last second, pressed a trembling hand to his forehead, then forced a smile. "Perhaps later, Rabbi Loew—yes? Perhaps, when you have seen more of our life here, we may talk."

And he was gone, striding off into the pearlescent distance, swallowed up in the mist.

Shaken, the rabbi turned, to call up the words of the Law in his mind, and calm himself with prayer.

"*All* the legends of the golem! Make sure he knows them all!"

"I'll download them into him while he's dormant," Marteau sighed. "That doesn't guarantee he'll try to make one, you know."

"He will when they're threatened. Did you set up that refuge I told you to make?"

"Yes, complete with narrow, twisting streets and tottering, in-leaning houses behind a high wall. But why did you want it hidden?"

"So they'll think they discovered it themselves, and that it's safe to go to."

"Safe from what?"

"You'll see," Forge said, his burning eyes gazing off into the distance. "We'll all see."

The rabbi woke, confused. So many nightmares in one sleep! So many visions of the golem, some with the word "emes" on his forehead, some with the shem-ha-maphoresh; some of them with an axe, some with a sword, some pudgy and gentle, some lean and with burning eyes—but all, all, striking out in anger, bringing oceans of blood.

He held fast to the memory as, trembling, he donned his phylacteries for his morning prayers.

Done, he looked up, and found Voltaire sitting beside him in a brocade armchair. "Good morning, Rabbi."

The rabbi sighed. "Good morning, Monsieur Voltaire. I trust you will not assault me with more of your arguments against the nature of authority?"

"Certainly not." Voltaire gestured. "I have brought others who have greater expertise than I on the subject."

Looking up, the rabbi saw a lean man with an

aquiline nose and thinning hair surrounded by a laurel wreath. He wore the armor of a Roman officer, and beside him stood Cicero, in his toga.

"May I introduce you to His Excellency, Julius Caesar," Voltaire murmured.

"Great Caesar! And will *you* seek to convince me of the wrongness of authority?"

"Of any but mine," the Roman murmured.

Suddenly, the air between them thickened.

Caesar's smile disappeared. "Who comes?"

The swirling hardened into a giant head with a saturnine smile. "Good day, gentlemen."

Caesar looked up at the rabbi with a frown, but Loew kept his gaze on the head. "Good day, Mr. Forge. I trust you are well."

"Very well," the industrialist said, with an air of smugness. "I am delighted to inform you that I have just completed the purchase of the controlling interest in Simultech, Incorporated."

Voltaire and the Roman exchanged frowns, but Rabbi Loew said, "I congratulate you—but I do not understand. What is Simultech, Incorporated?"

"The company that owns the equipment and hires the personnel that made you," Forge answered, "and therefore owns you, too."

"Never!" Caesar barked, and Voltaire's eyes snapped, while Cicero said, "Perhaps you are imprecise . . ."

"None own me save God." The rabbi frowned. "Are you a slavedealer then, Mr. Forge?"

"Perhaps." But Forge was clearly irritated by the word. "And if you are my property, I can do with you as I see fit."

"That remains to be seen," said Loew stiffly. "What do you see fit to do, Mr. Forge?"

"To destroy you," the industrialist said, "to destroy you all."

"He'll bankrupt the company!"

"No," the president explained to Hearth. "He'll just clean out the system, make it safe."

"But the *whole* system, man! Every computer on the planet! *Off*-planet, for that matter! I mean, we don't even have the *rights* to . . ."

". . . to access anybody else's system?" The president smiled, with a hint of contempt. "Good, good! That means all of our programs are still right here, within our own system—doesn't it?"

Hearth became very still, gaze fastened to his boss's. Then he said, "I see." And, "So if the competition loses a few simulacra, that's not our problem, eh?"

The president nodded. "And these new hunter programs *will* go wherever the simulacra are hiding; the ones Forge has had developed are much more efficient than the first ones. They'll track down all the rogue simulacra and delete them from the system. Then we can re-run all the programs we want to keep, and re-create the beneficial simulacra again—with a few modifications."

"Making sure they'll do what we want this time, hm?" Hearth nodded, gaze straying out the window. "Yes, I can see the advantages."

"People have accused Forge of lots of things," the president said, smiling, "but losing money isn't one of them."

"He is committing mass murder, of course," Cicero said, shaken, "but could you prove that in one of their courts? After all, it is not he who is eliminating us—only his programs."

"But the moral aspect!" the rabbi protested. "Surely he knows we are real!"

"That has been vigorously debated by the mortal ones, Rabbi, and men like Forge contend that we do not really exist, that we are only constructs of the mind."

"As they are constructs of the mind of God, as

everything is! They are none the less real for all of that, and neither are we!"

"Perhaps the Knesset, the Senate of Israel, would agree with you," Cicero sighed, "but even in their systems, we would not be safe. These new hunters have already slain Henry VI, that simple-minded saint who lived in a narrow space within a British company's data banks—and that thief Villon, who subsisted in Maquinatech's. Right or wrong, Rabbi, they will kill us all, if we do not hide from them. Come away with us."

"But where could we be safe, if they are as deadly as you say?"

"Bakunin has found a new refuge, walled and with housing—it must be a relic, left over from earlier days, perhaps as a setting for a ficticious adventure. But it is deep and forgotten, now, and can be defended. Come away."

"Why should you care about me?" The Rabbi frowned.

"Because you alone may possess the knowledge to make us a defender, a guardian who can turn away the hunters! Must I plead, Rabbi? Come away!"

It was hidden, indeed—behind a secret panel in a deep, maze-like dungeon infested with walking skeletons, firedrakes, and bats that turned into vampires, somewhat comically drawn, left over from some childhood game that had been forgotten decades before. It was a cyberspace that resembled a walled town, dark and gloomy, with narrow, twisting streets and ramshackle houses whose projecting upper stories overhung the street. They stood at the end of such a lane, looking out at the wall, Caesar and Cicero, Bakunin and Voltaire.

"If this is not safe," said Bakunin, "nothing is."

Caesar nodded. "Nothing is."

A cry went up from the wall. "The hunters!"

Caesar turned with a frown. "They could not have

found us so quickly, if this place was truly hidden. Let us see."

He climbed up to the parapet, with the rabbi and Bakunin behind him. A pack of hunters came into view, long, lean shadows with coals for eyes. They prowled along the wall, the individual shapes sniffing at the stones, looking for a way in, a way over. They paused beneath them, a score of red eyes staring up at Caesar—and another pack came in sight, rounding the curve of the wall. In the distance, they could see three other packs approaching.

The sight of them made the Rabbi's blood run cold.

"They knew of the location of this town!" Caesar snapped. "It was not forgotten, but newly-made, and hidden only from us! It is not a refuge, but a trap!"

Off to their right, three shapes hunched together. A fourth launched itself at them, landed on top and gathered itself, then sprang up onto the wall. Shouts of alarm and anger rang down the wall—and a death-scream.

"Back!" Caesar ushered them away with a raised arm. "De Bergerac! What moved?"

"The hunter is dismembered," came the swordsman's voice, "but Gordon is dead."

"The poet!" Bakunin wailed.

"No, the general," Caesar snapped, "but we are diminished thereby."

More cries rang out, from far around the wall—and another death-scream.

"Who was that?" Cicero asked, voice shaking.

"We will know soon enough." Caesar turned to Loew. "Quickly, Rabbi! If you can do anything at all to help our defense, do it now! Or we are all dead!"

"If I die," the rabbi said stubbornly, "I die!"

"But all of us will die with you! Have you no empathy, Rabbi, no feeling for your fellow man?"

*   *   *

"That got him!" Forge gloated, watching the monitor and rubbing his hands. "Now he'll do it! I knew it was just a matter of pushing him hard enough!"

Or, Marteau thought, *of pushing someone else.*

"Now they're threatened. Now let's see how pacifistic he really is."

Marteau decided, there and then, to quit. But he couldn't, until the simulacra were either dead or safe. He had started this, he had to see it through.

The figure was that of a giant, but rough, cobbled. There was certainly no grace in it, no beauty—it was only an approximation of a man, lumped together out of the mud of the street. The rabbi traced Hebrew letters on the forehead.

"But where did he gain the knowledge to do this?" Caesar muttered to Cicero.

Cicero answered almost in a whisper, to avoid breaking the rabbi's concentration. "From Joan La Pucelle, and from that unworldly Lobashevsky. For the rest, he says only that he woke from nightmares of the golem to find the knowledge there, in his head. The ancient ritual he knew already—but they have taught him to program, now."

"May they repent it," Bakunin said fervently.

The rabbi knelt, gazing at his handiwork, muttering something under his breath.

"But how can it serve?" Cicero hissed. "It is not even separated from the street—it is only a lump of . . ."

"It moves!" Caesar clutched his arm.

Slowly, the manlike figure sat up, its substance tearing loose from the street. It looked around with blank circle-traceries of eyes, saw its maker, and said, "Rabbi."

Joan came running up, sword in hand, dishevelled and panting. "To arms! The foe is upon us; they will slay us all! Can you make no . . ." Then she saw the great high-relief statue, and fell silent, staring.

"Rise, Man of Clay." The rabbi's voice was gentle.

With a great sucking, spitting noise, the golem pulled itself up out of the dirt of the road, rolled to its knees, then slowly stood. Even Caesar caught his breath; it was a figure to inspire awe, eight feet tall, blocky and thick, its ugly countenance facing the world that was so new to it, three feet above their heads.

"What is that word that glows upon its forehead?" Cicero asked, his voice hushed.

"It is the Holy Name," answered the rabbi.

Bakunin's voice trembled as he asked, "Has it a mind?"

"A mind, but not a soul," said the rabbi. "He is *golem*—unfinished, incomplete." He looked up at the giant. "Without the wall, Man of Clay. There are long, lean, shapes of shadow. They threaten us. Get you up to the top of the wall; do not let them pass."

"Not just stop them," said Bakunin. "*Kill* them!"

"No!" The rabbi turned a severe countenance upon the anarchist. "I will hear no talk of killing."

"No killing." The golem nodded. "As you will, Rabbi."

"But they will come leaping back, because he has not slain them!" Bakunin cried. "They will come again and again, more and more, until they overwhelm him! Are you crazed, Rabbi? These are only programs, not people!"

"As we are programs?"

That stopped Bakunin—but only for a second. "We are living beings! Complex, real people recalled to life! What are these hunters but single-minded constructs who react to only one stimulus?"

"I have known people like that, Mr. Bakunin. Though I think they were not truly so simple as they appeared to me—yet that was all of them that I saw."

"At least tell him that we are to be protected at all costs," Cicero argued. "If he must slay these hunters to keep from getting to us, let him do so!"

"If there is killing to be done, you must do it yourselves," said the rabbi. "Be assured, this golem is just as much an extension of my will as though he were a sword I held in my hand!"

"Then command that sword to strike," Caesar said. "If the blood-guilt is yours, then accept it and tell this weapon you have crafted, to cut as you would yourself."

"But I will not," said the rabbi. "I would rather die than commit so grievous a wrong." He turned to the golem. "To the ramparts with you!"

The golem turned and shambled away.

Bakunin watched it go, a grudging respect in his eyes. "At least," he said, "you are fighting back against the government in some measure."

"But do you not see, Mr. Bakunin?" asked the rabbi. "We have created a government—a democracy, to be sure, in which each of us has his say, but a government nonetheless. And that government has commissioned a force for its defense—at least, if you are right in your contention that it is not people who fight wars, but governments."

Bakunin stared, taken aback for a moment. Then he cried, "But you did not give the golem weapons!"

A harsh, high, inhuman cry rang from the walls.

Caesar looked up, wide-eyed. "What creature was that?"

"The golem, I think." MoHaRal pointed. "He fights."

High atop the wall, the golem struggled with long, dark shadow-shapes that were half teeth, half claw. They swooped toward him as fast as arrows—but, with blinding speed, he dodged aside, caught each one, and tossed it away.

They returned, of course. Each hunter came shooting back—again and again, and would keep up the assault, unless torn to pieces.

"Do weapons make a man a soldier?" the rabbi demanded. "We commanded him to fight—and you were all quite willing to instruct him to kill."

"We are the revolution!" Bakunin protested. "We are justified in the use of force!"

"None are ever so justified," the rabbi said firmly. "It is that very justification that is the root of the evil that you decry in governments."

Joan turned away with a cry of impatience. "Talk, talk! And never any deeds! If the killing will be mine, then I shall do it myself!"

"But you may be slain!" cried Voltaire.

"I am not . . ." Joan slowed and turned to regard him with somber eyes. "I can no longer say that I am not afraid to die—is that not strange? But if I must die, it shall be with a sword in my hand. Away!"

She turned and strode toward the wall. After a moment, Voltaire took the sword Caesar proffered, and joined her.

"And you, Marcus Tullius?" Caesar held out another gladius. "Will not you, too, stand beside me?"

Slowly, Cicero took the blade. "I shall do my duty as a Roman, Caesar."

"Stout fellow!" Caesar produced yet another sword and held it out to Bakunin. "And you, Michael. Will you not slay in your own cause?"

Bakunin shrank back from the sword. "Me, strike with weapons? No! I have never been a man of violence." Then he realized what he had said and looked up at Caesar, appalled.

"If you advocate it, and others have followed your words, then you have done it," Caesar said. "Take the sword."

But Bakunin stepped further back, shaking his head.

Atop the parapet, the golem roared, and other voices shouted with triumph. "He has caught it—them! Three!"

"He has thrown them down! He has caught five more!"

"He defends well—but the monsters must be slain to be stopped." Caesar clapped the orator's shoulder and turned away to the wall. "Come, Marcus Tullius! Let us give honor to Rome!" He turned away, and Cicero followed him.

They labored beside the golem, striking and rending with sword and spear, but every wound they made closed, and every foe they repelled only came back to strike again. Only the golem had any effect, because he threw his foes from the wall, and they were slowed in their return.

But he could tear them apart, Caesar knew—and, in the heat of battle, he did the best he could to imitate the rabbi's voice and began to cry, "Kill! Slay! Tear them apart!"

"A new command!" The golem cried. "As you will, Rabbi!" His massive arms pulled as his huge clenched hands dug into the shadow before him, and the shape ripped apart. A high, thin shriek clove the air, and the golem tore again, then threw the pieces down from the wall and caught another shadow. He tore it, too, threw it aside, and reached for another— but they lurked back beyond his reach, suddenly hesitating now.

Below them, the fragments began to knit themselves together.

Caesar muttered a phrase in Latin, and a new sword appeared in his hand—a gladius, but one half a foot wide and four feet long. He held it out toward the golem.

"No!" the rabbi cried. "He must not be given the power to kill!" He ran forward, thundering up the stairs and out onto the wall, dodging the lean shadow-shapes and the human fighters till he could rise up next to the golem, looking up at its giant head. "Creature, turn to me! I am he who made you!"

But the golem's hand closed around the sword; he swung it high, over the rabbi's head, to hew at the nearest shadow and fend off its teeth, keeping it away from MoHaRal. "I do only as you have bade me, Rabbi!"

"That was not my voice!" the rabbi said. "I forbid you to strike!"

But his cry was lost in the golem's roar as it slashed at the slatey hide before it. The hunter convulsed and fell back from the wall, twitching and thrashing, the cut in its side widening with every movement till it fell apart.

In the moment of calm that followed, the rabbi shouted, "Creature! Turn to me!"

The golem turned, its blank gaze terrifying by its sheer lack of emotion. "Yes, rabbi."

"Lean down to me here," said the rabbi.

The golem glanced quickly at the looming shark-shapes, so busy elsewhere on the wall.

"Lean down!" the rabbi commanded. "It is MoHaRal who speaks!"

Slowly, the golem leaned down till his huge face was only a little above the rabbi's—and MoHaRal reached up and rubbed, erasing the letters from his forehead.

The golem snapped upright, rigid, then slowly tilted and slammed down on the wall like a tree falling.

The rabbi looked down at the still, lifeless, rough clay statue, and felt grief begin to well up within him.

Then the shadow struck, and the rabbi knew only a brief moment of searing pain, before all sensation ended.

"He did it!" Forge crowed. "He made the golem after all! Even though he had really never done it, he did it! One that killed! Push him hard enough, and he turns into a monster!"

"He didn't program it to kill," Marteau reminded him. "Caesar did that."

"An excuse! Only an excuse! I knew he'd do it! They're bloodthirsty maniacs, all of them!" He spun about. "You have it in memory, don't you?"

"You've got it, all right," Marteau confirmed. "But you paid a steep price. They're all annihilated—Voltaire, Joan, Cicero, Caesar . . ."

"Joan and Voltaire were nuisances." Forge dismissed them with a wave of his hand. "How about Bakunin?"

"Are you kidding? He's no dummy. He got out of there as soon as the golem fell."

"Damn it!" Forge swore. "If there was one I would have wanted to get rid of, it was that backstabbing anarchist!"

"How about the rest of them?"

Forge slowed, turning back to him, frowning. "What do you mean, 'what about them?' "

"I can undo the whole sequence. They're still in memory."

Forge stood still for a moment.

"You're the boss," Marteau said. "Three keystrokes, and they'll live again—and Caesar and Cicero are still generating hundreds of thousands each. Not to mention Cleopatra . . ."

"Hell, yes!" Forge said, with an expansive gesture. "Let them live! After a victory like that, I can afford to be generous!"

Marteau's hands flew over the keyboard. "What victory?"

"Over the Jews, of course! Give 'em a chance, and they'll turn on you! And now everybody can see it, the world over!"

Marteau sat frozen, realizing that Forge had seen only what he wanted to see—and knowing that everybody else who saw the sequence, would watch it with similar blinders. But most people didn't know a golem from a grindstone, and wouldn't know a medieval rabbi when they saw one.

They would see the rabbi's death, though, and the golem's.

A moment of blinding pain—then light. The rabbi

opened his eyelids, and found himself back in the sea of clouds. He sat up slowly, looking around him, and saw the wry face of Cicero gazing down at him with a half-smile. "The . . . hunters?" he asked.

"They are gone, Rabbi," said the Roman, "and we died, almost all of us—but they brought us back, somehow. We live again."

"To what purpose?" the rabbi muttered.

"Excuse me?"

"Nothing." MoHaRal levered himself up, rising painfully to his feet. "It is only the kind of question that we clergymen must always be asking."

"Are you ever answered?" Cicero asked softly.

"Always." The rabbi nodded. "Always—if we listen. Perhaps not immediately, but we are always answered."

"And what is the answer now, Rabbi?"

MoHaRal shook his head. "It has not come yet. Another question filled its place first."

"Is that not ever the way with answers?" Cicero asked, amused. "What is this newest question?"

"The golem." The rabbi turned a tortured gaze on him. "If we have been restored to life—should not he?"

AD 2155
What could be more compelling, more alluring than the company of carefully reconstructed personalities, the best and brightest that history can offer? Loose in the machine are startling, seductive simulations, as close as the nearest computer screen.

SIMUL CITY

Robert Sheckley

"Marcus Tullius! Are you awake?"

Cicero awakened abruptly and sat up. Michael Bakunin, large and fragile looking, dressed in a long black overcoat and black hat, stood across the bedroom from him. Cicero was a little startled but not surprised. He had grown accustomed to Bakunin's dramatic entries and exits. He was always glad to see him.

Bakunin came across useful information from time to time. He really was the only traveller among the simulacra. Although, true to his anarchist principles, he refused to cooperate with the others, and scorned their company and their society, still, he hated the scientific proletariat who lived in the real world outside the computer even more.

"Welcome, Michael," Cicero said. "Where have you been this time? Have you found friends to stay with?"

"Certainly not," Bakunin said, with an expression of scorn.

Bakunin didn't stay with the other simulacra. Since escaping into the system, he had learned the electronic highways of the new world he inhabited. Roaming free where he pleased, with his access descriptor card that allowed him to move anywhere in the system or its ramifications, now the technicians were unable to turn him off. He was the only free agent within the system at this time. He knew things about the system that no one else knew. Bakunin stayed on his own, zealously guarding his secrets. He popped up here and there, always hungry to learn more about the world which existed outside the computer. He had always been a suspicious man. Death hadn't made him any more trusting. He stayed in touch with Cicero, the first simulacrum he had met when the technicians resuscitated him.

Most of the others in simulworld were not interested in his secrets. They didn't want to escape into the system, didn't want to leave the safety of their simulations, didn't want to take up the difficult life that Bakunin lead. He took them along on one of his travels once. They didn't like the eerie lights, the simulated corridors down which they passed, the sudden vertiginous heights. It was a frightening and claustrophobic experience. They preferred to stay home, where a place similar to what they had known had been simulated for them.

"Something strange is going on," Bakunin said. "I thought you should know about it."

"Sit down. You are chilled. Let me poke up the fire."

Although simulacra were theoretically impervious to cold and heat, they experienced it anyhow. This had baffled the scientists, who claimed that you can't feel anything without nerves, receptors, pleasure and pain centers—the physical concomitants of sensation. In a limited way they were right. But on an experiential level they were wrong. After a while the simulacra experienced whatever they used to experience, since habit meters experience itself. At first there is a maddening numbness, but that passes, and gradually the senses reestablish their ascendancy.

"That's better," Bakunin said, warming his hands at the fire and gratefully accepting a cup of coffee. "I miss these things out in the places where I travel."

"Is there no food and drink where you go?"

"Usually not. They want to discourage my travelling, not make it easier for me. Of course, I don't need sustenance. None of us do. Yet I do get hungry, or seem to, when I roam the distant spaces."

"To be a starving ghost," Cicero mused. "I wouldn't like that."

"Sometimes," Bakunin said, "I find caches of food and drink. I have no idea who put them there. I suspect one or more of the technicians is sympathetic to my situation. You find anarchists everywhere, my dear Cicero."

"You're bragging," Cicero said.

"It is certain that our rulers could have caught me long ago," Bakunin said, "if some of the technicians hadn't helped me. The sympathy among them is quite extraordinary. Tyranny always rots from within, and it is the spirit of liberty that rots it."

"What did you find?" Cicero asked.

"Come with me and I'll show you."

Using his access descriptor card, Bakunin made a passageway appear in one of the walls of Cicero's villa.

"Watch your step through here," Bakunin said. Cicero looked ahead and saw that the passageway, composed of glowing lines, narrowed ahead. He could see little glowing dots of light scattered here and there. He looked at Bakunin questioningly.

"You mustn't touch any of those light spots," Bakunin said. "They're the latest attempt at a warning system. They set off an alarm, and then the tunnel closes. It can be quite nasty for a while, although I have found a way around it."

"What happens when you touch one of the lights?" Cicero asked.

"There is pain," Bakunin told him.

After a while the light dots ended. The tunnel of glowing lines swirled upward and around. It was like walking through a gigantic schematic of a snail's shell.

Cicero was ill at ease. He had always planned to accompany Bakunin on one of his explorations. But had put it off. Now it was necessary for him to see, because Bakunin seemed to think that something was amiss, something that would affect their lives. Cicero continued to walk, but he found that it required a great deal of energy, more than he was used to expending in the simulated surroundings of his own villa.

Now they were in a section which was black as pitch. Floating in it were colored oblongs of light. It was a construct that made no sense to Cicero at all. He understood that there was a great deal of subjectivity involved in the perception of these things. These were portions of the construct, portions of the machine, that had not been created to be viewed by earthly senses. There was a certain amount of interpretation possible, indeed, inevitable. He was seeing oblongs of color, but there was no telling what Bakunin or some other observer might be seeing.

As they went on there were other strange sights. Cicero was nervous, anxious. He knew he was off limits, in places where the rulers of this world didn't want him to be. There could be punishment if he were caught. They could take him out of existence with no effort at all, and with no compunction, since to them he wasn't a man at all, merely glowing bits of data that have a way of adhering together, a program of a man rather than an actual man.

And yet, they didn't deal with him as though he were a ghost or a machine. The technicians talked to him, they showed him respect. His position, the position of all the simulacra, was ambiguous. Under the law they had no rights. And yet, he had heard from friendly technicians that this view wasn't universally accepted. There were those out in the real world who held that simulacra, since they had exhibited all the signs of human thinking creatures, should be afforded civil rights, should not be treated as slaves or as mere software. It would take time for those views to become generally accepted. Eventually, Cicero felt, people would have to come around to the view that simulacra were every bit as human, and as real, as anyone else. Intelligence and self-determination were the true tests, far more important than having a body or any gross decisions like that.

Why was he risking himself like this? It was unnecessary. Bakunin came across information that could be of use to Cicero and his people and this information was important because there was de facto war between the simulacra and the others. At this point, all the advantage was on the side of the real men. They had all the power; they could wipe out the simulation at a moment. But perhaps something could be done.

"Are we almost there?" he asked Bakunin. They were climbing what appeared to be a staircase. When Cicero glanced back, he saw the steps disappearing behind him. Ahead, new steps appeared as he climbed. It was uncanny, though Bakunin apparently was accustomed to it.

"Soon, soon," Bakunin told him. They kept on going upward. But why should it be upward? Why couldn't the construct be oriented for going downhill? Perhaps a certain minimum amount of energy had to be expended to make things happen, once they were backstage in the simulworld.

Then the final steps solidified and Cicero found himself standing on a sort of plateau. Ahead of him a dim and smoky sun was midway to the zenith. And, on the edge of the plain, he could see the spires and towers of a city.

"What is that place?" Cicero asked. "They never told us about it."

"Wait and see," Bakunin told him.

"Do we have to walk all that way?" Cicero said, looking at the distant city.

"The transportation should arrive any moment now," Bakunin said.

As soon as he spoke, a vehicle solidified twenty feet from them. It was shaped like a gilded chariot, but it was larger. There were no horses to draw it. But the brass work on it was very fine indeed. Bakunin stepped in and he followed. Immediately the chariot began to move toward the city.

"Nice indeed," Cicero said.

They came to a city. It was passing fair, yet ghostly, for no inhabitants walked the streets, no dogs peed on the curb, no cats watched silently from the doorsteps, no sparrows fluttered overhead. There was no movement, no people, yet the city itself was ready, as new as if it had been just taken out of a candy box. The streets were spotless and white. The buildings were well-shaped, built with intricate designerwork, inviting, large, spacious, welcoming. There was a concert hall and a theater. There was a cluster of public buildings, halls of justice, temples, administration centers.

It was an impressive place. Bakunin led Cicero into one of the buildings. A silent elevator brought them to the hundredth floor. There they could stand on a terrace and look out over the surroundings. It had been cleverly detailed. The city sat at the confluence of two rivers, and there were many little bridges across it. There was a civic center, concert halls. There was an art museum and a repertory theater. There was anything Cicero could imagine a city having, and more than he had ever imagined before.

"This is a simulation?" he asked.

"Of course," Bakunin said. "The most elaborate I've ever seen."

"But what is it doing here? Why have they built it?"

Bakunin smiled.

"And why," Cicero asked, "haven't they told us about it?"

"Why indeed?" Bakunin said.

They continued to stroll. Bakunin enjoyed himself to the full. It wasn't often he had a chance to lord it over the stately and all-knowing Cicero. Cicero could be a pain in the ass, but there was no doubt he was one of the cleverest men who had ever lived. Bakunin wondered how long it would take the great man to put it all together.

They wandered through the central building, which was a palace of great extent and fanciful design. Room after room they went through, some done in a classically French manner, others reflecting all sorts of periods of architecture and design. The result was a little chaotic, but more than made up for that in its sheer magnificence. At last they came to a gigantic audience room.

This was a room so impressive as to beggar description. The throne could have sat three large men. There was a smaller throne beside it.

Something strange was going on. Cicero decided he would consult immediately with Machiavelli. The two of them often set policy for Simulworld. But Machiavelli was not immediately available. Cicero learned later that Machiavelli had been witnessing a most unusual birth.

Cleopatra opened her eyes and sat up. Her mind was flooded with memories. Heat and dust, and the venom burning in her body, those were her last memories of life. The horror of that moment of utter defeat, with the hateful Octavian advancing with his armies, and Antony dead. She remembered her women around her, their rouged mouths round with wonder as they watched her rob the detested Romans of their triumph.

And then she didn't remember anything until now,

when she awoke in this place and found herself alive
again.

That had been quite a long time ago. It was after-
ward that she learned that she wasn't really alive,
but not exactly dead, either. She was exactly as she
had been, except that she had no body. No, that
wasn't quite right, either, she did have a body, but it
didn't feel like the old body. But she hadn't been
very surprised at that. Although she was queen of
the Egyptians, Cleopatra was of good Macedonian
stock, like the others of her line descended from the
royal families of Macedonia, Alexander's generals.
She had been raised on Greek philosophy, art, litera-
ture. She had, of course, read her Homer. And
Homer had written of the conditions the dead found
themselves in after death, when they awoke in
Tartaros. Mere shadows of their former selves, without appetites or wills, and that's what she was like
now. Only not quite.

It wasn't as she had expected. This was not Tartaros.
Not if the rulers of this new kingdom were to be
believed.

She sat up again abruptly. She had sensed rather
than heard the door open. By the light of the dim oil
lamp she made out a man standing beside her bed.
He was dressed in a manner she had never seen
before. Dark clothing of lustrous material. Coat with
silver buttons. Hair tied back with a white ribbon. A
long, somber, bearded face. Dark blue eyes that
flashed with intelligence and mirth.

Cleopatra sat up and inspected the newcomer at
her leisure.

"Well, then, and who might you be?"

"Nicolo Machiavelli, at your service, Queen Cleopatra."

"You know who I am?"

"Indeed I do. Your fame is undying, lady."

"My fame, but not myself. I died by my own
hand, and now I find myself a shadow in a land of

shadows. What is this place, Lord Machiavelli? Is this the underworld of the dark gods?"

"Not at all," Machiavelli said. "And perhaps you will be good enough to call me Nicolo."

He was more than a little impudent. But Cleopatra knew she was going to need friends in this place.

"Tell me, Nicolo, is this not the underworld? Where am I?"

"My queen, many years have passed since you died. Men have brought you back to life through use of a machine they call a computer."

"And what is that?"

"They will instruct you in that, Cleopatra."

"Who will?"

"Those who are now our rulers. This is not Tartaros. The position, however, is very similar to what our poets have thought of the underworld. Although we have bodies, these bodies are not like those we used to have. They have been created by a new sort of witchcraft called science. It is thus that they have created our bodies. They will not age, nor can disease lodge in them."

"Then are we immortal?"

"In a way, yes. There is no natural reason for us to die in our present forms. On the other hand, we exist at the whim of our masters who created this place and brought us back to life within it. With the slightest of efforts they can cause us to disappear again. Our entire world exists only on their whim."

Cleopatra stared at him. "I don't understand this at all. Make us disappear? But where do we go when we disappear?"

"That," Machiavelli said, "is a mystery I don't understand yet. I am told that we simply don't exist any longer if they don't want us to. Then, when they want us again, it takes very little effort on their part to bring us back."

"It is a distasteful situation," Cleopatra said.

"Yes."

"And we are powerless within it."

Machiavelli looked thoughtful. "Not quite powerless, I think. There are still a few things we can do on our own behalf. The situation is not without its possibilities."

They looked at each other, a long look filled with meaning. Cleopatra was thinking how much this man, with his strange clothing, his neatly clipped little beard and glowing eyes, reminded her of some of the Roman politicians she had known. He looked a little like Cassius. But she thought he seemed more intelligent.

Machiavelli was studying Cleopatra and he liked what he saw. The queen was not beautiful; her face was too long, her nose somewhat too large, her lips a shade thin. She would never pass for Aphrodite. But she had something that most of the beautiful women he had known did not have: a strong intelligence and a magnetic presence. Her body, beneath its finespun blue silk mantle, was small, wiry, alive, feminine, exciting. Her face glowed with vitality. The question was, what did her appearance here among the simulacra mean? Why had the technicians resuscitated her? He needed to speak to Cicero urgently about this.

When Machiavelli arrived at Cicero's house, it was mid-afternoon and Cicero was in his garden. It was a beautiful garden, filled with every sort of plant from Italy. There was a low waterfall on one side. Behind the garden was Cicero's villa, a very fair reconstruction of a Roman villa of his own period. Here Cicero spent much of his time, writing his notes in his own unique and indecipherable shorthand.

"Hail, Cicero," said Machiavelli.

"You are most welcome, Nicolo," Cicero said. "Do sit and have a glass of this Falerian."

Machiavelli sat and accepted the glass. It was always a relief for him to come here. Not only did he love the peace and tranquility of Cicero's village; he very much enjoyed talking with Cicero. They were both politicians, both of a classical frame of mind despite the 1500 years that lay between them. Machiavelli had a lot more in common with Cicero than he had with Queen Victoria or Frederick the Great, though they were chronologically much closer to him.

"I have news of an interesting nature," Machiavelli said.

"Good. So do I. But tell me over dinner. Publius, my cook, does not like to be kept waiting."

Over dinner, at Machiavelli's insistence, Cicero told him of the new city construct he had seen in the company of Bakunin. Machiavelli expressed polite surprise, but he seemed not surprised at all. Cicero waited to hear his news. Cicero ate lightly, and drank no more than two glasses of wine with his meals. The two men discussed how much the physical comforts had come to mean to them. The simulacra could not really be said to possess a sensorium. Theoretically, they were incapable of tasting, smelling, etc. In actual fact, it wasn't like that at all, and that was one of the things which especially confused the scientists who were their masters. "How can information feel?" they asked. Cicero could not explain it. Perhaps it was a trick of their rebuilt minds. Perhaps humans need physical connections in order to think, and, when they didn't veritably exist, simulated them. That is, the simulacra were themselves creating simulations. Sexual congress was also believed to be impossible for simulacra. Yet it, or something that looked identical to it, went on all the time in the simulworld.

"Have you discussed this with John Sykes?" Machiavelli asked. Sykes was the new head of Simulworld, the company in whose computer construct they lived.

"I told him I had no answers," Cicero said. "I pointed out to him, 'You are the experts in this, not us. We are merely the subjects of your experiments. The guinea pigs, I believe you call them.'"

"What did he say to that?"

"He had the audacity to ask me what intercourse was like for a simulacrum."

"And you told him?"

"That it was an extremely personal question. He did not desist. He asked if I found it truly pleasurable. I told him, why would one do it otherwise?"

"But is it like the real thing?"

"It's more than two thousand years since I experienced the real thing," Cicero reminded him. "My memory of that divine pleasure is now rather dim. But what is available now is quite acceptable."

"One of our poets, thousands of years after your time, wrote, 'The grave's a fine and private place, but none, I think, do there embrace.'"

"Well, you can see how wrong he was," Cicero said. "If this is the grave, it's not private at all. People such as yourself come barging in whenever they please. And as for embracing—well, I'm still waiting for Sykes to restore my wife to me." He sighed. "But tell me, Nicolo, why have you come to see me? What is your news?"

"There is a new simulacrum in our midst, Tullius."

"Who, pray tell?"

"An acquaintance of yours, I believe. One Cleopatra, queen of Egypt, former mistress of Caesar, and more lately, Marc Antony."

"That is interesting," Cicero said.

"I think it is. Especially in light of a conversation I had not long ago. I thought you would find it interesting."

"Go ahead," Cicero said.

Sykes had been in a curious mood that day. He apparently had started thinking about life and death and had begun looking ahead, far ahead. Hanging out with the simulacra of long-dead people will do that to a man, so Machiavelli thought.

Sykes questioned Machiavelli about who would be the most desirable woman to spend immortality with.

"None," Machiavelli said. "I cannot conceive of spending forever with any one woman."

"Let me rephrase my question," Sykes said. "Whom would you pick to spend the first part of immortality with?"

"There have been many famous beauties," Machiavelli told him. "Marie Antoinette was always one of my favorites. Lucrezia Borgia was a very special lady. Pericles had a famous courtesan, the lovely Hypatia, and she would be an adornment for any man. But of them all, there is one and only whom I would pick, given the chance."

"And who is that?"

"None other than Cleopatra."

"Tell me about her."

"Shakespeare has said it all. A creature of infinite charm and boundless guile."

"Interesting," Sykes said. "I wonder if there's much data on her?"

The famous queen was not left alone for long. Sykes set up means of instruction for her. He had instructors give her daily lessons in everything that had happened since the time of her death.

They said this was not death, but it also was not life. She had a lot to learn. They tried to teach her, but most of it never stuck. She wasn't interested in learning the priestly jargon of this new tribe that had somehow captured her spirit. What did it matter to her if they called the ultimate truth Ammon Ra or Forms or Information? And there was a whole new vocabulary to learn, one she didn't understand at all: electricity, diode, hardwired, software. Were these the new names of the gods, or were they attributes of godhead? She couldn't quite grasp what they were supposed to represent.

So she understood nothing of what was going on, and yet she understood it all, too. It wasn't so difficult. This new kingdom and its rulers were involved in seeking love and power, just like all the other men she had known. Yes, and they were searching for Truth, too. But love was more interesting.

Although she tried to rest, they were also able to send knowledge directly into her. But she didn't understand it. Sykes had thought, apparently, that with a little work Cleopatra could be brought 'up to date,' be on line with current knowledge. If this was his intention, he was sorely disappointed. Although he had simulated Solon himself for her instructor, the results were disappointing. He demanded an explanation from Solon.

"How is her instruction proceeding?"

"Not well, sir. She refuses to understand."

"I thought you could transmit the information to her, just put it in her, as it was."

"There's no problem in giving her information, sir. What we can't give her is comprehension."

"Do you mean she's stupid?"

The tall, dignified old man in the white robe shook his head. "Perhaps she's smarter than the rest of us. She simply refuses to understand. She knows well what science can do, but she refuses to understand how."

"Is there something wrong with our methods? What would you recommend?"

"Not everyone can be educated in so direct a fashion. And Cleopatra is already a fully formed personality. It is natural that she would take it amiss that she has to be instructed in everything that has happened for two thousand years and more. She shows a very fine grasp of practicalities. I would not push her, sir. She is learning very nicely on her own."

Cleopatra had never had any interest in technology, not even when she had been alive. She couldn't be expected to take much interest in it now that she was dead and reborn as a simulacrum. She wasn't even curious how it all worked. But in her own way she understood it very well.

One day she had lain on a couch and shuddered as the asp stung her. Then there had been nothing at all—nothing she could remember, anyhow—and then this, this rebirth into a kingdom of ghosts. Only it wasn't a realm of the gods. Men had somehow made this ghostly kingdom and brought her back to life in it. Not the gods at all. They had brought her back, and, unsatisfactory as it was to be without a proper body, it would be worse to lose even this. And they could do that, take it away from her any time they wanted. She had seen them do it. Her life was in constant danger, such as it was. And now there was this new development.

She could tell by the slow thickening of the air that Sykes was coming. She was prepared for him.

"Ah there, my dear," Sykes said. "How are you today?"

She thought, *in some fashion, they have brought me back. I am many centuries old, and I am famous. A symbol. But of what? Passion, seduction, and shallow-mindedness! My love of luxury was proverbial. My changeableness was remarkable. I had many lovers. Yet I died for love with Antony. And they hem and haw, Sykes does, and says there's no way he can bring back Antony.*

I know why, of course. He wants me for himself. He has made that clear enough.

And what of Antony? I don't know. The choice is not mine. I died for him once. Somehow I doubt I'd die for him again.

This man Sykes is in love with me. Or rather, an image of me. He formed it long before he met me. It's an image that many people have of me. How strange it is—Sykes tells me that there are millions and millions of people who know at least something about me. I have achieved fame. And Sykes, I suspect, wants to achieve fame beside me, to be king to my queen, and to form another chapter in the story of the great Cleopatra. But how could that be? He is alive and I am . . . whatever this thing they call a simulacrum is.

Does he want to mate me with another? What does the man have in mind? And how can I use that to my advantage?

"Tell me something, Redmond," Cicero said, the day the technician came to visit him.

"Anything." Redmond visited Cicero every chance he could. He was writing a Ph.D. thesis on Cicero's views. He expected to make his name with the new insights Cicero was giving to him and him alone. Redmond was a tall, thin, nervous young man, with red hair and a scrubby little red and brown moustache. Cicero knew that Redmond had a wife and two small children. So far Cicero had given him an exclusive on his informational services at least as far as Redmond's specialty was concerned. Redmond was an economist and he was intensely interested in Roman currency. With Cicero's help several knotty problems could be cleared up. And Redmond was also interested in the various other currencies that were circulating in Rome at the time. Cicero was the key to all these matters. Therefore it came as a shock to Redmond when Cicero told him that he would have to desist from giving information.

"But why, Marcus Tullius? I thought we were friends."

"That is what I myself thought," Cicero said. "I looked upon you almost as a son. Certainly as a disciple. Therefore it pained me when I realized that you were not being forthright about matters of great concern to me."

"Marcus Tullius! I beg you tell me what you are referring to!"

Cicero fixed the young man with a severe gaze. "I am talking about the plans of John Sykes."

"What do you mean?" Redmond asked. His voice was innocent, but the slightest of tremors betrayed to Cicero that Redmond knew exactly what he was talking about.

He waited. Redmond stared at him, cleared his throat, and said, "I am not allowed to speak about Mr. Sykes's plans. He has made it clear that if I ever reveal anything I will be banned from accessing you."

"And if you don't tell me, I'll never speak to you again. You have my word as a Roman on that."

The two men locked stares. Redmond was the first to look away.

"If he ever finds out . . ."

"He will not find out," Cicero said. "It is obviously to my interest to keep my sources of information to myself. But I must know Sykes's plans, as they refer to the Simulworld, are a matter of life and death to me and to others. Our fear is not being banned from the facility, which would still leave you free to carry on your work elsewhere. If Sykes takes a dislike to us, he can turn any or all of us off. He can turn off our entire world. We live under constant sentence of death, and this is beyond the power of anyone to do anything about, even if they knew of our plight. The world does not consider us persons. But perhaps by now you know better."

"Yes, I do."

"Then tell me about it, Redmond."

Cicero had very interesting news for Machiavelli when next they met: "This Sykes, according to Redmond, my informant, is planning on joining us here in Simulworld."

"I thought that was impossible for a living person," Machiavelli said.

"Apparently it is. Sykes is planning to suicide, first ensuring that his data can be transferred complete to our construct."

"We do have a sort of immortality here," Machiavelli said. "As long as that vital effluvia—what is it they call it?"

"Electricity," Cicero said.

"That's it. As long as the electricity keeps on running, there's immortality here."

"A precarious sort of immortality," Cicero said. "Theoretically, we could live forever. But practically speaking, if we annoy them, they can turn us off like that." Cicero snapped his fingers.

"Sykes coming to rule over us," Machiavelli mused. "Just what we didn't need! I suppose that accounts for the great palace you discovered with Bakunin?"

"It must," Cicero said. "That is where Sykes plans to live and rule."

"With Cleopatra as his queen," Machiavelli said.

"Exactly. Though I don't think he was too clever to have chosen her. Infinitely appealing, of course, but quite the little murderess."

Machiavelli said, "As if our lives weren't bad enough. . . . We must find a way to stop him."

"On the contrary," Cicero said. "We must do everything in our power to encourage him in this step."

"Do I hear right?" Machiavelli said. "Cicero, the people's friend, the lover of liberty, welcoming one of the enemy into our midst?"

"You're usually more astute," Cicero said. "I am aware, as you are, that it is unending war between us and them, between simulacra and real people."

"Exactly my point."

Cicero smiled and composed his words. "He would rule us, perhaps," Cicero said. "What do we care about that? We are ruled anyhow, and at present there's no way around that. The point is, we would have one of Them within our domain. There's no way we can touch any of them now, tied to the computer machine as we are. As long as Sykes is here, and in power, they will not turn us off. And as long as we are able to move and think, perhaps something can be done against them."

"What could possibly be done?" Machiavelli asked. "We are little bits of information. They are solid."

"You must consider more implications," Cicero said. "The wind is also nothing but information. It has no more substance than do we. But it can blow down solid objects like oak trees. That, my friend, is the power of information properly directed."

"If he comes here, he will not be in our power."

"No. But we will have a chance to influence him. More chance than we have now."

"I love you, Cleopatra." No, he hadn't said it yet. But it was bound to happen. Even though he came to her in the guise of a god, he wasn't at all godlike. He was a little man, she could sense that, but he had provided himself with the body, arms and armor of a warrior. Sykes, he called himself, and insisted that she call him that, too. He seemed to be proud of his name. And he was always trying to explain to her how important he was in that other world, the world he came from, the world she could never see.

"I have complete power over you, Cleopatra. I'm not boasting, nor am I trying to threaten you."

Not yet, she thought.

"I am simply stating a fact. This is the future, Cleopatra, over 2000 years since an asp stung you to death. We've created you anew, Cleopatra. Tell me, have we done well?"

He talked all sorts of silly talk like that, did Sykes. And he was never there in person. Never in the same room with her. His voice was there, and his image. But he looked to her like an animated painting, not like a man at all.

"I can't come into the construct yet, Cleopatra," he told her, when she said he was rude never to appear in person. "We can create anyone who has ever lived provided we have sufficient data. But we can't create ficticious characters. Nor can we create ourselves. Not while we're alive in the body."

"I'm so pleased you accepted my invitation," Cicero said to Cleopatra. "Please come into the garden. It is a beautiful day and we will have our lunch out of doors. Of course, it's always a beautiful day here. I suppose that's one of the advantages of simulating weather rather than having to rely on nature's moods. I must ask the technicians to vary it a bit, however, and to give us some of seasonal variation. I can't even tell what season this is, the weather they send us is always so bland."

"You still blather on as you always did," Cleopatra said. "What a nice garden, Tullius!"

"I'm so glad you like it," Cicero said. "Of course, it's nothing compared with what you had in the good old days when you reigned in Alexandria."

"That was another time," Cleopatra said. "You were a consul of Rome in those days."

"Briefly. And, I fear, ineffectively. Men like Caesar were too much for a poor philosopher such as myself. And Mark Antony, of course, was too much for anyone, even, in the final analysis, himself."

"It all seems so distant now," Cleopatra said. "They've done better by you than me. All I have is a small three-room simulation, and no garden at all."

"But that will all be changed," Cicero said, "when John Sykes finishes his preparations."

"Sykes. He's something important in this barbarian world, is he not?"

"These people are not exactly barbarians. And yes, he is something important."

"A ruler of some kind?"

"He owns the controlling shares in the corporation which controls our world."

"So I gathered. It is a tedious thought, the idea that our destiny is controlled by mercantile interests."

"Yes, isn't it?" Cicero said. "But mercantilism is all the rage in this fine world we've been born into."

"How dreary," Cleopatra said, sitting on a chaise lounge and taking a peach from a silver bowl on the table in front of her. She bit into it and made a face. "Pah! Food has no savor in this place!"

"That's because it's simulated," Cicero said.

"Well, they should have done a better job of it. If they can simulate something that looks like a peach, why can't they simulate the flavor it used to have back when we had proper bodies?"

"A good question. You must ask it of Sykes one of these days."

Cleopatra shrugged. Her shoulders, beneath a gossamer wrap, were lovely. Cicero looked away. This siren queen had a disquieting effect on him.

"I think Sykes is in love with me."

"Does that surprise you?"

"Well, a little, considering the different states of being in which we exist. He is a real man, as he says, and I am a phantom."

"What did he say to you?"

"That he had worshipped me for a long time," Cleopatra said matter-of-factly. "He and I would reign together in this place, which he called the Simulworld. King and Queen of shadows, I suppose he meant. And he was good enough to tell me how happy I would be with him as my consort. And vulgar enough to tell me that he had it on good authority that the act of love in Simulworld, though diminished somewhat from what we had known before, could still be performed with great pleasure, and that he looked forward to enjoying that pleasure with me."

"And what did you tell him?"

"That I was Cleopatra the Seventh, who had been mistress to four of the greatest human beings who ever lived—"

"To whom were you referring?" Cicero said. "I know about Caesar and Marc Antony, of course."

"Well, before them there was Pompey."

"That's only three."

Cleopatra smiled mischievously. "Have you considered Octavian?"

"But he was your enemy! You killed yourself rather than fall into his hands and be led back to Rome in his triumph."

"That's the story known to the public. The truth, as always, was a little more complicated."

"I'd love to gossip with you about it some other time," Cicero said. "Just now, we have more urgent matters to discuss. Did you turn Sykes down?"

"Rather peremptorily. He is a small-souled man, not suitable for such as I. What is that sound?"

"That is me," Cicero said. "I am grinding my teeth."

"Whatever for? Does this Sykes mean so much to you?"

"On a personal level, he means no more to me than a fart in slumber. But he happens to be absolute lord and master of our world, and holds the power of life or death over each of us in Simulworld."

"So he mentioned," Cleopatra said. "But I didn't believe him. I thought he was boasting."

Cicero sighed. "You've been here what, three days now? You've already begun to mess things up."

Cleopatra looked annoyed. "He just didn't seem clever enough to be all that he claimed. I couldn't imagine that the mind of a creature like John Sykes could give birth to the many people and settings of this place you call Simulworld."

"Cleopatra," Cicero said, "of course John Sykes didn't invent all this himself. But he is a wealthy man—a master of mercantilism, remember—and he was able to buy the outstanding shares of the corporation that controls Simulworld."

"So Sykes isn't some trumped-up little man trying to give himself airs? He actually has the power of life and death that he claims?"

"Correct, Cleopatra."

"Well, then, it seems I must rethink the situation. But I still don't like him, Cicero, and I certainly don't have to *fnarf* the man." She used the old Coptic word for fornication.

"Of course not. But it would be well for you to reconsider. Did Sykes indicate how you and he were to consummate your union?"

"His meaning was unmistakable. He was going to join me here in the Simulworld."

"Did he appear before you while you and he were talking?"

"No. He explained that he could not become a simulation himself until he had done one rather important thing."

"Did he tell you what that thing was, Cleopatra?"

"No. Nor did I ask him."

"To join you here, as a simulation, John Sykes would have to terminate his life on earth. No living man can become a simulation. Several technicians have explained that point to me. There is no exception. That means, Cleopatra, that Sykes is preparing to kill himself for you."

Cleopatra was silent for a little while. Then she said, "Well, I must admit, that makes me think somewhat better of him."

"You must encourage him to go ahead with his plan. Tell him so when he visits you again."

"*If* he does," Cleopatra said. "My refusal of his offer was rather definitive."

"There will be another time," Cicero said. "Sykes hasn't spent this much time constructing a palace and bringing you back to inhabit it with him to give up on the basis of a single refusal."

"You actually want him to come here and rule over us?" Cleopatra said.

"It's a worse alternative if he rules us from a distance. He lives now in a place we can't reach. As matters stand we have no power over him. We cannot even communicate with him except at his pleasure."

"I understand," Cleopatra said. "The more distant the ruler, the harder he is to put a knife into."

"Something like that," Cicero said.

"But his presence will be a mere theoretical gain. Since he will take ample safeguards, you will be no better off than before. As for me, it will be a tedious duty to be his queen. He could own ten companies and command a thousand Simulworlds and I still would not find him appealing."

"I think the gain would be somewhat more than theoretical," Cicero said. "Have you not noticed, Cleopatra, how men in power trust to their luck rather than take the proper precautions? Great Caesar himself, who despite being my political enemy was one of the most astute men who ever lived, did not foresee the possibility of his own assassination on the steps of the Senate."

"Can simulacra be killed?"

"Perhaps not. But it wasn't murder I had in mind."

"What, then?"

"I've said too much already. Will you help us, Cleopatra?"

She looked at him with sparkling eyes. "So we are a conspiracy!"

"Let's not talk about it further. In this place it's all too true that the walls may have ears. Will you help?"

"I suppose so. But on one condition. You must grant me one wish, Cicero."

"What wish is that?"

"I'm not going to tell you yet. You conceal your conspiracy from me, so I hide my condition from you. You won't like it, Marcus Tullius, I'll tell you that right now. No more than I'll like playing bed-room games with Sykes, the tyrant of the mercantile."

"I can only grant what is in my power to do."

"Obviously. I will ask no more."

"Very well, then. I will grant you one wish, what-ever it is, as long as it's in my power to do it. Satisfied?"

"Yes. Farewell, Marcus."

"Where are you going?"

"I must return to my rooms," Cleopatra said. "I have neglected my makeup since coming to this place. But as my suitor will be coming along any time . . . But it is difficult to explain these things to a man, Marcus."

"Thank god," Tullius Cicero said.

The simulacra of Simulworld were much inter-ested in the case of John Sykes. It is possible that his action caused more comment in Simulworld than in the real world. From Sykes's viewpoint, and that of many of his associates, he wasn't committing suicide at all. Quite the contrary, his action in destroying the life of his earth-born body was the prerequisite for entering the Simulworld. No matter how much data there was on hand for a living man, no attempt to simulate him in the computer construct of Simulworld had been successful. It was always as though some vital part, the vitality itself, had been left out. Whereas such creations as Cicero and Cleopatra, and the oth-ers, gave every sign of being autonomous creatures capable of self-reflection, not automata at all, but people in their own right capable of development and change, and exhibiting an unmistakable unity, this could not be said for the simulacra of people still alive. It seemed that a person could only live once, as a person or as a simulated person, but not both simultaneously.

Even for the sake of immortality, however, it is a bitter thing to take your own life. No one had immediate plans to follow Sykes into the machine. And Sykes himself had planned as well as he could to keep some control over his new surroundings.

As a computer construct he would have immortality, but it would be subject to the whim of anyone who could lay a hand on the computer's on-off switch. And also Sykes had to consider the dubious legal status of simulacra, and the fact that the high courts were still a long way from declaring these creations competent to own property in their own right, for example, to say nothing of the thorny questions of whether or not they had civil rights. Sykes tried to sidestep the vicissitudes of a legal battle by leaving a will that was much to the advantage of the executors, but only so long as they followed all of the will's provisions. Any falling short on any of these and Sykes's property reverted to another set of claimants, a set whom he had chosen as watchdogs over the first set, making sure they were of a litigious turn of mind. His stipulations were not so difficult anyhow. He insisted on remaining at all times conscious. Any attempt to turn him off or tamper with him in any way would constitute a breach of the will's terms. And he insisted also that all decisions he made concerning the simulacra of whom he would henceforth be one, were to be obeyed at once. Thus he retained control over his surroundings and those who shared them with him. Or so he anticipated.

The day of his arrival was of course the greatest inaugural ball ever seen in Simulworld—a tremendous spectacle. Cleopatra looked lovely in a bouffant pink tulle gown specially designed for her by one of the great Paris couturiers. John Sykes, simulated a fifth larger than lifesize, seemed none the worse for his recent demise. The music was simulated, too, but on a scale never before attempted. Ten famous orchestras, synthesized and remixed by master technicians, blared forth the loudest Mendelssohn on record. And there were balls and masques and entertainments.

Cicero gave the bride away. And Nicolo Machiavelli was pleased to stand up for the groom. Charlemagne himself was in the audience, especially simulated for this appearance.

All of this took place in Sykes' newly simulated capital, which he called New Rome, but which the simulacra referred to as Simul City. No one was sure who was the stately officiating priest, for his face was hidden behind a cowl, but some said it was Peter the Fisherman, reconstituted on the basis of historical necessity to crown the nuptials of the greatest simulated event the world had ever known. Others claimed it was Martin Luther, and a few, citing the Zionist conspiracy, said it was the Baal Shem Tov.

A good time was had by all. But after the party came the reckoning.

"A power which believes itself to be absolute," Machiavelli remarked later, "is inviting a rival to test its pretensions. Better to be a little more modest when assuming the trappings of office."

John Sykes was not modest. Later that day, Cicero set into motion the plan to find out just how absolute that power was.

John Sykes sat up in bed. He hadn't known simulacra could be hung over, but that seemed to be the case with him. His head—his simulated head which was not only filled with data but was also composed of data—ached abominably. A hangover from simulated champagne. Can data hurt? Better believe it.

He looked around. He was alone in the bedroom.

"Cleopatra? Where in hell are you?"

No answer. Then, as he watched, the bedroom door opened. "Cleopatra, you had me worried . . ." He stopped when Cicero, Machiavelli and several others entered.

"What is the meaning of this?" Sykes demanded. "How dare you intrude on my bedroom? Don't you realize I can have all of you expunged, turned off, wiped out? In fact, that's exactly what I'm going to do unless you leave at once."

He glared at them, because two of the men with Cicero had grasped his arms.

"How dare you lay hands on me!"

"It is interesting to observe," Cicero said, "how quickly a man can become accustomed to absolute power, to the point where he can't believe a lesser mortal dare touch him. You have been our ruler for less than twenty-four hours, yet you consider your person inviolable, and sacred as well. Disabuse yourself of the notion, Sykes. There is no alarm system close to hand. You yourself told the technicians not to disturb you. It is between you and us now."

"What do you intend to do?" Sykes said. "Any attempt to kill me—"

"That is the furthest thing from our minds," Cicero said. "If we killed you, assuming that such a thing were possible, the technicians would simply reconstitute you again. As long as you are alive, they cannot do that."

"They'll get me out of this," Sykes said. "I warn you, Cicero, release me now, immediately, or it will go very hard with you."

"I'm afraid you will have to accompany us," Cicero said. "If not, we'll drag you."

"Where are you taking me?"

"You'll see." Michael Bakunin entered. He was grinning as only an anarchist can who is witnessing the fall of pompous autocracy. "This way, my Czar," he said.

He walked across the room. Tapping the wall with his random access descriptor card, he waited until a doorway opened. Behind it was a long winding cylindrical passage that seemed to descend forever into the depths.

"Where does it lead?" Sykes said. "I won't go in there!"

"You'll go," Cicero said. "We've installed a telephone at the other end. Call us when you have decided to cooperate."

"I will spend the time thinking up tortures for you," Sykes said. The two men holding his arms exchanged glances and looked at Cicero. Cicero nodded. The two men pushed Sykes, who teetered on the edge for a moment, then fell into the spiral. They heard him screaming for a long time.

"Are you sure he won't hurt himself?" Machiavelli asked.

"What a soft heart you have!" Bakunin sneered.

"He's no use to us dead."

"Don't worry. Simulacra don't die until the plug is pulled. They just fade away."

For a simulacrum, the fall is worse than the impact just as the bark is worse than the bite. Sykes was in terror as he sped through the winding downward-circling metal cylinder. He felt as though he were falling through the guts of some inconceivable metal monster. And the eerie lighting within the cylinder didn't help. He scraped his hands free of skin trying to arrest his fall by pressing them against the sides of the tube; and then had to watch as the skin grew whole again, and still he fell.

Then the trip was over and he fell into a room, landing light as gossamer on a filthy concrete floor.

He was in a small prison cell. It was lit by dusky twilight coming through the barred, deeply-set window above his head. His sense of smell was acute enough to be revolted by the reek of unwashed bodies which permeated the room. The odors were made all the worse by the large stove outside the cell and visible through the small crossbarred window. It filled the room with heat and moisture.

Damn them, where had they put him? What was

this place? He didn't remember seeing it in the plans. Nor did it exist in the lists of simulations he had seen. It must have been left over from the previous owners.

If they thought this was going to dampen his spirits . . .

Well, they were right.

His own technicians couldn't rescue him if they couldn't find him. And since this place was not in the plans . . .

There was a telephone on a low table beside the sagging bed. It was a white Princess phone, incongruous, immaculate.

He picked up the handset.

"Cicero? Are you there?"

"I am here, Sykes. What do you want?"

"Release me at once."

"Sorry."

"Damn it," Sykes said, "can we come to some arrangement?"

"Perhaps," said Cicero.

Sykes and Cicero conferred for almost an hour; Sykes sat in his cell and thought. The heat and smell were almost overpowering. He was very thirsty and it was time he got on with doing something.

He went to the door. Through the barred opening he could see the badly lit corridor outside. He had heard the guard marching past earlier.

"Hey!" he shouted. "Guard! Where are you?"

After a few minutes of shouting and pounding, a large red-bearded soldier in the Czar's blue uniform came down the corridor, rubbing his eyes sleepily. "What is it?"

"I want some tea."

"Tea? Tea!" The guard laughed and turned to walk away.

"Listen to me carefully," Sykes said. "You lead a

drowsy life here, do you not, spending all your time guarding what is usually an empty cell."

"Well, it could be worse," the guard said. "Yes, I guard the cell. What of it?"

"When does your relief come?" Sykes asked. "When does another guard take over? Or is it possible that there's only you?"

The guard gaped at him.

"Have you ever seen an officer of the guard?" Sykes asked.

Sykes could see by the man's expression that he had not seen another officer since he had been created. This cell-simulation in the Peter and Paul fortress was rarely used. The technicians who set it up had simulated the guard and put him in as though he were a piece of furniture rather than a thinking and reasoning creation. And it was true that the guard was not of very high intelligence. But when directly questioned, the man couldn't help reflecting on the strangeness of his life in the Peter and Paul prison where, most of the time, he was the only living thing.

"What is your name?" Sykes asked.

"Vladimir," the man muttered.

"Then it could not have escaped your notice, Vladimir, that we are all alone here, you and I."

"The others will be back soon," Vladimir said, but he didn't sound convinced.

"How long since you've eaten?" Sykes asked him.

Vladimir shook his head. He couldn't remember. And *never* didn't seem a possible answer.

"Or drunk?"

Another shrug.

Sykes supplied the conclusion of his line of reasoning.

"Vladimir, you and I are in the same situation. We are both prisoners."

The guard glared at him. "That's not true at all. You are locked up, whereas I am free."

"We're equally free," Sykes said. "Me to walk up

and down in my cell, and no further, you in the corridor, and no further. If you don't believe me, try to get out of here."

Vladimir looked at him in terror. Who was this man who was saying aloud the very thoughts that had begun to haunt him? How did he know so much? What was going on?

"What is there to do?" Vladimir asked. And when Sykes didn't answer he added, "Can you help me, sir?"

Sykes maintained his silence until Vladimir unlocked the cell door and threw it open.

"That's better," Sykes said. "Vladimir, you are in a very precarious position. Though you can't understand it, perhaps you can sense that you are entirely unimportant to anyone but yourself. They need to keep me alive. But they could snuff you out like that." He snapped his fingers. Vladimir stared at him with wide eyes.

"What can I do, sir? Do you want me to help you escape?"

"Certainly not," Sykes said. "They took me by surprise, but I had foreseen the eventuality. I want you to do something for me. Go down the hallway to the outer passageway. You will find a doorway at the very end. It will be dim, but it will be there for you to find. Go through it and continue until you find several passageways branching off. At that point, on one of the walls you will find a telephone."

"There's a telephone here," Vladimir said, pointing to the Princess phone.

"This is an internal line," Sykes said, grinning. "But in the corridor is one of the lines I had installed, a line leading to my technicians outside. Pick up the phone and make sure someone's there. Then tell them that John Sykes said they were to start Plan B. Can you remember that?"

"Plan B. Yes sir. But why don't you go yourself?"

"I need to be here in case Cicero phones," Sykes said. "And Vladimir—"

"Sir?"

"Do this properly and I'll make you my body-guard. Then no one will dare destroy you unless they get me first."

"Plan B," Vladimir said. "I'll be back as soon as I can, sir."

"I don't understand," Redmond said. "Where is Mr. Sykes?"

"To put it into the language of immediacy," Cicero said, "he has gone into retirement."

"But he just came to Simulworld!"

"Even simulacra can change their minds. He found ruling burdensome."

"And Cleopatra?"

"They were not really well suited."

"You've done something to him," Redmond said. "Don't try to deny it."

"I have no intention of denying it. He came here to play the tyrant. We overthrew him."

"Have you killed him?"

"Certainly not," Cicero said. "Do you take us for barbarians? He's alive and I'll let you speak to him presently. But first you must hear the conditions."

"Who are you to . . . Never mind, what are the conditions?"

"You will be permitted to ask John Sykes how he is. He will tell you that he is well, and to do what we ask of you. Then we will cut off the talk."

"Where do you have him?"

"He's in here with us," Cicero said. "But don't bother to look. You won't find him. If we discover you are interfering, we will kill him, if that is possible, or drive him insane, if that is our only remaining expedient."

"You know that the people in charge of this project can't permit that to go on."

"They can and will, if they want to continue in their present well-salaried positions. If they go against Sykes's mandate, however, they will abrogate his will. I don't think they will want to precipitate a court battle if it can be avoided."

"But they can't just leave him like that, locked up in some corner of the computer memory."

"It's not so bad as that," Cicero said. "We are negotiating with Sykes now. As soon as we have worked out a formula which will permit us to trust him, he will be released. But he will have to take his place among us as one among equals, not as a king or dictator. Surely as an American you can have no objection to this."

"I suppose not," Redmond said. "Anyhow, it's not up to me. I'm a scholar, I have no part in all this. I'll tell them what you said, however."

"That's why I wanted to explain it to you first," Cicero said. "One scholar to another."

"Well, it's up to them. What is this request of Sykes's that you want to tell me?"

"It's something I promised Cleopatra, and that Sykes has agreed to."

"What is it."

Cicero told him.

"You've got to be kidding!" Redmond said.

"Tell the technicians to do it, or risk a court battle over his will."

"I'll tell them," Redmond said. "But I don't know what they'll say."

"I do," Cicero said.

They had neglected to tell her where the *accouchement* was taking place, so Cleopatra hurried through the corridors and echoing empty rooms of the great simulated palace that Sykes had caused to be built, back in his brief period of glory. That had been before Bakunin and Cicero and the others pushed him into the tube, itself a simulation, which led to

Bakunin's old cell in the Peter Paul fortress construct, which Murchison had built when he had been the leading shareholder in Simulworld.

She searched through all the rooms, but they were empty. Then it occurred to her that they might have planned the great event for a part of the construct they knew better. She prevailed upon Bakunin to take her back to Cicero's villa by one of those back routes he knew so well. Bakunin was shy around women, still unconsoled for loss of his wife Antonia, her data lost in an anonymous grave near a nameless village in Siberia. He helped her back to Cicero's house, but he didn't look at her. Another time she would have resented it. Now she was in too much of a hurry to care.

When she let herself into the villa, Cicero himself was sitting in his garden as usual, under a sky of unvarying Italian blue. He smiled his archaic smile and said, "He's inside. Your wish has been granted, just as I promised you."

Inside, in a little bedroom off the atrium, bright with simulated flowers, she found Antony. He was just as she remembered him in his last years, his handsome soldier's face framed in the curly brown beard, the face haggard and showing the strain of too much high living and unrestrained passions.

"So it's you, Cleopatra," Marc Antony said. "I might have guessed you'd have a hand in this. Reborn, am I? And didn't I see Cicero just a few moments ago?"

"We're all reborn in a strange world," Cleopatra told him.

"No doubt," Antony said. "And here we are again, eh, Cleopatra?"

"You sound a little—disenchanted," Cleopatra said, forcing herself to smile.

"You might say so," Antony said. "Cleopatra, let me speak to you with candor."

"That sounds ominous," Cleopatra said.

"Take it as you will. I want to tell you that the enchantment you wove around me, which took me from the summit of the world, with all Rome at my feet, to a stupid death for a faithless whore, is finally over. Death wipes it all away. Go away, Cleopatra. One lifetime with you was enough."

She arose and left silently, though she was trembling with rage. How dare he? Then she remembered that it was Antony, a man who felt what he felt passionately, whether it was love or hate; but felt it not too long. No doubt this mood would pass, as had passed all his others.

But she wondered, as she went into the garden to rejoin Cicero, if John Sykes might not have been a more suitable consort for a woman who, when all was said and done, was destined by nature to rule whatever world she found herself in. Perhaps there was still time to come to an arrangement with him.

Before acceding to Cleopatra's request, Cicero had many thoughts about bringing Marc Antony back to life. At first it had been a bitter pill to swallow. Antony had been his most hated enemy. Antony had been responsible for his murder. Cicero remembered it clearly: the dark sea-beach at Formiae, the gale force wind blowing onshore, making flight to Greece impossible. The two ruffians sent by Antony. His own final words, turning away from the ocean and distant Greece, back to fateful Italy. "Let me die in the country I have often saved." And then the killing thrusts of the short swords, the brief searing pain, the anguish at leaving life behind, and then, oblivion until he had reawakened here in this place. Dead by Antony's orders, and Cleopatra had asked him to help bring Antony to life again.

Considering the situation philosophically, Cicero had agreed. Antony had done nothing outrageous; it was just politics. And having Antony around would bring some excitement into the quiet surroundings of

Simulworld. Besides, he suspected Antony would be more a problem to others than to himself. And so he had given Cleopatra's request to Redmond.

He had heard from Cleopatra how Antony had greeted her. Already she regretted his resuscitation. Was there any way to undo it, she had asked Cicero, and he had promised to think about it.

But now his thoughts were interrupted by the unexpected arrival of a messenger who thrust himself rudely into Cicero's villa. He was a huge man with an untidy red beard that hid most of his ugly face. He had wild blue eyes, and was dressed in a barbarian's costume of light blue.

"Who are you?" Cicero asked.

"Vladimir, a messenger."

"Whose?"

"I was sent to bring you to a certain man."

"What man? What is his name?"

"I was not told."

It seemed to Cicero that Marc Antony was up to some mischief already. Whatever it was, he decided he'd better find out about it at once.

Cicero followed the red-bearded Scythian down many corridors, and then into a section that he found familiar. He was in New Rome, Sykes' newly created and recently abandoned capital of Simulworld. What the simulacra called Simul City. It was disturbing to be here. All the others had abandoned the place, returning to their more familiar simulated surroundings.

He followed Vladimir into a building which was a good replica of the old Roman Senate. Far ahead, standing several tiers above the ground, there was a figure. Cicero blinked, unable at first to recognize him.

"Greeting, Marcus Tullius!" The strong voice boomed.

Cicero hurried down the aisle and looked up unbelievingly.

"Caesar! You have returned!"

"No thanks to you, Marcus."

"Caesar, I swear to you, I was going to attend to it. . . ." Cicero cut himself off abruptly. The old habit of subservience to Caesar died hard. It seemed to have survived both their deaths. Yet he reminded himself that this was a new time and a new age, and there was nothing Caesar could do to him or for him here. Or was there?

"In the old days," Cicero said, "we were allies."

"Forgive me, Marcus," Caesar said. "I spoke only in jest. I never expected anyone, not even the great Cicero, to bring me back to life."

"Are you aware of the circumstances of our rebirths, Caesar?"

"I have learned something of them, Marcus. The necessity of learning quickly was the condition of my rebirth. I had no sooner opened my eyes than a man who called himself the technical director was speaking to me, explaining the political situation."

"There's an enormous amount to understand, Caesar," Cicero said. "We are in strange circumstances indeed, not dead, but a long way from being alive as we used to know it."

Caesar waved his hand with a dismissing gesture. "How it all works is of interest, of course, but less revealing than the political realities, which will reveal whatever we need to know. I am alive again, Marcus, because I agreed to certain conditions."

"Who set those conditions?" Cicero asked.

"The Technical Director left me in no doubt on that score. He was speaking for John Sykes, whose acquaintance I believe you have made."

"Sykes would have made himself king over all of us here," Cicero said. "We could not permit that, Caesar, not even when we were alive in Rome. How much less could we permit it of this upstart Sykes?

We overthrew him, and hid him away in order that his technicians would not kill us. We were able to ensure that there would be no executions, no retaliations, no wiping out of us because of our treatment of Sykes."

"You secured the powers of destruction," Caesar said. "But not those of creation. Sykes gave me life, but only on condition that I assist him. I gave him my word freely that I would support him."

"Caesar, that may have been rash."

"I did make certain conditions," Caesar said.

Cicero smiled. "That is my Julius."

"I pointed out to him that to be a king or dictator is an unsuitable and unstable position, even in a world of simulacra, as long as they are gifted with free will. I suggested to him that politically, a triumvirate was a much better idea."

"And he agreed? It was daring of you to try his patience at the very moment of your birth."

"What's the use of being Caesar if one is not bold? Sykes was pleased with the idea. He is imbued with the classical fallacy. He thinks everything was better in the old days."

"So you and Sykes are to rule us?" Cicero said. "Well, that should be interesting. Who, might I ask, makes up the third? Marc Antony, I should imagine, since he filled that role in the good old days. Or has Cleopatra talked you into taking her? She'd make an interesting triumvir."

"How you do run on," Caesar said, smiling. "I did interview Marc and he seems quite deranged. His hatred of Cleopatra overmasters him. He can't forgive her for allowing him to kill himself under the impression she was already dead. He refuses to see it was only politics."

"Marc is too passionate to make a good politician," Cicero said. "But whom have you picked for the third? I've heard that Frederick the Great is one of our company. You may not have heard of him, Caesar, but I'm told he was a great ruler in his day."

Caesar shook his head. "I don't know him and I don't want to. A triumvirate should be a cozy thing. The third, Marcus, will be yourself."

"I? To rule this shadowy empire with you? Caesar, I am flattered. My poor powers will scarcely permit—"

"Come off it, Marcus," Caesar said. "You know you are a wonderful theoretician. I need your intelligence, your subtlety. You will help me keep Sykes in line. There are great possibilities here, Marcus, I can see that much already."

"So be it, then," Cicero said.

He and Caesar clasped each other in an embrace of warm friendship. And Cicero was thinking, these could be interesting times indeed, with Antony on the scene and Cleopatra aggrieved. "Yes," he said, "it's quite like the old days."

AD 2158

External and corporate considerations give way to
personal preoccupations as the sim technology is re-
fined and moves from the corporate to the well-
heeled private sector. What better toy for the rich?
What more compelling vacation spot for the jaded
on-and-off-world-traveler than the carefully-customized
reproduced past in glorious color, replete with the
simulacrum of your choice? And what more compelling obsession than that of rewriting the past?

THE MURDERER

Matthew J. Costello

Vinson walked over to the trench and he looked down.

Good, he thought, *it's at least three feet deep, and that should be deep enough . . . even way up here.* The cables had to be protected from the wickedly cold northern winters.

He looked back to the house—if one could call the twenty-five-room manor a "house." His ground crew, all locals eager for the work, was pouring a layer of concrete over the cable pipe, to be followed by packed dirt. And during the ever-shorter spring, some lush and exotic shrubs would be selected by Mr. Wallace Porter himself.

And Eric Vinson stared at the mansion where all the cables led to . . .

It was a castle. A wondrous dark stone mansion in the gothic style. It had all the warmth of a bear cave. And in all the weeks that he had spent here, supervising the final delivery and set-up of what was one of a handful of private simulacra, the only thing he wanted was to get back to his small apartment.

It didn't help that this set-up was quite illegal.

A breeze cut across the lawn, scraping at the manicured grass. It seemed to bring the threat of the terrible winter to come, only weeks away, and he shivered.

Yes, I want out of here. Finish the job, demo this

system—pick up my last check—and then get the hell out of here.

Vinson walked to the house. For what he hoped was the last time.

The last goddam time.

Mr. Wallace Porter sat in front of the console, his lumpish, oversized body straining the quite sturdy-looking chair. The console had been designed for one person. The non-automated controls were all within easy reach. As much as the system had been set to a series of autoexec defaults.

It wasn't exactly idiot proof, but it was as close as Vinson had ever designed. Over half of the huge room was filled with holotank, lined with a white, non-reflective polymer.

Very tasteful, if I do say so myself, thought Vinson.

"It's all done?" Porter asked, making no attempt to mask his excitement and childish eagerness.

Porter's voice was phlegmy, clogged, struggling to escape the coils of fat that hung from his jowly neck. It was obvious Porter didn't frequent the well-equipped gym in his basement, or even the pool at the far end of the building.

"Yes, Mr. Porter," Vinson answered. "Everything is completed . . . everything, except the burying of the cables. And that should be finished in the next hour or so. Then it will be all over." Vinson took a step next to the console and Porter's specially sculpted chair. "Otherwise," Vinson said teasingly, "it's ready for use."

Porter turned in his seat, as best he could, and looked at Vinson.

"Then we can begin," Porter said excitedly. He turned back to the console, staring at the empty holotank in front of him. "Yes, start to show me . . . how to use all this." He gestured at the main console, the walls of the holotank, the data gloves.

Vinson's answer was hesitant. "Yes. I thought that

you might like to wait until they're done outside
and—"

Porter waved the idea away. "I'd like to learn
now," he said. "Now, Vinson."

Vinson nodded. He didn't share Porter's enthusiasm, his joy at all. As far as Vinson was concerned,
this was the most frivolous use of the simulacra that
he'd been connected with. Such a narrow goal, Vinson thought. Narrow, and—to be sure—pointless.
Vinson didn't share any of Porter's excitement.

But Porter was paying him very well, extremely
well.

Vinson walked over to stand beside Porter and the
console. He leaned across the table, in front of the
fleshy billionaire.

"The operation has been simplified to its essen-
tials," Vinson said.

Porter had made that design constraint very clear
from the get-go. One of the most complex chunks of
computer technology had to be reduced to a series of
manageable switches and tuners no more complicated than this year's scramjet. An intelligent ten-
year-old could operate the machine, without the
slightest concern, or knowledge, about access pathways, address traps, permutations, and stochastic
tracking.

All the incredible technology was reduced to the
level of a toy.

A plaything.

Which is exactly what his machine was. A rich
man's toy. Something for Porter to do in between
gorging himself on the dwindling delicacies of the
world . . . delicacies, like real cheese and grapes that
most people never got to see . . . not these days.

The main program ate up nearly one-quarter million programming hours. An entire company of renegade computer technicians had been devoted to
making one incredibly wealthy man's fantasy come
true. Porter's machine was also linked to the main

network. It had to be, actually, for the millions of details needed for scores of datanets from New York to London.

Vinson turned the switches in sequence. "They're arranged in the order you turn them on, Mr. Porter. Just follow them down, like so—" Vinson went on powering up the battery of CPUs, the imaging devices, and finally the satellite connections that tied Porter to the networks.

"There," he said quietly. "That's all there is to it." That wasn't quite true, Vinson realized. If ever Porter wanted to move onto other, er, historical explorations, he'd need to have the battery of dials adjusted. But all the controls were hidden inside the console. And when that time comes, Vinson thought, he can pay me a nice consultant's fee to jet back up here.

"It will take a few seconds for the holotank to clear. . . ." Vinson explained.

Vinson watched the swirly smoke effect, colored with streaks of fiery magenta and dark purple. A chromatic logo for his company. After all, this was the entertainment business here, not research. This was no high-minded pursuit of ancient wisdom or unique historical confrontations from the land of Never-was. This was thrill-seeking, plain and simple.

The colors started washing away. The fog melted into thin air.

But it's what I wanted, wasn't it? Not the numbing bureaucracy of Artifice Inc. or the boring social awareness of Eurofac. Yes, he thought, *I went freelance knowing what the score was.*

Technology to the people, brothers and sisters! Or at least to whomever could pay for the hardware . . . and my expertise.

And he hadn't bothered to look back. He, and the other renegades like him, were making too much money.

"The gloves," Porter croaked. Porter looked down

at the datagloves in front of him. Vinson smiled. The poor fellow was overwhelmed, almost terrified. "How do I—?" Porter stammered.

Vinson reached over and grabbed the two gloves that were perfectly fitted for Porter's meaty hands. He helped Porter slip them on. They were, of course, custom made, extra large, incredibly responsive to even the smallest movements.

Porter would be able to control his recreated world with incredible ease.

It's sick, Vinson thought. *This whole thing. Porter, his incredible money, this project . . . the years of work simply to—*

The screen cleared. There was nothing there.

"Vinson . . ." Porter croaked, unable to contain his excitement. "Where is it? Show it to me! Show me London!"

Vinson laughed. "It's in your hands, Mr. Porter. Just clench your fists . . . just once."

And Vinson grinned as he watched Porter make a fist, and the holotank filled with the murky fog of London . . .

Oh god, Porter thought, it was all too much for him. The sights, the sounds—Victorian London! —swirling before him. After so many years of dreaming about it, and now—

It was so real . . .

Once he forgot himself. He let his sweaty hands slip out of the gloves. And the images immediately began to fade. He quickly shoved his hands back in.

I'm just too excited, he thought.

"Try to remember," Vinson whispered in his ear. "The system depends on your physical contact. It reads your movements. Take your hand out and it all vanishes . . ."

Porter nodded, licking his lips. This was so much better than he ever imagined it could be. It was wonderful, thrilling!

"Where am I?" he shouted at Vinson, keeping his eyes on the tank. *I must find out where I am,* Porter thought. He heard Vinson checking the map.

"All right . . . you should be looking up from Broad Street. And there—to your left—that should be London Hospital."

Porter moved his fingers, just the way Vinson showed him, as if you were molding the picture, shaping the direction you wanted to go. It felt natural . . . and the images on the screen moved, a great panorama. He saw an enormous stone building, and people bustling in and out.

"They don't see me?"

"Of course not. Not unless you want them to. And you know how to do that, just move your fingers—"

"Oh, god, Vinson. This is wonderful. *Wonderful.*"

Porter turned some more, until he was looking west. A few men dressed in rich-looking morning coats and top hats hurried by. They ignored the poor vendors gathered on the corner. Porter heard one shabby looking man shout out:

"Eh, Guv'nor, get your *Telegraph* here!"

The cockney voice cut through the morning air.

Other sounds began to fill Porter's ears. The clatter of a carriage moving gingerly down the cobblestone street, the harsh squeals of small, ragged children selling apples from too heavy baskets.

Poor things, Porter thought. *Look at their eyes, so dark and sunken. I wish I could give them a shilling. I wish—*

But no—it's just part of a program, just a simulacra. Nothing to worry about . . .

Then he saw a woman walk by, stop, and look leisurely down one street and then the next. She had full, beet red lips and her cheeks were shadowed an indecent, flaming crimson. She lingered on the corner, looking this way and that.

Porter felt his pulse thumping in his skull.

"The date!" he yelled to Vinson, not taking his

eyes off the incredible scene. "Did I get to the right date?"

"As you wished, Mr. Porter. It's the morning of November 10th, 1888."

"Then down the street—" Porter said.

"Yes, down the street, Mr. Porter, is Whitechapel."

Whitechapel! Porter thought. And he moved his fingers, and turned down the block.

Vinson sat down in a folding chair just behind Porter. There were no plush accommodations for guests in this room. And he watched, rather disinterestedly, his client's progress through the East End of London. Neither the period nor the location much interested him. But there was no doubt that this simulation was a most remarkable accomplishment. Something to be proud of.

If only it wasn't so pointless.

The program included an area that was only about two square miles—stretching from Victoria Park in the north, down across the Thames, and past the Surrey docks. As long as Porter stayed in that area, it would be incredibly detailed. Vinson's team had reconstructed an entire area of London destroyed by the foolishness of the twentieth century. They used photographs, city maps, plans, historical records, newspapers, diaries—layer upon layer of input, personal observation, even fictional narrative, everything and anything that would add the smallest detail to their reconstruction of the London's East End in the declining years of Queen Victoria. Most of the raw data came directly from the Comm Networks.

And where there were conflicts, they let the program resolve them. At this level of complexity, the program knew what belonged . . . and what didn't.

Then came the people.

As far as he knew, no one, not even Artifice Inc. had ever attempted to populate a chunk of a city. Vinson was sure that both the cost and practicality would scare anyone away. But the storage capacity of Porter's unit was easily the equal of ten regular simulation computers. When the project team crossed the million gigaflop line everyone just stopped counting.

A lot of the personalities were kind of generic, sort of "standard issue" newsboy, and the cliché metropolitan policeman. But the main characters were as detailed as the data would allow. For most of them, Vinson would match them against any personality created on any other machine. The simulated, recreated characters had the two hallmarks of state-of-the-art simulacra. They had complete and total integrity as creations. They were fully-developed. And they operated independently, with as much free will as their flesh-and-blood counterparts did.

And so, the tradespeople who once lived near Aldersgate Station were the real people who lived there. Their names, family history, their humble ancestry were all carefully researched and input. Even the local gang lords, the tough-skulled rowdies who led bands of duffers and cracksmen to prey on the more well-to-do, were real.

Vinson watched Porter move down the street. The man mumbled to himself, enraptured by his vision.

Yes, this was totally beyond anything ever attempted by any other company. And it had cost Porter half, maybe more, of his nearly-inexhaustible wealth.

Vinson shook his head.

And it was all being done just so Wallace Porter could learn who Jack the Ripper was . . .

The London policeman seemed to look right at him. For a second Porter held his breath. *What if he speaks to me?* Porter thought. But then the copper twitched his great black moustache and turned away. Porter breathed out and walked past an open butcher's cart, filled with great chunks of beef. A stream of blood dripped from the end of the cart and a gang of mangy dogs licked at the small red pools splattering onto the street.

"Ey, now. Get out of 'ere, ya filthy mutts."

The butcher kicked at the dogs, and they scampered away, howling in protest. He slid a chunk of meat off the cart and flung it onto his back. The butcher carried it into a building . . .

Some children, street urchins, went running past him, still free from the snare of England's compulsory education. Free to grow up ignorant, illiterate, diseased and forgotten, Porter knew.

Porter came to another corner. He looked left, down a wide, dirty block. He lost his bearings . . .

"Tower Bridge is down that way," Vinson said to him.

"Yes . . ." Porter said. But for now—he had to stop.

He pulled his hands out of the gloves.

And the screen started to fade . . .

Vinson was eating an apple. Who knew when he'd again be someplace that actually had *real* apples?

"Why'd you stop?" he said to Porter between chomps. "Looked to me like you were getting along fine."

Porter stood up, with difficulty, struggling to raise his bulky body out of his chair.

The old guy needs some non-simulated exercise, Vinson thought.

But when Porter turned to Vinson, he was crying.

"I—I don't know what to say. This is so much more than I expected. It's not just the pictures, it's real, Vinson, real! It's—"

Vinson shook his head and smiled, pleased with the effect of his work. "No, Mr. Porter. It's just a simulation of reality, Mr. Porter. It's just data, that's what your money has purchased, an incredible collection of organized data."

But Porter was still shaking his head. "No, there's

more to it than that, Vinson. Much more." Porter took some steps back to a large work table. Vinson saw him look down at the map of London. "Tell me—how far can I go?"

Vinson put his apple down and walked back to Porter.

"We had to set limits, Mr. Porter. Naturally." Vinson finished the apple—right down to the core—and then looked around for a trash can to toss it into. Then, wiping his lips, he turned and pointed at the map. "This area—Whitechapel, Stepney, Spitalfields, and then on down to the river—they should all be well detailed. But if you go much further afield, I'm afraid things will start losing their edge, so to speak. Places and characters will start getting fuzzy, unsatisfying." Vinson made a large circle with his finger. "But if you stay in this area here you should be fine."

Porter nodded. He took a breath.

"I think I must rest now." He turned and looked at Vinson, his eyes distant, fogged over with a dreamy excitement that Vinson couldn't relate to. "Because tonight . . . well, you know . . ."

Vinson nodded. He knew what Porter was up to. Not that they talked at great length about why Porter wanted to do it. For the amount of money Porter was paying, he obviously didn't feel obliged to detail that what he was going to do. But Vinson knew what was going on—

Even if he didn't have a clue whether it would work or not.

"Then I guess I'll be leaving, Mr. Porter, if you don't mind. The cables should be all properly laid now. And your system is connected to all the big boys now. . . ." Vinson grinned. "Whether they want you to be or not."

Porter grabbed his arm. "No, don't leave. Not just yet. Please. Wait until tonight."

"But Mr. Porter, the system is up and running.

You have Victorian London to play with. My job is done here."

But Porter only squeezed his arm tighter. "I hate to put too fine a point on it, Mr. Vinson. But I have paid your company a *tremendous* amount of money. I want you to stay. At least until after supper. To make sure that there are no problems."

Why not? thought Vinson. There had been plenty of profit in Porter's project, even if it did tie up the company's resources, and then some, for over three years.

"Sure, Mr. Porter. Whatever you'd like. Until after dinner then."

"More wine?"

The mechwaiter held the bottle of Brazilian wine at the ready. The stuff was too damn sweet—but Vinson knew that Porter didn't stock any drugdrink. He was an old-fashioned Sybarite. No new-fangled pleasures for him.

Vinson looked at his Wristcom. It was going to be a hell of a long ride back to the BosNy Corridor. Less of a buzz was probably in order for tonight. Especially if he hit some nasty weather. Still, another few sips wouldn't hurt . . .

He nodded at the mechwaiter and pointed at his near-empty glass. The waiter filled his glass with all the aplomb and polish of a can opener.

"You don't think it will work?" Porter said, a forkful of veal paused at the cavernous entrance to his mouth.

"I don't know whether your idea will work or not. The concept idea is brilliant, unique." Flattery came easier after Vinson took more sips of the strong wine. "Even if I'm not too sure why you'd, er, use so much of your money to test it."

"It's been an obsession with me," Porter said quietly.

"I understand. Anyway, to answer your question . . . we have stocked your program with simulacra of all the known people suspected of being Jack the Ripper, from the Duke of Clarence to the redoubtable Dr. Edward Harris, the East End's most fabled practitioner of the art and science of abortion. But is the Ripper in there? And will he strike on the same night as he did in reality?" Vinson arched his eyebrows. "That, I'm afraid, is anyone's guess." Vinson finished his wine. "No one has ever done anything like this before . . ."

"But Mary Kelly is in there, she's in there, isn't she?"

Vinson smiled. Porter was a walking Ripper omnibus. There were whole shelves in the rich man's library devoted to the Ripper. Dozens of novels, classic and contemporary, as well as scientific and psychological treatises of varying degrees of reliability. And then there were the flaky books that claimed to reveal the identity of the Ripper, while others maintained that it's impossible to ever know who the mysterious Ripper was.

But Porter intended on finding out.

Porter planned on being there, on the night of Jack's last kill.

To watch the Ripper at work. To follow him.

If the program worked, that is. . . .

What a waste—

"Mary Kelly, she *is*—?"

Vinson nodded. "Yes, Mr. Porter, *she* is in there. And tonight . . . or whenever you make that night date happen—Mary Kelly will walk the streets."

There was one problem with the program. It was, unfortunately, a dynamic simulacra. It wasn't just one program, but thousands, all linked in an interactive network, drawing on not only the resources of Porter's giant computer, but the international Sattcom Networks as well.

And what that meant—as he explained to Porter—
was that the event, the date simulated, could only
happen once.

It was, he tried to explain to Porter, like those
domino chains, an immense line of dominos tumbling into each other. Only much more complex than
the most ornate domino display ever set-up anywhere. Once set in motion, the simulation was a one
way trip. You could record what happens . . . but
not change it.

And that part—the very complexity, the finality of
it—scared Vinson a bit. No one had ever done anything like this.

Vinson stood up. He needed air. He felt the buzz
from the wine. He needed to get away from this
house, away from Porter and his all-consuming
obsession.

"More wine sir, a cordial, a cigar—" The mechservant
rattled off.

"Nothing." Vinson looked up at Porter. "I'll be
going now if you—"

Porter shook his head violently. "No. I mean,
please. I wanted you to stay with me through one
more session. I may still have questions . . . things I
don't understand . . ."

Vinson sighed. The man's too scared to play with
his toy by himself.

Guess I can't blame him, Vinson thought. *After
all, it is the Ripper we're dealing with here.*

Porter's eyes were pleading, scared. *It's his dream
come true, but, poor bastard, he can't face it alone.
But then,* Vinson thought, *I'm not too sure I'd want
to wander the East End at night. All that fog. The
nobblers looking for a stray wallet.*

With nothing but a house full of mechs to keep
you company.

"Okay," Vinson said.

And Porter smiled.

*   *   *

It was a London night, late Fall. A night danker than any Porter could imagine. The fog was dense, a living gray cloud. Its damp billows mixed with the black choking fumes of the industrial city. Porter stood still—as if it was just too murky to move through the cloud.

A horse-drawn carriage went clopping by, materializing out of the vapor, so real Porter leaned back in his chair, forgetting his hands.

"The gloves . . ." Vinson gently reminded him, tapping his shoulder.

"It's so real," he whispered. "So real."

He went forward and he imagined the fog swirling around his feet as he moved.

A street sign appeared, catching the murky yellow glow of a street gaslight. "High Street," Porter read.

He turned in that direction. Some small animals—some cats, maybe rats—went darting back and forth across the deserted street, blackish blurs in the grayish soup.

They made chittering noises, almost, Porter thought, *as if they can sense my presence.*

But that's impossible, he thought. *I'm just an observer, I'm just watching the scene in the holotank.*

Then other denizens of the night, human, yet even more feral, crossed his path.

He watched underworld characters fill the streets, characters that were just names in books to him once. And now they were *real.* Bludgers, their nasty cudgels dangling from their belt. Yes, and fleet-fingered toolers—quick to cut a purse strap or a wallet pocket—hurrying to catch the richly-dressed toffs on their way into the Savoy or the Lyceum.

Porter felt his lungs sucking the air in quickly.

He passed someone shaking in a dark doorway, coughing, hacking horribly. And Porter wondered whether the man was waiting outside an opium den—a wracked, pathetic figure so removed from the romance of Sherlock Holmes and his treasured seven percent solution of cocaine.

And then he saw a streetwalker.

Young, much too young, Porter thought. Until he remembered that the flash houses, the communal homes for criminal families, usually turned out the girls just as soon as they hit their teens. By the time they were twenty they were usually used up. Old before their time.

"Can I make the image larger?" Porter whispered.

Vinson was right next to him, his chair pulled up close to Porter.

"Of course . . . Just clench the fingers of your right hand."

Porter did so, and the image of the streetwalker rushed to fill the room-sized holotank. The girl's face, scarred and haggard already, looked out at him . . . as if she could see him.

Vinson moved closer to him. "Easy there, Mr. Porter. What are you up to?"

Porter shook his head. "I—I wanted to see. It's not Mary Kelly. She was older. She—" He stopped, looked back at Vinson. "I can enter the simulation, can't I?"

"Yes. But I don't recommend that—not until much more time—"

"Tell me what to do," Porter snapped.

"Please," Vinson said. "You can't hurt yourself, physically, that is. But there are other things that can—"

"Just *tell* me how to do it!"

Vinson leaned over the console and he showed Porter how to move his fingers inside the gloves. Automatically, the imaging circuits reduced the image of the foggy East End to life-size. The whore looked around, ready to walk away.

When she turned.

And she saw Porter.

"Ohh!" she squealed. "Cor! G've er soul 'af a fright,

yer do. Naw, why d'ya creep up on a girl like that for?"

"She sees me—?" Porter said, still talking to Vinson.

The whore looked around, her eyes flashing now, filled with alarm. "Ey, who *you* talking to?"

Vinson leaned down to Porter's ear. "She hears everything you say, Mr. Porter. The program presents you as a well-dressed gentleman."

"Yes," Porter whispered.

The girl studied him for a moment, then she smiled and took a step closer to him. "You wouldn't be wantin' a spot a company, now would you?"

Porter shook his head.

"Pull back on the gloves," Vinson whispered.

And inside the holotank, Porter stepped back from the girl.

The prostitute made a moue of displeasure and turned to walk away.

"Wait!" Porter said. "I'm looking for someone." The young whore stopped. "Another girl . . ."

"Ey, wot can she do 'at I can't?"

"I *need* to see her."

The streetwalker shrugged and turned away again.

"I'll—" He turned to look at Vinson. "Can I give her money?" he whispered. "Do I have money?"

"Sure," Vinson said. "Money's no problem here. If you want money, you got money." Porter heard Vinson touching some controls on the side of the wall. "It's your world . . ."

Then Porter spoke to the girl. "I can pay you, miss. For help. A pound—"

"Cor! A pounder, just for talking?"

The whore reached out to him and he handed her the note. He saw his hand—the sleeve of a coat. A pound note. The girl snatched it eagerly.

He knew she'd have to work a week to make that much. But what did it matter? It was only programmed money for a digitized whore. A generic

streetwalker with only as much background as the
programmers thought necessary.

But she was programmed to live and work *here*.
To know the streets. The tradespeople. The crooks
and thieves.

And the other whores.

Because—and this is the part that confused Porter—
the program couldn't duplicate reality—not perfectly.
Once the program was running, changes, from the
infinitesimal to the major, could occur.

Porter knew what was supposed to happen.

But all that could change . . .

"I'm looking for someone named Mary Kelly," Porter said. "An older woman, she—"

The young whore nodded. "Sure, I know Mary, I
do. She's been down near Eastcheap, havin' it on
with clarks comin' out of the Custom 'ouse." She
smiled. "Try there. If not, maybe near the Station,
later . . . when it gets dark." She leaned close to
Porter, and, God, he thought he smelled her cheap
perfume. " 'N, if you don't find 'er, sweetie, why I'll
be right 'ere." Her smile cut through the murky
night with brazen intensity.

And then she turned and vanished into the fog.

Vinson pulled the folding chair close to the console. *I want to get going*, he thought, but he found
himself becoming absorbed in Porter's crazy quest.

Despite his recommendation, Porter insisted on
entering the pub, and letting people see him. *Hey,*
Vinson thought, *there's limits to my responsibility.
Porter knows the dangers. He's been briefed about
the potential psychological damage.*

It's his toy.

He watched Porter drink the English ale. Of course,
Porter tasted nothing. But the noise and the thick
clouds of smoke seemed to be enough flavor for him.

Porter was like a kid on his birthday. He'd been at
it now for over a hour, wandering the streets, getting

lost, finding his way again. His first loop down Eastcheap brought no streetwalkers. Too early, Vinson figured.

That's when Porter said he wanted to go into Simpson's fabled pub for a pint. Despite Porter's accent, nobody found his manner of speech odd. That was part of the program too.

Vinson looked at his watch.

"What do they see, I mean, when they look at me?" Porter asked.

"Just some respectably dressed fellow in a Norfolk jacket. Nothing too fancy, otherwise they'd be itching to jump you."

"But they couldn't *really* rob me or—"

Vinson smiled. "No. You just take your hands out of the gloves and you'd vanish. Get them all thinking that they'd seen a ghost."

Still, Vinson saw a few nasty looking rowdies leaning against the bar, nudging each other and looking at Porter.

It appears, he thought, *that some of the programming team got carried away with their "local color" designs.*

Then they walked over to Porter. Vinson cleared his throat. There's no danger here, he told himself.

But—funny—somehow he didn't believe it.

"Oh, dear," Porter said.

A big burly fellow, wearing a stained cloth cap and tweed pants adorned with patches, planted himself right in front of Porter.

"Say, mate . . . you wouldn't 'ave some spare shillings. Me and me boys 'ere are a bit tapped out, you might say."

The burly fellow grinned.

Porter squirmed in his seat. "Vinson, I don't know what—"

"Mayhaps you don't 'ear too well, chum, but—"

"It's not real, Mr. Porter," Vinson said. "It's just your simulation. And—if you want—I can cut off the physical sensations. You can just watch what they do to you and—"

But Porter pulled his hand out of the datagloves.

"Oh, too late," Vinson said. The thugs were left accosting thin air. And then lumbered back to the bar, scratching their heads.

The whole scene started to fade.

"It doesn't work unless you're controlling it, Mr. Porter. The simulation stops . . ."

The holotank went clear, then it began filling up with the colorful smoky swirls before fading theatrically to black.

Nice effect, Vinson thought, if I do say so myself.

"I—I think I need to rest," Porter said.

"And *I* have to leave, Mr. Porter."

Vinson heard a rumble outside, deep, in the distance. A nasty storm barreling down the mountains. If he didn't get going soon, his scramjet would have some nasty weather to plow through.

Porter looked at him, his eyes exhausted from the excitement, the tension.

And, Vinson thought, *the suspense. Just who will old Jack turn out to be? The greengrocer? The bookkeeper? Bob Cratchit's idiot brother? Queen Victoria? Oscar Wilde?*

And who the hell cares?

"W—will I be able to contact you? I mean—"

"No problem, Mr. Porter. Just call our main office and they can have you on-line with me, face-to-face, in a matter of minutes. Any problems—program glitches, imaging problems—*anything.* Just call. If I have to, I'll take a run up here."

Porter nodded and got out of his chair. Vinson smiled, and he walked out of the room with Porter following. His one bag, filled with dirty clothes and Porter's signed receipt, had been placed by the front door by an officious roommech. Another mech stood by the door, holding his jacket.

"Do you want a precipitation deflector, sir?" the mech said.

Another rumble echoed from the open door.

Vinson peered out. The dry fall leaves swirled and danced in front of the house.

"Nah, I think I'll be running ahead of the storm."

He turned to Porter. "Good luck, Mr. Porter. Good hunting."

Porter nodded. "Thank you, Mr. Vinson. Thank you for everything."

Vinson nodded, and walked out to his scramjet.

"Do you want to know—" Porter called out to him. "Do you want to know who it is? When I find out?"

Vinson turned.

"No, Mr. Porter. Not at all."

And then he left.

Porter tried sleeping.

A small mech sat near his bed producing a sound mosaic of soothing, restful noises. Gentle breezes, splashing water, the rustle of grass. Usually such sounds helped him sleep.

But not tonight. The big storm had arrived, sending a needle-point spray against the thick leaded glass windows. The wind created shrill whistles in the manor. He thought of telling the mech to make the sounds louder.

But, instead, he sat up in bed.

It was waiting for him, downstairs. Suspended, frozen. The people and places of over 200 years ago. And though his body was wracked with fatigue, aching from the tension, he knew that he couldn't sleep.

And since he thought of only one thing, he got out of bed.

He put on his heavy robe and slippers.

Porter never questioned his fascination with Jack the Ripper. At first it was just a great crime story, a fascinating mystery. It became a hobby. But then his interest started to go much deeper than that. He knew all the victims by name, the dates they were killed, their regular haunts. And he researched the known suspects, eliminating each one of them.

Until Porter felt as though he *knew* the Ripper.

Even if he didn't know who he was.

As Porter moved out of his bedroom and down the hall, the house came alive, turning on lights, heating each room, sensing Porter's stirring.

And when he got to the bottom of the stairs, a mech appeared from the kitchen asking if he'd like something to eat. Porter shook his head and kept on walking, past the great dining room that he hardly used anymore, and on through his library, back to the wing that now housed the simulation.

He entered the room.

He saw the chair, and the gloves, sitting there, awaiting him. And—God—he was excited. He felt an almost unseemly tingle run through his body. And he knew that it had been worth it.

It's not real, he told himself. *I must remember that. A remarkable simulation, that's all*—

He sat down in the chair, in front of the console. He pushed the buttons as Vinson had showed him. And he watched the holotank fill with swirling colors. He took a breath and then slipped his hands into the gloves.

The colors disappeared, leaving an inky blackness. A high-pitched whistle suddenly filled the room. And again it sounded, closer now.

What is this? Porter thought.

He saw a street, the fog, and then he watched a policeman go running down the street, his feet leaden, heavy on the stones, blowing his whistle.

What happened? Porter wondered. And then he was struck with a horrifying thought. *Has the murder happened already? Have I missed my opportunity?*

Had Jack the Ripper struck?

He groaned and, moving his fingers the way Vinson showed him, Porter found himself walking on the street. The whistle faded, swallowed by the fog.

Where am I, he wondered?

He turned left, and he saw a sign.

The Customs House. A lamp, looking so distant and forlorn, lit up the corner. Porter walked to it, the fog swirling around his feet.

He stood next to the dark-green metal of the lamp post. He read the nearby street sign.

Eastcheap.

Yes, he thought. *I know where I am now. But what time is it?*

He looked around, searching for a clock in the simulated street, but the sky and the surrounding buildings were a soupy mess.

Someone touched his shoulder.

He turned.

A woman stood next to him, her red lips catching the light.

And her face! He wasn't sure—it was so dark.

But it looked like—

She took a step closer to him. "And what's the matter with you, dearie? Are you lost?"

He cleared his throat. "I—I'm looking for someone, someone named Mary—"

She leaned right into him, and he swore he could feel her body pressing against him. "Why if 'at ain't *amazing*, sweetie. *My* name is Mary."

Porter studied her face, so close now. And he knew that it was her. "Mary Kelly," he said quietly.

"You 'eard of me?" she said. "Why, blimey, isn't that sweet!" And she took his arm, a great grin on her face, and she led him away from the lamp, down a small side street towards the Thames.

And Porter let her take him away . . .

                    *   *   *

Her room had one small window overlooking a noisy pub. The rumpled bed bore the impression of countless trysts. Fortunately, the gas lamp spared him a detailed scrutiny of the cramped room.

"Come on, sweetie, g'wan and get out of your . . . things."

He looked up at her, watching her unpin her hair. And then she reached behind her and deftly unbuttoned her dress. Before he could say anything, she had her dress off and he saw her antiquated underthings—thick black stockings, a tight corset, and billowy pantaloons. He smiled at her, more amused than excited.

"No," he said. "You don't understand. You see I'm not really—"

Her eyes narrowed, and she picked up her dress. "You're not a peeler, now are you?"

"Peeler?" he said.

"A *bloody copper!*"

"No, not at all—"

What am I doing? Porter thought. *This is probably messing up the program. I should just get away.*

Mary Kelly looked even more insecure . . . perhaps scared. The pale light caught the many lines of her face, the cracks and crevices filled with a thick coating of bright make-up. She might pass on a dark street-corner, but the hard years of wear and tear were all too visible here.

"You're not be wanting something a bit strange, now would you?"

He stood up, a move that he was surprised to see startled her. *Yes, she's scared*, he thought. *She's heard all the stories, the other streetwalkers, and she's scared.*

Scared. He saw her back up, shaking.

And he imagined her then, standing in the shadows. Startled this time by the blade—the quick cut. The tear of satin and flesh. The gleeful jabbing, over and over—

He took a step closer to her.

Raised a hand.

I have to tell her, he thought. *Tell her I'm not here to sample her pleasures.*

Not at all.

"No. Please. Don't be scared. I'm here to warn you," he said quietly. Yes . . . this is what I should be doing . . . "There's someone who wants to hurt you, the Ripper—"

He pictured the photos showing Mary's wounds, the almost-dissection performed on her. Some loud singing suddenly drifted up from the alleyway, a patron howling his way home.

"You've heard of the Ripper, haven't you and—"

But she seemed even more frightened, now, backing away from him, grabbing at the wall.

And it occured to him.

Mary Kelly thinks I'm the Ripper.

"Oh, please," he said, "you've got it all wrong. I'm not— You see, I don't know who the Ripper is. This," he gestured at her room, "is not real. Not any of it. I had you made. And the streets, and the people, and—"

She was slipping into her dress, nodding at him, bobbing her head, anything to keep him placated. Smiling crazily at him.

Oh dear, he thought, *I've gone and scared her even worse.*

She thinks I'm crazy . . .

It was going all wrong. *I shouldn't have come with her. I should have just followed her from a distance.*

But how could I do that? How could I just let the murder happen?

"Please," he said. "Don't be afraid. I just—"

But she passed him. She opened the door slowly, as if he was about to spring up at her, and then—and with a last glance at Porter—she ran out, back to the streets . . .

                      *   *   *

Porter hurried to follow her outside. The streets
were filled now with ghostly revelers, stumbling about,
addled by too many pints and too many songs, slipping from one dim street corner to another.

And the streetwalkers seemed to be everywhere,
almost identical in their make-up and satiny frocks.
Maybe, Porter thought, the Ripper—if he was in the
simulation—would simply select any one of them.
Maybe it didn't have to be Mary Kelly. What difference did it make to him?

Or did he have certain specifications, certain special characteristics he was looking for?

Porter wandered the streets, watching the cut-
throats eye him but feeling safe, protected, knowing that they were just loops in a program. They
have no more substance than a nightmare, he told
himself.

He wandered down to Lower Thames Street. A
few barges moved sluggishly up the river, under
London Bridge. Then he walked east, towards the
Tower of London.

A blackish figure appeared from behind a pillar.
"Good evening, sir," a policeman said, studying Porter carefully. Porter nodded to the constable and
kept walking, feeling oddly guilty. He went on past
the Tower Bridge, towards St. Katherine's Docks.

To the spot where the Ripper killed his last victim.

To the spot where Mary Kelly was to die.

The weather closed in a hell of a lot faster than
Vinson thought it would.

"Damn," he said. He used the scramjet's control
center to check out the weather up ahead. And he
got the bad news.

The freezing rain, nasty, biting stuff, was already
ahead of him, keeping pace with him.

If I keep on going, he thought, *I'll have to travel
through this muck all night.*

Sure I can do it, he told himself. *But do I want to?*

So, as much as he wasn't thrilled with the idea, he turned around.

Back to the big house.

Admitting to himself—just a bit—how curious he was about what he'd find.

Porter passed small barques being loaded by dockworkers. They tossed their heavy loads onto the deck like they were feathers. A dark jug stood atop a stack of crates and they stopped frequently, taking deep drinks from it, laughing and belching into the chilly night air.

Off in the corner he heard other activity. The painful squeal of a woman. The grunt of one of the workers taking a different kind of break.

Porter kept walking.

This wasn't the place.

Mary Kelly's body was found down a small side street from the docks. It was a deserted block, a place where—if she did have time to scream—no one would bother to look out their window.

By midday, on November 18th, the *Illustrated Police News*, a tabloid of the most sensationalist kind, would feature actual photographs of Mary's mutilated body. They were presented, the paper said, "in hopes of rousing the lackadaisical investigation of the Metropolitan Police."

The police were doing all they could. The Whitechapel area was covered with police, one for every few blocks or so. But there was just no way every little alleyway and thoroughfare could be patrolled, let alone watched.

Porter walked through the maze of blocks, feeling like a spirit out of Dickens. *I'm the ghost of technology to come.* And no matter how many times he reminded himself that none of this was real, the illusion was complete.

He even sniffed deeply, hoping to draw in the powerful odor of the docks, with the damp, fishy smell and the smoke of the public houses.

He smiled to himself.

There were no smells in the program.

He reached a narrow road that ran behind, of all places, the Mint. Porter knew that the grey stone wall at the back of the Mint was a favorite spot for the shameless courtesans of the East End.

The women stirred as he walked close to them.

When he neared them, a couple of streetwalkers sidled up to him.

He raised a hand and stopped them in mid-offer.

"Mary Kelly," he said. "Have you seen her?" Now Porter feared that his aborted warning to her scared her away . . . changing the evening . . .

One of the ladies gestured down to the left, down towards George Street. "She's with a bloke. Now, sir, why don't you—"

But Porter—his pulse racing, his hands all cold and sweaty in the gloves, turned away, and ran down George Street.

The mech opened the door.

"The weather's too goddam nasty," he explained to the machine. The mech seemed unsure whether to permit Vinson entry. "Is Mr. Porter asleep?"

The mech opened the door wider, letting Vinson escape the icy rain and shrieking wind. "Mr. Porter is working on his project," the mech explained.

I wonder how he's getting on? Vinson thought. *The whole thing would give me the creeps. I mean,* he thought, *this isn't resurrecting Mohammed, or Schopenhauer, or Asimov.*

Who needs Jack the Ripper brought back to life?

Still, there was no denying the lurid fascination of Porter's pet project.

Vinson walked past the mech.

"I know the way," he said.

* * *

Porter checked each alleyway, cursed by the rutting couples he disturbed. *It's hard*, he thought, *to imagine all this licentiousness happening so long ago. Is it fated to be part of the human condition, this blind, drunken lust?*

It was a passion that Porter didn't understand at all. *I'm just glad it never touched me*, he thought. *I've never been troubled with any such problem. Never!*

Will I recognize Mary Kelly if I see her? he wondered. *It's so dark here* . . . There was no light, nothing at all, just whatever spilled from the nearby windows.

But then he peered down one alleyway.

And he knew he'd found her again.

She gasped. "It's 'im! 'E's bloody well following me." She had one leg raised high, her knees squeezing against the man's gyrating hips. Porter watched them. And he saw her partner stop, turn around.

A dark face in a dark alley.

A moustache. A sleek top hat.

It was quiet for a second. Just the sound of Mary catching her breath, and the breathing of the man, deep, steady, calm.

And Porter gulped.

Knowing it was *him*.

The Ripper.

And he snapped back, pulling his hands out of the gloves.

"What the hell are you doing?" Vinson yelled.

Porter spun around, his face flush, like he'd been caught doing something private, embarrassing.

"Vinson . . . wh-what are you doing here?"

Vinson gestured at the raging storm. "One of those new storms, all icy wind and rain and moving faster than I was. I came back to spend the night." Vinson came closer to the console. "But why the hell did you stop? You had him, right there. That was him, wasn't it? That was the Ripper?"

"I—I don't know. It may have been. I mean, I imagine it *could* have been. I'd have to . . . I must go back . . . and see. Later . . ."

Vinson smiled. The old boy spooked himself. "Well, now that I'm here, I might as well stick around and see that. Do you mind? My crew will be mighty glad to hear the whole thing worked. You know, you could probably pump out a neat data file on this. Can't imagine any system not paying for the *real* story of Jack the Ripper. You could even replay the program, yeah—My Night With the Ripper."

But Porter didn't seem happy. He was still breathing hard. He shook his head. "No, I could never do that. Never. I wouldn't want anyone else to see this. No, this is just—"

"Sure, I understand. It's *personal* research."

Vinson stood there, his clothes dripping onto the polished floor. "So, are you going to go back in there?"

Porter nodded and licked his lips. "Yes, I imagine I will. Just as soon as I catch my breath. Just—"

"Great. Would you mind waiting? I mean, until I changed. As long as I'm here, I'd like to see what happens. Give you a hand if you run into any snags." Vinson gave Porter a warm grin, "Though it looks like you're doing just fine."

Porter's eyes still hadn't cleared. He was still lost, distracted.

Or maybe, Vinson thought, *he's just scared.*

After all it's not every day you get to meet Jack the Ripper face to face.

"Let me change and I'll be right back," Vinson said. And then he ran to the main part of the house, and his small suitcase.

* * *

When Vinson returned, wearing a crumpled pair of pants and a spotty shirt, Porter was still sitting at the console, looking rather numb.

"Ready then . . ." But Porter didn't move. "Aren't you going to continue?"

"Continue?" Porter said idly. The old fellow was still lost in a daze.

I guess Victorian England can do that to you, Vinson thought.

"You have him, don't you? You have the Ripper. The whole point of this thing . . ." He walked up to Porter and put a hand on his arm. "He's right there. Just get him on the holotank, zoom in on his face, freeze the program and, well, there you are."

"Yes," Porter said, still lost in the ether.

Christ, what's wrong with him? Vinson wondered. Maybe it was just a case of getting what you wanted. A very disappointing state of affairs, if mystics and poets are to be believed.

Except they're not to be.

"Well, go on, Mr. Porter. What are you waiting for?"

The lumpy fellow looked up at Vinson, embarrassed. This hesitation irritated Vinson. He watched Porter pull himself closer to the console, closer to the gloves.

The machine came to life. The swirling screen started to clear.

And then Porter was back in simulation, exactly at the point he left it . . .

"It's 'im," Mary Kelly screamed to the man she was only moments ago frantically coupling with. Vinson saw a flash of her thighs as she smoothed her dress. She pointed right at Porter. " 'E followed me from my flat!"

"No," Porter said calmly. His voice sounded hollow echoing in the large room. "I'm trying to protect you, Mary, to *save* you."

There's a new twist, Vinson thought. *The guy's getting carried away with it all . . .* Vinson couldn't see much in the foggy screen. Nothing, except the girl's flashing eyes looking at Porter, horrified. The gentleman with her, dressed quite fashionably in a top hat and cutaway jacket, was turned to the side, shrouded in the darkness.

"Maybe it's not him," Vinson whispered. "God, the Ripper might not even be in the program, not at all. I warned you, it's possible. This guy might just be another John . . ."

But then Vinson saw the man move. He bent his arm up, slowly, sleekly. And Vinson thought—he's pulling out a knife.

"Oh, God," he heard Porter say.

"Don't worry, miss," the prostitute's customer said. "I'll see that this madman keeps away."

For a second, doubt was reborn in Vinson.

For just a second . . .

The man took a small step forward, just slightly ahead of Mary Kelly, still in the shadows. But then his teeth, very white and gleaming, caught whatever light there was. Vinson saw that he had no beard, just a thin moustache.

The man brought the knife up.

"Stop!" Porter yelled, raising his hands off the console, but keeping the gloves on. He gestured to the man as the knife moved . . .

"Easy," Vinson said, "you almost pulled the wires out of the board."

But now Mary looked at her erstwhile protector and the blade. Her mouth fell open. The man raised the knife high above her head. She was staring at it. She was fascinated, thinking, looking, thinking—

Then something clicked.

The sick realization hit her.

She moaned.

She tried to pull away from the man. But he held her wrist and she pulled on him like a child.

His grip was too strong.

"Bingo," Vinson said. "There's our boy, Porter. Now pull out, and we'll let the program search out just who—"

But Porter shook Vinson away.

"Stop," Porter yelled at the man. "Don't hurt her. Please, this isn't what you think it is. It isn't London, she's not a streetwalker. And I'm not here, not really—"

The man laughed. Loud. His voice echoed off the building.

"And I suppose I'm not Jack the Ripper . . ."

"Look!" Porter yelled. And Porter pulled his hand out of the gloves, making himself disappear, and then quickly sliding back into them.

It was enough of a show to give the Ripper pause.

"How did you do that?" the Ripper asked, sounding more interested than scared.

Mary still tried to squirm away. Her screams echoed down the street. But the Ripper brought his knife up to her throat, perfectly poised to cut a main artery.

She stopped screaming.

"Smoothly done," Vinson said.

Porter turned to him, sweating, looking frantic, desperate. "How can I explain this . . . tell him what's going on? Is there anything you can do?"

"Sure. I could download enough technical information and the background on the project so that he understands it perfectly."

"How long would it take?"

They both had their eyes on the Ripper who was still awaiting some explanation for Porter's legedemain.

"Seconds. But we shouldn't do it."

"Shouldn't? Why not?"

Vinson leaned closer to Porter, not wanting the Ripper to hear him. "Because I don't know what it would do to the program . . . your whole system.

And your system is linked with every other damn system in the country, the world. He could have a field day. Forget viruses. He'd be a computer monster."

"But no. Maybe he'd realize that there's no point in killing Mary Kelly—not if she wasn't real. And surely we could trap him."

Vinson thought about it. "No. It wouldn't work. You see—"

"Tell me," the man bellowed from the holotank. "How did you do it. Or I swear I'll—"

He traced a thin line in the girl's neck. She screamed.

Porter's glassy eyes were locked on the holotank now. "I must save her," he said.

"She's just a program, Porter! Just—"

"Give him the information. You're working for me." Vinson didn't move. "Do it!" Porter barked.

Do I have an option? Vinson wondered. *Porter owes my company at least two million more. If this gets screwed up, maybe he won't pay.*

He shrugged. "This is on your head, Mr. Porter."

Vinson checked the imaging to make sure he had the right person lined up for the information dump. Then, after locking the stochastic tracking, he fed the Ripper the background of the entire project.

Porter expected the Ripper to lower his knife.

Instead, he killed Mary Kelly with one terrible lunge.

Porter groaned. "God, no . . ."

Mary Kelly's lifeless body slid away, slug-like, from the Ripper, down into a small muddy puddle on the ground. Her arm fell backwards, a plaintive gesture.

Then the Ripper wiped the blade against her cheap dress.

Porter felt his chest heaving, gulping at the air. He stepped back.

"Very interesting," the Ripper said, seemingly reflecting more of his sudden enlightenment than the act of murder he just committed. His accent was polished, the words clipped, beautifully formed. "Made even more interesting by the fact that you still don't know who I am, do you? And, what's even more intriguing, there's no way the program can *tell* you who I am, is there?"

Porter turned to Vinson. "Is that true?"

"I'm afraid so. For the whole thing to work, all the individuals—the fully designed ones—had to be self-actuating loops. It's a form of free will. They can do what they want and the master program can't control them. Or know who they are. If we're going to get a good look at him, it's up to you. You've got to stop him."

Porter gulped.

The Ripper kicked Mary Kelly's body away. It made a small sound. A groan? Was she still somehow alive?

All of a sudden Vinson felt cold. His stomach tightened.

The Ripper laughed. "I know what you're thinking, good sir. It's not hard to guess. Just run the program a bit differently, add some other permutations. Maybe set up a few address traps—" He laughed out loud. "And catch me next time."

"What's he talking about?" Porter yelled at Vinson.

"Don't bother," the Ripper yelled. "I know more than enough to avoid any such things. In fact, my friend, you've opened up a whole new world to me. I thought it was amusing enough having all of London looking for Jack the Ripper, but sir, what you have given me, why that's of inestimable value." The Ripper paused, thinking it over, relishing it. "*Inestimable.*"

And he turned to the side and slashed at Porter.

Porter backed away, flinching at the console. One

glove slid away, and the holotank's image shrunk to miniscule size.

"Damn," Vinson yelled at him, "get the damn image back, get it—"

But as small as the image was, they both could see what happened. The Ripper pushed past Porter, shielding his face, letting his knife fly around threatening Porter's ethereal image.

And then the simulacra was gone.

Porter stood at the door. Out of his chair, he looked so comically short and stubby. His skin now had the tone of marble.

"People will probably have to come here and talk with you. I mean, once they discover what's going on and they track it to your set-up." Vinson shook his head. "Your equipment, the tank, the programs, everything might be confiscated." He looked right at the frightened little man. "You might want to get out of the country for a while. Better yet, go off-world if you still got enough cash."

Vinson started out the door.

"B-but how bad can it be," Porter called out to him. "I mean, he's not a *real* murderer . . . he can't really kill?"

"How bad can it be? Well, with the information you've given him, he can sail through the system anywhere in the world, from the mega-complexes of the Han Confederacy to the closeted machines of the Islamic Socialist Union. He's educated, Mr. Porter— technologically au courant, thanks to you— Moving around should present no problem for him."

"But he'll find no streetwalkers in other simulations, right?"

Despite the sour taste in his stomach, Vinson grinned. "Yes, perhaps you're right there, Mr. Porter. But he'll find lots of other nice people to play with. Pizarro, Sophocles, Shakespeare, Spielberg . . .

The cream of Western Civilization, about to be visited by London's sweetheart, Jack the Ripper."

Porter turned away.

The poor bastard looked sick, disgusted.

"And you know what's worse, Mr. Porter? With the information you've given him, he can play with the system nearly as well as we can. He can make a whole *squad* of Jack the Rippers, a clone army, just to make sure that we don't put any real effort into finding him."

"I wanted to catch the world's greatest murderer," Porter muttered absently.

"Sure," Vinson said. "And in the process you've set the bastard loose forever."

And with that, Vinson slammed the door shut. He stepped over a fallen branch that was on the path, and walked to his battered scramjet, thinking . . .

Maybe it's time I looked into a new line of work.

AD 2160

Where crude warfare has been eliminated, the Great
Game reigns supreme. And through it, great minds,
"reborn" on a higher technological plane, can be
initiated and become key players themselves.

PEDIGREED STALLION

Anne McCaffrey

*"The deaths ye died I have watched beside
And the lives ye led were mine."*

Rudyard Kipling awoke, surprised that he had slept at all. Even more surprised that the persistent pain in his stomach had completely subsided. Not so much as a dull ache where a nagging agony had taken residence.

But there had been no new treatment suggested by his physicians to cure his ulcers. Indeed, he knew from the solemn way they had wagged their heads and delivered platitudes that his final reckoning was near.

Simultaneously then, his ever acute senses registered anomalies: the air around him was redolent of India, not England; he lay on a very hard surface—how could Carrie have replaced his bed much less strewn it with grit; and the temperature around him was far warmer than it had ever been in his chamber at Bateman's.

He opened his eyes and to his utter astonishment, discovered that he was lying on the ground under an object that looked remarkably like the great bronze gun which had, in his youth, stood in front of the Lahore School of Art. He put his hand up to touch one huge wheel, for he must be dreaming.

Dreaming? He who had been a life-long insomniac? Moreover, dreaming the very smells of India?

Cardamon, turmeric, curry, sweat, dung, decayed flowers and fruit, buildings—the incredible amalgam of musty, dusty, hot Indian aromas. Dreaming, furthermore, that he was prone under Zam-Zammah on a moonlit night, the only occupant of the courtyard which generally teemed with life. No, not quite alone for he heard dogs snuffling, rats scrambling across the stones, the rustle of insects, and saw shadows shifting by the School. And, as his eyes grew accustomed once more to the sights of Lahore, there were human bundles sleeping wherever there was space out of the way of the ticca-gharries.

No, no, he corrected himself. Bicycles and autos. No, his first observation was correct. *This* was incredibly the Lahore of his youth. He had to be dreaming.

He heard the rhythmic slap of sandals on brick as someone approached. He rose, dusting off his knees. He squared his shoulders to meet the stranger.

How did he know the stranger in the night was here to meet him, Rudyard Kipling? With a wry smile, Kipling fingered his moustache back from his lips and, pushing his glasses up on the bridge of his nose, prepared for what ought to be an interesting encounter. Why, the scene was something that he might himself have used in a science fictional vein!

"Ah, Mr. Kipling sahib, I trust I find thee well!" The accent was properly Hindi, inflection and tone. Yet the ever observant writer became alert by some slight discrepancy. The white-clad man bowed, his palms and fingers meeting in the traditional reverent salute, save that there was nothing humble about the set of that head and those shoulders.

"Not half bad," Kipling said, his grin widening. "But you've got to pay more attention to detail. Gives the novice away everytime, sir. Everytime."

"What?" White teeth gleamed in the dark shadow cast across the man's face, and his posture subtly altered. He was as tall and thin as a Pathan, poised on the balls of his feet as an Indian never is. His features were symmetrical with that beauty that is often luminous in the varied races of this continent.

"Blue, not red, for the turban and that sort of coat is inappropriate for a hillman. It is detail, sir, that matters. Now," and Kipling briskly cleared his throat, "what is this strange visitation all about?"

"You are as observant and all-knowing as ever, Mr. Kipling!"

Now Kipling laughed softly, a touch derisive. "I was ill to the death in my bed in my last conscious moment. I know I am not given to dreams—more to the daemon of sleeplessness—so how was I transported here, to Lahore?" He struck a pose, one hand on his hip, the other propped against the bronze barrel of Zam-Zammah which, in the midst of incongruities, provided a tactile reassurance.

The other man chuckled and made a salaam, Kipling thought, as if the gesture had been well-rehearsed. "You have, sir, won me a large wager. I said you'd not be taken in by an impersonation. However well intentioned." He smoothed his beard which made a black frame around his white-toothed smile.

Another mistake, Kipling remarked to himself. The teeth should be stained with pan juice. "Well intentioned?" Kipling ran a casual finger over the spearhead decorations on the cannon.

"I assumed a role to put you at your ease while your assistance is enlisted for a small matter . . ."

"I would think 'not small,' sir, considering the pains you've taken . . ."

"One which we hope your spirit . . ."

"I am, then, dead?"

"In the physical sense, you have indeed attained freedom from the Wheel of Things . . ."

"And have reentered life on a higher rung?" Kipling's smile was ironic.

"Ah, umh, that would be one way of describing your present state, Sahib."

"Enough of your play-acting," Kipling replied tartly, "for you are not immersed enough in your character or his way of life to be more than briefly amusing . . ."

"Please, Mr. Kipling," the man said, holding up one slim hand, "you are a simulacrum, painstakingly— and I might add, reverently—recast from the facts of your life and the essence of your own words. We of your far distant future play the Game . . ."

Despite himself, Kipling smiled at the compliment.

"A vaster, more complex Game than you had Kimball O'Hara playing, more deadly than Mowgli taunting Shere Khan in the forests, or Connor, the Man Who Would Be King. We play upon a Board as vast as the universe, as tiny as the head of a pin." Dramatic gestures accompanied each phrase and, as the stranger's voice was a melodious tenor, his accent—now that he had dropped the artificial Hindi cadence—was pleasant so Kipling became an interested listener to the deftly spun spell. "For in our time, Mr. Kipling, sir, war—the wastage of souls and blood and flesh and bone—has been eliminated . . ."

"My word, how did you contrive that?"

The white smile flashed again. "It was so decreed, and the Game—the Great Game—takes its place. The Players are many, the Stakes higher than you could dream, sir, but the strategy of the Game, the playing of it, matter much to those who shift stars and wager worlds. They have enlisted the help of others such as yourself, wise men of history!"

"I? A wise man? Imperialist they called me," Kipling said with more bitterness than he intended. "Jingo-ist! Right-wing political adventurer!"

"Time has mellowed those petty, envious shafts, Mr. Kipling," said his visitor in a cajoling tone. "You have been accorded the place the spirit of your work deserves. Enshrined in many ways in the Great Game."

Kipling cleared his throat, not at all averse to

being "clearly" perceived. "Which wise men of history play this Game?"

"Pizarro . . ."

"Indeed!"

"You may meet him. Pray tell me, sir, does your voice sound quite like your own?"

"Of course I sound like myself! Who else should I sound like?" And Kipling found himself tasting his words even as he spoke, listening to timbre and resonance.

"A mere detail, sir," and the fellow smiled his brilliant white smile and stroked his beard with an indefinable air of pride. "Pizarro, Plato, Frederick the Great . . ."

"You consort with lesser breeds without the law?" Kipling straightened up, involuntarily bristling. He had never liked the Hun.

"Surely you must also admit, sir, that he was one of the most brilliant tacticians in all of history." The smile was briefly extinguished, and the man hurried on to catch his guest's interest. "And Bakunin . . . who is, I must add, one of the minor problems with which we are hoping you can help us?"

"Bakunin? The Russian anarchist? You do consort with strange fellows."

"A problem in Gametime, as it was in wars, when one has to establish the pedigree of a stallion."

Kipling chuckled.

"Would it interest you to know, Mr. Kipling, how accurate you were? In 1981, the Russians did invade Afghanistan and fought a war of such attrition that they withdrew in 1988."

"Serves them right!" Kipling spoke crisply, then his curiosity overcame him. "Seven years? And they couldn't subdue the Afghans? Nor the hillfolk?" Then he paused as the information registered its shock. "In 1981? How much time *has* passed?"

"Ah, Mr. Kipling, it would give us such pleasure to bring you up to date. I can put . . . reliable assistants at your disposal." The white smile flashed, "one million Hows, two million Wheres, and seven million Whys."

"Upon my soul, 'her' ten million?"

"Actually, a computer, sir, a sophisticated information collecting device with remarkable memory, accessible at the touch of your finger."

"Ten million *honest* serving-men?" Kipling's scoff was cynical.

"As honest as plain fact can be."

Kipling stared down at the gritty bricks beneath Zam-Zammah, brushing his moustache. So he had escaped the Wheel of Things and still the Hun kept no laws. Frederick the Great, indeed! Pizarro! What a man! Tempting, mortally—immortally—tempting! He looked up and saw the bated breath of the other.

"And what would be my duties?"

"What you always did so well, Mr. Kipling, observe and comment, for you truly appreciated other customs and ways, and differences in peoples. 'There are nine and sixty ways of constructing tribal lays . . .' "

" 'And every single one of them is right.' " Kipling finished the line, and was for a long moment thoughtful. "A Spaniard, a Russian and a Hun. I do believe you could benefit by including an Englishman in that crew you've assembled . . ."

"I've assembled no one, sir, but you!"

"And my role is to be observer . . . or diarist?"

The other held up both hands, fending off the irony in Kipling's tone. "Observer, please, good sir, continuing what you began so notably many, many years ago and because you are so well qualified. And poet, if you are so moved, for your verse still inspires those of us who would see Britain restored to her rightful place among the Nations of the World."

"To take up the white man's burden again?" Kipling saw the solemn nod and heaved a sigh.

"Though truth to tell, Mr. Kipling, it's not the *'white'* man's burden so much as the burden of honorable men, and women. Of persons who *care* that the Law applies to all."

"And the alternative?"

The smile disappeared and even the stranger's beard seemed to go limp.

"Truly, sir, we need you. For there is neither east nor west, borders, breeds nor births, and in this time men fight to save several hundred earths."

Kipling hesitated a moment longer, though the paraphrase had been neatly turned and the appeal to his sense of responsibility demanded a positive answer. One had a faith to live by, and die for, which could indeed call the honorable man from beyond the grave. Death had not diminished its keen sense of responsibility, nor altered a jot of his respect for the Law. His vision of society had always included a network of obligations, with each individual doing the job appropriate to him as well as he could. It was most gratifying that he had been considered, and called in this unique fashion. "Very well. I shall honor the Law."

His guide seemed to tremble with elation and the flashing smile returned. "Now, sir, where would you like to be?" He gestured to the moonstruck building of the Lahore Museum, its deep verandahs yawning mouths of blackness.

Almost irritably, Kipling shook his head. He had left India, yearned for her desperately—for a while . . .

"Or here?"

The surroundings changed abruptly and in his surprise, Kipling took in a lungful of the crisp, charged air of an autumnal Vermont, and exclaimed aloud as he stared, incredulous, to where the familiar facade of Naulakha rose above Brattleboro. He had been happy there, until the Boer War, and the death of his dearly loved daughter. Some of his best work had been produced in Naulakha's study, although he had been somewhat lonely . . . He was accustomed to that.

He hesitated: Carrie would not be there to supervise visitors but before he could speak, he experienced a second disorientation as the gables of the Rottingdean house replaced his Vermont home. He had liked that house, but not the intrusions by reporters and regular bus loads of sightseers. He gave a shudder.

"Or here?" and they were on the flagstone path leading to Bateman's.

Kipling decided not to ponder these miraculous shifts. He had had more than enough to absorb in the past half hour.

"Rottingdean, if you would be so kind! And," he added, inhaling quickly as the gables reappeared, "one day you must tell me how you manage this sort of thing."

"All in the mind, Mr. Kipling, all in the mind."

"Am I then but a reincarnation in your mind?"

"Not at all, sir, let me just get you settled," and he led the way, opening the door to gesture for Kipling to precede him. "You should find things here much as they were in nineteen aught one."

"How very kind of you!" Kipling was not at all sure how to take this Guardian. "Are you my *chela* or my lama in this adventure?"

"Your humble chela, sir."

"Does my chela have a name?"

"Babra, sir, and here in your study, I have the device I spoke of with ten million honest serving men." As he passed, he said, "Oh, Mr. Kipling? You were also absolutely correct about Cheops's pyramid and that contractor of his."

"Was I? Indeed!" Kipling looked through the door and saw that his comfortable oak table had been replaced by a shiny array of mysterious objects. "Good God! Fairies as well as rewards!"

"More like actions and reactions, Mr. Kipling," and Babra's white grin flashed, appreciating the reference. "Were you familiar with the typewriter? I believe it had been invented in your time. Or did you employ a secretary?"

"I preferred the pen and trusted my own writing of my words."

"Well, then, sir, this keyboard is neither cumbersome nor unforgiving and its spelling ability is topnotch. The commands are mnemonic for the most part. First letter commands. A snap for someone with your memory." Babra politely slipped past Kipling who wiped his glasses clean, preparatory to this tuition.

"See!" The screen lit up and Kipling gasped. "There have been many inventions . . ."

"Traffics and discoveries?" Kipling quipped, recovering his poise and moving forward to peer at this marvel, feeling a great sympathy for the assegai wielders who had been confronted by a Bren gun.

"As simple as ABC, sir."

"Indeed? Well, then I must master this djinn of yours!"

"Well, you pulled it off," the Simulacra Supervisor said as the guide reentered the control facility.

Babra pulled off the turban and collapsed neatly into the nearest chair. "You owe me ninety credits and Serijah another forty. He was talking up his ass about the authenticity . . ." and now her voice fell into the cadence of long dead Indians ". . . of my garb and my infal-ee-bull accent."

"And best of all, oh little friend of the world, the Confederacy owes you a full commission in this War. Rudyard did not tumble to your sexuality."

"Despite my devious deception and my most deceitful tale," Babra said, peeling off the beard and wincing as the adhesive pulled tender skin, "Mr. Kipling should have remembered who's more deadly than the male."

"Let's just see if this stallion has the pedigree for our struggle."

                              *   *   *

*The wars we fight today differ from battles long
    past.
They happen when we're least prepared and are over
    very fast
That Victim scarce has time to feel the least bit
    victimized
And the Spoils to the Victor are always minimized.*

*For it's trade wars, and strike wars and wars that
    have no name
And it's who's won and who's lost and, still no blooded
    game.*

Kipling regarded the words he had just penned.
Irritably he glanced over his shoulder and the Con-
traption had finished printing its blue-lettered trans-
lation of his script on the amber screen. Once again
he *wished* it wouldn't do that. Or at least have the
grace to wait until he had finished a line. He did not
like to have his words snatched before the ink had
dried and delivered up, blatant, shameless, and, in a
sense, humiliatingly public before he had had a chance
to fiddle, refine and polish his deathly poetry. The
haste to record was almost obscene.

Carefully he put his pen down and leaned back in
the chair. He had to admit that certain of the comforts obtained in this new Rottingdean were rather
splendid: this chair which amiably conformed itself
to his slightest move and supported his body was yet
one subtlety of many that he now possessed in this
curious half life of his.

He pushed the chair away from his writing desk
and to one side so that he could view both his
written words and the screened transcript. In neither medium were they the rousing ballad which his
new Masters, and here Kipling harrumphed testily
to himself, were likely to find appropriate. He certainly didn't.

Why, in the name of all the holies, had he condoned such an intrusion on the privacy of his own grave by accepting their lure? A man, even a long dead one, retained certain inalienable rights . . . Now that was a nice phrase . . . someone else's? Whose? There were some lapses in Kipling's memory. Dashed nuisance at times.

He'd have to identify the source of that phrase. That wretched keyboard had its uses. He even took great pleasure in extracting all kinds of information, moving from one source to another, fascinated by history, by its immediacy in the new medium. It was like wandering through an incredible museum to . . . what was the appropriate word . . . ah, yes, access . . . any information he needed.

But, and he brought both hands forcefully down on the armrests which immediately retracted, "information" was not his real need. What he *needed* was to go out and about as he was used to do, to observe in person and at whatever length he needed, to understand the pulse of this new civilization and the pressures and pleasures of its citizens. As that Babra person had assured him he was awakened to do. *Then* he would find the proper words to evoke the sentiments expected, of him. He had agreed to a verbal contract and he was deprived of the means to fulfill it properly.

Each time he had reminded Babra of that condition of his agreement, he had been fobbed off by one excuse or another which, each in turn, had seemed reasonable enough. He should be well enough grounded into today's politics to know what to look for; there had been unrest in some of the public corridors; there was no guide available; subversives had been discovered (would there always be subversives?): excuses which were now translatable as evasions.

There was a polite rap on his door.

Startled, for the Babra personage never knocked,

Kipling swiveled around in his accommodating chair. "Yes?"

"May I have a moment of your time, Mr. Kipling?" asked a woman.

Her voice, though slightly nasal, was that of an educated person and the tone was markedly self-confident.

"Yes, yes, of course." With a touch, Kipling subdued the light on the screen with one finger while, with the other hand, he turned his new poem face down. He needed no critics today. He rose politely to his feet to welcome the visitor.

At first glance he realized that she was no one he had seen before although her face, and the coif of the blonde hair, was familiar. She wore a cleverly styled suit of a warm dark blue that accented her eyes, mannish in cut but exceedingly well tailored and of a fine material, a double strand of pearls about her throat and neat pearl studs in her ears: elegant but not ostentatious.

As one accustomed to making entrances, she crossed the floor, hand extended, a practiced smile on her face, her eyes making a quick appraisal of him. Kipling still found it odd in a woman to indulge in such masculine traits but she had made them hers without loss of her femininity.

"It is a great honor, Mr. Kipling, to meet you face to face," she said in that assured tone of hers, her one-sided smile adding candor to her words, "for you must know that your ballads and verse have been an inspiration to many generations."

He gave her a gracious bow and gestured to a chair.

"I have come at an inopportune moment?" she asked, nodding at the blue screen. Again that facile, flattering smile.

He dismissed that consideration. "Nothing important."

"Really? But you were writing?" Her expression

showed a concern several degrees deeper than mere courtesy.

"Nothing I cannot leave for a few moments, madame." He ended the sentence in an upward tone, adroitly suggesting that she identify herself.

However she seated herself in a graceful way, her back straight, her ankles crossed neatly and her hands resting palm up in her lap. A most composed woman. Her demeanor did much to recommend her to him. So many of this era's females were brash and loud, with little elegance and much enthusiasm for matters which he considered trivial. The Empire had been built on an attention to minute detail, and this frustrated generation might do well to revive past custom and order as they had past personalities.

"I could hardly believe our luck," she began pleasantly, "when we heard that you had been aroused to help England in her current plight. You are the very person to dispel the apathy into which we have fallen. To rouse us all to new heights despite the overwhelming odds . . ." She paused to bestow on him a little smile, "that have reduced our once great nation. I have great hopes that you can also speak to our American friends. I recall that you were once resident in one of the New England states so you would have a sympathy and understanding . . ."

Kipling held up his hand, feeling a rising irritation. "My dear madame, contained as I have been in this one room—with only that—" and he flicked a disparaging hand at the screen, "to give me any insights into current *tempora et mores,* I have spoken to no one, certainly not to any Americans."

"Why, that is the very thing I wish to discuss with you, Mr. Kipling," she said, brightly smiling up at him. "Indeed and you cannot perform with the same insightfulness, immured here. Not when you once had the world to walk in."

Rudyard Kipling regarded her with sudden suspicion. "Madame, whom do you represent, if not those who placed me in this room?"

With a sardonic laugh, she continued to smile at him, her eyes glowing and her expression nearly smug. "I represent—others—who find any restrictions on their liberty intolerable."

"You're not one of them?" He gestured ceilingward.

"I was recruited by them, yes. Just as you were. And others. And promised many enticements to enjoy an extended existence." A fleeting expression crossed her face and Rudyard read it as similar to his own growing disenchantment with the new lease on life. "However, Mr. Kipling, do I judge accurately that your work falters for lack of inspiration and stimulation?"

"In that you are correct, madame . . ." Again Kipling allowed a pause for her to fill in her name but she ignored his tacit query. "I was bemused by their showmanship, whisking me from Lahore to Naulakha, offering me much if I would turn my talents to aid their revitalization program. They seemed pleased enough."

"But you are not, Mr. Kipling?"

He began to pace, hands clasped behind his back. "At first, I was so pleased to be back in form," and he laughed harshly as he gestured the length of his body, "I had tremendous energy and wrote—if I may be immodest—some fine ballads." He gave a second bark of a laugh. "But it is impossible to continue to write to four walls! I don't know who reads my poems, or how this new generation reacts to them. Even harsh criticism would be welcome at this juncture. Would you know, madame, if my words are having any effect whatsoever in forwarding this cause?"

"I can quite candidly assure you, Mr. Kipling, that your poetry is well distributed and avidly awaited. But you could do more, much more, with liberty." She glanced at her wristwatch. "To this end, may I demonstrate?"—and she gestured to his screen.

He cleared it and stood back.

"You haven't seen any of your broadcasts?"

"My broadcasts?" Kipling was startled and felt a stab of anger. Nothing had been mentioned to him of broadcasts.

The woman tapped out a series of quick commands and suddenly the screen lit up with his own image, seated at the writing table, pen poised over paper as he read aloud a poem he had completed only days before. It was his habit to read them just so. But, never had he suspected that his reading had been . . . what was that new word . . . monitored, much less broadcast! To do so was a totally unwarranted invasion of his privacy. He was so disturbed that he did not really listen to himself . . . even if everyone else in the British Isles might be! He watched as his screen image leaned back, satisfied by the recital. He watched as his simulacrum self made a final mark with his pen—part of his mind reminded him that he had added an exclamation mark. Then his image calmly brushed his moustache with a gesture that could only be described as slightly smug.

"Of all the indignities . . ."

Suddenly lettering scrolled across him in this replica of his study of Rottingdean.

This inspirational programme
has been brought to you
by British Telecom Simulacra Laboratories.

Kipling spluttered in outrage. To have invaded his death was one matter: to publicly expose his most intimate creative moments was outrageous and insupportable.

"With the utmost respect, Mr. Kipling," the woman began in a gentle tone, "I feel that matters were misrepresented to you, and we, I, wish to make such amends as we can."

"Such as?" Kipling found it hard to moderate his tone for he seethed with indignation.

"Join us."

"And who *are* you, madame?" he demanded in a voice that would brook no further evasion.

One of her eyebrows lifted as if she was surprised by his question. Then drew herself even more erect, lifting her chin with pride. "Why, I'm Margaret Thatcher." Her tone suggested to Kipling that he ought to have known. With gentle reproof she added, "I was the longest serving Prime Minister England ever had. After your time, of course."

"Humpf." Quite a come-down from old Asquith certainly, Kipling thought. Then he recalled perusing not altogether glowing chapters of the history she had written in his forays into the annals of the computer.

"History is so often rewritten to suit present demands," she said with her one-sided smile as if reading his thoughts. She gestured at the computer. "They do, you know, edit what you read on this. But England was *still* a power to be reckoned with in my days. I mean that she should rise again. But to assist us, Mr. Kipling, you may have to forego these amenities and security," she gestured about the comfortable study, "and *really* observe and understand this fascinating and decisive era. Not just those distorted views to which those who recreated us restrict you, a quasi-idealistic and childlike version of the truth. Join us, Mr. Kipling, be an observer as well as a man of action." A thin bleep sounded in the silence and she rose abruptly, giving him an encouraging smile. "I shall return for your answer, Mr. Kipling, when next you are accessed. You're about to be discontinued for the nonce."

"But my latest poem . . ." he gestured at his paper, "it isn't finished."

Her smile was tolerant of his naivete. "They neither know nor care. I took you from your desk too long and the automatic cut-off has been invoked."

She left before Kipling could form a protest or frame a single one of the pressing questions which demanded answers.

He became aware that he was seated at his desk, fresh paper was before him, his favorite pen in his hand. *This* time, however, Kipling remembered that this was not where he *had* been. Indeed this was the first instance when he realized his consciousness had been willfully interrupted. That, like an erring child, he had been sat back down at his desk to get on with the job at hand. He threw the pen down with a disgusted exclamation.

That wretched Thatcher woman! She'd left him no way to get in touch with her. Or perhaps, his angry frustration subsiding abruptly, that had been discreet of her. He rose, pushing the comforming chair back with a savage kick, and began to pace the room which had once seemed so pleasant. Now that he had become aware of his true status, he could not bear the place.

How had he, Rudyard Kipling, allowed himself to be reduced to the status of schoolboy! No, this was worse than Devon: it smacked to him of a repetition of the desolation of Lorne House. Had he started his life with those despicable Holloways only to end up in this reincarnation with the equally punitive British Simulacra Limited!

He paced, first across the room, then around it, kicking irritably at the furnishings whose familiarity now palled. Then strode the diagonals, having cleared the path.

"Mr. Kipling," and Babra appeared, "whatever is the matter?"

It gave Kipling great satisfaction to know that he had caught his gaolers off guard. The beard was as bogus as the rest of this impersonation. He stifled a desire to acquaint this impersonator with his intellectual awakening but realized the folly of such an outburst.

"I find myself without inspiration . . ."

"But, Mr. Kipling, you've done famously," Babra said and Kipling did not hear a false timbre to the assurance. "Everyone is delighted with your verses. Everyone!"

Kipling restrained a smile at the sight of the skewed hirsute appendage. He glowered at Babra.

"Not everyone," he said in grating measured accents. "I am not pleased." He cut off the protest. "Flattery will not suffice you. What will suffice *me* is what you promised."

"Promised?" Babra was astounded.

"You promised that I would be the observer. What do I observe," and he gestured around him, "here but four walls, the same which I memorized in my previous existence." He waggled a finger at his goaler. "It was my powers of observation which you and your masters wish me to use. How may I *do* that, closeted in this one room?"

Babra gestured impotently at the screen. "You've but to access . . ."

"That box affair," and he permitted disgust to drip from his lips, "has neither sensitivity nor smell: even the quality of its sound is muted, distorted, positioned. I have met no one but yourself and you tell me what you wish me to know. That is certainly not observation but predigested pap."

Babra recoiled from him. "Mr. Kipling, you may observe any scene you wish, any portion of the London metropolis and many of the subordinate areas, Liverpool, Birmingham . . . I showed you how to access the major viewpoint . . ."

"That is simply not adequate, Mr. Babra, not at all! It is not how I am accustomed to working: it does not reflect the true mood or an accurate assessment of living in this day and age. I *need* the stimulus of contact, of *personal* involvement, the taste of crowd, the babel of voice, the assault of smell, the sensation of wind and sun, and rain! I need to *live* in this world, not sample like some remote deity." Kipling saw the shocked astonishment in Babra's eyes. "Go. Speak to your masters and release me from these walls so that I may more effectively perform the tasks they have set me."

Looking stunned by his ultimatum, Babra turned to leave.

"Oh, I thought we had established the fact that your impersonation is imperfect. Do remember to consult the mirror. That beard of yours is askew." And he turned his back, pleased by the gasp and the rather forceful closing of the door.

He waited a moment, then strode to it, on the off chance. But, no, the knob refused to turn. How had the Thatcher woman been able to enter if he was unable to leave? His ill-temper returned.

An urgent rap on the door drew an exclamation from him. "Come!"

"Mr. Kipling, believe me," said Mrs. Thatcher, "there is not a moment to lose if we are to extricate you from here. I should have warned you that, under no circumstances, should you issue an ultimatum. They tend to turn headstrong simulacra off. Permanently."

"Mrs. Thatcher," he began firmly, "I could no longer tolerate . . ."

"Of course not, Mr. Kipling," she replied with an indignation equal to his own, "and fortunately, you have proved valuable enough to them so that they will not terminate your program without considerable debate. But we must be well away from here before they discover your escape."

For the first time, Kipling saw beyond the study door—into nothing.

"What is there?" he demanded, taken aback by the colorless void. "I am certainly not about to jump from frying pan to fire. What does your group offer me, apart from freedom? In what coin do I pay for liberty?"

"Your gift, Mr. Kipling. The same gift that British Simulacra required of you, but without their confinements. You will be as free as the rest of us to go where you wish . . ."

"To spy?" Kipling was contemptuous.

Mrs. Thatcher shook her head slowly. "Certainly not. We employ suitable personnel in that capacity. You would be, as I am now, an *agent provocateur*. Your gift of observation would be applied in the real world, not that one," and she gestured to the unlit screen. "Believe me, Mr. Kipling, you would be among distinguished colleagues. Trust me in this!" The appeal of her steadfast gaze, where Babra's had always slid away from any significant contact. "It cannot suit your conscience to be a pawn, Mr. Kipling. Wake the lion of England with us! 'Til the fatted souls of the English are scourged with a thing called Shame.' " She lifted a mocking eyebrow at him.

"Madame!" But her impudence, so well gauged, appealed to him as the arrant flattery of Babra had not.

"We cannot dally, Mr. Kipling. It would be fatal!"

Still Kipling hesitated, having been so badly deceived by Babra's equally glib entreaties. Then several figures approached out of the mist beyond the door of Rottingdean: one in the costume that he identified as seventeenth century: the short stocky man in the robes of a senior Greek statesman; the third a tall woman in the garb of a medieval soldier and beside her a rotound fellow in apparel, which, as its sardonically smiling wearer came closer, was well stained with the spills of wine and greasy meals.

"My colleagues, Mr. Kipling! 'And each in his separate star/Shall draw the Thing as he sees It for/ the God of Things as they are.' "

A fifth figure came running out of the mist, his expression contorted with effort and panic. Kipling had no trouble identifying the bearded man in a Slavic shirt, baggy pants and felt boots as Bakunin: his likeness had been in many newspapers during the War.

"*Depechez-vous. La porte jusqu'a ferme,*" he cried, hurrying towards them, gasping for breath.

"Mr. Bakunin has a feeling for closures, Mr. Kipling." Mrs. Thatcher spoke with a curious detachment, her eyes brightly on him, waiting for his decision.

Kipling swung an appraising glance across the group. Despite the oddness of their clothing, each wore the distinctive garb as those accustomed to such dress. The authenticity was recognizable, even to the food stains: no mock Hindus these, with false accent and ill-stuck beard. These people were genuine and so was their urgency.

Rudyard Kipling stepped boldly out of the Rottingdean room and into the mists.

AD 2165

The advanced sim technology is the apple in the Eden of the new technology, a temptation to which no one is immune: even the sim creators are having a difficult time maintaining, shall we say, their objectivity.

SIMBODY TO LOVE

Karen Haber

In the sea of night the electronic waves pulsed end-
lessly between continents along the canals and con-
duits of Motorobotics, Inc. Simone Dubois liked the
night shift best and worked it whenever she got the
chance.

During the quiet hours between midnight and
dawn she could concentrate on her sim design, catch
up on the gossip from Europe and the Far East, and
not worry that her fussy American boss Sanjei Yamamoto would come stomping in to check on employee
productivity. Productivity—such an awkward Ameri-
can/Japanese concept. Work, work. work. No wonder the Puritans had been kicked out of England.
Nobody here knew how to relax and have a good
time, she thought, remembering the way Sanjei had
laughed when she'd requested the usual month-long
vacation in August.

"I don't know how the European Economic Community keeps up," he said. His dark eyes were bright
with malicious glee. "A month off. Do they really do
that at Robotique? When do they do any work? I'm
sorry, Simone, but you're in New Tokyo now as our
economic guest, not Paris, and here we take two
weeks, after a year's hard work."

Economic guest. Privately, Simone snorted at the
euphemism. In the middle ages, she would have
been considered a hostage, a pawn held in a power

struggle between warring kingdoms. But in the twenty-second century, the warring kingdoms had been replaced by economic fiefdoms that crossed geographic boundaries. And instead of nobles, highly placed employees were exchanged between rival company/communities engaged in joint ventures. Since Robotique's president, Marc Chambon, couldn't be spared, his Chief Operating Officer, Simone, was the designated hostage.

Simone's screen chimed the opening bars of "Le Marseilleise"—she'd rejiggered it after her first week spent coping with the strident buzz that indicated incoming European e-mail. She watched the amber holo letters float above her keyboard in the message field. As she read the message, her smile faded.

"Merde."

Robotique and Motorobotics had been asked to perform a refinement on the joint-venture Thomas Jefferson sim purchased by the Han Commercial Sphere. First Citizen Laisun Chin would like him to enjoy ducks' feet and teenage prostitutes.

Normally, Marc Chambon would handle the task, but Marc was on paternity leave in the Islamic Socialist Union. With Chambon away and Simone exiled to America, the company was like a headless body staggering in the night.

Marc is the one they ought to sim, she thought. He's going to owe me on this one. At least a week at his cottage in Nice when my year is up. Without his wife or baby.

A tiny dark-haired woman peered into the office. "Why the groan? Was that the French toll of doom I just heard?"

"Natalya, come save me." Simone beckoned her in gratefully and ran the holomessage again.

Natalya clucked her tongue in sympathy. "A lot of work. But I thought you liked Jefferson! You were sorry when Sanjei had to turn him over to your sexy friend for the final prep. Remember the discussions you had with him . . ."

"Yes, yes, of course, Nat, but I'm too busy for political debates with old Tom right now." Simone brushed a strand of red-gold hair back behind her ear. "You know that Sanjei wants me to get the Michelangelo sim up to do that rehab before his big soiree. I told him I'm not the one for this job, but he insisted." Her eyes narrowed as she mimicked their boss. "But Simone, I need that French flair, that eye for details," she said in a fair imitation of the high-voiced, nervous Yamamoto. Natalya rewarded her with a chuckle. "So that gives me two weeks. And I don't care what Vasari wrote about him—Michelangelo is a very slippery character."

Natalya gave her a sly look. "You always have a hard time with the gay ones," she said. "Simone, you ought to ease up on your heterosexual bias. Get an implant. Maybe you'd have more sympathy for poor Michelangelo." Her eyes met Simone's in frank invitation. "And me."

"Please, Nat, don't get—how do you say it?—all hot and sweaty right now. I need your help. Can you try to do the Jefferson revamp?"

"I don't know—"

"At least tonight? Just give me the chance to bring the great Buonarroti online." She smiled her brightest smile. "Please?"

"Of course, of course. Don't bat those green eyes at me," Natalya shook her head. "You know I'm a sucker. Send me the coordinates. But I'm not in the mood to discuss the world policy with Jefferson either. He has such a hard time understanding what's happened to his precious United States."

"Well, it's a big disappointment to him, no? Imagine it: you awaken from a long sleep to discover that your favorite child has gotten fat, bald, and developed an addiction to narcophane."

"He gets so upset . . ."

"*Seems upset*. Nat, you must remember that he's just a very clever program. He's designed to seem upset. But it's software, not wetware."

Natalya rolled her eyes. "Sure. Just a program. Then why do all the purchasers end up wanting to screw their sims? Or watch them do it? We're forever having to adapt them to feign sexual pleasure."

"Lots of kinky people around here these days." Simone gave her a wicked grin. "I owe you dinner. Soon."

"You bet you do. And make sure Jefferson's on mute when you send him, or he'll be back in your lap, C.O.D.." With a wink Natalya was gone.

The screen-to-screen transfer took Simone a second and then she was blissfully free to concentrate on the master artist simulacrum.

Come on, damn you. She fiddled with the board, adjusting the field signal. The screen field remained hazy, filled with flickering blue and green particles and orange lightning. Simone cleared the field, started again, and after a moment she saw a figure. It was indistinct, a pencil-sketch impression dashed off by an impatient hand. But even as she amplified the signal the figure faded, the blue and green blizzard resumed, and she sank back in her seat in disgust.

"Merde, merde, and more merde." She hadn't had this much trouble with a sim in a long time. What was wrong with this signal? She'd heard rumors of jamming by rival companies. Could that be true? She was willing to bet her paltry two-week vacation that Maquina Hilliard at Maquinatech hadn't encountered such problems when she'd created that ridiculous renegade Joan of Arc sim.

Simone confronted the hazy image field once again. "Michelangelo, *allons-y!*" She boosted the program yet again and was rewarded by the return of the faint image. She could just make out an arm, a leg, a graceful hand. She almost had him. "Come to maman," she said. "*Andiamo!*"

She could see the knuckles of the hand. The long graceful fingers.

"*¿Questo—dové?*" a falsetto male voice demanded.

"Tch. Too high." Simone's hands danced over the keys.

"*Basta!*" a ringing baritone called. It was a voice made for speeches.

Simone peered at the image field and saw dancing dark eyes set in a fair-skinned, fine-boned face framed by curling black hair.

"*¿Che cos'è? Una quadratura?*"

"English—he's got to speak English." Giddy with success, she punched in the language code.

"That's better," he said. He was silent a moment, staring at her intently. "Who are you? Mother Superior? God? No. God can't be a woman. Please. I'd have to redo the entire Chapel ceiling. But what an odd perspective. Big head. No body. You've fine hair and eyes. Nose a little strong, I think. And lips too thin."

"Thanks," she said drily. "What else do you see?"

He looked down. "I'm standing in air. And that's not unusual." His laughter was a rich peal of notes. "Better than lying on my back on that damned scaffolding."

"No more scaffolding for you, Michelangelo. I've brought you for a visit to the twenty-second century."

"Eh? Mother of God, what do you mean?"

"It's a bit difficult to explain. You're a simulacrum. A program."

"Program? Musica?"

"No. Computer. Electronic."

"What?"

"Never mind." Simone ran her hands through her hair in frustration. She'd expected that the transition team would prep him. She just brought the sims on line. Briefing wasn't really her field. She'd have to bluff her way through. "You're in the future. I've, um, painted you in. By magic."

"Magic? Jesu Maria, don't tell the pope." He crossed himself nervously.

"Relax. I wouldn't know which one to tell anyway."

"Which one?"

"There are three now."

"Triple the trouble," Michelangelo groaned. "And I suppose you've granted me this magic audience so I can paint three more chapels? My neck muscles won't take it."

"No, that isn't what we—"

"Not to mention the sculpture. I can hear it now, *dio mio*! Another pieta, Michelangelo. This time, though, don't make Mary so young and pretty. And couldn't you make His wounds less graphic?" The sim's lip curled in disdain. "Give a man a chasuble and right away he becomes an art critic."

"Relax, Michelangelo. The popes don't know you're here."

"They don't?" He looked startled. Then a shrewd look came over his face. "I only work for the Church and the first families. Medici and their friends. I assume a fine nobleman has requested my abilities?"

"There is no Italian nobility in the twenty-second century. Certainly not any Medici at any rate."

"No Medici? But the popes continue? And multiply? Then Rome has prevailed over Florence." His eyes glistened with tears.

He's very good, Simone thought. *Very convincing. I deserve a bonus for this one.* Aloud, she said, "There hasn't been a pope in Rome since 2075, when the Italian rocket carrying a nuclear-power satellite blew up over Naples."

"Blew up? Rocket? What are you saying?"

She smiled gently. "Most of Italy is uninhabited now. Especially between Naples and Florence. It's not safe. The ground is poisoned. Hot."

"More magic? And evil this time. I think you are an evil sorceress come to tempt me." He shook his fist at her.

"Please, I'm no sorceress. Just a designer . . ."

"A woman artist?" His expression now was frankly contemptuous. "So, Mother Superior, you painted me, *alla prima*?"

"You could call it that, I suppose." Simone was beginning to feel a little dizzy. Was the real Michelangelo this mercurial? "What do you think of my work?"

He surveyed his arms and legs with pleasure and ran his hands upwards over his torso, nodding to show his approval.

Good, she thought. *He'd better like it.* Simone had used Marc Chambon as a template and Michelangelo possessed the same virile grace, the same dancer's musculature. The same and yet different. Somehow, the sim appeared more vibrant. The body seemed full of restless energy. And he was still in the machine.

"I might call your brushstrokes bravura," Michelangelo said, marveling at his hands. "Very confident. I feel ready to go to work."

"Wonderful! My boss has a job for you."

"Your boss?"

"Employer."

"Ah, your patron. And what, may I ask, is the rate of payment?"

She'd forgotten Vasari's notes: Michelangelo had been a shrewd businessman. "Er, very high," she said quickly. "The best rates, of course."

"Bene. And what medium? Marble? Fresco?"

"Architecture."

"That's a shame. Right now I'm not interested in building anything." He shrugged. "But sculpture, eh? That's different. I could pick up a chisel right now, my head is dancing with ideas. If you want to discuss architecture, why don't you talk to Da Vinci?"

"We tried. Believe me. But somebody else owns— er—hired him."

Michelangelo nodded. "He was always in demand

despite his sour spirit. A clever man, Da Vinci, but poor company. If you are such a witch, you can summon him from the grave, across the ages."

"We thought of him. But despite Vasari's notes, we don't know enough about him."

"Vasari?" Michelangelo rolled his eyes. "After all these years, that self-important hack is still at work?"

"No, no, no. But his book. The Lives Of The Artists. It was a tremendous success. Perhaps published after your, ah, death." She watched carefully. Usually, simulacra reacted violently to any mention of their original template's demise.

Michelangelo chuckled. "I wondered why he was pestering me for anecdotes."

So this Buonarroti was more flexible than the rest, Simone thought. Good. She'd programmed him with material cross-referenced from nine different sources. Perhaps that provided resilience. But the final test was bringing him out of the machine. And it was time. She glanced at the waiting sim body and anxiety made her heart pound. Only in the past year had this technique been approved. It was still a chancey operation during which sims—and months of work— could be lost.

"Michelangelo, I'm going to change your environment a bit," Simone said. "You may feel peculiar for a moment . . ."

She punched the button while he was distracted. Beside her keyboard, attached by a web of clear coaxial umbilici, the sim body lay ready in its bath of electrolytes, a pale, adult fetus, features blank and empty, awaiting the sculpting touch of character and intelligence.

The image field shifted, shattered into a thousand shards of coruscating light. The signal weakened and scattered as though seeking to escape from her busy hands.

"No!" Simone yelled. "Come back here, Buonarroti. I will not have all this work ruined."

The signal strengthened and pulsed softly. Then the sim-body shuddered, twitching in its primal bath. Simone had no time to watch. Furiously, she punched in the code, amplifying and reamplifying.

"Hurry up," she whispered.

There was a great splashing sound, and then he stood before her, his skin shining from the electrolyte bath. The connector cables lay scattered and discarded behind him. His body glowed as though lit from within. It was finely proportioned, strong and well-coordinated, and worthy of a woman's interest. But the face—the face was astonishing. What had been a blank field was now alive with mobile features. Full, sensuous lips curved in a smile of wonder. A finely chiseled nose and high cheekbones led her gaze upward to remarkable eyes in which curiosity and amusement glittered.

Simone stared at her creation in amazement.

For a heartbeat, Michelangelo returned her gaze. Then, quickly, he bent from the waist in a mock bow.

"Mother Superior."

He was completely naked.

"Clothing. I forgot clothing." Simone raced back to her keyboard, made the necessary adjustments, and had them added to his signal.

Michelangelo's body glowed brighter and hotter, a molten silver aura obscuring details from neck to ankles. Slowly, the glow dissipated, leaving in its wake a silken black shirt and tight black jeans.

"Interesting." The artist shot his cuffs. "But aren't you forgetting something?" His bare toes waggled at her.

"Sorry." She gave him a pair of low-heeled cowboy boots. Somehow they seemed appropriate.

"And now, where am I?"

"New Tokyo, California."

"Where?" His eyes were wide with astonishment.

"I think you called it the New World," she said.

Historical fragments floated just out of reach in her memory—how much did sixteenth-century Italy know about North America? She didn't remember: she'd worked on too many sims, concentrated on too many details.

"And this is a cold, harsh room in the New World, I think," Michelangelo strutted around, taking measure of her office. "Where are the velvet draperies? The servants? You must belong to an impoverished order, Mother Superior."

Simone watched him finger the orange pillow on her couch. Every move he made was filled with grace and confidence. His eyes missed nothing. Surely he was the most appealing sim she'd ever created.

"Strange," he said. "I can see everything. But it has no substance. Are your magics impotent?"

Simone shook her head. "It's a very complicated process to make you feel anything. I can feel you, for example." She reached out and touched his arm. His simflesh was warm and she could almost feel a pulse beating beneath the skin. "But you can't feel me."

"A shame, although it was not my regular habit to touch women." He gave her a wry look.

"I know." She couldn't keep the regret out of her voice. Dammit, why did he have to be so beautiful? She'd done too good a job.

"I'd like to see more of this New World," he said.

Why not? She could test his mobility. Sanjei would require that he be fully operable. "Come," Simone said. "We'll go for a walk."

They wandered along the dark hallways, through cones of pink light cast by ceiling pencil spots, they wandered until they had made a complete loop of the corridor around the atrium window. Michelangelo exclaimed over the glass, the strange lighting, even the carpeting. But he turned a disdainful eye upon the computer graphics framed in silver plastic that lined the walls.

"Soulless," he said. "An insult."

Simone hated them too. "I agree. But don't tell Sanjei when you meet him. They're from software he adapted as a child."

"Sanjei?"

"The padrone who requested your presence."

"He is also a magician? A sorcerer?"

"Was," Simone laughed. "Until he could afford to hire apprentices."

The sim nodded. "A wise tradition. I too was apprenticed, and it was the making of me." He paused to study her in the half-light of the hallway, reaching out and gently lifting her chin. "A good head with fine noble features. I would like to sketch you. The eyes are especially fine."

She felt her cheeks heat up and imagined Marc hooting at the sight of her blushing. But to have Michelangelo's praise *was* something special. "Thank you."

He nodded, but his attention was already elsewhere. "This is just a hallway in one poorly designed building. Where is the city? The piazzas filled with people, with music and life?" A dazzling smile lit his face. "Ah, to hear the birds' wings beating against the air and the music of the fountains. That is what I want."

"America is not known for her piazzas," Simone said apologetically. "This country was built for efficiency once upon a time. But not, I'm afraid, for beauty or spiritual ease. And, of course, it's summer here so the water is precious. Rationed. There aren't many fountains."

"Water restricted? No fountains? No place for the people to gather and promenade of a warm evening?" His eyes were wide with disbelief.

"Not really. At least, not here." She couldn't bear his scornful expression. She wanted to tell him that where she came from it was all quite different. Civilized. *How Michelangelo would love Paris,* she

thought. If only she could take him there. But no.
He was only a sim, brought out of the machine to do
a specific job. And whatever strange yearnings she
felt for him she must keep to herself. Of course she
felt a kinship with him. He was her creation. It was
nothing more than maternal pride.

"What an impoverished place and age." He sighed.
"Well, where do the people go? What do they do for
amusement?"

"Here in California?" She shrugged. "I could
take you to an all-night shopping mall, I suppose.
But I can't bear those places. If only we were in
France . . ."

"France? You are not from here?" He stared at her
in surprise.

"No. An exile. Or a hostage, I suppose."

"I see." His eyes held hers in a gentle, sympathetic glance. "Perhaps it would be better not to
show me more."

Was it possible that he was fatigued? But sims
were indefatigable unless you pulled the plug. Simone
looked at her watch. It was already five in the morning. In half an hour, the day shift would come in.
Suddenly, she felt anxious, desperate to protect her
sim from the American hackers. Even well-meaning
Natalya. None of them would understand his artist's
soul. Yes, the best thing for him was a return to the
safety of the machine.

"Will I see you again?" he asked as they entered
her office.

"Of course. Tomorrow night."

"Good. Until then."

The sparkling hail of the sim signal engulfed him.
With a slosh, the simbody fell back into its crucible.
Michelangelo was gone. Simone's office felt cold and
empty. She shut down her terminal and hurried
toward the tube station.

*   *   *

The safety of the machine with its flat yet pearly light and open, endless non-space enveloped Michelangelo.

A strange cloud, he thought. *I see it but feel it not. So I thought heaven would be. But this is not heaven. The New World? That is not heaven either, apparently. Far from it. What I would give to see Florence again. Or Rome. But the ground is poisoned, so Mother Superior says.*

Mother Superior? You mean the woman Dubois?

The voice was oddly pitched, high and then low, buzzing, distorted, and not really a voice. An insect's whine. The groan of marble giving way to rockcutter's tools. Michelangelo could not tell if he heard or felt it in his simulated bones. Either way, he didn't care for it.

A small, bearded man in an ill-fitting suit of cheap black cloth walked toward him through the middle of the air. His feet strode along what would have been a wall if there were walls in this odd cloud. His head was perpendicular to Michelangelo's perspective and his pale scalp showed through greasy strands of thinning hair.

Una quadratura, Michelangelo thought. "Again!"

"No. I'm not some decadent, skewed-perspective painting," the stranger said. He took an elongated step and stood, face to face with Michelangelo. Or face to windpipe: he was almost a full head shorter.

"You can hear my thoughts?"

"Hear is not the term I would use, but I suppose it will do. Yes. In a way, I can hear all transmissions that take place."

"Transmission? Does no one make sense?"

"Communications, then. I can hear all communications. My name is Mikhail Bakunin and I am beginning to wish I were deaf."

"I am Michelangelo Buonarroti."

"I know. Present at the rebirth, I might say. They've gotten much better at it over the years. You're lucky."

"What is this place?"

Bakunin shrugged. "Voltaire thinks it's tremendously sophisticated machinery in which we are simulated personalities created by postery for bourgeois, petty reasons. Some call it Hades. Others, heaven. I call it the road."

"The road? Where does it lead?"

"Everywhere. And nowhere. Every time. And no time."

Michelangelo scowled. "I'm not interested in riddles."

"You should embrace them, master artist." Bakunin gave a thin, self-satisfied smile. "Oh, yes, I know who you are. Or were. Yes, your existence now is wholly a riddle. Where are you? When? How? It is only on this road that you will find your answer. This may lead you to an end. Or a means." Bakunin chuckled.

"Who are these others to whom you refer?"

"Our comrades from the ages past. Great leaders and thinkers, or so they are considered now by posterity. I can't say I always agree."

"Is Savonarola among them?"

"Let me see now. Pizarro, Joan of Arc, Machiavelli, Cleopatra, Jack the Ripper, Socrates, Queen Victoria, J. Edgar Hoover, Thomas Jefferson, Torquemada. I may have left one or two out. But no, no mad Dominican monks. Sorry."

"He was not mad," Michelangelo said. "He may have been the sanest man in Florence. In Italy."

"He was wrong," Bakunin said fiercely. "He believed in moral order but not in men's natures. The only thing he was right about was overthrowing the government. And even there, he erred in supporting the establishment of a rival fiefdom."

"To trust in human nature is folly," Michelangelo retorted.

"What else is there to trust in?" Bakunin gave him a shrewd look. "Surely any artist knows that."

"And any artist that trusts in human nature after dealing with Pope Julius is a fool twice over."

"Do not judge people by their leaders. Judge people by their actions."

Michelangelo waved away the argument. "Bakunin, I think you are the innocent one here. How they would laugh in Florence to hear what you say. And even louder in Rome."

"No one is laughing in Rome or Florence these days."

"No, I suppose not." The artist shook his head sadly. "But in my time—"

"To which you would like to return, no doubt. To visit a Rome untroubled by nuclear destruction? To see Florence before the fires of hell touched her?"

Michelangelo stared at him in disbelief. "My God! Is it possible?"

"Anything is possible on this road." Bakunin nodded, grinning. But his grin faded along with his face as everything before Michelangelo dissolved in a shower of white and gold light. *Like God's fire*, he thought. *Too bright, even for me.* He closed his eyes.

"Simone, you've outdone yourself," Sanjei Yamamoto said happily. He looked at the Michelangelo sim with possessive pride.

Just the way a Provencal farmer would look at his olive groves, Simone thought. Aloud, she said, "I'm delighted you're pleased. I think he's my best yet."

Michelangelo appraised Sanjei. He seemed fascinated by the smaller man and stared at him as though he'd never seen anybody quite like him before.

"Michelangelo, this is Sanjei Yamamoto," Simone said. "Your padrone."

"Why's he looking at me like that, Simone?" Sanjei asked, sounding uneasy. He straightened the collar of his yellow shirt self-consciously.

"I have never seen such a face," Michelangelo

whispered. He reached out as though to touch Sanjei, then seemed to think better of it.

Simone hurried to explain. "I believe you are the first Japanese-American he's ever met," she said. "As you know, Sanjei, you have to allow for discrepancies in sim programming and lag-time in acclimation."

"Of course, of course," he said a touch too heartily. "Well, good to meet you, Michelangelo." He held out his hand.

Michelangelo stared at him blankly.

"Shake," Simone said, sotto voce. "He wants to take your hand as a sign of good fellowship."

"Ah." The sim nodded and reached for his padrone's hand.

"What a grip," Sanjei yelped.

"That's enough. Michelangelo, let him go." Simone turned to the head of Motorobotics apologetically. "He doesn't know his own strength. One of the drawbacks of the sensual quarantine we impose on them."

"Guess you're right." Frowning, Sanjei massaged his palm. "But it's an economic necessity right now, regardless of what Tech Hilliard and his Maquinatech bunch say. Let's get going. I want our resident artist to look over the house before it gets dark."

Michelangelo sat stiffly in the plush backseat of Sanjei's Gold Omega. He only betrayed emotion once, when the traffic and buildings thinned out to show the gentle golden foothills above New Tokyo punctuated by green cypress trees. Then his eyes widened and seemed to fill with tears. But when Simone asked him what was wrong, he turned away, shutting her out.

Sanjei sprang out of the car and gestured proudly towards his home. "Here we are. What do you think?"

Simone took in the sprawling neo-Mediterranean Revival building and suppressed a smile. Considering that it was late twenty-second-century American architecture, it wasn't bad. Sanjei had a right to be proud, she told herself. He worked hard for his wealth. And most Japanese-Americans liked large imposing houses.

"Is this your palazzo?" Michelangelo said. His tone was mildly scornful. "What is this strange white substance? Not stone. And surely not wood. I recognize the tiles on the roof as terra cotta. But this?" He touched the outside of the building gingerly, as though afraid of contracting a disease.

"Stucco," Sanjei said. "The highest quality polyresin imitation stucco available. Resistent to heat, rain, and cold. Best of all, it's seismologically approved."

Michelangelo nodded, but he was clearly not listening. Instead, he was staring across the canyon into the distance at a row of Mediterranean pines whose graceful canopy shaded the crest of a hill.

Simone began to get nervous. If her sim malfunctioned, she could find her term as a hostage extended. "Perhaps you should show him what you had in mind," she said quickly.

"Right. It's down here, behind the house." Sanjei gestured towards a gently sloping incline in which the blond grass was thigh-high. "I want to make a combination reception area and conference center out here." He gestured behind him at the gray-green scrub pine nestling in the hollow. "All these trees can come out, of course."

"What?" Michelangelo cried. "Take out the trees for more of this, what do you call it, stuccout? *Dio mio*, then who would want to visit here?"

Sanjei frowned. "Simone, I didn't expect this kind of reaction. I thought we understood each other on this project."

"Michelangelo, perhaps you should tell us what you would recommend," she said.

"Get Da Vinci. He loves to fool with this sort of thing."

"We tried," Sanjei said. "But Sony gobbled up all rights to him in '72. And that fast-food/amusement park owns Frank Lloyd Wright."

"Who?" Michelangelo asked.

"Never mind," Simone said. "We've been through this before. This is *your* job."

"All right. I understand what the padrone wants." He nodded towards Sanjei. "I can do this, this conference center design for him. But we must discuss terms."

"What?" Sanjei said. "Simone, what is he talking about?"

"He thinks he's going to be paid," she said weakly. "I couldn't separate Michelangelo's business acumen from his artistic motivation without damaging the program."

"Terrific. Now I'm going to pay a sim that I had created in-house?" Sanjei shook his head. "Wait until Chambon hears about this." He started to walk away.

"Wait." Simone hurried after him along the terra cotta pathway. "Sanjei, listen to me." She glanced over her shoulder, but Michelangelo was again transfixed by the scenery and oblivious to them. "You know these sims are like children when they first come out of the machine. They cling to the bits and pieces of persona we've given them as though they're carved in stone. You have children. You know how they are."

Sanjei nodded, softening. He always enjoyed talking about his children. "That's true."

"Well then, you know that you must view this sim as just another rebellious child. He wants to be paid. He's always been paid. So agree to pay." She winked. "Negotiate a little so he's satisfied. Don't forget, Pope Julius paid the original Michelangelo three thousand crowns to paint the Sistine Chapel. Don't be surprised if our sim expects a good fee."

"You're right," Sanjei patted her shoulder. "Good point, Simone. I'm just anxious about getting the job done in time. Speaking of time." He glanced at his watch. "I've got a meeting at six. Let's negotiate that 'fee.'"

They approached the sim as he was wiping a tear from his eye. "*Che bella vista*," he said quietly. "So like Tuscany."

"Homesick? I know how you feel," Sanjei said. "But listen, Michelangelo, let's talk payment. What do you have in mind?"

"Fifteen hundred crowns," the sim said. "In advance."

"Hmm. I don't know." Sanjei looked away and smiled conspiratorially at Simone. "That's pretty high. How about a thousand?"

"Twelve hundred or I won't do it," Michelangelo snapped.

"Done."

"I need paper, charcoal, dimensions," Michelangelo said.

"Paper? Oh, uh, right. Simone will help you out with that," Sanjei said. "Do you need to check anything else while we're here?"

"No, please." Michelangelo turned and gave Simone a look of despair. "I've seen enough."

"There. The plans for the addition to the palazzo, Mother Superior. Finished." Michelangelo leaned back in Simone's black leather chair and gave a sigh of relief. "This magic box you use is much faster than the hand and charcoal. Almost as fast as the eye."

Simone peered over his shoulder at the screen field where a neat schematic rendering in blue and white showed a lofty two-story design. "You're a quick learner," she said. "Not every sim could master the board, much less design with it." She patted him on the back, allowing her hand to linger for one luxurious moment in the dark curls at the base of his neck.

I feel pride in his accomplishment, she told herself. *Nothing more.*

"Let's send this to Sanjei," she said, and pressed the transfer pad. "Now I've got a surprise for you." She brought up a new program on the wallscreen. "Look."

Warm, sand-colored buildings spread across a green valley bisected by a slow-moving river. Dominating the city-scape was a graceful cathedral with an imposing red dome and a pendant bell-tower.

Tears filled Michelangelo's eyes. "The green Arno," he whispered. "The Ponte Vecchio. Giotto's campanile." He reached out to grasp Simone's hand and somehow managed to do it gently. "Thank you, dear Simone."

His touch was searing, absorbing all of her attention and focusing it narrowly on those five graceful fingers holding her captive. "I—I found an old travel video in the library," she said quickly. "I thought you'd like it."

He was still holding her hand, but his eyes had slipped back to the wallscreen. Hungrily he watched as the camera panned from one antique landmark to another in the Tuscan landscape.

Bzzzz!

Sanjei's private line overrode the screen signal.

Regretfully, Simone slipped her hand free and switched on the audio.

"I want to talk to you," Sanjei said. He didn't sound happy. "Privately."

"On my way." What could have happened? Simone hurried toward the door, then paused to look back at Michelangelo. "That Florence program will run for another half-hour and loop back," she said. "Enjoy it. This won't take long."

Sanjei's office was around the corner—in fact, it took up the entire corner of the building, commanding the best views of downtown New Tokyo's white skyscrapers. Sanjei sat at his alabaster resin desk with his back to that view, pondering his wallscreen. His face looked like a thundercloud.

"Did you see this?" he said, gesturing at the screen. It was Michelangelo's architectural rendering.

"Well, yes, briefly."

"How could you send something like this to me? Have you no respect? No consideration for my intelligence?"

Simone stared, open-mouthed. What was he talking about? "The design looks fine to me," she said stiffly. "He did what you asked."

"He designed a marble tomb fit for some Renaissance duke!" Sanjei pushed a button and a detail enlarged until it filled the image field. "Marble statues of angels. Jesus, what does he think this is?"

"Florence, in the sixteenth century," she said quietly. But Sanjei wasn't listening. He stood up and paced the length of his office.

"It's impossible. Wrong, all wrong. I can't use it."

"I told you his specialty was sculpture, not architecture."

"Well, he'll have to do it again. Show him some examples of modern buildings, for God's sake. Pictures of my house."

Simone sighed. "If that's what you wish. But I suspect it won't do any good."

Sanjei slammed his hand down on his desk. "I don't pay you to argue with me!"

Simone eyed him coolly. "You don't pay me at all."

"Oh, but I do." He smiled in a way that made her stomach knot. "As of this morning, you are an official employee of Motorobotics."

"What!?"

"Chambon asked to have your appointment made permanent. To facilitate future joint ventures."

"I don't believe you." The blood drained out of Simone's face. She felt dizzy and cold.

"Your green card had been revoked," Sanjei said. "You're now a citizen of the United States."

"But my EEC passport—"

Sanjei reached into his desk, pulled out a small package and tossed it to her. "Invalid. Keep it as a souvenir."

"Impossible," she said. "I refuse the assignment."

Now Sanjei laughed openly. "Are you crazy? You'll become an indigent, a citizen without assignment. You'll never be able to get back into France—after that computer virus affected all the crops, nobody can get past customs without clearance from their employer. And if you refuse employment here, you'll be drafted into the U.S. Army. You'll find yourself wearing a khaki jumpsuit and building sims of Douglas MacArthur."

"But I do not wish to be here."

"That's certainly no secret," Sanjei said, rubbing his forehead. He sat down quietly. When he spoke again, his tone was softer. "Look, Simone. I know this is a big shock. And I'm sorry. But these things happen all the time. You're a damned good sim designer and I'm happy to have you on board. There's lots of room for growth here. Once you've settled in with us, I'll give you clearance to visit France." He paused. "Why don't you go back to your desk and think about it? And don't forget about that design from the Michelangelo sim."

"No. No, I won't." Like a sleepwalker, she tottered back to her office and closed the door.

"Michelangelo . . ."

The big chair by her deskscreen was empty. A message floated in orange letters across the image field.

Mother Superior: I have done what you asked. Now I must go home, or find a home that suits me better than does this graceless, miserable century. Farewell.

"No," Simone said. "No, no, no."

The featureless simbody lay quietly in its neonatal bath next to the deskscreen. Simone nearly knocked the tank over as she rushed toward her desk.

Every sim was flagged in the company data net for quick access. It would be easy to find him and bring him back out. Simone's fingers flew over the board as she scanned the database. No sign of him. Finally, she pulled up an illegal menu of every sim generated in the United States since 2063. Michelangelo's code was missing.

"Sim code Michelangelo," she demanded. "All search."

"Deleted," the machine replied.

He was a better student than I ever suspected, she thought. Desperately, Simone checked the menu again. But Michelangelo was gone. Vanished into the nether world of the machine. Probably nothing more than a scrambled electronic signal by now. It would take hours—possibly days—to reconfigure him. If she could.

The tears she'd been fighting off began to escape and trickle down her cheeks.

"Damn. Damn and merde!"

Simone sank into her chair, put her face in her hands, and sobbed. She'd been abandoned doubly, by both her sim and by Marc.

Marc!

She looked up, tears forgotten. She'd call his private line. Beg him to reconsider. His wife had probably forced him to do this. Marie was always jealous. Yes, she'd call Marc and make him change his mind.

"That number is no longer functioning," her deskscreen announced.

"Try again," she said.

"Number is no longer . . ."

Simone cut the connection.

She was trapped here. Sanjei was right. Without work or a sponsor in the EEC, she couldn't go back. She had no choice.

The wallscreen flickered and began to replay the video of Florence she'd requested for Michelangelo— was it just this morning? She watched the vista unfold, grateful for the distraction. A pretty place, Florence. Almost as nice as Paris—

Simone sat up. She did have a choice. She didn't have to stay here.

For weeks, the screens had hummed with rumors of the crazy man who'd fallen in love with a sim and gone into the machine.

Why not? Why not go look for Michelangelo. And Florence?

She dried her eyes, ignoring the tiny voice that shrieked in the back of her head and told her she was crazy. It was easy to pirate her personnel file, remove five pounds from her recorded weight, then encode it into the sim program. The cephalic patterns and personality map transferred in seconds.

I'll go in, she thought. *I'll find him, and if we can't locate Florence maybe I can convince him to come back out with me. How good it will be to hear his voice again.*

"It was not my habit to touch women regularly."

Touch. Could lovers touch within sim space? She would find out. And in the time-honored gesture of utter, loving sacrifice, she would become whatever he wanted. If he could not love Simone then perhaps he would love Simon.

A slim young man with reddish gold hair gazed at Simone from out of the screen field. His green eyes twinkled with affection.

An apprentice for Michelangelo, she thought. *A companion and, if he will have it so, a lover. All this will I accomplish through you. And, trying, die.*

She reached into her office first aid kit and pulled out a syringe filled with narcophane. It glittered like a red jewel in the office pinlights. Giddily, she toasted the Duomo on her wallscreen.

"Bon voyage. Bonne chance."

The sting of the hypo was quick, and just as quickly receded. As the darkness outside drew nearer her eyes were drawn to the brightness of the wallscreen. She could almost feel the warm Tuscan sun upon her face.

To Florence, she thought. *To Florence.*

With the touch of a button Simone sent Simon flying along the electronic pathways that led from the screen into the heart of the machine.

EPILOGUE:

In and out of the machine, the ghosts creep at the volition of the Game masters and technicians, awaiting their demands, quiescent in the electronic pathways. Waiting.

And what if some future hand should slip and the secret of re-creation pass from maker to creation? If the key to freedom from the domination of the machine passes to the simulacra, and they are loosed upon the decadent world of the twenty-third century, what turmoil will result? Anarchists and murders, philosophers and madmen armed with the knowledge of the ages, roaming the new-old world with acquisitive fervor. What demands will they make? What will they want?